Acclaim for *Other Times*

'Thomas has the rare ability to recreate the very sounds and smells and atmospheres of a long-lost world. These range from the crowded beach at Bournemouth on the last warm day of the phoney war ('Children, donkey rides, any more for the Skylark, ice-cream, fish and chips') to Bairnsfather and Molly's cut-price wedding with round paper scraps from a hole puncher for confetti. This is a tour-de-force of imagination and story-telling and, for me, one of the most satisfying reads in years. I cannot recommend it highly enough' *Daily Mail*

'Thomas's descriptions of people and place are as good as ever, and he brilliantly captures the atmosphere of the time; the interminable wait for something – anything – to happen, in the freezing winter of 1939/1940. This is an engrossing book, immaculately researched and extremely readable' *Bath Chronicle*

'When it comes to telling a thoroughly good tale, few do it better than former Barnardo boy Leslie Thomas . . . Stirring together a little modern history with a whole raft of laughter and tears is a recipe for writing a surefire winner' *Yorkshire Evening Post*

'A genuine warmth and humour . . . the pages keep turning . . . Thomas, as ever, tells a cracking yarn' *Mail on Sunday*

Other Times

Leslie Thomas is one of Britain's most popular authors. His boyhood in a Barnardo's orphanage is described in his hugely successful autobiography, *This Time Next Week.* He is the author of numerous other bestsellers, including *The Virgin Soldiers*, *Tropic of Ruislip*, *The Magic Army*, *Arrivals and Departures*, *Chloe's Song*, *Dangerous Davies and the Lonely Heart* and, most recently, *Other Times*. He lives in Salisbury and London with his wife, Diana.

Also by Leslie Thomas

Fiction

The Virgin Soldiers
Orange Wednesday
The Love Beach
Come to the War
His Lordship
Onward Virgin Soldiers
Arthur McCann and All His Women
The Man with the Power
Tropic of Ruislip
Stand Up Virgin Soldiers
Dangerous Davies: The Last Detective
Bare Nell
Ormerod's Landing
That Old Gang of Mine
The Magic Army
The Dearest and the Best
The Adventures of Goodnight and Loving
Dangerous in Love
Orders for New York
The Loves and Journeys of Revolving Jones
Arrivals and Departures
Dangerous by Moonlight
Running Away
The Complete Dangerous Davies
Kensington Heights
Chloe's Song
Dangerous Davies and The Lonely Heart

Non-fiction

This Time Next Week
Some Lovely Islands
The Hidden Places of Britain
My World of Islands
In My Wildest Dreams

LESLIE THOMAS

Other Times

Published in the United Kingdom in 2000 by
Arrow Books

5 7 9 10 8 6 4

First published in the United Kingdom in 1999 by
William Heinemann

Arrow Books
The Random House Group Limited
20 Vauxhall Bridge Road, London, SW1V 2SA

Random House Australia (Pty) Limited
20 Alfred Street, Milsons Point, Sydney,
New South Wales 2061, Australia

Random House New Zealand Limited
18 Poland Road, Glenfield
Auckland 10, New Zealand

Random House (Pty) Limited
Endulini, 5a Jubilee Road,
Parktown 2193, South Africa

The Random House Group Limited Reg. No. 954009

www.randomhouse.co.uk

A CIP catalogue record for this book is available from
the British Library

Papers used by The Random House Group Limited are natural, recyclable products made from wood grown in sustainable forests. The manufacturing processes conform to the environmental regulations of the country of origin

Typeset in Baskerville by
Palimpsest Book Production Limited
Polmont, Stirlingshire
Printed and bound in Germany by
Elsnerdruck, Berlin

ISBN 0 09 941523 2

Dedicated to Jean Ratcliff and the Lady Taverners in recognition of the work they do with needy children

Author's Note

My thanks to David Penn and Chris McCarthy of the Imperial War Museum, and Major Denis Rollo of the Royal Artillery Historical Trust, for their help; to Tony Richards, City Librarian, Southampton, and his staff. Also to the many people, particularly in the Southampton and New Forest areas, who so willingly shared their memories with me.

There are those who will think of this story as a tale from history; to others it will seem that it happened only yesterday.

1

It seemed somehow unfitting that everything should be so docile along that coast; a washed-out autumn sky reflecting in an uncaring sea, birds flying much as usual, offshore a minesweeper rocking as if asleep. Not a foot trod on the shingle. There were small chuffs of wind. It was an empty morning.

At seven o'clock the men stumbled from the two huts. Not for the first time Captain Bevan thought how difficult it was to make a parade from only sixteen soldiers, two excused boots.

They formed up in two blank-faced ranks, not particularly straight, in front of the sandbag rampart around a solitary Bofors gun, its feet spread out on last summer's seaside rose garden, its camouflage netting like an old woman's skirt. Bugles, even if militarily appropriate, were not allowed. Under the Defence Regulations, no one, on pain of arrest, was permitted to sound a siren, hooter, whistle, bell, horn, gong or bugle. The silence irked Sergeant Runciman; an army should be noisy, at least have a certain amount of din. Whoever heard of a hushed army? He had unearthed an old bird-scaring rattle in a barn; it still worked when he privately swung it and he had suggested its use for rousing the men in the morning but a check on regulations by Bombardier Hignet, the sage of the orderly room, revealed that doing so would signify a gas attack. So Runciman had to shout at the door of each of the huts. Gunfire, as morning tea was traditionally called, was brought in an aluminium bucket by the NCO of the overnight guard. If the hot water had failed in the wash-house, which sometimes happened, the tea was also used for shaving, giving some men brown chins.

Although they were designated a troop of the Royal Artillery it was not easy to think of these men as troops; so few and so disarranged were they. They now paraded in front of the slim-barrelled, lily-snouted gun, on the oblong of asphalt once a playground but with the swings and seesaw banished and only the metal stumps remaining. In wartime children, like everyone else, were expected to make sacrifices.

The men's shadows were longer than the men for it was October and the sun was becoming later and lower. When Runciman, a regular soldier, gave orders his short, sturdy body tensed and then trembled as he shouted, as if it vibrated with the effort even though it was only an everyday drill. Now he ordered the small parade to attention for Bevan's inspection which the officer carried out without fuss. There was little point in making any. Eight men were missing; three on leave, one on compassionate leave because his wife had gone off, and four still in Aldershot Military Hospital following the intense sickness that had decimated the unit and others in the area, two weeks before, when a Maltese civilian cook had reached his limit and dropped senna in the midday stew. It took longer to train a cook than a gunner and army cooks were in short supply. There were insistent queues at the latrines and some who had not eaten the stew pretended to have done so for the sake of going sick. 'Men are crapping everywhere, sir,' reported Runciman soberly.

'It's just as well the Boche didn't attack,' Bevan had said. 'The country would have been left defenceless.'

There seemed not the remotest chance of the Germans attacking, by air or any other means. The war had been on, if not actually being waged, for almost two months. Since the initial official fears had diminished and then disappeared – Southampton, whose six jovial barrage balloons they could see from the gun site, had confidently expected six hundred deaths from bombing in the first twenty-four hours – a deathless quiet, oddly near to a disappointment, had fallen across Britain. Air-raid wardens and fire-fighters had searched empty skies; cardboard coffins had remained unopened. People began to ask what had gone wrong.

Gulls were squawking above the parade and Runciman needed to out-shout them. The men's movements, like their eyes, were dull for there had been a dance in Lyndhurst public hall the night before. They left-turned, right-turned and about-turned, and the sergeant marched them up and down a bit on the asphalt and then silently on the grass, more to get them moving than anything else. Captain Bevan returned Runciman's salute and said: 'Carry on, sergeant' before striding off towards his office. His pace diminished to a walk.

He sat at his adjutant's desk wondering where Eve was, what her baby was like. He expected to get a letter from a divorce solicitor before long. That is what she wanted. They had been oddly grateful to the Prime Minister, Mr Chamberlain, when he announced the Declaration of War on Sunday 3 September, because it meant that they could part more easily, logically and, oddly, with less pain. Eve had been in the rocking chair, her belly swollen, her face washed out. He sat upright, facing her and the situation; they had studied each other with a mix of sorrow and relief. Those vivid moments after 11.15 that morning had meant many things to many people, fear, sadness, deep uncertainty; for them it was a convenient excuse.

Eve had been his second wife; Margaret, his first, had died five years after their marriage. Eve was still at school when he first went to work on her father's estate on the border of Hampshire and Sussex in the late 1920s. Bevan had only been aware of her in the holidays, a tubby tomboy who somehow, almost miraculously, became a slender young woman.

'Everyone still calls me Lumpy,' she laughed to him.

'It doesn't apply any more,' he said.

She had offered him a lift home from the county ball, a night for long-dressed ladies and uniforms. She wore a silver gown. It made her eyes seem grey.

'I know my father got you to join his silly soldiers,' she said as her Ford bumped over the estate roads in the dark. 'Territorials seem a little ridiculous, don't you think?'

'He doesn't think so. He's still keeping a watchful eye on Germany.'

'The uniform suits you though. White tunic and all that.' Her tone softened. 'Uniforms suit tall men. All soldiers should be tall.' He grinned in the dark of the car. 'And your medals. They don't look so cumbersome on you. My father loves his medals.'

'He loves the army.'

'Do you?'

'In peacetime it's interesting.'

'And war?'

'Necessary.'

She pulled up outside the stone cottage where he had lived with Margaret and where he still lived. 'Can I come in and see?' she asked.

'Yes . . . yes, of course.'

When they were in the ordered sitting-room she picked up a wedding-day photograph of himself and Margaret. 'What was she like?' she asked. 'I did see her once or twice.'

He was pouring drinks. 'Quiet,' he said.

'Like you.'

'I suppose so. Some people say quietness is the ultimate intimacy.'

'She died in an accident, didn't she.'

'Yes, one night on the road from the village.'

She took the glass and sat on the arm of the one big chair, her silver dress folding in columns down her legs, her eyes deep and her smile elfish. 'I've been in here before, you know,' she said. 'Several times.'

'You have?'

'I've even spied through the window.'

He sat down opposite her. 'Why?'

'My friend Clara and I,' she said, revolving her drink in the glass. 'I had a big crush on you. So did she. We used to call you Valentino, handsome but silent.'

Bevan laughed outright. She extended a hand and he touched it with his. 'My apologies,' she said.

'Don't. I'm very flattered.'

'We saw you through the window once while you were trying to teach yourself to dance. We heard the gram playing and we thought you had a woman in here. But there you were, book in hand, trying out the steps. It made me feel odd, very sad.'

She dropped her eyes but when she looked up he was smiling at her. 'I never did learn properly.'

'You danced very well tonight,' she said. 'Even if I had to ask you. Thank God for the Ladies' Invitation Waltz.'

She handed him her glass and he refilled it. 'You know I am sailing to America at the end of the week,' she said. 'On the *Aquitania*.'

'Yes, I heard. How long will you be away?'

She shrugged. 'A couple of years, I don't know. It's my father's idea. It's to make me into a well-rounded woman, as he says. As if being known as Lumpy were not enough.'

He handed the drink to her.

'Do you want to hear about my secret visits?' she asked.

'If you want to tell me.'

'I had such a pash on you. Silly, I suppose, but there it is. I was only fourteen. You hardly ever locked your door and when you weren't here I came in and just played at being here with you – you know, making your meals and getting your slippers, games like that.' She hesitated, then finished her drink. 'I must go,' she said as if it were a sudden decision. He took her to the door. 'I even got into your bed once,' she said. She leaned forward and kissed him and he returned the kiss.

'Have a good time in America.'

'I wish I weren't going.' He saw she meant it then. 'When I come back,' she said, 'I expect you to ask me to marry you.'

When she had gone Bevan finished his drink thoughtfully. He took off his white mess jacket and, with a wry smile, jingled the medals. He left them attached to the jacket and put it over the back of a chair.

It was raining on the cottage window now, splattering the small panes. There came a timid knock at the door. She was on the step, her hair and her silvery dress getting wet.

'That silly car ran itself into a hole,' she said, avoiding looking at him. 'And I'm soaked.'

'I can see,' he said. She fell into his arms. He folded them about her. 'It will be ages,' she sniffed. Her face powder had streaked, her rouge was smudged. 'I'll be away years.' She walked into the room and he closed the door. Without looking at him she began to take her dress off. 'It's sopping,' she said.

In later times whenever he thought about her he always saw again how, pale and young and naked, she had put on his white mess jacket and, with the undistinguished medals bouncing over her breast, had marched laughing up and down the room. Then she sat on the bed, rolled sideways across the cover and said: 'We'd better not do anything while I'm wearing all these bits of tin.'

Later she said: 'I wouldn't dare tell you what I imagined when I crept into this bed that time. Things you would never dream for a fourteen-year-old called Lumpy.'

'You're not Lumpy now,' he said holding her.

She giggled. 'Only where I am supposed to be.' She eased her breasts towards his face. 'Kiss them, please. I always wanted you to give them a kiss.'

They lay together until morning. In the first light they made love again. 'Have you had many girlfriends, James?' she enquired. 'I mean serious girlfriends, you did this sort of thing with.'

He laughed. Soon she would be gone. 'I was married for five years, remember. After that I decided to concentrate on my work here.'

'My father is going to make you his land agent, you know. When Roberts retires.'

He knew. 'That should see me through for life,' he said.

'There is the matter of marrying me,' said Eve. 'You promised.'

'I promised to ask you,' he corrected. 'When you get back. By then you will probably have changed your mind.'

'Oh, I hope not,' she said.

Bevan left the office door open to the October mild air. Bombardier Hignet would soon be released from gun drill, and would make the first cup of coffee. There were some important-looking papers on the desk, none of them important. One concerned a new issue of waste-paper baskets and filing trays marked 'In' and 'Out', and another the looming visit of a military chiropodist. The door faced east and if he stood he could see the Needles, the toothy end of the Isle of Wight. A fresh, sunny wind came in the door ruffling the wall calendar. The *Daily Express* lay folded on Hignet's desk. Bevan walked over and casually opened it. On the front was a propaganda photograph of George Formby, with his lemon grin and ukulele, entertaining troops – amused British and bemused Frenchmen – in France. The RAF had dropped leaflets over Germany advising the enemy to surrender. There was an advertisement for the benefits of Bovril and another for Cherry Blossom boot polish.

Runciman, always the professional, was giving sharp orders to the seven men of the gun crew, so sharp there was scarcely an echo, and Bevan went to stand at the door to witness the soldiers go through the pantomime around the Bofors. The two gun layers, Purcell and Brown, wound the handles for elevation and for line from bucket seats on each side. Bairnsfather, the loader, said they reminded him of his mother and the woman next door both swinging their mangles on opposite sides of the back fence. It was Bairnsfather who loaded the ammunition, clips of four shells, into a hopper and operated the firing pedal. Cartwright and Ugson were the ammunition carriers, Ugson being relieved of his duty of observer once they were in action. Then Sergeant Runciman watched the sky and controlled the gun from his position to the right of it. Hignet's task, to his intense embarrassment, was to sweep up imaginary empty shell cases. They had another similar gun but it had gone to be mended. The remaining weapon could not be fired even for practice because they were surrounded by a retirement area and residents had complained to the War Office that it shook their beds and bungalows. When they needed to rehearse with loud ammunition, alive or dud, they had to take the weapon to the slopes of Salisbury Plain, several miles to the north. Many people hardly knew there was a war going on.

Now the sergeant was snapping through the action drill. Bevan watched the coned barrel of the forty-millimetre quick-firing weapon elevate and then traverse, it seemed to him, almost eagerly as if the gun itself felt that this might be the real thing. It nosed around the sky apparently sniffing for enemy aircraft. Gunner Ugson, the observer, knew there was sod all up there. It was an excellent gun and had been in use with the British Army only since 1937. They were lucky to have it for Bofors were in short supply. There were less than a hundred in the country and this pair had happened to be unloaded at Southampton at the start of the war. It was a Swedish invention and the Swedes were neutral, had preserved their private peace, while selling the weapon to the Germans, the British, the French and anyone else who would buy. Bevan knew what was coming next in the drill and he half turned away, grateful that no outsider could see. It was so diminishing. He heard Runciman snap through the final sequence of orders and then bawl: 'Fire!'

'Bang!' shouted one soldier. Then because the Bofors was rapid firing – ostensibly capable of one hundred and twenty rounds a minute – three other men each shouted: 'Bang! Bang! Bang!' Even at a distance he could see how embarrassed, how crestfallen the crew were. Not a gull swerved nor squawked. Bevan shook his head and wondered, not for the first time, about the strange state they were in.

* * *

'There's only so many times you can say "bang".' Runciman took his forage cap off and sat deflatedly in the chair Bevan indicated. 'Or *ways*.' Bombardier Hignet poured him a cup of coffee as though it might be seriously beneficial.

'War?' Runciman said to Bevan. 'Call this war, sir?' He had been a soldier since the early 1930s.

'It's a trifle quiet,' admitted Bevan. 'But I don't know what we can do about it, sergeant.'

'What I say is, if we're going to have a blasted war, let's *have* one. Let's get over there and get at them. Why don't we bomb them? Set the Black Forest on fire, sir. That should burn nicely.' Hignet, as though taking a note of the notion, scribbled on a pad. Runciman went on: 'Christ, there's some bloke in Parliament who says we can't bomb the Krupps Armaments Factory because it's a *private company*. Ever heard anything like it?' He caught sight of the front page of the newspaper and snorted. 'Leaflets! Dropping leaflets.' Even more scornfully he surveyed the photograph. 'And George Formby.'

'He's a secret weapon,' offered Hignet, who had glasses, was overweight and was thought to be intelligent, which was why he was in the orderly hut.

'Fear of retaliation,' suggested Bevan. There was rarely acknowledgement of rank in office conversations, only a casual reference to it as a title, almost a nickname. Captain Bevan was sometimes 'sir', and Sergeant Runciman was occasionally 'sergeant', but Bombardier Hignet was rarely called anything to his face. 'If we do bomb them,' said Bevan, 'Chamberlain's afraid they'll bomb us twice as much.'

'My dad's bigger than your dad,' grumbled Runciman. With a sort of plea he confronted Bevan. 'What am I going to do with them today, sir? They can't pick up any more litter. They've painted everything in sight, some of it twice, and I can't put them weeding again.' He turned his face to Hignet as if he, as a last resort, might understand: 'These are fighting men.'

'Sandcastles,' suggested Bevan feeling foolish. 'The CO thought the sandcastles we had last week were a good idea. Build up a castle and work out how to attack it.'

'And it's nice on the beach,' put in Hignet peering out through his schoolboy spectacles towards the sea. 'Fresh air, sunshine.'

Runciman scowled towards him. 'We've done the digging holes and filling them up again, we've painted the coal white,' he said returning to Bevan. 'If we build sandcastles will you come over and take a look?'

'Of course. Why don't you build some sort of model of the Maginot Line. A bit of it. There was a diagram in last week's *War Illustrated*.'

'I saw it,' said Runciman. 'I expect the enemy did too.'

'Then we can work out how the Germans can outflank it and get into France.'

'Through Holland and Belgium,' murmured Hignet. He looked down at the newspaper as though washing his hands of the matter, but then added: 'Easy.'

'Easy,' agreed Runciman. 'So easy it don't seem to have occurred to the High Command.'

'Or anybody else,' put in Hignet. He regarded Bevan half seriously. 'You ought to warn them, sir.'

The sergeant, who did not like the bombardier butting in, stood and drained his coffee. There was plenty. Rationing was six months away. 'Right, sir, I'll march them up and down for a while, get them nice and loose, and then I'll set them digging the Maginot Line.'

'I'm going over to the mess,' said Bevan. 'See if I can find the old man.'

'Golf,' said Hignet studying the picture of George

Formby. 'Leaflets,' he sighed. 'We ought to drop George Formby over Germany.'

'He's usually back earlyish,' said Bevan defensively.

'Golf, that's it,' said Runciman putting on his forage cap, straightening it fiercely and going out. 'Get the men playing golf.'

When he had gone Hignet sighed: 'The sergeant wants action,' as if it were beyond him. 'They say they're actually sending some men home, back to their jobs, because they haven't got anything to do in the army.'

'*You*'re not going,' said Bevan. 'Hitler may strike at any time.'

It was very strange but James Bevan had known the house since his boyhood. It was called Southerly and faced the English Channel with a blanket of now badly cut lawn going down to the edge of the sand-and-shingle beach. As a thin, tall schoolboy on steamer trips from Southampton, to Bournemouth or Weymouth, he had always looked out for the flag, a blowhard Union Jack, flying from a white pole in the garden as if it were starched, wind-stretched even on the most unflappable summer days. The flagpole was still there, its paint splintering, but without the flag. Authority had taken it down.

Nothing surprised him these days. A deluge of regulations, some of them very curious, had issued from Whitehall as soon as hostilities had begun. They had probably been making them up, collecting and collating them, storing them, for decades. Unauthorised flags were not to be flown or shown. The Government could seize, at no notice whatever, *anything*; anything from a horse to a house. Officials could demand to be told private information, even private thoughts or desires. A citizen could be thrown into prison for fourteen years for failing in their duty to their country, although many citizens were uncertain as to what this duty might be. The drawing of maps and sketches was forbidden and if a person took a newspaper out of Britain it would be confiscated, although it could be readily purchased again in another country. Britons could still holiday in eternally neutral Switzerland where they could view German troops drilling just across the border and this had proved a popular attraction. Former soldiers came back with opinions that the enemy's goose-stepping not only looked ludicrous, but was also exhausting and could cause injury. At home a farmer could neither kill a pig nor indulge in the unlikely pleasure of smoking a cigar in an open field at night. Woodpigeons were to be exterminated but carrier pigeons became official property. Loitering beneath bridges or alongside railway lines was not allowed, nor was scraping gas-warning yellow paint from pillar-boxes. Staring at police officers or army sentry-boxes was highly suspect.

Even as a boy, James had been attracted to the house, Southerly; its fine windows and white, spread shutters, its outlook to the sweeping Channel, its windy weather-vane on a jaunty turret and its flag. Once, when he was on holiday from school, he had taken the train from Southampton, an unusual solo expedition, and had crawled like a sniper through the hedge and watched people standing on the lawn. There were ladies in extravagant hairstyles and the sweeping skirts of the early century, men formal and upright in the evening, set about in groups, conversing, laughing politely, with drinks in their fingers and servants carrying more glasses on trays. He remembered how enthralled he had been to spy on the genteel scene. He had lain concealed, the bracken scratching his bare knees, until it started getting dark and the people drifted into the house. One man lingered, a lone shadow, and was joined by a lady wearing a creamy dress who came through the half-light like a moth. The man was apparently waiting for her and, while the boy lay hidden and excited, they kissed with passion. James heard him say: 'It won't be long, darling. Not long now. Soon she will be gone.'

Wide eyed and worried he had travelled home, wondering what precautions he ought to take to save an unknown woman's life. But he told no one and did nothing although he kept an eye out for sudden, suspicious deaths in the *Southampton Echo*. Then there had been the time when he went with a Sunday school to Southerly for a Christmas tea and a magician. The ceilings were painted with idyllic scenes but so lofty that they were scarcely discernible.

On that October morning in 1939, however, it had become an officers' mess. Previously it had been a small and choice hotel, with views of the Isle of Wight and the lofty liners setting out on their luxurious voyages, but it shared the abrupt fate of hundreds of hotels within hours of war being declared.

'Threw the guests out in the street,' said Josef, the sole surviving servant, who now fulfilled multiple functions; porter, doorman, cellarman, waiter and informant. 'Defence Regulations, indeed. Old ladies, eighty and more, old gents. It was like the Nazis, sir, in Czechoslovakia. But this is England, and I don't care who hears me say it.' He glanced around as if he did. 'Some had been here years. It was like their home.'

Josef had more eyebrows than hair. He was short, stout and lined. He operated professionally from a low, almost secret room and at night he had to go outside and climb a fire escape to reach his quarters. He had a wireless set as big as a cupboard with wavebands for Delhi, Honolulu and Melbourne. 'I've had the police in just to make sure I'm not a spy,' he told Bevan with a certain pride. 'But it's not a transmitter and I'm not doing anything illegal, nothing that's going to endanger the country. I'm a Jew and I don't trust those Narsties.'

He had certificates pinned around his room certifying that he had listened to Stockholm, Helversum, Madrid and other places. 'I've never got a peep out of Honolulu or Delhi or Melbourne,' he admitted touching the face of the set a little sadly like someone who loved a child which had failed to come up to expectations. 'I get Berlin though. Clear.'

'Weren't the police worried about you listening?' said Bevan.

'Berlin? Worried? I'll say. Well, they've got to worry about something and it makes a change from telling people their blackout curtains don't fit. Coppers walking around in their tin helmets. Like I say, there's no law against it. The Jerries play the best Yankee music and I turn a deaf ear to their Nazi rubbish. They're saying that this war was started by Jews. Well, I don't know anybody who started it.'

After the parade had been dismissed and the gun practice was over, the Bofors's barrel shrouded by camouflage netting, Bevan went through a rusting gate in the hedge before the house. There was another entrance, at one side, crudely widened for military vehicles.

Thirty or more officers of several unconnected units dispersed along the neighbouring coast shared the mess; sappers engaged in digging tunnels without end, and ordnance types who had spent weeks taking apart a squadron of clapped-out tanks and trying to put them back together. Everyone was trying to look busy. Josef strolled out of the house and stood surveying the seashore as if he owned everything as far as his eye could see. He plucked a late daisy from the lawn and examined it.

'Shame we can't show the flag by the beach any longer, Josef,' said Bevan.

'Identification, sir,' sighed Josef. 'If a U-boat came up the Solent and saw the Union Jack he'd know right away it was England, now wouldn't he?' He glanced at Bevan as if he did not expect to be believed. 'Your boss is just back, sir.'

Major Durfield had wedged his backside in a chair, with a pot of coffee in front of him. He called for an extra cup. 'You know what I hate about this war?' he said to Bevan. He was nominally in charge of the artillery troop and another further down the coast which gave him ample excuse to dawdle between the two. He produced a flask and emptied a splash of whisky into his cup, making a token offer to Bevan before quickly slipping the flask away in an inner pocket.

'What's that, sir?'

'Golf,' said Durfield. 'Bloody golf.'

'Is it harder?'

'It's harder because the eighth at New Milton runs parallel to the road, right alongside. If you play early, which I have to, bearing in mind my duties, the damned people going to work, I suppose they're going to work anyway, some of them actually *bawl* at you from the bus. Obscene gestures, waving fists out of the windows. They seem to think I shouldn't be playing. Because it's wartime, for God's sake. They don't realise that when *I'm* locked in combat with the Hun they'll still be in their cosy factories, having their tea breaks, gossiping and going on their communist strikes.' He leaned forward as if ashamed of what he was about to divulge. 'Today, Bevan, I even hid in a bunker so the bastards wouldn't see me. Playing with a Navy chap straight home from convoy duty. He thought I was mad. I made him hide with me.' He laughed sourly. 'Like being in the damned trenches.'

'Good practice, sir.'

'I wonder if it is,' said the major. He put his cup down and tapped his nose confidingly. 'I wouldn't be surprised, Bevan, if this lot wasn't all over by Christmas.'

'Oh, the war. Who's going to win?'

'No winner. A draw, a tie. Hitler will talk to us and we will talk to Hitler and everyone will call it a day. We'll all be reasonable. Not everybody is against Germany, you know, not everybody in Parliament.'

'But it would happen again some time.'

'But not necessarily with the Boche, maybe with the Ruskies. At the moment the Germans are wedged between Russia and us, remember, and we've always feared the Reds. But by then you and I may be too old.' He surveyed Bevan. 'What are you now?'

'Thirty-nine. Old as the century, sir.'

'Right. Well, when it happens again perhaps we can sit back and simply observe. Personally, I had enough of the First War. Did you catch that?'

'Yes, I did.'

'You were young.'

'I'll never learn,' Bevan laughed ruefully.

'You've parted from your wife, haven't you?'

'Yes, sir.'

'I've parted from three of the buggers.'

They finished the coffee and refused Josef's offer to make another pot. 'Let's get out of here before all those oily armourers, or whatever they call themselves, come in, mucking up the cutlery,' said Durfield. 'The rate they're working on those tanks they'll be ready for the next war. Why the War Office had to cram half the British Army down here I'll never know.'

Bevan followed him into the shabby lobby. Durfield always stepped out in a commanding way, all that was commanding about him. With every day of military occupation the house was becoming more ill used. There was a pile of bicycles, another of gas-mask containers, and an incident with a fire extinguisher had ruined the fabric covering of one wall; a fallen chandelier stood propped like an open umbrella.

'I've known this place for years,' said Bevan.

'You mentioned it before. Pity it's such a mess. But at least it's being used. Half the hotels they emptied in such a hurry are still empty, those bloody Whitehall numbskulls don't know what to do with them. I'm glad they've somehow left this chap Josef. He's a Jew, isn't he? Jolly useful though.' He stood and straightened his uniform, and for a moment looked almost important. 'I've been meaning to inspect the turret, take a look at it. That knobbly bit on the end of the house. Those air-raid-warden johnnies want to use it unless we need it. We ought to *make sure* we need it. They're civilians. Don't want civvies spying on everything we do.'

Bevan followed behind his expansive backside, then overtook him and opened a scraping door.

'It's up here, sir. I remember going up when I was a kid.'

The tower smelled dank, so enclosed that the emulsion on the walls fragmented on their shoulders. Bevan pushed open the door at the top and they went in. The major, patting the dust from his uniform, resounded in the empty place. His subordinate walked towards the windows, the sun filtered by the grime on the glass. He picked up a yellow page of newspaper. 'Watch it,' said the commanding officer. 'Somebody might have wiped their arse on that.'

Bevan had already checked. It was the sports page of the *Daily Mail*. The headline said: 'Cricket and Football to be Cancelled.' It was dated the previous 31 August. He screwed up the page and wiped one of the windows. A finger of sun drifted in.

'It's not too bad up here,' said Durfield sniffing around. 'Cleaned up it would be a good place for something or other, even if it's only to have a crafty nap. We must make sure that those ARP twerps don't get their hands on it.'

When he had rubbed most of the grime from one pane Bevan worked the newspaper over another so that they each had a peep-hole. 'Our Bofors looks good from this angle,' approved the commanding officer. 'Although how they can say it fires a hundred and odd rounds a minute defeats me. The bloody thing's hand loaded. It can only manage eight. When's the other gun back?'

'Thursday,' said Bevan. 'They promised.'

'Some promise,' sniffed Durfield. 'I doubt if they know how it works.'

Bevan was eyeing the coast laid out before them, the very cloth of England, green and brown, with a faintly glistening sea; Christchurch Bay, grey serrated with silver. The minesweeper was still lolling out there, not doing very much, and a solid merchant ship followed by a smaller one, already trying to keep up, was in the Solent heading for the sea.

'Bugger going to sea,' said Durfield. 'Those U-boats are bastards.'

Bevan said: 'You can see for miles, can't you.' He looked towards the old hump of Hurst Castle, then west to Hengistbury Head where the Saxons landed. Then there were the bungalows of England, squat and untroubled; Milford-on-Sea, Barton-on-Sea, row after white row.

'What's going on down there?' asked Durfield. He pointed to the beach. 'Are those our bods?'

'Yes, they are.'

'What are they up to?'

'Building sandcastles, sir.'

'Oh, right. Good, good.'

*   *   *

Gunner Bairnsfather was one of the few men in the troop who could drive a car, for he had been a baker's roundsman. The unit had a 1938 Ford, whorled with camouflage. 'Look at it, sir,' he said running his thumb around the contours of the green and brown paint. 'Old Jerry could spot this a mile away.'

Bevan grinned. The gunner was young but almost bald, his fair, wispy hair merging with his pale pate.

'Everybody in our family's like this,' he had boasted in the barrack room, hands fumbling for his spindly strands. 'Even my mum.'

The strategic lesson with the sandcastles had gone well. The men had sat around contemplating their system of redoubts with a pride recalled from childhood beach days, patting pieces here and there, excavating careful moats, ensuring the sand was sufficiently damp and adhesive. Sergeant Runciman looked for once fulfilled and swung a child's tin beach bucket he had found, a summer relic. The handle was snapped but the bucket had Snow White and the Seven Dwarfs painted around it and between them they had a competition to see who could recognise and name the dwarfs. There was even some sharp argument. Gunner Brown said: 'You, Cartwright, you wouldn't know fucking Bashful if 'e shouted at you.'

'You'd know Dopey, Brown.'

Bevan strode over the shingle to the sand and was asked to adjudicate who had built the best tower. The lank Gunner Purcell, called Persil, won. They had each put a silver threepenny bit in the kitty and he now gathered the tiny coins with a swagger. 'I was always good at sandcastles,' he said.

They had gone through the textbook tactics for overcoming fortified points, some of which had been in the army manual since before the Boer War. Runciman had skipped the section on the deployment of horses.

The day had remained soft and the men had enjoyed wasting time on the beach. Some had even taken off their cumbersome regulation boots and paddled in the shallows when the lecture was finished, splashing each other with their toes.

'War's not too bad sometimes,' philosophised Bairnsfather as he opened the car door for Bevan. 'Nice morning on the sands. Go for a ride in the afternoon. It's the fighting I don't fancy, sir.'

'Some people say there won't be any,' said Bevan.

'What do you think, sir?'

'I don't know. Ask Hitler.'

They were going to drive to Southampton to pick up a bag of documents from the London train. Bevan was glad of the trip.

'It could be worse,' said Bairnsfather as he bent and turned the starting-handle. 'We could be looking for jobs.' The engine fired and he patted the shivering bonnet. 'There's a million and a half on the dole.'

'The army's full,' said Bevan.

'And doing Sweet Fanny Adams,' agreed Bairnsfather. 'Still *something*'s got to happen *sometime*.' They drove away from the coast, through the serene bungalows, towards the New Forest.

'You know, there was a famous cartoonist with the same name as you,' Bevan said.

Pigs and ponies were at the side of the narrow way, cottages with deep-thatched, rounded roofs crouched behind the autumn trees. The scene was grey and yellow. 'No relation,' said the gunner. 'My mum tried to make out he was, like in the street, but she was just showing off the way women do.'

'He was famous in the last war.'

'I know, sir. Old Bill. I can't fathom how anybody could laugh about all that mud, all those bangs. If we ever get into action, I hope nobody's there to make fun of us.'

The road went like a finger across the forest. They did not see another vehicle until they were almost at the Southampton junction where they came upon a squat Bren-gun carrier tipped into the bracken-lined ditch. Bairnsfather enjoyed the sight. 'How did they manage that? I'd like to drive one of them. Right down the middle of our street.'

'How was the dance last night?' asked Bevan as though he would have liked to have been there.

'It turned into a booze-up, sir,' said Bairnsfather. 'They wouldn't let us on the dance floor because of our boots. The ruddy caretaker said we'd damage it.'

'So you didn't dance?'

'Took it in turns, sir. There was a local civvy and we kept him in beer while we borrowed his dancing pumps. They didn't fit everybody but we managed. In the end we all got on the floor anyway, for the Gay Gordons, all sozzled.'

'That didn't do the floor much good.'

'No, sir. And I've still got the bloke's shoes.'

A locomotive oozing steam stood against the platform, its green Southern Railway carriages strung out to the very extreme of the station. People were hurrying with suitcases, porters pushing barrows of luggage and handling passengers aboard. Under the clock the apparently anxious stationmaster checked an outsized silver pocket watch, looped on a heavy chain, like a starter in a race. Flag in hand the guard stood dumb and grumpy because blowing a whistle was prohibited; it now meant incendiary bombs. The railwaymen missed their whistles. 'Christchurch, Bournemouth, Poole,' he bellowed.

Towards the end of the train a first-class carriage

door was open and, near it on the platform, a tall man in a pin-striped suit and carrying a bowler hat stood in conversation with a young woman in a smart pale costume. Their talk was apparently deep. Not until the guard shouted finally did the man briefly embrace her. She kissed him and then he boarded the train leaving her watching. He slammed the door like an emphatic goodbye and Bevan saw the brief white wave of his hand from the dimness of the corridor. Slowly the woman raised her hand.

Sandbags were piled over the stationmaster's office making it like a pyramid; there were also some around the ticket windows and the Nestlé's chocolate machine. 'We had a few bags left over,' said a porter to Bevan. 'If Jerry comes, we might need that chocolate.'

The Military Police office was also sandbagged. There was only a small aperture and the door was locked.

'Sorry, sir,' said the corporal from inside. 'We got a couple of drunk and violents so we had to see to the door.' Bevan peered through the fortified hole. Two handcuffed sailors were lying full length along two benches; a military policeman sitting on one whose face was anguished, and a tubby girl in ATS uniform with fine thighs straddling the other who looked less perturbed.

The papers they had come to collect were in a War Office canvas bag and they were handed over by the MP. 'Caused ructions on the train,' he said nodding over his shoulder to the restrained sailors. 'Called the guard a conchie.' He lowered his voice. 'Mind, he is more or less. Reserved occupation, on the railway. But he says he'll be a conscientious objector if needs be. He don't believe in war.' Again Bevan peered around the MP's shoulder at the two ratings. The military policeman said: 'I don't believe in war, neither. But I've got to, sir. I've got to.'

'We all have,' said Bevan. He signed for the bag and left.

As he turned the corner outside the station he almost collided with the young woman he had seen on the platform. She was now preceded by a grey-uniformed chauffeur carrying her suitcase. Bevan, trying to avoid the couple, dropped the War Office bag, almost on her feet, and she picked it up. Her face had been serious, almost stern, but now she smiled. 'Secret documents?'

'Highly,' Bevan smiled back. 'About the unit rations.' He thanked her and took the bag.

'I promise I'm not a spy,' she said.

There was a Rolls Royce. The chauffeur put her suitcase down and opened the door for her. Then he put the case in the front and climbed into the driving seat. The car, polished blue, eased away.

Bevan saw Bairnsfather's face pushed against the windscreen of the army car. 'Now that was *nice*,' said his driver as he got in. 'What I'd give to have a spin in that. I've seen it around where we are. It can't go far on the petrol ration.'

They began to drive through the downcast streets of Southampton. Its docks had saved it from the worst ravages of the 1930s depression, particularly its ocean-liner terminals; the travelling wealthy had saved the jobs of working dockers. But the war had brought melancholy; there were half-finished buildings, including a nearly-completed new cinema now shrouded in corrugated iron. Few vehicles were in the street. An Austin propelled by gas with an inflated bag on its roof stuttered in front of them.

'They'll be putting up sails next,' muttered Bairnsfather.

But once out of the city centre they could see the grand spread of the docks, the upstanding masts and funnels of ships and the fingers of overhanging cranes. An ocean liner rose above them all, stripped of her luxury, waiting for troops to embark. They had painted her grey, grey as the sky, grey as the city, grey as the war.

'I was born in Southampton,' said Bevan.

'Yes, sir, I heard.'

The officer scanned the streets through the windscreen. 'Take the next turn on the left, then left again. I haven't been here for years.'

'My old man was a gunner in the First War,' said Bairnsfather. 'Stationed at Rochester. A Zeppelin came over one night but they had no ammo. It hadn't turned up or something. All he could do was look at it. He said it looked so pretty in the moonlight, it would have been a shame to shoot it down.'

He negotiated the corner, despite the sandbags from a police telephone box having slid into the road.

'This is it,' said Bevan, still leaning towards the windscreen. 'It's not changed. The one, two, three, fourth house along.'

They pulled up among the damp orange leaves at the kerb. 'That's the house.' Bevan pointed across the street. 'The one with the big tree in front of it.' How well he remembered that tree.

'We lived on the top floor,' he said. 'My mother was a music teacher.'

On impulse he got out of the car. Bairnsfather watched him as he walked across to the house and thought how some men were so solitary. Bevan stood in front, below the tree, then, as though on a second impulse, walked up the short, unkempt path to the front door. The paint was as faded as it had ever been. He put out his hand and touched the wood and, to his surprise, the door opened with the pressure of his hand.

Bevan stepped in. There was a room facing him where Mrs Colbourn had lived with her doomed dog.

He turned and stared up the narrow staircase to the middle landing and, as though drawn, went up the uncarpeted steps. The house echoed and smelled as if it were unoccupied. His boots sounded loud on the wooden treads.

On the middle landing was another dusty door. Mr Whistler had once lived there, forever complaining about the noise of Vera Bevan's violin lessons. The upward steps had some shreds of carpet still fixed to them, a piece on one stair, then, after several bare threads, another piece. After all these years, twenty-five now, he could not believe that this was the remnant of the blue carpet once fitted there, the carpet which his younger sister Agnes had used as a toboggan run, sitting on a tin tray and skeltering down to the landing below.

He could see her doing it now, laughing, bumping, legs flying. Sadness came over him.

He mounted the stretch of stairs. If anyone appeared he would pretend he was a billeting officer who had come to the wrong house. He reached the top landing, their landing. The door to the apartment was six inches open. Gently he pushed it and the room so well remembered opened out in front of him.

Almost fearfully Bevan stepped in, only one step, a wait and then another, walking into a half-forgotten life. This had been the big room at the front of the house with the bay window where he and Agnes had spent so much time looking into the street below. He went to the bay and stood sadly remembering her excited squeak, her lively face, her spirit, her adventurous dreams.

He turned away almost militarily from the window and went across the bare room. One by one he went through each of the other doors, into the parlour where his mother had given her excruciating lessons, the kitchen with an electric cooker where two gas rings had once been, the three bedrooms, his mother's, his and the little one for Agnes.

For a final moment he went back to the window. The horizon of the house tops was much the same, the sky showing between the chimney-pots. He could see Bairnsfather standing beside the camouflaged car below. Bevan was a generation older and the young soldier and his barrack-room comrades were his responsibility. There might come a time, perhaps soon, when they would be called to face action, even death, together. He would need to look after them. The thought brought him back to the present and he went out of the door closing it carefully and pensively behind him.

The land lying back from the southern coast had seen much of the history of England. After his landing and battle at Hastings in 1066 the concern of William the Conqueror had been to make secure the meadows of the south so that he could feed his horses. Without grass his army could not move. Thirteen years after he became King William of England he returned to the same places and, to the west of them, cleared the peasants from their hovels and fragments of land to make a chase, a hunting ground, which he called the New Forest.

Alf Unsworth had been taught so at school and now he lived and worked every day in the middle of his history lesson. The magistrates' court where he made his policeman's way that autumn morning also housed the Verderers, where men with archaic titles made rules for the one hundred and forty-five square miles of woodland and moor. His steps took him through the familiar sloping street, as quiet as it had ever been that wartime morning, the pubs and the shops deep under their thatches, the hotel with its white tablecloths visible through mullioned windows, the sturdy church, its churchyard spilling down to the wall leaning over the road. Alice Liddell, who had been in real life the Alice of Lewis Carroll, was buried there and Detective Sergeant Unsworth occasionally thought that Lyndhurst had a touch of the oddities of Wonderland.

The coming of the war had, for a brief time, seen a decrease in the incidence of crime, both local and national, as though wrongdoers had resolved to contribute to the common effort. But, as with the population generally, the novelty had worn off with the non-arrival of Armageddon, and criminals realised that with petrol rationing, the threat of shortages, and the useful blackout, there were advantages for their trade.

Buildings summarily vacated by wartime decree, hotels, colleges, and offices evacuated by civil servants (to areas that were often to prove more dangerous) were a real proposition. Doors were faulty, windows left unlatched, and contents lying unattended. Good beds were spirited away, dining tables, chairs, cutlery and crockery; typewriters were whisked from windows and filing cabinets carted boldly from main exits. It was a major redistribution of property. There was also the even more profitable pilfering of plumbing. Taps and lengths of chain and plugs were all commercial items and the lead, the bluey as it was known, was the most commercial of all.

On this mild grey morning Unsworth had the circumstances of a number of these burglaries on his mind. He doubted if they would be solved, if arrests would ever be made, and he knew that locals were not involved, poaching being more in their line. It was the Southampton gangs, supplemented by soldiers, sailors and airmen, on leave or off-duty. Men who might be called to die for their country were not necessarily law-abiding.

Unsworth had a naturally serious face. Today, if it were even more set, it was because his twenty-year-old son was going into the navy. A German U-boat had that week evaded the anti-submarine nets at Scapa Flow, in the Orkney Islands, and sunk the prime British battleship *Royal Oak* at anchor. Eight hundred and thirty-three men had drowned only yards from the shore. He and Ellen, his wife, together with Alan, his son, had listened to the news bulletin. It gave the fewest possible details. Disasters were not dwelt upon. That morning they had eaten breakfast together, conversing as if Alan were embarking on a pre-war hiking holiday, then shaken hands at the railway station. He knew that Ellen would be tearful over the washing-up suds, praying for an arranged peace although, as she said, she personally had no time for that Hitler.

As he walked a wavering figure on a bicycle came into his view at the top of the angled street. The rider launched himself down the hill and approached, legs recklessly spread out like wings on either side of the machine. 'Good morning, vicar,' said Unsworth when the man had braked. They liked each other. 'We're in more or less the same business,' George Goodenough had once said to him. 'Both of us try to catch sinners.'

His long clerical chin supported a grin. 'On the trail of malefactors, Alfred?'

'Off to court, reverend,' said Unsworth.

'Ah, the sword of justice.' Goodenough's bicycle was balanced by the deeply scratched toe of his left shoe, the other leg remaining thrust out into the street. His church was in a village two miles away. 'We are having to move evensong to three in the afternoon,' he said as if hopeful that Unsworth would turn up. 'This blackout business is causing havoc, you know. Last Sunday one of our regular worshippers was struck by a mystery bicycle. Almost rent her asunder.'

'It's doing more damage than the actual war,' said Unsworth.

'Darkness over the land,' sighed Goodenough. He gave a push with his toe and continued down the hill, legs still projecting. Unsworth wondered if he rode that way in the blackout.

His policeman's task that morning was to apply for the remand of a Pole arrested while siphoning petrol from cars parked after dark in quiet villages. It was Monday and the usual blank-faced parade of weekend drunks trooped singly into the dock; drunk and incapable, drunk and disorderly, drunk and indecent (urinating outside the fire station), they came and went, each half a crown lighter in pocket apart from the urinator who was fined five shillings. 'The fire station,' said Lady Violet Foxley, the chairman of magistrates, 'is an important part of the country's defence.'

The next accused was short and so familiar to the court that he was followed spontaneously by an usher with a wooden footstool which was placed in the dock so the accused could see the magistrates. 'I was on war service, ma'am,' he announced.

He was fined the usual five shillings for poaching. 'I was looking for enemy parachutists,' he said without much hope.

'And something for the pot,' added Lady Violet. She had known Catcher Hurrock since he was a schoolboy with a catapault, just as she knew all the local people. Her stern exterior was softened by cheerful eyes.

'Next case,' called the clerk. Then, with difficulty: 'Wladyslaw Tyssowski.'

Unsworth rose and the Pole went into the dock and looked about him with high-cheeked hauteur, eyes bright and belligerent. The charges were read. Siphoning petrol from parked vehicles including a police patrol car. 'Can I check the spelling of the name?' said Mr Deemster, the clerk. 'It has become so difficult these days.'

Unsworth spelled out the name. The Pole looked pleased. 'Wladyslaw was a Polish king,' he said.

'I have to apply for a remand in this case, Your Worship,' said Unsworth to Lady Violet.

'Does he have a fixed address?'

'Warsaw,' said the man in the dock.

'He is living in lodgings, ma'am,' said Unsworth.

'Is he likely to abscond?'

'Escaped from Poland,' interrupted the accused.

Everyone looked at each other. Lady Violet hesitated, then said: 'Seven days in custody.'

'I think we will be able to proceed then,' said Unsworth. The man in the dock raised his fist and shouted: 'Polzka!' as he was led away. The Pole's place in the dock was taken by a soldier. Unsworth made for the door as Bevan came through it.

Unsworth never forgot a face. He turned from the door and sat in his previous seat.

'Your name?' the clerk asked the soldier.

'534869, Gunner Bairnsfather, Harry, Royal Artillery, Your Worship,' said Bairnsfather noisily coming to attention in the wooden dock.

'You are charged with the theft of a pair of shoes, valued at five and sixpence, the property of John Barley at the Public Hall, Lyndhurst on 14 October. How do you plead?'

Bairnsfather's chin rose. 'Not guilty, Your Worship. All a mistake.'

In the dock he said: 'They wouldn't let us dance in our army boots, so this chap was lending us his shoes. He went off without them. He'd had a few. I was just keeping them for him. They wouldn't even fit me.'

'I know Barley,' said Lady Violet. 'He's very forgetful, particularly in certain circumstances.' Leaning over the bench studying the soldier closely, she decided she liked him. 'Case dismissed,' she said. 'Make sure he gets his shoes back.'

'I think I know you,' said Unsworth to Bevan when they were outside. 'Jim . . .'

'Bevan,' said the army officer. 'And you're Alfie Unsworth.'

'Right,' said Unsworth. 'Totton Road School.' His naturally serious expression relaxed into a smile. 'Remember the *Titanic*?'

'Will I ever forget it.'

On that April day in 1912 they had been taken to see the wondrous *Titanic* in the dock at Southampton; flags and pennants streaming in the smoky morning, funnels tall and upright, awaiting her first and last passengers.

There were two hundred children on the quay, their faces raised to the great wall of the hull, the bow like an axe. Alfie had stealthily moved through the mackintoshes. 'Keep this for me, will you,' he said to James. 'Be a pal.'

James took the object, a small brass wheel. It weighed down his pocket. 'What is it?' he whispered.

'Souvenir,' Alfie whispered back. 'Don't show nobody.'

James promised. He took the wheel home and put it under his bed. His mother was taking a violent violin lesson in the rear room. He had his tea and then took out the brass wheel again. At nine o'clock he looked from the window and saw Alfie in the street. He went down the long stairs to the front door.

'Got it?'

'Yes. Here.'

They were standing conspiratorially behind a steaming horse that had been left in the street with its cart while the driver delivered coal.

'How did you get it?'

The other boy took a long time to look up. 'I *got* it,' he said. 'One day I'll tell you how.'

The wheel was three inches in diameter with a short stump of metal axle through the middle. The street gas lamps reflected in its buffed and burnished surface. 'Brass,' said Alfie running his finger around the rim. 'Best-quality brass that is. They use gold with it.'

'Gold?'

'So I was told.' He held the short axle with two fingers. The wheel revolved easily. 'See that,' said Alfie in a moment of prophecy: 'If that wheel was under the sea for years it would still turn. Easy as now.' The boys looked at each other. The horse at the front of the coal cart softly deposited a load of dung. Alfie said: 'You know the ship's got watertight doors. This wheel comes from them.'

The coalman, ebony in the lamplight, emerged from a house across the street, an empty sack over his shoulder. He wore a skullcap of leather with another sack like a cape over his shoulders, sweat glowing on his black brow. 'What you two up to?' he asked. Alfie had already passed the wheel back to James who hid it behind his back. 'Waiting to pick up the dung,' Alfie said.

'All I do is help people grow their rhubarb,' grumbled the coalman. 'I ought to charge.' He climbed behind the horse, lifted the heavy brake, and the animal plodded off, the cart creaking, through the damp evening street.

Alfie said to James: 'You're my friend.' James nodded. Alfie patted the wheel. 'Hang on to it for me.'

'I'll keep it under my mattress,' promised James.

'I'll remember this,' said the other boy. He held out his hand and they shook seriously. Alfie turned to study the pile of dollops on the road. 'I'll have that lot,' he said. 'The woman next door will give me a ha'penny for that.' He glanced up with an expression of fair play. 'Unless you want it.'

'No. No thanks,' said James. 'We've only got window-boxes.'

'Just take a bit.'

Resourcefully he turned and dodged to a dustbin beneath the gas lamp opposite, lifted the lid and took out a screwed-up newspaper. 'This'll do,' he said. He spread it out on the road and, using a piece he tore from a page, picked up the warm ginger dung, oval piece by oval piece, and piled it at the centre of the paper. 'Good stuff,' he said expertly. It did not make a large heap and he seemed halted by second thoughts before tearing off another section of the newspaper, placing one piece of dung in it and handing it to James who took it dubiously. The fruity smell filled his nose. 'That's for you,' Alfie said. His eyes hardened. 'Hide the wheel. Don't ever tell.'

He loped off along the gas-lit pavement, the droppings steaming in the newspaper, like a boy carrying a bag of fish and chips. James, with the twin burdens of the wheel and the solitary nugget, turned back towards his home. He dropped the dung in the hedge of the small front garden. His mother would not appreciate him bringing it back.

From their earliest days James and his sister Agnes had lived with the sounds of their mother's musical tuition. Vera specialised in beginners. Agnes was two years younger than her brother, conceived during one of their father's brief but romantic visits. She grew to hate the violin.

As James entered the apartment on that evening, the stolen wheel beneath his school jersey, the dying scrapes of the day's last lesson were shivering through the dim interior. Agnes was sitting in James's room as she often did since it was the most distant from the source of the noise. 'Why doesn't she ever get someone who can *play*?' she complained. They were both quiet children and they enjoyed each other's reserved company, reading or drawing or making up games. Sometimes, in the school holidays, James was allowed to go by train on short journeys to Portsmouth where he saw the ships of the British Battle Fleet, and sometimes to the New Forest. But usually he was at home with Agnes. Living on a top floor was different from living at street level. Sometimes they played houses, as mother and father, using her dolls as children. In the game Agnes sometimes pretended to be a violin teacher and her antics made them stuff his bedclothes in their mouths to muffle their laughter. As part of the games too they often climbed into his bed, as parents might do, the dolls all tucked up for the night.

They had never heard their mother perform anything more than the scales, exercises and simple pieces required in her teaching; when she was alone she never played. Sometimes they wondered if she *could*. When they asked her to play to them she invariably held up her long fingers and said she was tired.

Their father Vincent had left home, so he claimed, on account of the violin. He was a languid, lazy and vulnerable man who believed he suffered from acute hearing, the opposite of deafness. He finally left while his wife was instructing a particularly backward pupil. Years later when he was supposed to be dead he reappeared in James's life and told his son that he had been conceived on the very night of the new century, the New Year of 1900. Vera and he had returned from celebrating in the early hours. 'We danced the Turn-of-the-Century Two-step,' he remembered. 'And we made you later.'

2

How shocked and frightened the two boys had been when the news came out. The newspaper billboards said: '*Titanic* Sinks,' in terrible tall headlines. And already they were questioning the *watertight doors*! Hardly able to hold the *Daily Mail* between them they read the drama. Twenty-seven years later Unsworth remembered how it had been as he walked from the court to the police station.

'You've got to give yourself up, Alfie!'

'Me! What about you, Jim Bevan? You hid the wheel.'

'*You* pinched it.'

'I didn't. It was the other boy. It was him what thieved it.'

'Which other boy?'

'I'm not telling.'

'I only hid it,' said James.

'That's as bad. We'd both better go.' Unsworth's twelve-year-old face had collapsed with anguish. 'We could be hung, Jim. You and me both. There's 'undreds drowned.'

With this in mind they decided not to surrender to the police but to bury the wheel instead. They took it out into the forest on a bus and buried it secretly. After twenty-seven years neither could remember the place.

Unsworth knew when he got home that day Ellen would have been crying. She had dried her face but there were traces. She started weeping again when he embraced her. 'I hate the thought,' she sniffled. 'Our Alan on that horrible sea. Cold and horrible and grey it is.' She looked at him challengingly. 'It seems like only sailors are getting killed,' she sniffed. 'Hundreds, thousands, already. Soldiers and airmen don't get killed like that.' He regarded her sharply.

'Oh, Alf, he's our son.'

'He only went off today.'

'He said he'd phone as soon as he could. I hope the beds are not damp.' She was making tea.

'First he'll have to do weeks and weeks of training,' her husband said. 'Most of it on dry land. He may never go to sea at all.'

'He *wants* to,' she put in. 'I tried to tell him otherwise, but he *wants* to. He could have joined the police where he'd be safe.' He grimaced.

'Well, let's wait and see. He may end up in a comfy office in Portsmouth.'

'I hope to God he does.' She busied herself cutting the bread and butter and took out a fresh jar of home-made jam, breaking the seal. She stopped and regarded him hopefully. 'Can't you put a word in? Being as you're in authority. I mean you *are*. Or get *somebody* to. All the time I keep hearing of fellows who've got good, safe places, because somebody's put a word in.'

'I'll talk to the First Lord of the Admiralty,' he said patting her arm.

'Don't joss, Alf.'

She poured the tea, the same solid afternoon tea that they had enjoyed throughout their peaceful, peacetime lives. There was no rationing yet, only of petrol, and the shops were cheerfully full for the approach of Christmas. But she said: 'How long will we be able to eat what we like? In the last war, remember, they only brought rationing in when people began fighting in the food shops.'

He bit into a crust heavy with plum jam. 'You ought to make plenty of this next summer,' he said half seriously. 'Just in case. They can't stop the plums growing.'

'It's the sugar,' Ellen pointed out. The thought made her decide to tell him. 'I've got a secret hoard,' she said.

'Of sugar?'

'Of everything. Well, not everything, but a lot of things. Tinned.'

'Hoarding,' he said grinning, 'is illegal. I think.'

'It's in Alan's room. Under his bed. I'm not sure even he knew it was there.'

'I don't suppose Alan spent a lot of time looking under the bed.'

'He used to when he was little. For boonymen and suchlike. Later on it was for socks.' She began to rise from the table. 'I'll show you.'

Enjoying the conspiratorial intimacy of the moment, he slipped his arm about her comfortable waist. Her rounded face touched his and he followed her up the stairs, into the small bedroom on the landing which had been their son's ever since they moved into the house in 1929. Alan had been ten then and the room had fitted him. 'He'll feel at home if they put him in a submarine service,' Unsworth said.

'God forbid,' she said, her face again creased. 'Under the water is worse.' Sadly she surveyed the room with its group photograph of the Lyndhurst Cricket Club and the Portsmouth Cup Final football team of 1939. There was a model aeroplane, a Boulton-Paul Defiant and a shelf of boyhood books. 'He had a picture of Lana Turner,' said Ellen, 'but it looks like he's taken it with him.' In the dimness of the October day there was a bird singing in the tree outside the net-curtained window.

'Listen to him,' said Unsworth.

'It's that robin,' she said. She bent and lifted the hem of the quilt. 'Remember all the hours I took over this.'

She kneeled and from below the bed pulled a wide cardboard box covered with a tea towel which she took away revealing the tops of dozens of tins. 'That's enough for a siege,' he said kneeling beside her.

'That's exactly what it's meant for.' She began picking up the tins, one by one. 'Salmon,' she said. 'John West.'

'Took the best,' he read around the label. 'The choice cut.'

'I've got half a dozen of those. Then there's sardines here, and pilchards, and another half-dozen of corned beef, and baked beans.' One at a time, as though making moves in a game, she placed the tins on the carpet and manoeuvring the cardboard box to one side pulled another from below the bed.

'Chunks,' she said lifting a tin of pineapple. 'Eight, and I'm going to get some more. And these are nice cling peaches.'

'Salmon . . . peaches,' he said. He picked up a jar of fish paste. 'Months of Sunday treats.'

Neatly she began to pile the tins away. 'That's not what it's meant for, Alf. We'll be short of food before long.'

'What do we do if Jerry invades?' he teased. 'Scoff it all as fast as we can? Gobble up twelve tins of salmon and all the peaches before the Hun gets to Lyndhurst?'

He helped her push the boxes back below the bed and she carefully pulled the hem of the counterpane down saying: 'They'll never find them.' Her face straightened. He held her for a moment in the confined room with the robin still singing freely outside the window. He pushed her gently and lay on top of her on the single bed, their thighs slotting warmly. 'Who knows what's going to happen,' he said. 'Nobody seems to know, Chamberlain,

Hitler, nobody. I certainly don't.' He studied her close, serious face. 'Let's have some chunks now.'

'Keep your hands off them,' she said.

In the orderly room, when Bevan went in that morning, were the usual War Office directives; about stirrup-pump training ('How to Extinguish Incendiary Bombs'), fuel supplies to service units north of Edinburgh, the grade of accommodation to be offered to visiting entertainers ('There must be a bath in the vicinity'), and a warning headed: 'Mixing Socially With Other Ranks.'

Officers, it said, should use different bars in public houses from those frequented by their men and should never encourage other ranks to buy drinks; nor should a drink be offered, whatever the circumstances. '*Don't, because the soldier happens to be your father or brother, drink with him in a public bar. Find somewhere private. He is sufficiently proud of you not to want to behave in a manner unbecoming to your rank.*'

'Christ,' he breathed. 'Who thinks up these things?' Bombardier Hignet looked up from his newspaper.

'What was that, sir?'

Bevan passed the directive to him. 'It is bollocks, isn't it, sir,' said Hignet mildly. 'If you don't mind me swearing. Class bollocks.'

He rummaged in a pile of newspapers he kept in a corner. 'The other day there was a letter in *The Times*,' he said. He found it.

Sergeant Runciman appeared at the door to the small office as Hignet began to recite in an assumed élite and high-pitched voice: '*I note with sadness that the middle, lower middle and working classes are now receiving the King's commission. These classes, unlike the old aristocratic and feudal classes who led the old army, have never had "their people" to consider. This aspect of life is completely new to them, and they have very largely fallen down on it in their capacity as army officers. Man management is not a subject which can be "taught"; it is an attitude of mind, and with the old school tie men this was instinctive and part of the philosophy of life.'*

Runciman looked from the bombardier to the captain. 'Which class are you, sir?' asked Hignet.

Bevan smiled. 'Failed working class.'

All the men grinned. Runciman said: 'I thought I'd take them on a bit of a route march, sir. As much as they can manage. The first three miles, I estimate. Their poor feet won't last longer than that. But at least we've got all the stragglers and malingerers back.'

'Well, at last we'll have the numbers. It won't look like the dawn patrol,' said Bevan. 'Is Cartwright permitted to go getting off with old flames while he's on compassionate leave to look for his vanished wife?'

'I don't think it's something that's covered in King's Regulations, sir. He says he did look for his wife but he couldn't find her.'

Runciman went out. Bevan said to the clerk: 'I'm going across to the mess. Haven't seen the old man today.'

'Sick, sir,' said Hignet without looking up. 'Flat out in his quarters.'

'I'm the last to know.'

'You're in command now, sir.'

'Splendid!' Bevan banged his flat hand on the desk. 'In that case we'll get the men fallen in, transport them across the Channel, advance under cover of darkness and hit the Germans where they least expect it.' He paused: 'On the other hand maybe we'll simply do this route march towards Lymington.'

'Better, sir,' agreed Hignet. 'Attack at night is not up their street. Gunner Purcell and Gunner Brown are afraid of the dark.'

They had the second gun back now behind its rampart

of sandbags, and the unit looked quite warlike in the wintry morning, the full company parading under the twin barrels pointing towards the wide and vacant sky. From the orderly room doorway Bevan watched as Runciman got the men into order and snapped them to attention. Then he marched over and carried out his inspection. He took more care than usual because they were going out on the public roads.

Going along the front rank he reached Bairnsfather, leaned closer and lowered his voice. 'What happened to the local chap's shoes?'

'Back on his feet, sir,' Bairnsfather whispered too.

Bevan turned to Runciman and they traded salutes. Bevan stepped back below the elevated guns. The sergeant approached confidingly: 'I won't take them too far, in case Jerry comes.'

'If the siren goes, get them back at the double,' said Bevan endeavouring to look him in the eye. 'If necessary commandeer transport, a bus, anything.'

'Yes, sir,' said Runciman. He whirled towards the ranks. 'Parade! Parade . . . riiiiight turn!' His body stiffened, his hands shot down his sides. 'By the right . . . Quiiiiick march!'

Bevan watched them wheel away. He turned and walked towards the officers' quarters. He found Major Durfield sitting up in bed reading the *Daily Mirror* with a glass of whisky on the locker and the bottle on the floor only half concealed by the bedclothes. 'I'll be all right in a couple of days,' said Durfield weakly. 'Ready to resume command.'

He eyed the tumbler as though contemplating a swig but instead pulled himself up straighter in the bed. His pyjamas incorporated the regimental crest. 'What are the chaps doing?' he enquired as if it had been preying on his mind.

'We've got a full company, at long last,' Bevan told him. 'Everyone is back. Sergeant Runciman's taken them on a route march.'

'Where?' The CO looked alarmed.

'Towards Lymington.'

'God, I hope they don't frighten the civilians.'

Runciman personally doubted whether all the men would last the march. Lymington and back was beyond them. Those who had been taken to hospital after the senna-pods scare would be bound to drop out after a mile or so, probably in the area of the Cozy Café in New Milton. The men who had been excused boots were now wearing them and one, he noted, was already developing an introductory limp.

But all these worries were put from his mind by the appearance on the opposite pavement of a troop of uniformed Boy Scouts marching badly but stridently in the opposite direction. The tall person in charge, also in Scout array, was thumping the ground with the end of a stave as he strode. Runciman saw his own men were distracted. 'Eyes front!' he hurriedly bellowed. '*Left*, right, *left*, right, *left*, right.'

'*Right*, left, *right*, left, *right*, left,' responded the man leading the Scouts. He was bony as well as lofty, his legs like wire projecting from his shorts, his pointed hat like a steeple on a tower. He studied the advancing soldiers through thick spectacles, then, placing a whistle between his teeth, blew it shrilly and in continuing blasts. He removed it and squeaked. 'Boys – about turn!'

There was immediate confusion in the ranks of the youngsters; they turned and collided with each other, but the Scoutmaster stepped in, sorting them, pushing them, blowing his whistle in their faces, and giving orders. Runciman, still marching, glared professionally and bawled: 'Stop that whistle!' Then, with consternation, he realised that the Scouts were forming up to march behind his soldiers. 'Keep marching! Take no notice!' he snapped as he strutted. Most of the men could not see what was happening and the order created only uncertainty. They began to look over their shoulders and tread on the heels of those in front. 'Squad, halt!' bellowed Runciman.

The soldiers clattered to a stop but the Scouts following them kept marching, colliding with thc rcar ranks. Runciman was furious. 'You!' he bellowed at the Scoutmaster. 'You!'

'Me?' asked the thin man gazing around through fathomless glasses as if seeking who had called to him. One of the Scouts had fallen in the mêlée and was being lifted, snivelling, by others.

Runciman stamped up. 'Yes, *you.* Get your bleeding kids off the road!'

'Only one is bleeding,' pointed out the man. He had a Continental accent. 'This is the boy who has fallen.'

'There is a war on . . .'

'I know, I know,' the man nodded sadly. 'Very well I know. My uncle is in prison.'

'You'll be in prison if you don't stop blowing that whistle and obstructing service personnel.' Runciman attempted emphasis: '*His Majesty's forces.*'

The Scoutmaster surveyed His Majesty's forces who were, to a man, looking unbelievingly over their shoulders at the confrontation. 'Eyes front!' Runciman bellowed.

'They are obedient soldiers,' observed the Scoutmaster as they did it.

'Unless you get these kids off the road,' threatened Runciman, 'I will call the police. You can be arrested for blowing a whistle, you know.'

The man blinked and appeared impressed. 'You are able to call the police?'

'I can and I will. The civil authority.'

'Ah, we don't want the police. We are afraid of the police.'

'Then get off the road.'

Runciman strode away. 'Squad, quick march!' His face was scarlet. The men marched out gamely. The Scouts formed up on the pavement. 'Troop, quick march!' shouted the master. The Scouts strode alongside the soldiers. Runciman was speechless. 'We are not on the road,' pointed out the man Scout.

'At the double!' ordered Runciman desperately.

The troops began to trot. Several people had stopped to watch and a woman shouted: 'We pay rates for these roads.'

The Scouts broke into an energetic trot keeping abreast of the soldiers. Runciman was outraged, pointing at the man in charge but incapable of forming the words. 'Squad . . . halt!' he eventually shouted, almost sobbed. The men obeyed, falling against each other. The Scouts stopped on the pavement. Runciman stamped up to the thin man. 'Bugger off!'

'Time to bugger off, boys,' said the Scoutmaster looking about him mildly. 'We must bugger off for the soldier.' They had apparently arrived at their destination anyway. They turned and trotted in through a wide gateway and ran up the resounding gravel drive towards a building. The tall man saluted Runciman with the two-fingered salute of the Scouts and turned after them.

'Dib, dib, fucking dob, dob, dob,' muttered Runciman. He felt shot to pieces. He turned the marchers about and set them off in the direction from which they had come. 'We might as well go home,' he grunted. 'These people aren't worth fighting for.'

* * *

The commanding officer was still not very well. The unit did not have its own medical officer but one strolled over from the tank-dismantling quarters, gave him an aspirin and advised him to rest. Durfield insisted his place was with his men.

'It's a sort of rag-tag-and-bobtail school, so I understand,' he said when Bevan passed on Runciman's report. The CO was propped breathlessly against his desk, like a commander who had just come through battle. 'Aliens and suchlike. My view is that if they want to come here they ought to bloody well behave themselves. Go and have a word with them, Bevan. Put them in the picture.'

Bevan took Bombardier Hignet with him. Gunner Bairnsfather drove them to the grey building a mile away and they left him in the car. A group of boys cautiously approached. They wore blue jerseys and shorts.

'Are you a troop?' asked one.

'How do you mean, a troop?' Bairnsfather swallowed.

'Soldiers are troops. You are a soldier. You are a troop.'

'Oh, yes. Well, I am a troop.'

'Do you kill people?'

'Not so far.'

'Can we ride in this car?'

Bairnsfather glanced quickly towards the grey building. Bevan and Hignet had gone inside.

'Jump in,' he said. He took them for a bouncing ride up and down the road outside. When he returned there were more boys waiting and, Bevan and Hignet not having emerged, he gave these a trip, and then a third group. When he came back he found an orderly queue and continued the excursions until everyone had been in the car. 'I've got to wait now,' he said.

'For your Obergruppenführer,' said one.

Bairnsfather blinked, then said: 'Yes, him.'

Bevan and Hignet had walked into the echoing and shabby hall of the building where a sturdy, wild-haired man was awaiting them. He wore spectacles held together with tape and an old-fashioned frock coat. 'Ah, captain,' he said shaking hands with Hignet by mistake and then rectifying the error. 'Welcome to Jerusalem.' The voice was deeply Scots. 'I am Henry MacFarlane. I'm the headmaster . . . the superintendent.'

He led them through a door which he had difficulty in opening although it was not locked. Hignet stepped forward and opened it easily. 'I'd never make a soldier,' laughed MacFarlane. 'Apart from being too old.'

The room again was wide and shabby, cobwebs hanging like old banners from the high ceiling. 'We have no means of reaching them,' said MacFarlane seeing Hignet's upward look. There was an old metal army desk painted green with two chairs placed before it. MacFarlane hurriedly brushed each seat with his hand sending up two whiffs of dust. He smiled apologetically. 'We cannot afford charladies.'

They sat down. 'In a trice we will have some coffee,' said the superintendent as if glad of some certainty. 'It is being prepared.'

'Thank you,' said Bevan. There was a pause, MacFarlane studying them. Tentatively Bevan leaned forward. 'I telephoned because of the unfortunate incident yesterday when my chaps were marching and they somehow got mixed up with your boys.'

'Oh, the lads enjoyed it,' enthused MacFarlane as if the troops had provided free entertainment. 'They could talk of nothing else at supper.' He dropped his voice confidingly. 'Some of them have had quite exciting lives, dodging Hitler and so forth. They are accustomed to the military. Being here tends to be a wee bit dull.' As if to justify his presence Hignet produced an army notepad and a sharp pencil. Bevan said: 'Would you mind if the bombardier took some notes, sir? We'll probably have to put on a report. The army is keen on reports.'

'Ah, yes. Go ahead, go ahead,' said MacFarlane. 'War is full of reports.'

'Could you tell us something about the er . . . school,' suggested Bevan. 'How many lads do you have here?'

'Sixty-three. We will get more, I expect, once the war really gets under way. A lot more. These boys are mostly from the overrun countries, Poland, Czechoslovakia, Austria. We also have some gypsy lads from Spain. They're little devils. They have all lost – well, in some cases, mislaid – their parents, their families and somehow somebody has got them here to Jerusalem House, more or less to safety, unless the Führer catches up with them again. They are here until they are sorted out, until somebody finds somewhere for them to go, more or less permanently, we hope. We are supported by various organisations, religious and otherwise, and we get some government help, although civil servants don't appear to know what to do about the situation. There is, by the way, a collecting box by the door on the way out.'

'Yes,' said Bevan. He turned to Hignet. 'Note that, bombardier.' Hignet returned an uncomfortable glance and saying: 'Yes sir, right sir,' wrote something down.

Bevan said: 'I appreciate the work you are doing, Mr MacFarlane. But my commanding officer asked me to come along and clarify the situation. Yesterday was somewhat embarrassing, you understand.'

'I can see! Soldiers harassed, ambushed by Boy Scouts!' He guffawed and opened a drawer taking out a small brass bell. 'I'll get Herr Rohm in. And I think it's time for some refreshment.' He rang the bell and, as though he had been listening at the door, the lofty Herr Rohm, still in his Scouting clothes, entered with long strides. With almost manic enthusiasm he shook hands, went to the wall and with one bony hand practically flung a heavy chair to the side of the desk. 'It was good action yesterday,' he smiled. His hair was black and greased into a parting. His thick, seemingly blank spectacles were almost hypnotic. Bevan found himself searching for the eyes behind them.

'Action was the word, I suppose,' said Bevan. 'It was very uncomfortable for the men and for Sergeant Runciman.'

'Uncomfortable,' mused Rohm as though he were not sure of the word. 'Well, it was good practice, was it not?'

'For fighting the Germans?' said Bevan stiffly.

'Oh, sir, I know the Germans. Better than your Runciman does. I have seen Germans running down the street.' He paused and wiped his greased hair with a pale hand. 'In my direction.'

MacFarlane had eased back in the chair, enjoying the scene. There came a knock at the door and he shouted: 'Come in, bring the refreshment. We need refreshment.'

The door opened and Bevan and Hignet half turned out of politeness. MacFarlane continued his beam and Rohm's glasses shone. Through the door, manoeuvring a trolley on which were odd cups and a battered metal coffee pot, was one of the most beautiful women Bevan had ever seen.

'This is Renée Williams,' said MacFarlane waving a hand towards her. 'The lass who helps us here.'

Bevan had never seen a woman less like a lass. There was a dark exotic air about her, her eyes were deep. She looked utterly out of place pouring coffee from a dented pot but she did it with elegance.

* * *

When they were in the hollow hall, preparing to leave, MacFarlane said: 'Perhaps you would like to take a peep around.'

Bevan was about to plead military duties but the superintendent added: 'Renée will show you.'

With a knowing grin slowly breaking across Hignet's face, Bevan said: 'Of course. It would be very interesting.' Renée Williams did not meet his eyes. She turned to look up the wide and barren staircase as if she wondered whether the soldiers would be able to reach the top.

'It's a long journey around this place,' she said as they went up, Hignet dutifully following. 'It was once a school, then a convalescent home, and now it is a school again. Of sorts.'

'Why is it called Jerusalem House?' asked Bevan.

'It was a religious place, some sort of seminary,' she said. Her English was careful. There was a trace of an accent.

He was going to ask her how she came to be there but she told him first. 'I was looking for something to do.' They reached the landing. The two men peered with caution over the banisters to the stony floor of the entrance hall far below. There was a rounded coconut mat like a target in the middle of it. 'Some war work, you know, and I heard they were looking for help here. My mother was Viennese and my father English. But I have lived mostly in Austria.'

The army boots resounded on the landing. The place was all but naked of furniture and decoration. In one corner was an old fire bucket. 'To catch the rain,' Renée indicated. 'The roof leaks. Everywhere.' She sighed and said: 'It is difficult. Not physically but just . . . well, hard.'

'Emotionally,' suggested Hignet who had not said anything until then. He looked pleased.

'Indeed. The stories you would just not believe. Hitler should be ashamed. They don't mention their experiences, now, not even to each other, how they escaped, and they hardly ever talk about their families, the missing mothers and fathers, either. They have blanked them out.'

Bevan had to say something. 'They're safe now anyway.'

Renée glanced his way. 'For the time being,' she said. 'Some of them thought they were safe before. Then it all caught up with them again.'

She pushed open a door and they followed her into a barren room, made all the more so by a tall, ornate ceiling and leaded windows. Some of the diamonds of glass were missing and they could feel the sharp October fingers of the wind. There were two rows of iron beds, each one with two folded blankets at the foot, a single pillow at the head. Beside each bed was a metal locker. 'Makes our barrack room look cosy,' said Hignet.

Renée said: 'The place was empty when they came. Nothing. They had to sleep on the floor until Mr MacFarlane begged some beds from somewhere.' Bevan walked to the window. Below he saw Bairnsfather letting six boys out of the car. 'We really ought to try and help out,' he said.

'We've got bugger all . . . nothing else to do,' said Hignet. Bevan glanced at him and he added: 'Not till the war starts up properly.'

She showed them another dormitory, identical except for a big wooden cross on the wall. 'This was the chapel before,' said Renée. 'We're not religious, we've got too many different religions to be religious, and Mr MacFarlane tried to get the cross off the wall but it's fixed there.' She went to one of the bedside lockers and opened the metal door. 'This boy won't mind,' she said. She took out three lead soldiers, all that the locker contained, and set them on the top. 'Left, right, left, right,' she said. 'Ben has his own army.' She replaced the soldiers carefully and closed the door. 'Most of them possessed nothing when they came here,' she said. 'Just the clothes they had and they weren't much. We have a boy here who will not even tell us his name. We know it but he refuses to be called by it. According to him he is just called George – after the King.'

She led them along another corridor which appeared to lead to empty rooms because the echoes of their voices and their footsteps became louder. They descended another set of stairs, almost as grand and just as void as the main staircase, into a large room with a vaulted ceiling and the heavy smell of cabbage.

Three long, scrubbed tables occupied most of the space. Lines of enamel mugs were already in place and two silent boys were putting out knives and forks. Both boys, small and dark, stopped what they were doing when they saw the soldiers. Their expressions were apprehensive. 'It's all right,' Renée said. 'These are our friends.' Women's voices issued, with the odour of steam, from an open door at the end. 'Lunch is at home today,' said Renée, 'because it's Saturday. Monday to Friday they have it at school.'

A woman pushed her damp head around the kitchen door and scanned them swiftly. 'Brown jobs,' she called to somebody inside. 'Army.'

The boys laying the table took no further heed of them. Bevan said: 'Are they . . . er . . . distributed to schools all around the area?'

Renée laughed wryly. 'All they've ever been is distributed, you could say.'

'Sorry,' he said. 'I didn't mean it like that.'

'Captain Bevan wouldn't,' Hignet said.

She apologised. 'I'm sorry also. Perhaps I become too defensive. The reply to your question, captain, is that they go to half a dozen schools. Those that will take them. Some are reluctant, they say it causes disruptions.' She laughed drily and muttered: 'Disruptions. The boys could tell them about disruptions.'

They moved out of the big room into the corridor again. 'Some of them, most of them, could speak no English when they got here. The schools complain that they have no facilities for teaching English to foreigners. It seems they can hardly teach it to the natives.'

'How do the other children treat them?'

'Refugees are a curiosity and they get bullied a bit, although they stick together to defend themselves. Children don't pick their enemies with care. Anyone will do who speaks in a funny voice.'

Bevan said: 'It's very sad.'

'It is,' she said. 'The Boy Scout troop is the only thing that we've been able to do. They enjoy it. Our Herr Rohm escaped in his Scout uniform, you know. He wore it across Europe to France. The Nazis respect uniforms. A vicar here gave him some equipment for the boys. Somebody gave some money.'

'I'm sorry about the incident,' said Bevan.

'Oh, they enjoyed it. It was their turn to upset soldiers.'

She pushed on another door. Into the chill air blew a stream of warmth. Sitting among piles of laundry, washed and unwashed, with a water boiler gurgling in the background, was a boy bending over a book with other books piled against some folded towels almost at his elbow. Bevan saw how Renée smiled towards him. 'Franz,' she said. 'This is Captain . . .'

'Bevan,' said Bevan.

She turned her eyes to Hignet who said hurriedly: 'Hignet . . . Bombardier.'

'Do you throw bombs?' asked the boy. There were dark circles around his eyes. His face was pale and serious.

'Bombs?'

'You are a bombardier.'

Bevan grinned trying to imagine Hignet throwing a bomb. 'Well,' said Hignet carefully, 'I haven't done so, not yet.'

'Franz does his homework in here,' said Renée. 'It is warm. But damp.'

'I am writing English,' said the boy. He held up the exercise book, Renée took it from him and showed Bevan. He looked over her shoulder aware of her closeness. The handwriting was firm and clear. 'Rudyard Kipling,' said Bevan. 'You are writing from *The Jungle Book*.'

The boy said: 'Yes. It is strange, an Englishman writing about the jungle.'

Hignet took a look. 'Better writing than most of our blokes,' he said.

They went from the room into the corridor. 'He's very clever,' said Bevan.

'He wants to be. He wants to be clever, above any other thing.'

'Does he know where his parents are?'

'They left him,' she said. Her face looked straight ahead and her tone sharpened. 'A family living in Vienna. When the Germans came they left him in the house alone. They went away.'

Hignet said: 'Blimey.'

'Exactly, blimey,' said Renée. 'It seems they escaped to America. There was a note sent to his aunt telling her where to find the boy so that she could look after him. She couldn't.'

'How old was he then?' asked Bevan.

'He is twelve now. He must have been ten.'

They reached the bare lobby in silence. It was almost

as if opening the big awkward outside door let in some relief. They each shook hands with Renée. 'Thanks for showing us around,' Bevan said.

'Yes, thanks,' said Hignet.

'You can see that war is not all guns,' she said quietly.

Bairnsfather had the bonnet of the car up and was pointing into the engine with the heads of five boys peering in with him. 'Right, lads,' he said in an authoritative voice when Bevan and Hignet approached, 'get your nappers out.'

'Nappers!' shouted one of the boys and they laughed as though it were the world's best joke. Each one solemnly shook hands with Bairnsfather before they went, only sparing Bevan and Hignet a glance. Seeing these children, these bereft boys, transported Bevan in a moment and for a moment back to his own past. The boy who had shouted 'Nappers!' did it a second time when they were almost at the door and they all laughed furiously again.

'Don't take much to make them laugh, sir,' said Bairnsfather as he drove the car noisily down the gravel to the gate.

Hignet said: 'Can you imagine what it's like for them in that place?'

Bevan could imagine it very well.

The mirror was Georgian, appropriated from Southerly almost as soon as it had been cleared of its elderly peacetime guests, an early example of war booty. It was not good as a mirror: the frame had lost most of its gilding and the glass itself, in patches, was bare of silvering. Now it occupied the barrack-hut wall and Gunner Ugson, known as Ugly, was trying to arrange a representation of his whitened body in the separate reflecting parts of the glass. His upper torso was creased into layers which no amount of army life had hardened.

He glared grimly into the patchy mirror confronting an incomplete and unappetising jigsaw.

Ugson was twenty-five and neither proud nor vain. 'My trouble,' he moaned as he shifted in front of the mirror in the hope of focusing on a more flattering view, 'is that I've got a woman's body. I've even got . . .' Unsuccessfully he attempted to select a softer word: '. . . tits.'

'You have, Ugly,' confirmed Bairnsfather who was on his bed moodily cleaning his boots. Ugson revolved towards him and Bairnsfather took a moment to study the twin raspberry snouts. 'And they're not at all bad, either.'

'You mean that?'

'I do, mate.' Bairnsfather looked around the hut for another witness. Purcell was spread on his bed staring into *Lilliput* magazine, which published photographs of girls in two-piece bathing suits. 'What do you reckon, Persil?' asked Bairnsfather. Ugson, not ungracefully, did a further half-spin.

'Reckon about what?' asked Purcell.

'That Ugly's got a fair pair of tits.'

Purcell closed the magazine as if offered the opportunity of a different treat. 'Not too bad,' he said. 'If we ever gets into the war, some place where there's no tarts, Ugly might come in useful.'

Bairnsfather returned to his boots, attempting to mirror his face in the toecaps. Purcell went back to the unattainable beauties in the magazine and Ugson, briefly, to his reflection. He returned and picked up one of Bairnsfather's boots, also looking into the toecap. 'No better,' he grumbled.

It was Wednesday, the day before pay day. The soldiers had clubbed together for a packet of Woodbines and Cartwright had gone to get them from the canteen. The hut accommodated ten men, a comfortable complement, each man with his jealously guarded bed space: his pit, as the bed was known, his metal cupboard, and a shelf like a canopy above which held his field-service marching order equipment – his backpack, filled with cardboard to keep its shape, his ammunition pouches, his gas respirator in its ungainly bag, and his water bottle – as in each man's cupboard were his best boots, his metal polish for cleaning his cap badge and brasses, his Blanco for his belt, his first-aid kit, which contained different-shaped pads and various lengths of dressings and bandages, and a small bottle of iodine, to be used in battle. He also had his housewife, complete with needles and cottons, his boot blacking and, preserved like relics, his civilian clothes.

The most warlike part of the soldier's equipment was locked away elsewhere. The Lee Enfield .303 rifles, deployed and discharged by generations of British infantrymen, were in their racks in the armoury. They were long, heavy and cumbersome, not much shorter than some of the smaller men required to use them. The weapon had a range of two thousand yards and a kick like a camel. 'Fired accurately, with co-ordination and skill, five .303s can be as devastating as a single Bren gun,' instructors invariably recited. At the end of the rifle a bayonet could be fixed, sharp and brutal. 'Whip it in, whip it out, and wipe it!' was the order that echoed in the ears of generations of men thrusting the deadly points into long-suffering sacks. 'Sacks,' pointed out Bombardier Hignet with doleful philosophy, 'do not bleed.'

Inside the green-painted metal door of his cupboard Bairnsfather had his family photos, taken with a Baby Brownie camera: his mother and his motorbike. There was also a pornographic picture, taken secretly and distantly, of a smudgy couple having sex in a field. A flash of anything so erotic, even though remote and ill defined, was rare and exciting and men would regularly sneak into the barrack room and peer at the forbidden anatomy through a magnifying glass provided by the charitable Bairnsfather. Such explicit and forbidden revelations were rarely available. Even now, on his bed Purcell continued to attempt a squint around the edges of the daring swimming suits of the models in *Lilliput*.

Gunner Cartwright had two photographs appended to the inside of his locker door, one of his disgruntled wife and one of the former girlfriend he had met while on compassionate leave. On his return, his hut mates had assembled to compare, in a friendly fashion, the physical attributes of each woman. 'I reckon she's got a bigger mouf than your missus,' Gunner Brown said to Cartwright.

'Women,' grunted Ugson now sprawled unattractively on his bed. 'After that doctor sod 'ad done his bleeding lecture yesterday, I never want to see another woman in my life. What women can do to your dicky is dis-bloody-gusting.'

'I didn't like them nasty pictures neither,' agreed Cartwright. 'All them swellings.'

'Nobody did,' agreed Bairnsfather. 'It's not pretty. And even a spoggy won't save you from the clap, so he says. The clap can get *through*. Even if you wore two, one on top of the other.'

'One's bad enough,' said Cartwright. 'Like wearing your socks in bed.'

There was a garrison concert that night and with the absence of anywhere else to go, but with a sense of foreboding, they smartened themselves and went across to the former garage which had recently become the military theatre and cinema. Its original name board 'Harrison' had been repainted with some ingenuity so that a 'G' replaced the 'H' and the word 'Theatre' added. But it was not something to which they looked forward.

'That's what's wrong with this country,' said Hignet as he joined them on the approach to the entertainment. 'Able-bodied men, compelled to put on uniform, parade around, fire guns, eat like dogs, sleep on wire beds and then herded into garrison theatres to hear some old, farty, woman sing Gilbert and Sullivan.'

'It might be all right,' suggested Bairnsfather trudging with no conviction. 'There might be a striptease.'

'Not interested,' said Gunner Ugson. 'Not after that lecture.'

'You don't have to believe everything they say, even if he is a medical officer,' said Hignet. 'They'll tell you anything to scare you, to keep you in order. It's the class system, mate.'

Bairnsfather said: 'Them and us.'

'Them and us,' said Hignet definitely. 'They try to keep you down, tell you to be nice lads and not get syphilis, and go over the top and bayonet the enemy. That's all we're good for. That's what they think.'

'Even if there's a stripteaser she won't show bugger all,' said Bairnsfather. 'Not a pimple.'

'It would only get you overheated,' said Hignet. 'Over-excitement is not good for us.'

'Stuck here,' said Cartwright. 'Doing sod all. No money, no crumpet, no war even.'

'You've got a missus *and* a floosie,' pointed out Ugson. 'I've 'ardly seen a woman's nipple since I was a baby.'

They all laughed sourly. The garrison theatre was nearing. The letter 'G' had fallen off the sign to reveal the original 'Harrison'. Hignet said: 'Typical, that is.'

'I bet that's all that will be coming off here tonight,' said Bairnsfather. 'No striptease, that's for sure.' They had the small satisfaction of being admitted free. Civilians were allowed to attend the show on a payment of threepence and some of the elderly local residents were already in their seats. Officers could offer a donation and sit in the front row. Few accepted the challenge.

Bairnsfather, Hignet and Ugson sat on chairs halfway up the hall. Cartwright sat at the back, because he said he might want to go. The curtains had been brought from somewhere else and did not fit; they were fifteen inches short and there were gaps at both ends. An upright piano, infirm and damaged, stood beside the stage. The ceiling and walls of the big building were lost in dust and dimness. Its former use was commemorated in an advertisement, painted on tin, on a side wall: 'Lubrication available. Shell Oils for your Motor.' An old hand-operated petrol pump leaned like a sick man and there was a stack of tractor wheels in the shadows.

For all its lack of promise the garrison theatre was filling quickly. No one had any money on a Wednesday. Hignet sniffed. The place retained the faint smell of benzol and grease. 'I'm going to get a car,' he said like a vow, almost to himself. 'The minute this war's over.'

'I had one,' said Bairnsfather. 'Well, a baker's van.'

'Nobody I know's got a car, ever had one,' said Ugson.

A man wearing a shabby coat, a fly-away collar and a pained expression came to the front of the curtains to desultory applause. He spread his hands unnecessarily because the clapping had ceased. 'Good evening, lads,' he said. 'I've come up here because I'm brassed off.'

'So are we!' someone shouted. There was more applause and some heartless laughter.

'I'm brassed off with this *piano*.' The man took an ill-tempered swipe at the cowering instrument raising dust as he did so. 'I was promised a *grand* piano.'

'That's the grandest piano you'll get!' shouted the same voice.

'You'd better come on the stage,' the man bawled back. 'Clever sod.' His voice descended: 'I am an *artiste*. I have played at Croydon. And they provide me with this wreckage. However, I intend to go on. I do not want to let you down, lads.'

There was further insincere applause. The pianist failed to detect, or ignored, the mass sarcasm and with nose raised, as if to elevate it above the dust, he sat at the instrument and attacked it savagely. When they realised he was playing 'God Save the King' the men struggled from their chairs, stood at attention and sang without fervour. The anthem finished and they sat again with a resounding clatter and the pianist thumped into a music-hall song.

Three thin men in tights came on and danced. There were disbelieving groans from the audience and shouts of 'Nancies!' Afterwards a rotund woman appeared and sang old sentimental songs and a man with a red nose, which kept slipping, told old jokes. A ventriloquist took the centre stage, his wooden partner on his knee. The dummy's leg fell from its bright trousers.

Because of the short stage curtain there was a preview of the lower part of each act. The audience stirred with interest when two sets of pink, plump limbs appeared set in white socks and black dancing shoes, an interest that descended to another widespread groan when the performers were revealed as a pair of rounded ten-year-old girls. One had a bloodstained bandage around her knee. She grimaced theatrically throughout their stiff tap-dance and joined sulkily in 'The Good Ship, Lollipop', blowing up in tears at its conclusion and hobbling from the stage leaving her smirking partner to make a solo curtsy.

The pianist reappeared and announced: 'Now we have

an act *not* on the programme. Private Willy Hardy is going to read a poem.'

'Fuck me,' said Bairnsfather. He put his face in his hands.

Private Hardy shuffled into the limelight. He was so small he might have escaped military service by claiming to be a boy. His face was puffy pink and his eyes shone behind spectacles. From his pocket he took a sheet of lined paper and unfolded it. 'My poem,' he squeaked. 'My poem is called "A Warning to Hitler".'

Bairnsfather said: 'Fuck me,' again and Hignet said: 'Me too.'

Hardy piped again: '"A Warning to Hitler",' and, after a breath so deep his body appeared to expand, he plunged into his performance:

> 'Adolf, we are ready.
> Our resolve is steady.
> We can bear the brunt.
> You ugly Nazi cunt.'

There was uproar. Hoots and wild cheering filled the building; men were on their feet shouting: 'More! More!' Hignet beamed: 'That's a *lot* better.' But hope for a second verse was smothered by a hurried advance on to the stage of a uniformed padre. He tripped but recovered. 'In the name of God – stop!' he shouted giving the poet an unchristian shove.

'Which God is that?' bellowed Hignet half getting to his feet. The padre rounded on him and Hignet's belligerence shrivelled. Adding: '. . . sir?' to his question he sank back into his seat. Private Hardy was cowering like a child against the curtains.

'These fellows don't want to hear this tommy rot!' the padre ranted at him.

'Yes, we do!' the audience howled back. But there was no more. Hardy was hustled away and replaced by the pianist who announced: 'Now for some community singing.' The end was in sight.

Those were famous days for singing. Community singing especially. There was even a song called 'Let the People Sing':

> Sing a merry song to cheer them
> Tell them that I love to hear them!

'Who?' asked Hignet as, after the concert, they went hunched and hands in pockets in the direction of the canteen. 'Who *is* this bloke saying he loves to hear them? Is it the King? *Who*'s sitting up there telling us how pleased he is that we're singing?'

'Some of them are all right,' argued Ugson lamely. 'I like "Run, Rabbit, Run".' He sensed the disgust in the turn of their heads. 'Well, I like it.'

Everywhere was black. The countryside, the sea, were as though they had been painted out. A few stars, crowded together in holes among the winter clouds, blinked.

Two dozen men were tramping along the lane so dark it could have been a tunnel. A cow suddenly mooed across a hedge startling the soldiers in front so that they fell against each other and ended in a pile. Bairnsfather said: 'They used to sing "It's a Long Way to Tipperary".'

'Your dad did,' said Hignet.

'That's right.'

'Marching.'

'That's right.'

They fell into silence as gloomy as the night. Bairnsfather

said: 'Next time I want cheering up, Hignet, I'm coming to find you.'

'Thanks. But you've got to look at the realities, chum. They're going to herd us to the trenches like they did the last lot, the last generation.'

'They're taking a long bloody time about it,' grumbled Cartwright. He had decided to stay at the concert after all. There was nowhere else to go. 'That's one of the reasons my missus is cheesed off. According to 'er I ain't a proper soldier 'cause I ain't shooting nobody.'

Bairnsfather began to sing, softly at first, to himself:

> 'Roll me over, in the clover,
> Roll me over, lay me down and do it again.'

The men tramping at the front took it up:

> 'This is number one, and my song has just begun.
> Roll me over, lay me down and do it again.'

From behind, like an elongated choir, the stragglers joined in.

'This is number two, and I've got her up the flue,
Roll me over, lay me down and do it again.'

Soon the song swelled, the young men, the soldiers, tramped through the darkness and, as if to give themselves courage and cheer, sounded the chorus:

> 'Roll me over, in the clover,
> Roll me over, lay me down and do it again.'

It was their marching anthem, a simple, singable, indecency that would take British armies through battles, deaths, continents, seas and on, after years, to some sort of victory. It meant something to them. They even halted to complete its singing before opening the door of the canteen.

The place was sponsored by the Church Army. 'Are you church or army?' asked Bairnsfather of the girl pouring the tea. The pot was huge – dull metallic – and the tea came out like leather. It seemed too heavy for her slim arm. 'Want any help?' asked Bairnsfather.

'I'll struggle on,' she said but without tartness. 'I'm doing my bit.'

She completed filling a dozen mugs and splashed milk from a jug into each of them. Recipients were required to spoon their own sugar into the mugs, the spoon being attached by a length of lavatory chain to the counter. Bairnsfather took his mug. Hignet had gone back to the hut early saying he had experienced enough excitement for one night. Cartwright had found a copy of the Church Army newspaper and was attempting to interpret it. Ugson was counting the spots on his chin.

'I'm not church or army,' the girl answered eventually. 'I'm Molly Warner.'

'That's like a film star's name,' said Bairnsfather. She was neat and confident, her almost black hair tidy, her pretty face polished by the steam of the big teapot. A comfortable girl. 'Do you like the pictures?' he asked.

'Doesn't everybody? I go three times a week.' She hesitated before going on but there was no one else who wanted to be served. 'Where are you from then?'

'Home or in the mob?'

'In the army.'

'Oh, just down the road. Royal Artillery. Ack-ack. The two Bofors guns.' He attempted to appear solemn. 'Defence of the Realm.'

She laughed. Her teeth were neat. 'And what realm

are you going to defend with those peashooters?' A soldier came and asked nervously how much the cakes were. She said they were tuppence and he went away to tell his comrades.

'I think it's a shame,' she said. 'They've got no money.'

'Pay day's tomorrow,' he said. 'We're defending the realm for two shillings a day, fourteen bob a week. Fancy coming to the flicks with me?'

'I might,' she said. The soldier came back and tried to charm her, asking if she had any older cakes. She gave him a tuppenny one for a penny and added another for free after testing it with her fingertips for staleness; he carried them, like prizes, back to his friends who shared them out.

'Those guns can't hit anything, can they?' she said.

'They might if it's flying low enough.' He grinned at her. 'I'm not supposed to tell you.'

'Careless talk,' she agreed.

'You won't tell the enemy, will you?'

'I don't know any of them to tell.'

A soldier sat at the canteen piano and began to play, not well, but softly, 'O, Danny Boy'.

'Will you come to the pictures? Tomorrow night.'

'Can't. Working.'

'Friday then?'

'All right,' she said. '*Goodbye, Mr Chips* is on. Robert Donat. My mum said it made her cry.'

'Oh, good,' said Bairnsfather. 'I feel like a good cry.'

When he returned to camp with the stragglers there seemed to be less darkness and more stars. They had to be inside the guarded gate by 23.59 – for the army there was no such time as midnight – or they were on disciplinary charge, Army Form 252. Bairnsfather was still thinking about Molly and even now worried that she would not turn up on Friday. He thought she would. She did not look the sort of girl to stand you up. Molly Warner, what a nice name. And what a doll. What a smasher. He did a little dance as he went along the middle of the lane and began to sing softly:

'Run rabbit, run rabbit, run, run, run.
Don't give the farmer his fun, fun, fun.
He'll get by without his rabbit pie.
So run rabbit, run rabbit, run, run, run.'

They were famous days for singing.

As they left the dimmed bus and walked into the blind street Molly held on to his arm saying: 'I still don't like all this dark.'

The cinema was only picked out by a dim blue bulb, like the one that marked the police station. Immediately inside there was a bulky curtain and then another to be negotiated before they arrived in the foyer where the lights were still low. As they went into the main auditorium their eyes were already used to the dark and, almost without thinking, Bairnsfather looked over his shoulder as they went down the aisle to view the back row of the one-and-threepenny stalls. Molly immediately detected his intention. 'I'd rather not go there, Harry. Everybody's . . . at it.'

'Nobody watches the picture,' he said attempting to agree with her. From end to end the row was full of couples already in deep and carnal positions. The thick kisses and deep sighs could be clearly heard over the notes of the theatre organ on the stage. An usherette appeared with a heavy torch and shone it like a threat along the line stopping some of the murmurs for a moment. Others were too engrossed to notice. 'Stop that,' she warned. 'You've come to see the fillum.'

'What's it called?' demanded a cocky male voice.

'*Goodbye, Mr Chips*,' said the usherette. 'Don't you know?'

'Goodbye, you've had your chips,' he shouted. The entire row was convulsed. The usherette swished her torch along the line like a probing searchlight. 'It's not funny,' she said. 'I'll get the manager. A girl had a baby in here last week.'

'Christ, that was quick,' the cocky voice responded. 'I thought it took nine months!' The usherette turned in disgust and followed Bairnsfather and Molly down the aisle towards the middle seats. 'This war,' she complained, 'Is turning people into savages.'

Bairnsfather cast another slightly envious look over his shoulder. Molly had already sat down. Around them most of the seats were occupied. The organist was playing community tunes and a brightly coloured ball was bouncing along the words spread across the screen: 'She was a sweet little dicky-bird, "Tweet, tweet, tweet," she went.' Around them some of the people were singing. 'Want a Wallsy?' whispered Bairnsfather. She squeezed his arm and said: 'Later.'

The organist finished his medley and like a drowning man descended slowly, mechanically, with his illuminated instrument into the orchestra pit, waving as he went. 'He's training to be in submarines,' said Bairnsfather. She giggled and began to get out of her coat. The cinema screen lit up and in its silver illumination he could see the contour of her face and her breasts. She held his hand firmly. The second feature began, a comedy set in a department store which they had both seen. They laughed a second time. Then came a short film which instructed civilians what to do if confronted by Nazi parachutists. 'Do not resist,' came the stern advice. 'But do not give them anything, food, drink, directions or your bicycle. If you cannot lock up your bicycle, let the air from the tyres and hide the pump.'

The audience remained serious and attentive. On Movietone News there was an item about the Women's Land Army in which a group of recruits was seen cutting their fingernails so as not to inconvenience the cows during milking. Then the King and Queen were shown talking to some naval officers and the cinema erupted with applause. The last item showed a grinning Hitler inspecting devastation in Poland. Everybody hissed.

When the main film began Molly curled herself down into the arm which he carefully put around her. *Goodbye, Mr Chips* was sad and Molly began to sniffle as she sank lower in the seat. Bairnsfather's eyes misted and he stroked her shoulder.

Robert Donat and Greer Garson embraced tenderly on the screen. There was a resulting commotion in the back seats, sighs and groans. Bairnsfather caressed Molly's neck and she eased her head into his hand.

Everyone stood rigidly for the National Anthem – some of the patrons were caught by surprise and swiftly adjusted their clothes – and then began to troop out into the blacked-out street. Molly's eyes were smudged and she realised it and smiled with embarrassment at him. 'I really enjoyed it, Harry.'

There was a café between the cinema and the bus stop. He had been thinking more of a pub but she extended an encouraging hand and they went in. Others from the cinema were there. An airman had a pair of white knickers clutched like a trophy in his fist. The girl with him asked for them to be returned and he politely gave them to her. 'Don't want you getting cold,' he said. She giggled.

Bairnsfather and Molly had cups of tea and a cream slice each. She insisted on paying because he had paid for the cinema. 'I don't even know what you do,' said Bairnsfather. 'I know you serve in the camp canteen . . .'

'That's just voluntary,' she said. 'I work in the Southampton library.'

He was impressed. 'It's only because people have gone off to the war,' she said. 'I just put the books back on the shelves and that sort of thing. Nothing very clever. I want to be a part-time nurse, in the VAD. What do you do in civvy street?'

'Bakery,' he said flatly.

'Crumbs!' she grinned. It was an old joke but he laughed with her. 'It's a skilled trade,' she said.

'I just delivered the bread. But I can drive, that's one thing.'

'When the war's over is that what you want to go back to?'

'I don't know. I can't think about it being over yet. I wouldn't mind just being a millionaire or something.'

She laughed and said: 'You're nice.'

They finished their tea and got up in time for the bus. It was crowded. The embracers from the one-and-threes of the cinema had claimed the upstairs seats and were continuing their passion. 'You'd think there'd be somewhere else they could go,' said Molly. She looked at him with a hint of warning. 'I wouldn't want to make an exhibition like that.'

'Nor me, neither,' said Bairnsfather.

They left the bus. 'There'll be another along in twenty minutes,' she said. 'It will take you right back to camp. We could go in and have a cup of tea, but we'll have to hush. They've usually gone to bed by now.'

There was a brick-built surface air-raid shelter in the street. They could smell it. There were movements and they saw that a couple were clamped together in the dark oblong of the entrance. As they walked past the man, an airman, said: ''Ere, mush, want to cover us up.'

'What for, mush?' asked Bairnsfather deliberately. Molly gave him a gentle tug.

'Well, we can 'ave a shag and then we'll cover for you when you 'ave one.'

'That's right,' said the girl from the doorway. 'That's fair.'

'No, thank you very much,' said Molly tersely.

'Hard luck, mush,' said Bairnsfather.

'Who's that erk calling mush?' he said to Molly as they walked on. They heard mutterings behind them. 'I know that girl,' whispered Molly. 'I used to go to Sunday school with her. Brenda Parkin.'

They had reached her front door. 'The war's changed everything,' said Molly. 'Everybody.' Her voice altered. 'Listen, can you hear that?'

He said gently: 'The balloons.'

'They sing, don't they,' she said. 'It's the wind in the wires.' They stared up at the dark sky. The barrage balloons were invisible but the sound came down melodiously to them. 'They're singing to us,' she said. 'Just like a lullaby.' She took her key from her handbag and touching her finger to her lips opened the door by the inch. She went in first. They were in a narrow hall, heavily warm after the chill of the autumn night.

Bairnsfather eased her against the wallpaper and put his hands around her waist and kissed her. The wool of her dress felt gently rough on his palms. He tentatively shifted them to the undersides of her breasts but without fuss she returned them to her waist. He kissed her again.

A deep and vibrant snore came from the dark upstairs. He froze but she only waited for it to subside and said: 'He's fasto.'

'Who you got there then, Desperate Dan?' The boy's voice came from the top of the stairs. They could just see him sitting in his pyjamas. Molly was angry but thought the better of it. 'You'll have to go, Harry,' she said. 'He's a pest.'

She eased him through the door into the short front garden and then into the street. 'He's a damned nuisance,' she said.

Bairnsfather was reluctant to let her go but she kissed him with finality. As she did so the door closed behind her. 'The little swine. He's locked me out.' She looked along the street: 'Here's your bus.'

'How are you going to get in?'

'I'll have to bang,' she said. 'Wake everybody. I'll clip his ear.'

They both turned away, he towards the bus and she towards the front door. She turned and blew a dim kiss towards him. 'See you soon.'

The airman and the girl were still in the shadowed air-raid shelter entrance. 'Aw, come on, mush,' said the airman. 'Do us a favour. Cover for us and we'll cover for you.'

'What am *I* supposed to do?' grunted Bairnsfather.

'I can manage two,' said the girl. 'Book-ends.'

'No, thanks,' said Bairnsfather.

'You could 'ave a wank,' suggested the airman.

'Bollocks,' said Bairnsfather. The bus was there. He mounted the platform. 'Bollocks to you as well,' called the girl.

To Ellen Unsworth war seemed very little different from peace except that her son had gone and the nights were much darker. She was grateful every night when Alf came back from his police duties and they were safe in their bed. She feared that a stray enemy bomb might blow him up or that an uncovered Nazi spy might shoot him.

That late afternoon she returned to their cottage carrying her shopping bag, the week's groceries together with two tins of sardines and another three pots of salmon and shrimp paste for the covert emergency store under Alan's bed. She wondered where her son was now, and tried not to picture him already in some throbbing submarine fathoms below the fearful ocean. In the shop she had heard a man talking carelessly about a ship called HMS *Terrible* and the name had upset her.

It was four o'clock, nearing darkness, and she felt glad to be home before the blackout. As she opened the front gate sounds came from the rear of the cottage. She *knew* this time it was a German parachutist and took one of the tins of sardines in her hand as a weapon hoping he might mistake it for a grenade, although she was not sure of the shape of a grenade. Rounding the side of the house she saw a shadow digging in the garden, no Nazi burying his parachute but her husband delving into the small space of lawn. Even in the gloom the line between the grass and the newly turned black earth was clearly definable.

'Why are you doing that, Alf?'

He straightened, aimed the spade into the ground and held his back with both hands. 'I got off early,' he said. They faced each other, no more than silhouettes in the gloom. 'A suspected case of sabotage turned out to be a kid given access to matches.'

'So you thought you'd dig up our lawn. We sometimes sit on that in the summer, don't we?'

He trod over and kissed her fondly. 'Why are you holding that sardine tin like that?'

'Oh,' she said looking at it with a little surprise. 'I thought you might be a German parachutist.'

'And you reckoned he might like sardines?'

'I was going to clobber him with them. Or pretend it was a bomb.'

He went back and picked out the spade, then cleaned it with the side of his boot. 'Now the mud's on your boot,' she pointed out. 'Cup of tea?'

'I'm ready for one.' He took his boots off on the step and followed her comfortable shape into the house. It was not cold for early winter, only dark. She waited while he drew the double blackout curtains and then lit the oil-lamp they still used in the kitchen. It glowed, contented and safe. She put the kettle on the range and he sat at the table. 'Digging's hard work,' he said. 'Being a copper doesn't keep you fit. I thought I'd turn over the ground now so that the frost can break it up. Think of all the veg we can grow in that patch. It was too small for a lawn anyway.'

'There was just room for two of us,' she pointed out. 'On the deck-chairs.' She turned towards the kettle. 'You know that postcard from Alan we got yesterday. It said *HMS*, didn't it. Does that mean he's on a *ship* already?'

'It's a training establishment. Don't worry. The navy call everything His Majesty's Ship.'

He saw her back sigh with relief and she said: 'I was worried.'

'Ellen, stop worrying. He's going to be all right. Everything is.'

She put the thick cup and saucer on the scrubbed wooden surface of the table and, without asking, cut him a piece of the fruit cake she took from a tin and cut another slice for herself. He put two spoonfuls of sugar in her cup and two in his. 'We might have to cut down on the sugar,' she said. 'Once this war gets going.'

Unsworth grinned. 'We'll grow sugar beet in the garden,' he said. 'That's why I was digging.' She returned the smile. He never seemed to worry.

'Sugar growing in Lyndhurst,' she said, then, after a sip of tea, asked: 'Where are you going to put the air-raid shelter?'

His eyes came up slowly through the wisps of steam. 'Air-raid shelter? We won't need an air-raid shelter. They won't bomb Lyndhurst. There's nothing here to bomb.'

Ellen said: 'They might, by mistake. They might accidentally miss Southampton. It's not far. They say those shelters are really cosy.'

'They cost ten pounds,' he said. 'And then you have to dig the hole and put them in yourself. Oh, if you live in Southampton you get one for nothing. And the council digs the hole. If you want one free we'll have to move to Southampton and wait for the air raids.'

In 1938 they had been offered a police house but they had decided to remain in the former forester's cottage. He had converted an abutting coal house into a bathroom although it still lacked running water. Jugs and hot kettles had to be brought from the kitchen. Alf would sit in the tin bath and she would pour the water over him. Then he would do the same for her. Improvements would have to wait until the end of hostilities; it was like that for the duration. There was only a chemical closet but at least they were spared the former penance of going to the lavatory at the bottom of the garden, a long journey in the dead of night.

At nine o'clock, as always, they listened to the news on the wireless. 'That George Flemming, the one in the grocer's,' Ellen grumbled. 'He says he listens to Lord Haw Haw from Germany. He thinks he's funny.'

'Some people do,' said Unsworth. 'There's no law against it.'

'Flemming says he seems to know everything, that Lord Haw Haw,' she said. 'He even knew that the town-hall clock had stopped in some place or other.'

'At least somebody noticed,' he said.

'I think he ought to be stopped.'

'Flemming or Lord Haw Haw?'

'Both.'

Like millions they made the nine o'clock news a meeting place, a rendezvous. It was listened to in homes and factories and pubs. The Finns were beating off the Russians who had invaded Finland, and they were exultantly using home-made hand-grenades called Molotov cocktails to destroy Russian tanks.

'How do they make those?' asked Ellen.

'Don't you try,' he said. 'Petrol and other stuff in milk bottles. You stick to tins of sardines.'

'I've got some half-pint milk bottles,' she reflected. 'I forgot to put them on the step for the milkman. They're very brave those Finlanders, aren't they.'

'Some people say they're doing the Germans' job for them,' he pointed out. 'It's the Russians the Germans are afraid of, not us, not the French.' The telephone jangled. 'Trouble,' he sighed and got up to answer it.

When he returned he repeated: 'Trouble,' and took his overcoat from the peg.

'Just before bedtime,' sighed Ellen.

'I know. I won't be long. Somebody's signalling enemy submarines. So the report says. They're probably trying to find a lost dog.'

Quickly they embraced and he went out to the little Austin parked at the side of the cottage. Despite his approaching middle age and his stockiness he was quick-moving. The bonnet vibrated violently when he turned the starting handle. The headlights were sliced, glimmering through grilles. There was a white line painted along the running board. He trundled carefully into the blackness of the road and turned towards the police station. He knew that she had extinguished the light and was watching him from the window.

Two constables were waiting. The sergeant was behind his heavy desk like a soldier manning a strong point. 'It's a report that somebody is flashing a light from that tower on the end of the big house on the sea front – that one called Southerly,' he said.

'But that belongs to the army. It's the officers' mess,' said Unsworth.

The sergeant said: 'High treason.' He handed Unsworth a square of paper. 'This is the informant. A Mr Niven, St Martin's Way. It's one of them bungalows. Says he was walking his dog and he saw this flashing light.' The sergeant thought of something else. 'There's that alien bloke lives there, if I remember. He listens to Berlin on his wireless.'

'I know,' said Unsworth. He went out with the constables and they climbed into a police car, a Wolsey, and drove off through the void. They were halted at bayonet point by a sentry at the camp gate. 'We're going to the officers' mess,' Unsworth said. 'Would you mind lowering that sharp thing a bit and getting the duty officer?'

'Who shall I say it is?' asked the man but still keeping the bayonet pushed towards the car window. Unsworth indicated his uniformed companions and said: 'It's not the Salvation Army.'

'There's such a thing as disguises,' said the sentry sullenly. He lowered the bayonet, however, and called over his shoulder: 'Percy, call the duty officer, will you.'

Percy, who had apparently been asleep, although it had to be standing up because there was no room to lie down in the sentry hut, moved clumsily and wound the handle of the telephone. 'Go through,' he said after he had delivered the message. 'Keep going as far as you can. But no further 'cause you'll be in the sea.'

Unsworth could hear the pair laughing as the car went along the enclosed lane. They reached the house and he saw that it was Bevan waiting for them. He shone a torch on him and then on his own face. 'Hello again,' Unsworth said as they shook hands. 'Have you been signalling to U-boats?'

'Not personally.' As officer of the guard he was wearing his heavy service revolver in its leather holster. 'Has somebody?'

'We've had a report that somebody here is flashing a light out to sea. You've got a chap from somewhere, haven't you, who listens to Berlin?'

'Josef. But he wouldn't be flashing lights.'

'Where is he?'

'In his room, I expect. He's finished work. He's the mess waiter among other things. He's been here years.'

'I'll have to see him.' Unsworth said to one of the constables: 'Go and get the bloke who reported the lights.' He handed him the slip of paper he had taken from the police-station sergeant. 'Mr Niven.'

Bevan went towards the outside staircase that led to Josef's room. He was about to call when Unsworth put a hand on his arm. 'Better to go up,' he said.

'Right. But he's harmless.'

'Somebody's been flashing lights.'

They went up the stairs and Bevan knocked on the door. Josef's anxious eyebrows appeared as it opened. 'Yes, sir?' There was American music in the background.

'Can we come in?' said Bevan. 'It's the police.'

Unsworth did not wait to be invited. He walked into the room and professionally looked about him. The blackout blinds were scrupulously drawn. The big-faced wireless set was broadcasting swing music. 'That's Munich,' said Josef without being asked. 'Tommy Dorsey Gramophone Hour.'

'Nice,' said Unsworth. 'Can I see your papers? Your passport.'

Bevan was standing impotently. 'It's all right, Josef,' he said eventually. 'It's only routine.'

'Have you been flashing lights?' asked Unsworth bluntly.

'No. Why should I flash lights?' said Josef. He opened a drawer below the radio set and took out some papers. Unsworth ran his eyes over them and said: 'We've had a report of lights seen, apparently signalling from this building, towards the sea.'

'Wasn't me, sir,' said Josef glancing at Bevan for support. He turned the wireless off. There was another knock at the door. The constable he had sent to find Mr Niven came in. 'He's downstairs,' he said. He looked sideways at Josef.

Unsworth went back down the stairs and Bevan went with him. Josef with a sigh closed the door so the light from the room would not shine out.

'He says it came from the tower, the turret on the end of the house,' said the constable.

'That's right,' said Niven who was wearing plus-fours, an air-raid warden's steel helmet and an armband both bearing the letter 'W'. He had a whistle on a lanyard around his neck. 'It was Morse.'

'You know Morse?'

'Well, it looked like Morse.'

Unsworth turned to Bevan. 'How do we get up to the turret?'

'I'll show you.'

They went through the front door into the lobby. Once he had closed it Bevan switched on a single baleful light. Unsworth stopped and looked around the dingy area. 'This used to be nice,' he said.

'You remember?'

'We came here on school treats.'

'We did.'

'Seems a long time ago now.'

Bevan led Unsworth towards the door to the turret. 'Funny you being here now,' said the policeman.

'Do you really think there's somebody up there signalling?'

'No, not a bit of it. People keep on seeing things. Jittery.' They had left Mr Niven standing outside blinking below his steel helmet.

'What was he doing out in the blackout at this time anyway?' said Bevan. 'You can't see the turret from any of the houses, it's too far forward.'

'Walking his dog, he says. I'll ask if he's got a dog licence. I can't go back empty-handed.'

They had paused outside the door. Bevan said: 'I'll go up first.'

'It's your tower.'

Scarcely had they mounted the first step than they heard a scraping from above. They still had to round the bend in the stairs to see the turret door. Both stopped at the sound. 'Rats,' said Unsworth.

'Big rats,' said Bevan. He felt a reassuring comradeship with the policeman. He went up the last few stairs and, at the top, drew his cumbersome revolver. There were more scrapings from within the turret room. Bevan pushed the door open, not violently but firmly, and they both moved quickly through it.

Major Durfield, the Commanding Officer, was sprawled in a deck-chair, a bottle dangling from his hand, his eyes opaque, his mouth gaping. 'Ooooooh,' he said engagingly. 'It's a raid.'

On the floor below the bottle was a bicycle lamp. It was still glimmering. Bevan looked helplessly at Unsworth who said: 'Looks like he's been taken poorly.'

An urgent voice came from the bottom of the stairs.

'Sir, are you there, sir?' Unsworth looked at Bevan and they both looked at the major who now had his eyes closed and had lowered the bottle gently to the floor. 'Yes,' answered Bevan. 'What is it?'

'Sir, there's a mine on the beach. About a mile away. A bloody great thing.'

It was. It lay above the tide mark, huge and round, its spikes protruding, lolling on its side like a great menacing pudding. Two policemen were examining it closely, one holding a torch, the other writing studiously in his notebook. They both wore steel helmets and carried their gas-mask packs at their sides. Unsworth shouted to them from the road. Everyone in the two cars got out and stood in a distant group.

'It's all right,' called one of the policemen to Unsworth. 'It's one of ours.'

'Where do we get them?' said Unsworth under his breath.

Mr Niven, who had inexplicably accompanied them, muttered heavily from below his warden's helmet: 'I was in the navy in the First War. If that thing goes off it will blow everybody's teeth through the back of their heads.'

'We've got to evacuate the area,' said Bevan. The nearest bungalows, with nightdressed and pyjama-clad people dimly at their doors, were only a hundred yards away. Unsworth shouted to the policemen on the beach: 'Get away from that bloody thing. Get back here.'

They grumbled as they climbed up to the road. 'We weren't going to touch it,' said one.

'We've got to get all these people from the houses,' said Unsworth. 'You, constable . . .' He pointed directly at one of the policemen who had climbed from the beach. 'Get to a telephone and call Lyndhurst.'

'Then call the camp,' said Bevan. 'Three, four, seven.'

'Do I ask for the commanding officer?'

'Yes . . . no.' He remembered Durfield sprawled in the tower. 'Call the sergeant of the guard. Get the men out warning people in the houses along the road. There's some refugee kids. Warn them. They're at a place called Jerusalem House on the shore road.' Thankfully he realised they were two miles away. The whole crowd, every eye on the sea mine, backed from the beach towards the first line of bungalows, their retreat slow as though they feared any quick movement might set it off. The cars backed up. 'What's happening?' demanded one of the doorway figures. 'Getting us out of bed like this.'

'You might have been *blown* out of bed,' said one of the constables uncompromisingly. 'It's a sea mine. It could go off any minute.'

'And blow all these houses down,' said the second policeman with some relish. 'Get some clothes on and clear out.'

Swiftly the faces vanished. The policemen went down the first line of bungalows banging on the doors that were not already open. 'Get up! Get out! Emergency!' they shouted. 'There's a mine going off any minute!' bellowed the malicious one.

An army dispatch rider appeared, performing a theatrical braking on his motorcycle. He handed Bevan a message. 'The bomb-disposal boys are on their way,' he told Unsworth. 'From Poole.'

'Let's hope they don't stop for a cuppa.'

'They make one hell of a bang,' said Mr Niven lugubriously. 'See how many spikes it's got.' He adjusted his warden's helmet. 'Sink a ruddy battleship, a dreadnought, that would.'

People were pouring from the houses now. Several cars

started up and they were scrambling into them. Women carried protesting cats and men tugged at sleepy dogs. 'Are there any children along here?' Unsworth demanded of a man puffing past and carrying a window-box. The man said: 'No. Everybody's past it.'

It was astonishing how quickly the area was cleared. The bungalows further back were being evacuated just as promptly. Nobody knew where they were going. 'The cemetery,' a woman shouted. 'That's safe.'

The soldiers and the police had retreated half a mile, checking houses as they went. More troops came from the surrounding units and were halted at a safe distance. 'The kids are all out of that school, sir,' said Bombardier Hignet abruptly appearing. 'That Jerusalem place. They've gone in trucks to Brockenhurst.'

'Looks like the bomb-disposal boys,' said Unsworth staring down the coast road.

'It's the canteen,' Bevan said.

'Christ. Make sure they keep as far away as possible. Behind that wall by the graveyard. Once they start drinking tea they'll all get careless.'

'Here's the squad now,' said Bevan.

Two dark blue vehicles pulled up dramatically. 'The navy's here!' shouted one of the bystanders. Everybody cheered. As they did so the mine exploded with the most powerful and frightening sound any of them had ever heard. The earth shuddered, ears went numb, eyes filled with grit. They felt a wave of hot air sweep over them. The pavement was littered with felled pensioners. People dropped on top of each other, every window for half a mile was blown in. Smoke welled up against the night sky, the air was stiff with cordite.

Unsworth picked himself up. Bevan got up after him. They all stood stunned; soldiers, sailors, civilians and police.

'Christ,' said Unsworth, the first to speak. 'So that's what it's like?'

The only casualty was Major Durfield. He had sprawled, forgotten in the moment, slumbering in the deck-chair in the turret. The mine exploding a mile away had only briefly roused him. He murmured: 'Come in,' and returned to sleep not knowing that a single loose pane in the turret window had fallen into the room with the blast and had cut his sagging hand.

Once he had been discovered, and in the absence of any more serious victims, the army ambulance team strapped him to a stretcher, and drove him urgently to hospital in Southampton. As they loaded him he stared at the assembled onlookers, many of them his own men. It was the first blood they had seen spilt by the enemy and that it was merely a gashed thumb did not diminish it. 'Could be internal injuries,' said the medical officer. He studied the commanding officer's distraught face flat on the stretcher. 'Inward bleeding.'

Major Durfield believed it. The rush and the expressions all around, the young soldiers and the old sweats, convinced him that, although he was feeling only a momentous hangover, things might be worse within his body. 'Sod Hitler,' he said bravely to Bevan.

3

As the year was nearing its end the coldest winter of the century was moving in. By mid-December every morning was rimed with frost, the sea lay flat under the spell of the cold, the sky like a blanket. 'I see Indian troops have arrived in France,' mentioned Bombardier Hignet, reading *The Times* in the orderly room. British ships were being regularly sunk by the enemy but there was little news of the army and air force and still very little for anyone to do. In France the opposing armies remained merely eyeing each other from their trenches.

'I hope they weren't wearing shorts,' said Bevan.

'Oh, they *were* wearing shorts all right, sir.' The bombardier held up the newspaper so the officer could see the photograph. 'Freezing their poor Indian privates off.'

Bevan had taken over temporary charge of the troop. The other distant pair of guns, the second half of Major Durfield's former responsibilities, had been moved. Bevan went out in the morning to look over the two under his command; it seemed as exciting as an empty football field. Major Durfield had only returned to collect his belongings and had gone on sick leave before either a new posting or a medical discharge. 'I can't raise any enthusiasm for this war, Bevan,' he had said poking his face from the carriage window at Southampton station. 'I did my fighting in the First War . . . Ypres, Loos, The Marne. I was there.'

Bevan saluted him as the train moved away. Bairnsfather

who had driven them watched it go and said: 'The personal tragedy of war.' They drove through the stark streets of the city. A stab of wintry sun made them seem colder. 'Want to go and see your house again, sir?' asked Bairnsfather.

Bevan grinned. 'Don't think so, thanks. I've seen it.'

'Where do you live now, sir? Like, where do you belong?'

'In the army,' said Bevan. 'I don't have another place. My marriage finished just before the war.'

'Oh, sorry. I didn't mean . . .'

'That's all right, Bairnsfather.'

'What will you do over Christmas?'

Bevan grinned: 'Look after the guns.'

The New Forest was stilled with cold, no movement in the trees, the long open spaces powdered with frost that stayed all through the short daylight. The icy air made the distance distinct and they could see a herd of deer, stationary as on a Christmas card, almost on the skyline. 'Can't say I've tasted deer. Have you, sir? Venison, don't they call it?'

'Nor me.'

'Maybe I'll take a deer home for Christmas. My mum can cook anything.' He smiled sideways. 'Maybe next Christmas, when we're all on rations.'

They drove along the coastal road. Every glazier for fifty miles had been brought in to repair the windows of the bungalows blown in by the mine. The new panes blinked sombrely in the winter day. 'That'll be good trade that,' said Bairnsfather as they passed some of the squat houses, their patches of front lawn as white as handkerchiefs. Nobody moved. Nobody ever seemed to move. The bungalows sat in dumb rows.

'Mending windows,' nodded Bevan.

'Those blokes are going to make a fortune if Jerry starts

bombing. And all the others in the building trade. I ought to have gone into that instead of delivering bread.'

The car rattled towards the camp. The scene was like a watercolour. The sea and the sky in almost a single wash, the huts and the vehicles and the guns lying as if preserved. It was too cold for anything to move. Bevan was wondering if anything would ever happen. Then the air-raid siren sounded.

As the warning wailed up and down, Bairnsfather swung the car through the camp gate so violently that he almost demolished the sentry-box and the guard staring apprehensively at the sky. Two other men clattered from the guardhouse and took up crouching positions with their .303 rifles pointing upwards. There were unconfirmed stories that particularly negligent and low-flying aircraft could be brought down by accurate rifle fire.

Bevan was glad to see the gun crews running from the canteen, grappling with steel helmets and clutching gas masks, as they made for the guns. The warning Klaxon was sounding. Sergeant Runciman was already standing at the Bofors and shouting, chivvying the men. By the time Bevan jumped from the car the crews were in their positions. Bairnsfather ran to his position as loader. 'Ready for action, sir,' reported Runciman.

Bevan returned his salute: 'Well done, sergeant.'

In that moment, he felt, there was a new feeling between them and he saw that Runciman knew it too. This could be the time when they stopped playing at soldiers and became the real thing.

Together they turned their eyes to the sky. The forenoon was pale as ice, with only a scattering gauze of cloud. There was nothing to be seen. 'Look at that lot,' said Runciman glancing behind him. Bevan turned and saw the retired inhabitants of the nearest bungalows assembled outside their houses, heads elevated, searching for the enemy. Two of the men had binoculars and one a telescope. 'They'll soon move when they see a Stuka,' muttered the sergeant.

But no dive-bomber appeared. Nothing appeared. Out in the sea a phlegmatic coaster ploughed a westward course. The men's eyes went from left to right and back to left again. Then Ugson shouted: 'Aircraft, approaching right!'

The gun layers swung their handles. It was low and coming from the west. The sergeant shouted the elevation, and the direction. Both guns swung, the crews gripped with excitement.

'It's a goose,' said Hignet.

'Bugger it,' Runciman spat.

It was undoubtedly a goose. 'Can't we have a crack at it, sir?' asked Ugson.

'No,' said Bevan resignedly. 'It's one of ours.'

He had not seen Renée since the morning they had visited Jerusalem House. He had often passed the place and once, with a sense of guilt, had surveyed it through his field-glasses. All he had seen were some small figures standing like old people in the cold. Now Bairnsfather was driving him past the gate. On impulse, Bevan said: 'Let's go in here for a minute.' Bairnsfather gave a private grin and turned into the gate.

She answered the door when he rang the large brass bell. Her almost mocking eyes met his. He was conscious of her delicate perfume. 'Ah, it is the army,' she smiled.

'I thought I would come and see that everything is all right,' he said. 'After the air-raid warning this morning and the mine. I meant to come before.'

She let him into the cavernous hall. He felt her warmth in the chilly place. 'The boys were all right,' she said. 'They filed into the basement like lambs. On the night the mine exploded we all went to Brockenhurst in the soldiers' trucks. It was very thrilling.' She smiled gravely. 'To most of these children it's not new.'

'They seem to be the only people around here who actually know what war is about,' Bevan said. She told him she was about to have a cup of tea. He followed her into the kitchen. It was empty and scrubbed, smelling of carbolic soap. There was a kettle on the range and she made two cups.

Renée said: 'We didn't see any German aeroplanes this morning.'

'False alarm,' he shrugged. 'We almost shot down a goose.'

She put her fingers against her mouth, laughed lightly, and put the cup in front of him. There was no saucer. 'You might have been able to eat it for Christmas,' she said. 'Do you get leave for Christmas?'

'I'll have to stay. The CO's just been posted, so basically I'm in charge. Some of the men will get leave. They're going to draw lots. What will you be doing?'

'I'll be here with the children. Where do you live . . . well, where did you?'

He grimaced. 'Just down the road, really. Southampton. That is where I was born. But my family have more or less vanished over the years. It's no difficulty for me to stay here.'

'You're not married?'

'I have been. Twice. My first wife died. My second wife and I parted. On the day the war started actually. It was a good excuse. And you?'

'I've not been married. I've been in love, but not married,' she said. 'I don't see the point of marriage while this war's on. The fewer things to tie you, the better.'

He had finished his tea. 'The boy who was doing his homework, Franz, is he still doing it?'

She smiled. 'Nothing's going to stop him.'

She led him through the building. It was very wintry inside. 'How is Mr MacFarlane?' he asked.

'He has gone to London and to Cambridge. He's trying to get more money to run this place.'

She pushed at a door and the warmth of the room came out to meet them. There were a dozen children, heads bent over books along the slatted table, with stacks of towels and sheets above and around them. Franz was still in his place at the far end. He stood solemnly and shook hands. The other children looked up from their books at Bevan and then, with a sort of admiration, at Franz. Bevan awkwardly tried to converse with them.

'Who made the mine go bang?' asked one.

Bevan said: 'It blew itself up.'

They seemed to think this was funny and when he added: 'We all had to run like mad,' they laughed outright.

'Haven't you finished school for Christmas?' he asked.

'We work still,' said Franz seriously. 'Because this is a good room. If you write and you read, you are warm.'

As they went out Renée said: 'He's right. As you can see the place is icy. The children are in here as well.' She opened the door he remembered as leading to the headmaster's study. There was a meagre fire in the grate and every space on the floor was filled, children sitting cross-legged, reading, writing in exercise books, playing with small toys. As they entered every face looked up.

'We have a fire in one of the other rooms,' said Renée. 'But no more, no others.'

'We've got coal and coke,' said Bevan. When he went out he said to Bairnsfather. 'These kids are freezing. They've hardly got any coal.'

'I expect there'll be some lying around somewhere, sir,' said Bairnsfather.

* * *

On the deep December nights a sort of domesticity folded over the camp. In each barrack hut an iron stove, round and jovial, glowed. Blackout shutters were placed early across windows and a heavy curtain pulled across the closed door. Along the wintry coast, in each unit, in each camp, soldiers settled down to another evening of peaceful war.

'Bombardier Hignet,' complained Bairnsfather. 'Can we have something else on the wireless. It's supposed to be meant for the whole hut.'

'I know, I know,' sighed Hignet. 'Doesn't anybody else here like Mozart?'

'We'd like Radio Luxembourg,' said Gunner Brown.

'Ruddy Mozart,' said Cartwright. 'It's only the same tune over and over again.'

The wireless was on a shelf above the bombardier's head. 'Vote,' Hignet said. 'Democratic vote.'

There were six men in the room. Two others were on guard duty. Two beds were vacant. 'Who is intelligent enough to want Mozart?' invited Hignet with scant hope. He smiled ghostily around the hut and raised his single hand. 'I don't understand you lot,' he muttered. 'We're fighting for civilised values not rubbishy dance music.' Cartwright had already moved towards the set and, reaching up, changed the station. A blare of music burst from it. 'Down! Down!' shouted Hignet covering his ears. Cartwright adjusted the volume. 'It's only a quickstep,' grumbled Brown. 'That Mozart was a Jerry anyway.'

'Austrian,' said the bombardier.

'Same thing,' said Brown.

'Why have dance music anyway?' insisted Hignet. 'Who is there to dance with?'

The answer defeated them only for a moment. Then

Bairnsfather slowly rose from his bed. 'Would you like to dance, Ugly?'

'Not much good,' said Ugson. 'Two left feet, me.'

'Carty, come on, have a dance,' challenged Bairnsfather. 'I won't hold you close.'

Cartwright eased himself from his bed. 'I might as well get some practice for Christmas.'

'Who said you're getting leave?' asked Hignet.

'Men with families get leave,' Cartwright said.

'Your wife's buggered off,' Brown pointed out.

'She might come back for Christmas. And I've still got a girlfriend.' Cartwright glanced uncertainly at Bairnsfather. The band broadcasting had begun playing another tune. 'Who's going to be the tart?' he said.

'You are,' said Bairnsfather firmly. 'I can't dance backwards.'

This time it was a waltz, which made it easier. After some grappling, like wrestlers trying to gain a first hold, the two soldiers held on as though holding each other up and with Bairnsfather counting began to revolve in the open space between the beds turning as they waltzed to the end of the hut. 'One, two, three,' counted Bairnsfather.

'Not too near the stove, mate,' muttered Cartwright. 'It's almost on my arse.'

Abruptly the door opened, the night wind blew in, the curtain was pulled aside and Sergeant Runciman, veined face raw with cold, ordered. 'Officer present! Stand by your beds.'

Bevan followed him into the room and the officer and sergeant stood, silent at the sight of Cartwright and Bairnsfather in each other's arms. 'Is this serious?' asked Runciman.

'Practising, sarge,' said Bairnsfather as he released Cartwright. Hignet turned off the wireless set. Runciman looked as if he were about to say something else, saw Bevan was grinning, and decided against it. 'Right,' he said instead. 'At ease. Captain Bevan wants to let you in on something.'

The expressions changed. Apprehension and dismay: were they being sent somewhere? Into action? God forbid, not just before Christmas.

'Right, chaps,' said Bevan. 'We're going to draw lots for Christmas leave.'

Relief went around the room. Bevan was conscious of the heat of the stove. 'It gets very warm in here,' he said.

'Can't control it, sir,' said Bombardier Hignet. 'Put a few shovelfuls on and it gets like the Congo.'

The others looked at Hignet as if they thought he might even claim to have been in the Congo. 'Right, sergeant,' said Bevan. 'Explain how we're going to do this.'

Runciman said: 'It *is* hot.' He drew his chin up. 'I have here a hat.' He held out the forage cap like a conjuror. 'And in this hat are eight slips of paper. Five are marked with crosses. Those are the five in this hut who will be on leave at Christmas. Seven days. The rest can go home for New Year when the first lot get back. All right?'

The soldiers mumbled. Cartwright said: 'I thought it was those with families, sergeant.'

'We've all got loved ones, Cartwright. Some more loving than others.'

'Yes, s'arnt.'

Runciman held the cap out horizontally before him. 'Right, one at a time. Pick one slip out. You first, Hignet, as you're the senior.'

Hignet moved forwards. He dipped in his hand. 'Fiddle,' muttered someone. Hignet pulled out a blank slip. He tightened his lips like a man being sent on a dangerous operation but who is aware of his duty, and strode briskly back to his bed space. Ugson chose next. He got a cross. So did Brown. Cartwright got a blank and Bairnsfather a cross. Both the absent men on guard, their slips drawn by Bevan, won.

'That's bloody *done* it,' moaned Cartwright when the officer and the sergeant had gone out again. 'I was just 'oping to sort things out at home.' He put his head in his hands.

'Come on, Carty,' said Bairnsfather. 'Christmas is miserable as sin anyway.' He became thoughtful: 'If you do my next two guard duties, you can have my leave.'

Cartwright slowly raised his damp cheeks. 'You're 'aving me on.'

'No, no, mate. Would I do that?' The others were staring at him. 'No kidding. I can't stand bloody Christmas anyway. All our family have is rows.'

'And you're getting busy with that nice girl,' encouraged Cartwright gently.

'Well.' Bairnsfather almost smirked. 'I *have* been invited around to tea.'

'Tea?' said someone.

Bairnsfather regarded them solidly. 'That's what I said. Tea.'

'That's serious,' said Hignet. 'Tea's serious.'

Hignet turned the switch of the wireless. It was time for the news. The announcer, with something like controlled eagerness, said: 'The German pocket battleship *Graf Spee* with British warships in pursuit has fled into the port of Montevideo, Uruguay. The navy is waiting for her to come out and fight.'

Molly Warner surveyed him from his cap badge to his glistening boots. 'You look ever so smart, Harry. Like you're going to get the Victoria Cross.'

'I'm just as nervous. Are my gaiters straight?'

'You couldn't look better.' They were walking below the wet trees of her street. It was afternoon and already dark. Her house was at the end of the terrace. 'My dad will like you. He approves of what he calls spit and polish.'

'Bull,' he said. She had her arm linked proprietorially in his. 'I like the feel of khaki,' she said.

'Was he in the army?'

'My dad? He did *something* in the Great War.'

There was no one else in the dismal street except an air-raid warden with an audible limp. He examined each house for chinks of light as he faltered towards them. 'There could be a raid tonight,' he said.

'Tonight?' said Molly. The man did not seem to be the type who might have accurate information.

'Any night,' said the warden. He straightened his steel helmet and polished his glasses before limping on dutifully, merging with the night.

'Just like my dad,' sighed Molly. 'Wishing something would happen.'

They had reached the door and stood for a moment. Bairnsfather stamped both feet to straighten his trouser creases and made sure his cap badge was level above his eye. Molly kissed him on the cheek and wiped the lipstick with her handkerchief. She put it away in her handbag and took out her door key. 'Don't be afraid,' she whispered.

As she opened the door the warmth of the house came out to meet them together with her pink, pinafored mother who said: 'Just in time for tea.' She swiftly inspected Bairnsfather. 'You *do* take tea?' she said.

'All the time,' said Bairnsfather.

'Do come in.' Her assumed voice did not fit the tight hall.

Molly looked embarrassed. Bairnsfather shook hands

with her father, then her mother, then her brother Ronnie who had jam on his face. 'Couldn't you wait?' Molly said to the boy.

'He stole it,' said her father. 'From under our eyes. Right off the plate.' He stared at a space in an arrangement of jammed scones. 'He's going to be a thief.'

'I haven't made up my mind yet,' Ronnie said.

'Sooner he's in the army the better,' said the father. He was a bald, slightly stooping man, with an old-fashioned moustache, straggly and wet, and a sagging woollen cardigan.

The mother poured their tea from a blue-patterned china pot. Bairnsfather was glad to see its strength. Genteelly she wiped the mouth of the pot with a napkin after pouring. She would get on with his mother.

'Where are you stationed?' asked the father.

'Along the coast,' said Bairnsfather.

'Well done. Never give away your exact location.'

'That's what they tell us.' He thought for a moment. His Royal Artillery flash was across his shoulder anyway. 'Anti-aircraft.'

'Ah, ack-ack. Seen any action yet? Had any casualties?'

'There's not been any action to see,' said Bairnsfather. 'Not around here. Our only casualty's been the CO who collapsed in a deck-chair.'

They thought it was a joke and they all laughed except the boy who shoved his father's arm so that his teacup wobbled. 'He was in the Great War,' he said pointing at his parent. 'He was what was *great* about it.'

'Stop being so rude,' said the mother.

'Thinks he's funny,' said the father grimly. 'Listening to those comedians on the wireless.'

'Why is there a shortage of knicker elastic?' said Ronnie. 'It's a riddle.'

'We don't know,' said Molly staring at her brother across the table. 'We just wanted Harry to meet the family.'

'I'm part of the family,' insisted Ronnie. He grabbed another jammed scone. His mother pulled the fruit cake from his vicinity. He said: 'Are you trying to get hot with him?'

Molly blushed and said: 'Stop him, Dad.'

'Have you got a rifle?' Ronnie asked Bairnsfather.

'Not on me,' said Bairnsfather.

'Could you arrange for him to be shot?' said Molly.

'They've cornered that Jerry battleship, the *Graf Spee*,' said the father. 'She's holed up in South America, in the River Plate it said, Montevideo, and our navy is waiting for her just outside. She can only stay so many hours,' he said. 'Then we'll get her.' He looked at the loud clock on the mantelpiece above the cheerful fire. 'Time for drill,' he announced.

There was dismay. 'Dad, you *can't*. Not now,' said Molly. 'Harry's come to tea.'

Her mother said: 'Can't we do it later?'

'Drill!' exclaimed Ronnie to Bairnsfather. 'You're going to laugh.'

'Shut up,' said the father. 'It's important.'

'Can't you let the baby sleep on?' said the mother. 'And Beryl.'

Bairnsfather began to look carefully from one face to another. Molly was crimson cheeked, her eyes rolling. 'It only takes a couple of minutes,' said the father.

'But . . . we're having tea.'

'Tea can wait. The Luftwaffe won't.'

Bairnsfather watched in amazement. A half-asleep child was brought from a cot upstairs and placed bodily in a container. There were straps at the back so the baby could be carried like shopping. Another child, a girl about three, came down the stairs and, dull faced, was fitted into a gas mask which looked like Mickey Mouse. The father said: 'To the shelter.' They obediently trooped out, through the kitchen into the garden, and into the Anderson air-raid shelter buried deeply in the dank earth. 'Dug that hole myself,' the father said nudging Bairnsfather. 'I don't trust the council. Glad to see you've got your respirator.'

'It's orders.'

'Quite right too.'

Molly, almost in tears, hung the grotesque baby from the straps. 'I'll kill my dad for this,' she said to Bairnsfather.

'Who's is the baby?' he asked.

'Not mine,' she almost snapped. 'If that's what you think.'

He allowed himself to be ushered into the shelter. 'It's my sister's,' muttered Molly. 'And Beryl is. Her in the Mickey Mouse. Betty's out working, so she says.'

The interior of the shelter surprised him. It was as enclosed and comfortable as a small room. There were four bunks, two on each side, one above the other, each furnished with an eiderdown and a pillow. At the far end there was space for a low table and a stool and on the table was a lamp and a single-bar electric fire. 'I've got it on the mains,' boasted Mr Warner. 'We can do toast against the fire.'

'*And* there's a kettle,' said the mother producing it from a primly curtained alcove that occupied the space below the table. 'It goes in the same plug as the fire.' For the first time she regarded her husband with some fondness. 'He's done it all.' Bairnsfather admired the curved and corrugated iron roof. There was a picture of Jesus hanging a little out of true on the wall. 'We're not religious,' said the mother. 'But you never know.'

'Pump the baby up,' said the father.

'It's nearly time,' said his wife. There was a hand pump attached to the child's encapsulating gas mask. The baby was staring suspiciously through the perspex visor at them. Molly's mother pumped air into its sanctuary. Beryl seemed to have noticed Bairnsfather for the first time and was examining him with Mickey Mouse eyes. Molly sat sulkily on the lower bunk.

'You can't be too prepared,' said the father. He indicated the metal door that could be pulled over the entrance but was now partially open. 'Once that's closed you're safe as safe. They can drop what they like, high explosive, land-mines, anything. I've left it open because it gets a bit niffy.' He looked around challengingly. 'Gas-mask drill,' he said. Glancing sideways at Bairnsfather he confided: 'I saw blokes gassed in the trenches. They turned yellow.' Nodding at the khaki respirator pack hanging around the soldier's neck, he said: 'Join in if you like. You can't get too much practice.'

They all began to fit the grotesque rubber, pig-snouted masks over their faces. 'I was sick in mine last time,' said Ronnie. 'It was full up.'

Bairnsfather reluctantly took his service respirator from its pack and put it over his head. It had a pipe that led to an air purifier in the haversack. The father jabbed his finger at it, his eyes extended behind his visor. He spoke from within like someone with no roof to their mouth. 'Nn . . . at's a ngood mas that ith.' They sat in odd silence for three minutes until Mr Warner took off his mask. They all gratefully followed suit, each one red faced from the constriction. Beryl's nose had run copiously and it had to be wiped. The baby was left in its capsule. Mrs Warner gave the pump a few more presses.

'I nearly spewed up again,' grumbled Ronnie. 'It was hard to scrape it all out last time.'

His mother told him to stop. 'We'll carry on with tea then, if we may,' she said with heavy patience. 'I'll make a fresh pot.'

They climbed up a short ladder and into the black garden. Bairnsfather felt he had to say something. 'You could survive in there for a long time,' he offered.

'Weeks,' said the father. 'I'm getting a wireless to put in there. We could listen to Sandy Macpherson on the organ while the bombs are dropping.'

They had painted some of the wild New Forest ponies with luminous stripes to prevent them being knocked down by vehicles whose headlights were masked. Part of the road was also painted with the new broken white line down the middle. Bairnsfather drove the lorry cautiously. They did not want accidents that night.

Ugson, who sat beside him, said: 'I don't see why we couldn't snaffle the coal from the pile in the camp.'

'It's painted white, isn't it,' said Bairnsfather. 'We painted the bloody stuff. They'd notice. Besides, we want a lot of it.'

Ugson whispered: 'This must be what going into action is like.'

'Nobody is going to start shooting at us,' said Bairnsfather. He swore below his breath. 'Look – coppers.'

There was a Wolsey at the junction with the main road to Brockenhurst.

A figure with a torch was in the road and waving them down. With foreboding Bairnsfather applied the brakes. 'Now, Ugly,' he warned. 'Don't start telling the truth.'

The policeman, steel helmeted, shone his torch into the cab. There were two others standing beside the car. 'Where are you off to, lads?'

'Brockenhurst, mate,' said Bairnsfather. 'Want a lift?'

It had only been a covering joke but to their surprise

the policeman said: 'Right, thanks. Just to the next telephone. It's about two miles down the road. The car's conked out. We haven't got a radio in this one.'

Bairnsfather swallowed. 'Right. Move over, Ugly, let the copper . . . officer get in.'

The policeman called to his companions and they shouted back and waved their torches. 'Good job you turned up,' he said. 'It's too far to walk at this time of night.'

Ugson was afraid and said with controlled desperation: 'My uncle used to be in the police.' Somehow they had to fill in the time. Bairnsfather was prepared to say they were going to pick up emergency supplies.

'Oh, which force?'

'North somewhere. Up by Manchester,' said Ugson. 'But he had bad feet.'

'My feet are terrible,' said the policeman staring ahead through the windscreen into the overwhelming darkness. 'That's why I couldn't walk all this way. I was thinking of joining the infantry.'

They laughed loudly, too loudly they realised and the laughs came to an abrupt end. 'You have to be out all hours, don't you,' said Bairnsfather patronisingly. 'Good job you're not afraid of the dark.'

The policeman snorted and said: 'Fine copper I'd be if I was.' They drove for another minute and the policeman said: 'What do you reckon about the *Graf Spee*?'

'Bloody good,' said Bairnsfather. 'Good for the navy.'

'Nobody else is doing anything,' said the policeman.

To their intense relief he then said: 'It's just along here. Can't see it in this dark, but it's not far. There it is.'

He climbed from the cab and slammed the door banging with his hand on the side as a thanks and a farewell. There had been no sound from the men in the back. Straight-faced and silent Bairnsfather drove on. After a mile he nudged Ugson and they both grinned.

They went in front of the first darkened cottages of Brockenhurst soon after, the white walls ghostly.

'Wonder when all the lights will go on again?' said Ugson.

'Not tonight, I hope,' said Bairnsfather. 'Not when we're trying to pinch a ton of coal.'

They went over the level crossing outside the station. The railway lines had a low glimmer. 'We'll all be able to see in the dark before this war's out,' said Ugson. 'We won't need lights.'

Bairnsfather hushed him as he slowed the truck and they sidled alongside the railway yard. 'It's just over the wall,' whispered Bairnsfather. 'Tons of it.'

He brought the vehicle to a halt, cursing the squeak of the brakes. He got out of the cab and went around to the back of the truck, banging his hand lightly on the canvas. Two white faces poked out at the back. 'That copper scared the daylights out of us,' said Cartwright. Brown still looked frightened. 'I want to go home,' he said.

Bairnsfather said: 'Let's get this done and we can all scarper.' He moved to the perimeter fence and motioned to Ugson who had climbed down from the cab. 'Give us a bunk.'

Ugson made a step with his hands and Bairnsfather put his foot on it and was lifted to the top of the fence. Brown and Cartwright helped to hold him. He blinked over the fence. They let him down carefully.

'There's a lorry right alongside the railway trucks,' he said. 'It might be full or it might be empty. Give me a bunk over.'

They regained their positions and this time Bairnsfather heaved himself to the top of the barrier and adeptly disappeared over the other side. Two minutes went by and his disembodied voice came hoarsely over the fence to them. 'It's full of bloody coal. We can half-inch the lot. Even the starting handle's there. Get up to the gate. It's a hundred yards down. Stay and watch out, Carty.'

Cartwright could not see to either end of the street. He squeezed his eyes closer. All was stationary and dark. Brown and Ugson crept clumsily along the wall until they found the metal gate. It was vertically barred but high and locked with a straight top and a straight bottom. Bairnsfather now stood behind it like a man in prison. He bent to examine the bulky padlock and its chains. 'It'll need a grenade to get through that,' he grumbled. 'We'll have to do what we thought, chuck the coal over the top, lump by lump.'

'Lift it off its hinges,' said Ugson like a man who had known the situation before. 'Four of us can do it. There's no stoppers on them.'

In the dimness Bairnsfather regarded him with respect. 'Ugly, you're a genius,' he said. 'Get Carty.'

Brown went back towards the army truck and returned with Cartwright. 'Two each side,' instructed Ugson. They positioned themselves at the sides of the gate, grasping the iron uprights. 'Right, now. Lift,' said Ugson. It was amazing how easy it was. The entire gate was raised readily. They lifted it clear and set it down without noise against the fence. Bairnsfather turned like a shadow and went back into the yard. They heard him turn the starting handle and the engine of the coal lorry responded. It began to come towards them. With its low lights it went through the gate and Bairnsfather halted it in the street. He jumped from the cab. They stretched to look over the tailboard at the piled coal. 'The gate,' said Bairnsfather. They turned, triumphantly now, and with another single heave and a few manoeuvres slotted the gate back in place. 'Are we going to bring their lorry back?' asked Cartwirght.

'You can, if you like,' said Bairnsfather. He suddenly thought. 'Christ, we've got two now. Who's going to drive this one?'

'I'll drive the other one,' said Brown without confidence. 'I've done it before. I know how it works. But you drive this one – with the coal.'

'Wartime criminals,' said Unsworth thoughtfully, 'never cease to amaze me.'

'What have they done now?' asked Ellen. She put down the teapot. 'They've sunk that German ship, you know.'

'The *Graf Spee*,' he said. 'Yes, I know. I heard it on the news at the station. She scuttled herself. Sank herself.'

'Can they do that?' She arranged his cup of tea before him.

He was not sure what she meant. It sounded as if she thought scuttling might be contrary to the rules of war. 'They just open the cocks in the bottom of the ship and down she goes,' he said.

'I hope they don't ask our Alan to do it.'

'You can't scuttle a shore base,' he said.

'Don't, Alf,' she said, half a protest, half a plea. 'I don't know about all these war things. I just worry, that's all.'

He put down the cup and patted her arm. 'Sorry, love. Well, the German commander decided he did not want to surrender so he sank his own ship. He also blew his brains out.'

'Oh, that wasn't very nice.'

'He decided it was the honourable thing to do.'

'So some of them *are*.'

'Honourable? I suppose so.'

'What were you saying? About criminals.'

'Oh, it was just a funny one. Last night somebody

took the gate off the railway yard in Brockenhurst and stole a whole lorryload of coal. They found the lorry at Barton-on-Sea this morning. On the front. Empty.'

'Coal may be getting short,' she pointed out. 'We ought to get some in.'

The bar of the Birchwood Hut, tight as a wooden box, was deep in the trees away from even one of the small hamlets. Four men whose peasant families had lived in the forest for centuries, in the case of Tom Dibben back to the time of King William himself, sat over their ale and decided that it was unlikely the war would be over by Christmas.

'Easter, I reckon,' said Tom.

'August bank 'oliday Monday,' suggested Catcher Hurrock. He had an air of authenticity and there were rural rumours that he was now working for the Government. His father and his grandfather had been snake catchers and he had followed that profession since leaving the village school thirty years before.

'Soonest over the better,' said Rob behind the worn and polished plank that was the counter. The Hut, as everyone called it, was little more than that. In summertime customers lined up to cross the front step, shuffled along a wooden passage hung with the aromas of animals and ale, put their jugs across the bar for a fill of beer, and then walked through and out at the back door. On good evenings they used to stand and drink on the grass behind the thatched and lopsided building. Women stood apart with half-pints of cider and children played games in the trees. Forest gypsies sometimes appeared silently and stood in a third group, their wives, children and dogs standing about them. In winter the single room of the bar was opened and a stove lit.

The place could only accommodate six men, perhaps a seventh if Catcher was there because he was small and thin.

Rob, the landlord, had been on the Western Front in the Great War. 'Never was any bad blood 'tween Jerry and us,' he said. 'Not the Tommies. We was told to fight 'em, and they was told to fight us, but that came from the 'igh ups. We didn't 'ave anything against them personal. They was just poor bloody infantry, samc as wc.'

'Words of comfort to the enemy, Rob,' suggested Unsworth entering from the passage.

''Tis true, Mr Unsworth,' said Rob stoutly. He put a pewter mug on the bar and poured Unsworth a beer. 'And I'll say it in front of a magistrate if needs be. At this time o' year the Jerries and us used to lob presents, cigarettes and that, to each other. Some of the trenches was so close you could throw a piece of cake, easy as throwing a grenade. They used to sing the same Christmas carols but in German, loike.'

The men shifted along the bench to make room for Unsworth. 'There was no Hitler in those days,' pointed out Unsworth.

'Ah, but there *was*,' said Tom Dibben. 'He was one of they corporals.'

'He should have stayed like that,' said Catcher. 'There's no evil in corporals.'

'When do you reckon it'll be over then, Mr Unsworth?' asked Rob. 'What do the police think?'

'They haven't told me,' said Unsworth. 'It hardly seems to have started yet.'

'I 'ope it *don't*,' emphasised Rob. 'We don't want it like it was in the first ruddy lot. Being sent out at five, even four, in the ruddy morning – and just to get mowed down.'

'Why did it 'ave to be that time? Five o'clock?' asked Catcher seriously. 'You'd think they'd 'ave given 'un a lie-in afore attackin' like that.'

'Aye,' said Dibben. 'Why din' they do it in the afternoon?'

'They reckon it was to catch Jerry while 'e was asleep,' said Rob. He gave a harsh laugh. ''E couldn't 'ave been more asleep than we was.'

Unsworth said: 'They won't let men fight like that again.'

'Should 'ope not,' said Catcher. 'Won't be any young 'uns left.'

He turned confidingly to Unsworth. 'You 'eard I'm on war work.' The others leaned closer. 'I s'pose I can tell?' he said, glancing at Unsworth.

Unsworth said: 'Careless talk costs lives, Catcher. You're not a secret weapon, are you?' They laughed but they still wanted to hear.

'No, nothin' like that,' said Catcher. But his doubt had increased. 'I better not,' he said. He reached into the old haversack he habitually carried and, first taking out a dead hare, followed it with a catapult. The forked wood was hardened ash, the rubber a quarter of an inch thick and the pouch big enough to take a missile the size of a walnut. He was a deadly shot.

'I been told to watch out for parachutists,' he said. Unsworth realised he had changed his story at the last moment and nodded. The others looked disappointed. 'We *all* been told that,' Dibben said grumpily. 'My old woman keeps a pan of water boiling. Chuck it over the buggers.'

Catcher felt deeper into his bag saying: 'That 'minds me.' He took out a sleepy brown-and-white puppy. 'Found 'un yesterday,' he said displaying the dog gently. 'Shit on the bottom o' my bed 'e did last night.' He handed the pup to Unsworth. 'Under the brambles I found 'un,' he said.

'Why are you giving it to me?'

''Cause you're the police,' said Catcher. The others laughed.

Unsworth took the dog with him when he left, putting it in the back of his car. It rolled to sleep at once. He was pleased that Catcher had lied. The catapult was for keeping large birds and animals away from places logically designated as emergency landing grounds for fighter planes.

He drove through the forest to his cottage. Ellen was getting his lunch. That afternoon he had to give evidence at the inquest on a man who had died after riding his motorcycle into a forest pond which his blacked-out headlights had failed to detect.

He handed the puppy to her. 'We might as well keep it,' he said. He hesitated, then said: 'It will be company for you, love.'

'Alan's coming home on leave,' she said beaming. 'Forty-eight hours. At Christmas.' Unsworth smiled. She lifted the puppy up to her face level. 'What are we going to call you?' she said.

'Catcher,' suggested Unsworth. 'That's where I got him.'

She was walking towards the camp, along the bare road, in the early afternoon when Bevan saw her. He started out to meet her but then stopped, enjoying the sight, her red coat against the wintry wash of the landscape. Only one vehicle passed her, a milk van which slowed. He saw her wave to the milkman. He picked up the telephone and turned the handle.

'Gate sentry.'

'Oh, bombardier. That is French, I take it?'

'Yes, Captain Bevan.'

'French, there's a young lady walking towards the camp along the sea road.'

'I've been seeing her, sir. Nice red coat.'

'Yes, it is. I think she will probably ask for me. Will you send someone over with her.'

'Yes, sir. Brown. He's not doing anything. He never is, sir.'

'You were lucky in the Christmas leave raffle, weren't you, French?'

'I'll say. I'm off tomorrow, sir. They're saying it's French leave.'

Bevan laughed. He replaced the phone and hurriedly straightened his tie and brushed his buttons with his sleeve. They must get a mirror in the orderly room. He was alone. He closed the door because the place suddenly felt cold despite the oil heater in the corner. Through the window he saw Renée approach the gate, speak to the sentry, and after a moment continue on her way accompanied by Gunner Brown. Even at that distance Bevan could see Brown was blushing. Then Sergeant Runciman appeared as if by some trick and dismissed the gunner, taking over the escort duties himself, striding with short regimental steps and apparently stilted conversation alongside Renée. They arrived at the door. Bevan sat behind his desk and unnecessarily studied a map. 'Renée,' he said as if surprised when she came in. Runciman threw up a sharp salute, did a military about turn and marched away.

'Good,' she said. She was like a summer's day. 'Now you're calling me by my name.' He sat her in Hignet's seat. There was no room to move it from behind the desk.

'Ah well, Captain Bevan . . . May I call you Bevan? I'd like to do that.' He smiled. 'I have to tell you something,

Bevan,' she said. She seemed embarrassed. 'A great pile of coal has appeared in the playground.'

'Good God! When?'

'The other morning. I saw some of the boys pointing out of the window and there it was – just as though some good fairy had been in the night.'

'Well, I'll be damned.' He began to grin, then straightened his face. 'I wonder how that got there?'

'Mr MacFarlane is not someone to look, how do you say it, a gift horse in the teeth. He said: "Thanks be to God," and called to everybody to take it into the cellars.' She laughed. 'All the boys were black.'

He shook his head. 'Maybe it was delivered by mistake.'

'We've got it now,' she said firmly. 'Everywhere is so lovely and warm.'

'Do you have time for a cup of coffee?' he asked. 'We will have to walk over to the mess.' She leaned and patted his hand as she might have one of her boys.

'I was on my way shopping,' she said. 'Another time.' At the door she asked: 'You said you are going to be here at Christmas?'

'All through,' he replied.

'You could come and visit us,' she said. 'Have Christmas dinner.'

'I'd like to, but I can't leave the premises. I'm in charge of the shop.'

She regarded him solemnly. 'Then I must try to come and visit you. You can't be alone.'

It took Bevan a moment to answer. 'I'd be delighted.'

She was already on her way, the red coat bright in the drab day. She paused and looked over her shoulder. 'I only wish I could find someone to thank for the coal,' she said.

He watched her walk towards the gate and then out

into the road, turning towards the first shops of New Milton. Bairnsfather and two others were cleaning the Bofors and they stopped and watched her go. When they saw Bevan they returned to their duty. He walked over and pretended to inspect their work. 'Can't get it any shinier, sir,' said Bairnsfather. 'My mother couldn't.'

'You're not going to see your mother at Christmas then?'

Bairnsfather shrugged. Cartwright and Ugson grinned from their side of the gun. 'No, sir,' said Bairnsfather. 'I'll miss the family fisticuffs.'

They all laughed. 'You'll miss hanging up your stocking,' said Bevan.

'Did you used to hang up a stocking, sir?'

'Naturally.'

'Oh, yes. I wasn't sure whether officers did when they were little.'

Bevan said: 'We used to get an apple and an orange and a penny whistle or something. And a lump of coal.' He looked steadily at Bairnsfather. 'Did you ever get coal, Bairnsfather?'

All three faces changed. 'Yes. Yes, sir. Always. I always wondered what it was for.'

'It keeps people warm,' said Bevan.

It was the coldest Christmas of the century, although it was not admitted because such matters were under the clamp of censorship. There was no mention of it on the wireless bulletins nor in the newspapers, in case it afforded comfort and information to the Germans.

Going to the village church that Christmas morning, however, the local people were well aware that it was bitter, even though, in the absence of official confirmation, they had to trust their memories for anything colder. It was also very beautiful. No one could remember such a finely painted Christmas. 'Fair day,' said Catcher as he and Tom Dibben and their best-dressed wives approached the lych-gate.

'Aye, full fair,' agreed Tom.

'Never seen it so much,' said Mrs Catcher who was called Mirabelle.

'Nor I, neither,' said Annie.

There had been no snow. It was too cold for snow. When it did fall they knew it would crack the bone-dry trees so you could hear them break like a gunshot a mile across the forest. Hoar-frost hung from branches and roofs and clothed the churchyard graves.

'Now Filbert Hand would like this,' said Catcher. 'Reckoned 'e played better in the frost.' Filbert's tombstone just inside the wall was carved with the shape of a winding wind instrument called a serpent and he had been a famous player. 'That serpent 'orn,' remembered Tom. 'A mile long.' He glanced quickly at Catcher. 'They reckon 'tis in there with him. Never been seen since.'

'Too big for in there,' said Mirabelle.

'Remember,' said Annie a little sadly, 'when we was young how we used to laugh when he played it at the concert.'

'Fit to bust,' said Mirabelle. 'All wound around 'im.'

'Could be took to bits,' said Catcher. 'I seen 'un in bits.'

'In that case they *could* 'ave put 'un in with 'im,' said Tom. 'Filbert was only little, weren't 'e.'

'That's what made him look so comic,' said Mirabelle. 'All wound up in 'is serpent.'

'They could 'ave,' said Catcher. 'But nobody ever told.'

The Norman tower of the church stood square against the Christmas sky, the paleness of the background and the low winter sun lending warmth to its stones. Fields, open moor and patches of forest, all laden with frost, were glossed pink. The road crackled under people's steady tread. The church bells called the worshippers. Until the war was almost over they would not peal at Christmas again.

There were more people than usual. Those who rarely went to church were drawn by the bells and the uncertain future, khaki soldiers and some airmen in their glistening blue; there were city children evacuated to what was to become a serious war zone, some of them now wondering why they had to go to church and spoil what had always been an enjoyable day. There were London civil servants, some in bowler hats, a strange sight to the countrymen, uprooted from their suburban homes, required to oversee evacuated official files that might be needed in a national emergency.

The only motor vehicle going to the church, crunching past the walkers on the frosty road, was the Rolls Royce bearing Lady Violet Foxley, her two army-officer sons and her daughter Penelope.

''Er ladyship,' said Mirabelle low voiced. 'And her boys.'

'And that Penelope,' added Annie. 'Twenty-eight, and still not wed.'

They stood asidc rcspectfully. Inside the warm car Arthur, the elder son, said: 'Don't knock any of them over, Mainprice.'

'I'll try not to, sir,' said the chauffeur, adding quietly: 'Seeing it's Christmas.'

'There's more than usual,' said Horace.

'Christians,' sniffed Lady Violet. 'For the duration.'

'Mother,' reproved Penelope.

The car came to a gliding stop outside the lych-gate. The people backed away while Lady Violet, in her customary violet and with a feather, stiff as frost itself, in her hat, was helped from the car by Mainprice. The chauffeur trod heavily on the foot of an evacuated child who cried out but Mainprice ignored it.

'Don't know why she needs manhandling,' whispered Tom at a distance. 'Rides to 'ounds all right.'

'Hush,' warned Mirabelle. 'You never know when you might be glad of 'er. She'm a magistrate.'

The Rolls Royce party had disembarked. Annie said: 'Don't see that Penelope very regular.'

'Down from London,' said Mirabelle.

'Long way to come, eighty, ninety miles,' nodded Catcher who had never been there. They watched the car ease away, the crack of the frost breaking below its wheels sounding above the soft engine. 'Can't 'elp wondering 'ow they gets the petrol.'

'War allowance, I expect,' said Mirabelle.

''Igh-ups get petrol,' said Tom.

They followed the tail end of the worshippers into the church. It was full of the robust feel of a Christmas morning, warmed by the congregation of two hundred and the efforts of a coke boiler which wheezed and smoked against the north wall as it had done for thirty years, leaving a waxy patina on the memorial tablets above it.

'I wish that stove would stop sounding like a bad chest,' said Lady Violet rising at the end of her initial private prayer from her reserved hassock in the family pew. 'It's worse than the organ.'

'Don't be unkind, Mother,' cautioned Penelope. 'Mr Singer is in the army and Mrs Singer does her best.'

'Not good enough,' muttered her mother. 'She should forget the organ and play the stove.'

Her second son, Horace, rather short in his lieutenant's uniform, rose from his hassock. His burnished Sam Browne belt squeaked and he glanced around worried that someone might think he was letting wind. His sister grinned and said: 'That belt, Horace.'

'You know it was Father's,' he said.

Penelope did not understand the war. To her it seemed merely an opportunity for people to dress up and talk endlessly about the same old battles, the same old foes. In 1935 she had spent a year in Heidelberg University and she had lost her virginity to a young blond Bavarian who was wearing lederhosen. They had been walking, striding, through pine trees and their clean, acid smell had intoxicated her. He had wanted to marry her and wrote often up to the declaration of war. His last letter had arrived on the Monday after hostilities began and the postman, seeing Hitler on the stamp, had consequently reported her to the police. She occasionally wondered where her lover was now.

There was a Christmas tree at one side of the church, the sharp winter light through the stained glass window clothing its branches with extra colours. It had been chopped down half a mile away in a patch of the forest where the church tree had been felled for many years. It occurred to Lady Violet that it was now perilously close to the stove.

She also thought how wonderful the scene was and, sadly, that by next year it might very well all be changed. By how much no one knew. Perhaps her sons would not be standing beside her, short haired, straight backed, straight-faced, wearing their Sam Browne belts. Perhaps Penelope would be nursing the wounded on some battlefield, although she personally doubted it. It was possible that Germans would be singing the carols. She wondered if they would install a new stove.

Mrs Singer, as a young bride in the 1920s, had leaned fondly against her husband in the organ loft as he played on Sundays and for generations of weddings and funerals. She had heard too many stories of the temptations afforded to church organists and she kept close beside him. Then she had tired of being a passenger on the long stool and had persuaded her husband to teach her how to play, at least after a fashion.

Now she launched into the Christmas Day processional hymn with attack and even some confidence. She had been practising it all the week alone in the dark afternoon church with only a bedside night-light as a companion. She felt that her husband, now a soldier training in the far north, would have been proud of her. When he had made his weekly call from a telephone box in a snowbound village he had hummed a difficult passage over the frozen wires to her and afterwards had little time for conversation because his pennies were running out and there was a large, shivering corporal waiting for the phone. She had kept the tune in her head and had bravely run back through the graves to the organ loft.

It was uplifting: 'Christians awake, salute the happy morn.' The bells ceased as the first notes swelled to the roof ribbed like the inverted hull of an ancient ship; the choir processed down the aisle, their cassocks white as sails, the boys apple faced, the men with expressions fashioned by age, experience and wrinkles. The Reverend Goodenough brought up the rear, singing a little absently, almost a mumble, worried about what he felt was his duty that morning. He hoped Lady Violet would not be present; the weather had brought a lot of illness. But he saw her hat feather almost from the door and the hope vanished. It was going to be hard, very hard.

'Christians awake,' the church resounded, 'salute the happy morn, Whereon the Saviour of the world was born!'

Penelope thought 'whereon' was a strange word to

have in a carol. It sounded like 'theretofore' and 'notwithstanding'. She supposed it was only there because it fitted. A lot of things were like that. This church fitted, the village fitted, Lyndhurst, the nearest place you could buy anything, fitted, Southampton fitted because that's where the picture house was, and from there, in the past, you could go on a cruise. London fitted because it was two and a half hours distant, just remote enough to be enticing. She was having an affair. The man was a civilian and was determined to stay one. He had medical papers although to her he seemed healthy enough.

They reached the end of the processional carol and the vicar called echoingly upon them to pray. He would have made a poor drill sergeant, Arthur thought, with that arching, aching voice. Did vicars *have* to have voices like that or did they train them?

'Let us pray': the invitation sounded like an echo of Arthur's thoughts. They had done justice to the first rousing Christmas hymn, the choir's vigorous voices almost trembling the tree, the organ galloping along gamely and the congregation not far behind. Now the people obediently crumpled to their knees. Lady Violet had the thought that the family hassocks, which had done duty since the coronation of King George V really needed refurbishing. Perhaps she would undertake it herself. It could be part of her war work.

The prayers were the familiar seasonal wishes to the vast unknowns who were not so fortunate as themselves. The people muttered the amens. Wives were mentally timing the poultry already sizzling in their ovens. Then the Reverend Goodenough, after offering a silent, private prayer on his own behalf, called: 'Let us pray for our enemies.'

Up came Lady Violet's head. 'What was that?' she enquired of her son. 'What did he say?'

'Our enemies. Praying for them,' responded Horace, peeping around his hands.

'What for? We want them dead.' Her head raised, she muttered: 'Stop praying at once.' Her family stopped. There were no other protests. The people always accepted what the clergy told them. 'Oh God, whose son Jesus Christ bade us to love our enemies, let us pray for those now ranged in war against us, that they may see the error . . .'

Lady Violet rose from the hassock and squatted with her arms folded belligerently. Hers was the first face the vicar saw when he eventually stood.

'I hope you sent Herr Hitler a Christmas card,' she sniffed as they were leaving after the service.

'I . . . I beg your pardon, Lady Violet?' His voice below the porch had become a mousy squeak. The congregation were respectfully queuing to get out behind Lady Violet and her family. Most now stood on their toes to see what was happening.

'I said,' repeated her ladyship loudly, 'I hope you sent Herr Hitler a card saying perhaps: "Christmas wishes to Adolf".'

'Oh, Lady . . . !'

'What's all this praying for the wretched enemy?'

Her sons were staring far into the outside sky as though expecting an air attack. Penelope stood behind her mother, enjoying it. The vicar's head seemed to be seeking shelter in his collar.

'Jesus,' said the parson so carefully that he might have been making sure he got the name right. 'Jesus said: "Love your enemies".' Her stone stare was still fixing him. He added: 'And so do several bishops.'

'Are clergymen exempt from military service?' asked Lady Violet.

'Er . . . Well, yes.'

'It's just as well, isn't it.' She turned stiffly and with her family marched through the frosty churchyard towards the lych-gate and the already steaming car. Lady Violet sniffed. 'He might be called on to bayonet someone.'

It was an old British Army custom that on Christmas Day officers should serve other ranks at the table. The interior of the mess hall used by the soldiers of all the units in that area was as homely as a factory although it was drooping with paper chains and greetings in tinsel. There was a Christmas tree in one corrugated-iron corner but it had sagged to one side like last night's drunk. Nothing could lend cheer to the long girdered room. Bevan was confronted with an almost silent group of soldiers, twenty of them, huddled like survivors at its centre. Two were wearing festive hats but the expressions below the coloured paper were grim. A grey-faced second lieutenant from the Ordnance Corps was already handing out plates of food and another officer, a captain, grumblingly carried a tray of bottled beer. All around, the tables left empty by the lucky men on leave lay like rafts on a deserted lake.

A cook in a white hat stood with a spectacularly spotty assistant behind a counter on which the Christmas dinner was piled, a Catering Corps sergeant sweating and fussing behind them. 'Morning, sir, happy Christmas, sir,' he said harshly as Bevan approached. 'One or two of the men have complained about their eating irons.'

'What's the matter with them?'

'Can't cut through the turkey, sir.'

'I'll see what I can do.' He went towards the clutch of silent soldiers at the room's centre. One man was sitting in isolation, distant from the others, hunched over his food as though inspecting it for bugs or saying a private grace. Bevan was glad to see Bairnsfather and Purcell were among the group in the middle. Hignet's parents had arrived and Bevan had allowed them to take their son to lunch at a hotel. 'Happy Christmas, sir,' said Bairnsfather. Some of the men from other units looked at the gunner with scorn and one said: 'What's happy about it?'

'And to you,' said Bevan as cheerfully as he could. 'Any complaints?'

'That bloke serving,' said Bairnsfather pointing to the Catering Corps private. 'He's got more spots than the pudding.' Nobody laughed.

Bevan surveyed the room. 'Why is that man sitting by himself?'

'He wants to,' said one of the other soldiers. 'He's been crying, sir.'

'Fancy fucking crying at fucking Christmas,' said another man balefully eyeing the cooling food on his plate. He glanced at Bevan as if regretting the swear-words, Christmas or not. Bevan said quietly: 'Yes, it's a fucking shame.'

He turned from the group and walked, bumping against empty trestle tables, towards the solitary soldier who did not appear to see him coming. He was a pink, podgy man. When he eventually looked up his pale eyes were wet.

'What are you doing?' asked Bevan.

'Sitting here,' said the man. 'Sir.' He remained seated.

'I can see that. Why don't you go over to the others?'

'Them,' said the soldier almost to himself. 'I'd rather sit by myself.' Bevan thought about it, then took the chair opposite. 'I don't agree with war,' said the man as if Bevan could do something about it. 'None of it. No wars, I don't care who it's against.'

'You should have registered as a conscientious objector.'

'And go before one of those tribunals? For a start you have to say you believe in God and I don't.'

'You don't believe in much then?'

'I just don't want to be here. In this hole.'

'Not many of us do,' Bevan pointed out. 'I think you ought to go across with the others. Stop crying in your beer.'

'I don't drink either,' said the man. 'Not beer. Sometimes I have a glass of sherry.' He looked up like a plea. 'I've passed exams,' he almost hissed. 'Accountancy. I wasn't a street sweeper, you know.'

'Well, I didn't know,' said Bevan as patiently as he could. 'But now I do.' He looked towards the entrance of the mess hall. 'Ah, look,' he said a shade desperately. 'Here's Father Christmas.'

'Who does he think he is?' The soldier watched sullenly.

'I've just told you, son,' said Bevan. 'He thinks he's Father Christmas. Actually, he's a serving army officer.'

He got up before he lost his temper and went back towards the soldiers sitting around the centre table. 'Santa's got presents for everyone!' bellowed the newcomer blowing his beard out in front. Bairnsfather started laughing – almost manically as if the ridiculousness of the situation had got to him – and it set the others off. They rallied; one man choked on his dinner and they laughed more. The chef advanced with a tray full of Christmas puddings, solid as ammunition. Two other officers had arrived; one had the face of a small cherubic boy, and began to clear the plates. 'There's sixpences in the pudding!' shouted the sergeant. 'Who wants custard?'

The dinner plates were quickly cleared, the young lieutenant amateurishly carrying a toppling pile towards the kitchen. The crockery spilled and splattered its congealed food across one of the vacant tables. A roast potato bounced like a ball. There was huge cheering. 'Oh, blast! Oh, dash it!' piped the young officer.

The pudding dishes were pushed around and Bevan followed them with a jug of hot custard, dripping yellow across the lip. It steamed as it spread across the black-brown lumps. At once the men began to search with their spoons for the hidden sixpences. 'Got one,' shouted Purcell. He put the small coin between his teeth and scraped the pudding from it. He examined it minutely and said: '1929.' Another man dug out a sixpence and one said: 'I'm saving to buy a car, a nice little runabout.' Bevan glanced sideways across the room. The solitary soldier still sat watching from his isolation. Bevan had one more try: 'Come on over!' he called.

'Is that an order, sir?'

'No, it's not.'

'Then I'll stay here if you don't mind.'

'Miserable bastard,' said Bairnsfather.

The other men hardly gave a glance before turning to the now jovial Father Christmas. He had been unsure of what his reception might be but, suddenly, as if they had decided to throw their desperate lot in with him, they were laughing and cheering each present as it was distributed. Bevan found himself beaming. It was like a children's party from long ago; coloured squeakers were blown, the sergeant cook donned a clown's hat and crimson nose.

Bairnsfather unwrapped his bright paper, produced a pair of ATS khaki knickers, pressed them to his nose and said: 'Lovely!' Purcell grabbed them, held them out and shouted: 'I know 'er!' More silly gifts appeared, a copy of *Comic Cuts*, a torch with no battery, a battery with no torch, a picture of Stalin, a bar of Cadbury's chocolate with a bite taken from it.

Then Sergeant Runciman arrived. He was carrying his bakelite wireless set, bending forward with its weight.

Two of the men took it from him. 'Put it on the table,' he breathed. 'The King's on in five minutes.'

After a moment of uncertain silence, someone said: 'What's he singing?' They all laughed but looked expectantly towards the wireless. 'That's a nifty one,' said one man. 'How long you had that, sarge?'

'Christmas present to myself,' said Runciman. 'Eleven pounds ten that cost, batteries extra.'

He turned the knob and a dim light appeared behind the glass tuning panel. Hands moved forward but he pushed them away. 'Don't muck about with it.' He turned the tuning knob. Nothing happened but a faraway crackling. Runciman put his head enquiringly around the back of the set. 'Is the wet battery all right?' asked one of the men.

'Just had it filled,' said Runciman. 'I hope the ruddy thing works.' He looked at his watch and said: 'Sod it.'

The soldier who had asked about the battery went around the back of the set and began tinkering. He seemed to know what he was doing. He unplugged the leads and took out the glass accumulator with its level of blue acid. 'Just been charged,' repeated Runciman. The soldier returned it to its space. 'And the dry battery is all right?' he said.

'New,' said Runciman. 'Came with the set. Ruddy thing.'

'There *was* a light,' said someone else. 'On the dial.' The soldier was twisting the connections at the back. He returned to the face of the wireless and turned it on. Immediately there came some gurgling music. Everyone cheered. 'Right on time,' said Runciman.

'It was my job,' said the man. 'I'll find it for you if you like.'

'No. I know where London is.' Carefully, as if conducting a dangerous experiment, Runciman edged the pointer around the dial. The sounding strokes of Big Ben came from the set. 'That's it,' he said proudly.

'This is London,' declared a profound voice. There was quite a long pause as if the announcer wanted to ensure that everything was ready. Then: 'His Majesty the King.'

'Att ... en ... tion!' Runciman abruptly bawled. The startled soldiers got to their feet. The man behind them, alone, remained sitting but nobody noticed. The officers, including Father Christmas, stood stiffly. 'At ease!' ordered Runciman. 'Stand easy.' They had just time to sit again.

George VI's voice, with its aching impediment, stammering and yet somehow steely, came from the wireless. No one moved, no one spoke. Every word was taken in. The men's faces were set. The beer bottles stood like unattended skittles. At the end of the brief speech the King somehow steadied his voice and recited: 'I said to the man who stood at the Gate of the Year: "Give me a light that I may tread safely into the unknown!" And he replied: "Go out into the darkness and put your hand into the hand of God. That shall be to you better than light and safer than a known way".'

There was a deep silence among the soldiers, then the National Anthem began to play. 'Attention!' shouted Runciman as if coming from a trance. The men were already on their feet.

Bevan could not get rid of the lump in his throat. He half turned and saw the solitary soldier still sitting in his isolation. He saw Bevan's glare and awkwardly, reluctantly, stood, crying like a boy.

The light of the cursory afternoon was already beginning to fade when Bevan went across the frozen asphalt to the officers' mess hall. It had once been a stable and stood apart from the main house, blacked out against the diminishing sky. There were no noises, even the sea was soundless, as his feet crunched towards the unwelcoming building. He opened the outside door and standing within the heavy blackout curtain waited. Childish shouts come from the other side.

He pushed the curtain aside. Three rowdy young officers were crouched behind a table turned on its side using spoons to lob lumps of Christmas pudding at another group entrenched behind an old leather sofa on the far side of the room. 'Boom!' shouted one. 'Got him, Archie!' There was a clutch of empty wine bottles on another table and the debris of a meal.

So engrossed were they in their skirmish that not one of them saw him. He stood for a moment while the pudding flew and some of the bottles rolled on to the floor, then he turned and went out into the cold again, wondering how they would handle a real battle.

Even after only moments in the building he felt the stark air hit him with new sharpness. He went towards the main house and then, as though he wanted to put off going into it alone on Christmas afternoon, he turned towards the garden and the beach.

Around the corner of the house Bevan was presented with a petrified scene: there was no trace of wind, the cold seemed to have melded everything, sky, sea, land; the distant island was reduced to a smudgy finger, its lighthouse spark the only break in the dimness. In the foreground the two Bofors were stood cloaked in tarpaulin like a pair of beggars. The sentry guarding them stamped up and down trying to keep warm, his puffs of breath firing into the air.

Bevan trod over the white-fingered grass, past the flagpole and then down onto the shingle which shattered below his step. The sea was so flat it scarcely nudged the shore; he saw that the fringes were frozen and pushing out his boot tapped out a pattern of small stars. A solitary oystercatcher, its orange beak bright as a flame, flew low across the water crying out like a carrier of alarming news. He looked up and followed it until it, and its sound, faded.

He was about to turn and walk back to the house when he saw her coming along the shore. She was wearing her vivid red coat. She called to him and he went towards her. 'I promised I would try and come,' she said.

'And here you are.'

'I am.'

There seemed nothing more to say. She took his arm familiarly and they progressed back along the frozen beach together, very slowly, looking down at the patterns in the thin ice at the water's edge. 'At least the school is warm,' she said. 'We must thank the Christmas fairy. Perhaps you can do that for us.'

'I think I know him . . . them.'

'Everyone at Jerusalem House had a good time,' she said. 'The Jewish children had never celebrated Christmas before.'

'It's time something turned out right for them,' he said. 'Is Franz still studying?'

'Every day,' she said. 'He was at his books when I left. He wants to be the cleverest boy in the world, he says. But now that the place is warm everywhere most of the others have stopped studying.' She laughed thoughtfully.

'What did you do?' he said.

'Me? Today? Oh, I had some sherry, two glasses, and some Christmas turkey and mince pies. And you?'

'Officers in the British Army serve the men's Christmas dinner, so that's what I've been doing.'

'We should go back,' she said. 'Now it's getting dark as well as cold.'

They turned, but towards each other. She suddenly lay against him, breathing as if exhausted, and put her flushed cheek to his. Then unhurriedly turning her head she kissed him on his cheek. He could feel the warmth of her coat and the heat of her lips. The ice was cracking below their shoes. The sentry guarding the guns abruptly halted his march and stood observing their embrace. He called out: 'Merry Christmas, sir.'

'Let's go up to the house,' Bevan said. 'There's a fire. I was going to listen to the wireless.'

She took his arm again. As they moved up the garden she took on a mischievous look and called to the sentry: 'Merry Christmas to you.'

'Yes,' called Bevan belatedly. 'All the best!'

'How long must he guard?' she asked.

'Two hours normally, but in this weather they take it in hourly stags.'

'Are you afraid the Nazis will come and take the guns?' Her smile remained.

'Not if they've got any sense.'

They went into the house. In the big sitting-room the fire was growling in the grate. Bevan threw two logs from the fireside bin on to it. At once they split and blazed. She began to take off her red coat. He helped her. She was wearing a pale blouse below a dark brown cardigan. Her skirt was full, like a Cossack's. She wore short boots lined with fur.

Her breasts were pressing the parting of the buttoned cardigan over the blouse. She and Bevan were standing very close. She did not move but eyed him, still with mischief. He put his arms around her waist and hers went to his neck. 'Merry Christmas, sir,' she whispered. She laughed at his expression and kissed him deeply. He was amazed that it was happening like this. He returned the ardent kiss and then touched his lips to her soft neck. 'I would like a drink, please,' she said.

There was a decanter on the sideboard. 'It's port,' he said. 'Is that all right? It's very warming.'

She said it was. She was regarding him, still archly. 'You are very afraid, Bevan?' she asked.

'Afraid?' He poured the port. The glasses were generous. 'No, I'm not afraid. A bit surprised. I can't remember ever meeting anyone like you.'

'Part of me is Vienna,' she said taking the offered glass. She raised it to him and he raised his. 'My mother's part. Part of me is English. Today I think I am Vienna.' She sat on the huge worn sofa which faced the fire and held out her hand to him. 'Has it been very sad for you today?'

'Up to now it hasn't been hilarious,' he admitted. He sat beside her on the deep, faded cushions.

'You miss your wife?'

'No, I can't miss her. She's gone.' He paused, then said: 'It was odd but when they played "God Save the King" on the wireless this afternoon, after the King's speech . . .'

'We heard it. Poor man. He tries hard to speak.'

'He does. But it reminded me. When my wife and I parted, on the day the war started, right after Chamberlain's speech . . .'

'You told me.'

'They were playing the National Anthem then. *We stood up*. Both of us. It seemed ridiculous. She was pregnant. And when it finished we never sat down again. She went upstairs and I got together my army things, and left the house.'

'To go to the war,' she finished thoughtfully. 'The theme music should have been more, well, dramatic then. Beethoven perhaps.'

'Not Beethoven. Not in the circumstances.'

'Perhaps Elgar.'

Nothing was said for a moment. Then she searched in her shoulder-bag. 'Did you have your dinner?' she asked.

'Oh, dinner? Yes,' he lied.

'I have brought you some cake,' she said bringing out a paper bag. 'Christmas cake.' He grinned and took it from her. He realised how hungry he was. Opening the bag she revealed a heavy slice of fruit cake, thickly iced and dark with glacé cherries. 'Thanks very much,' said Bevan. He took it from her. 'I didn't have a *lot* of dinner.' He bit into the rich cake and then again. She began to laugh. 'Delicious,' he said.

'You have eaten mine as well,' she giggled. Before he could apologise or even brush the crumbs from his mouth, she began to kiss him, picking away the crumbs with her lips. 'I will have my share like this,' she said. Her voice had become tender. She moved against him, pushed him deeper into the sofa and undid the buttons of his battledress.

She began to kiss him again, pushing her breasts against his shirt, the softness of her cardigan crushing into the rough military material. He folded her to him, kissing her hair, her neck and her lips. The fire crackled into a blaze.

'You can touch me, James,' she whispered. 'In fact I wish you would.'

'I want to touch you,' he said and did. He pushed his hands against the underside of her breasts and then gently to the front. Even under the material he felt her nipples harden to his touch.

'For this sort of thing it has been so long,' she said. 'Too long for me.'

It had been a long time for him too. The fire roared encouragement. He put his hands below the cardigan and ran the palms down her shoulder-blades feeling her glow under the soft blouse. They kissed again, fiercely, greedily.

'Anybody home?'

The inebriated voice froze them. They crouched low into the sofa, its high back to the door, and clutched each other. 'Anybody home?'

'Nobody,' the voice answered itself. 'Not one fucker. What a bloody Christmas.'

They felt each other's sigh of relief when the door was closed. 'He was an officer?' asked Renée her eyes wide.

'A very browned-off officer.'

'Where can we go?'

Her face was flushed, her eyes eager. 'Upstairs,' he answered. 'But it will be cold.'

'We will be in the bed,' she replied bluntly.

He gave her his hand and helped her from the sofa. Carefully they went to the door and into the bleak, empty hall. Icy air blew under the front door. 'Now,' said Bevan urgently trying to think where they could go. The upper floor had been unused since the house had been taken over by the military. Some of the rooms were locked.

Up the main staircase they crept like children playing a secret game. She began to giggle and he gently hushed her. To his huge relief the door of the first room at the top of the stairs opened. They went in. It was icy, the windows patterned like lace, the curtains stiff as cardboard. The double bed was piled with eiderdowns, blankets and caseless pillows. 'We must get warm again,' she whispered. 'In the bed.'

She was pointing as if giving an order. Briskly, professionally, she began to take the folded blankets from the mattress; she selected an eiderdown, picked up a second, pushed it against her nose and said: 'We will soon be warm.'

Outside the window a piece of ice clunked as it fell. Bevan realised there was an early petrified moon and it began to glimmer into the room. He turned towards the door. 'Do not worry,' she said. 'I locked it as we came here.'

They were standing on opposite sides of the wide bed. He moved around to her and held her against him powerfully while they kissed again. 'In the bed,' she repeated. 'We will take our clothes off in the bed. Remove your boots. They will not be comfortable.' She suddenly grinned. 'For you or for me. I will take them. And these strange ankle things.'

'Gaiters.'

Already she was on her knees undoing the laces of the service boots. He sat heavily on the chilly mattress while her dark hair cascaded over his khaki knees. She was very nimble, easing one boot away, pushing him back when he tried to help, and then pulling away the other. She unbuckled the straps on the gaiters and threw them aside sniffing: 'Gaiters.'

Then, almost without pausing, like someone getting on with an essential job, she unbuttoned his trousers and tugged them down. He stood like a boy letting her do it, tottering as he tried to keep his balance. She knelt again and ran her hands up and down his legs, the shins, the knees and the thighs. 'You are not too cold?' she enquired. Her deep, dark eyes came up.

'Not too bad at all.' His hands went to her rich hair and he caressed her. She herself used the movement to press her face to his groin. She kissed his erection through the service underpants. 'These are not pretty,' she said.

'Army issue.'

'I will take them from you.' She did it. He felt her hands warm on his penis. 'Not army issue,' she said.

In the cold room he felt himself perspiring. His hands trembled against her hair.

Swiftly she unbuttoned her blouse. The static flashed from it as she threw it aside. 'I am electric,' she said.

He said: 'I think you are.'

She dropped the long thick skirt and threw off her furry boots in almost the same movement. He stared at her in the moonbeams. 'Quick,' she said. 'Before we are icebergs.'

Then they were beside each other in the bed, the two eiderdowns over them, their bodies clinging. Warmth flowed from one to the other. She was wearing a garment he had not seen before. It was soft, almost woolly, covering her breasts and down to her thighs where it met the tops of the heavy, black lisle stockings. He felt all of her while she put her hands around his back and held on quietly to his khaki shirt-tail; her back, her buttocks, the tops of her legs and the thick stockings. They kissed with passion. His erection was against her thighs. 'You would like me to take these stockings off?' she said solicitously. 'I am warm now.'

'No, no,' he said. 'They feel very comfortable . . . comforting.'

'Which?' she asked.

Bevan said: 'Both.'

There was only moonlight but he could see her face, dark and lovely, against the uncased pillow, her eyes glowing as she watched him.

'Do you like this?' She pulled away a few inches so she could display what she wore. 'It was my mother's.' His hands went to the covered breasts. 'It is a very useful thing,' she said more slowly. 'See, here is a little button.' She pointed to one of the slim shoulder straps. 'And here is another. They undo very easily.'

He undid them, peeling the soft material away from

each breast as he did so. One at a time. With a grateful groan he lowered his lips to the nipples pointing at him in the dimness, kissing them in turn. She wriggled and pressed her mouth to his forehead. 'And more buttons,' she said in a few moments. 'In a secret place.'

Renée guided his hand down between her thighs and he felt the two small pearl buttons. His own heartbeats seemed to clang in the ghostly room. 'They are easy to undo,' she said. She put his fingers on them and he loosened each one. 'That's a good idea,' he said.

'My mother told me it was.' Now she whispered. She took him in her hands and guided him to her. Underneath she was warm and moist and she widened her arch to welcome him. They held each other like gentle wrestlers manoeuvring for a hold as they became joined. Outside the frozen sea reflected the silver of the moon.

Lying with her afterwards in the deep of the bed Bevan murmured sincerely: 'This is the best Christmas I've ever had.'

Alan Unsworth's able-bodied seaman's uniform, with its blue bell-bottoms and its pancake hat, looked incongruous against the winter landscape of the New Forest. His mother, using the family Brownie, had taken some photographs of him on Christmas morning and even she realised. 'Somehow it doesn't look right with all this frost and these trees,' she said. 'On land.'

'He should have joined the infantry,' said her husband. 'He could have been camouflaged.'

It had not been a great success; not as Ellen Unsworth had hoped at all. Alan had appeared breezily in his uniform and carrying his kitbag on Christmas Eve and there had been the anticipated excitement. His mother made a great, and occasionally tearful, fuss of him and it had been a relief when they had all gone to the Running

Hart in Lyndhurst where they listened to the carol singers and Ellen became a little tipsy on gin and tonic and had to be gently helped home. 'Run away,' she kept imploring her son as they stumbled through the chill darkness. 'Go absent. Desert. The war can go on without you.'

Christmas dinner had been interrupted by the entry of Catcher, the new small dog, with a dead rat. Unsworth had to go into the police station in the afternoon, called because a local burglar, overcome with remorse at the previous night's midnight mass, had surrendered and loudly owned up to his crimes. Irritably Unsworth took the man's protracted statement and asked: 'Couldn't you wait until after Christmas?'

'I might have changed my mind.'

Ellen and her son had listened to the King's broadcast while Unsworth was away. 'Poor King,' she said afterwards while she took the dishes from the table. Alan helped her. She began to run the hot water in the sink. 'I'll let them soak.'

'He didn't want the job,' said Alan. 'It was his brother clearing off with Mrs Simpson.'

'That flibbertigibbet,' said his mother. They returned to the sitting-room. 'The King doesn't sound well, does he,' she said anxiously as though her son might know more.

'Weak,' he nodded. 'He can't help it but the rest of them can, Mum. This Government's weak as water. Chamberlain. He needs that umbrella. God, he's wet.'

'He got us a breathing space,' she said cautiously. Both realised they had not had a disagreement since he was a boy at school.

'Munich,' he said bitterly. 'Kowtowing to that bastard Hitler.'

'Alan,' she reproved. 'I've never heard you speak like that before. All I think is that Mr Chamberlain gave us time to get ready, to build guns and planes and suchlike.'

'Well, I don't think we've done it,' he said. 'There's no guts, no inspiration. God, these politicians, these leaders. They'd show the white flag tomorrow. As long as they could keep their stocks and shares.'

'I don't like to hear you talk like that. I'm sure the King wouldn't give up. What about those lovely words at the end of his speech.'

'The man at the Gate of the Year,' he said slowly. 'I wonder who wrote that?'

'Yes. He was telling us to be brave.'

'It's not up to the King,' he said. 'It's the rest.'

They had both been relieved when Unsworth had returned from the police station. He sensed their discomfiture but said nothing. They listened to Arthur Askey on the wireless and opened their presents to each other and played cards. When they went to bed Ellen said to her husband: 'He's changed already, you know, our Alan.'

'Lots of people have,' he said kissing her on her chubby cheek.

'He thinks the Government is no good, it's weak. He thinks they're cowards.'

'He might be right.'

With sudden real anxiety she said: 'Oh, Alf, I don't want those Nazis to win. I don't want them here, doing their geese-steps through our Lyndhurst.'

He patted her face. 'We'll have to try and see it doesn't happen.'

'How?'

Unsworth said: 'I don't know, darling.'

It was with a sense of relief, almost escape, that father and son walked through the steely morning of Boxing Day to the Running Hart in Lyndhurst. They went silently downhill, below the burdened trees and bleak sky. A blue-coated sailor going through the white, inland town caught the attention of other people and an old couple, guiding each other along the stiff pavement, called out: 'God bless you, lad!' The two men paused and shook hands with them. Unsworth knew them by sight. They lived in a cottage on the edge of the forest and he had never seen them apart, going on their walks and their shopping, sometimes seeming to push each other along.

'They've been here for ever,' said Unsworth.

'I don't want to be,' said Alan.

'You don't?'

'No, Dad. I'm never coming back here. Not to live. No matter what happens. Getting away like this was right for me. I didn't realise it before but I needed it to happen. I don't want the rugby club and the cricket club and the young farmers' dances.'

'You'll miss the parish pantomimes.'

His son laughed. They went into the closeness of the Running Hart. It was only noon and the saloon bar had just opened. Alan said: 'I don't want to upset Mum.'

'Don't tell her then. Neither will I. Once you've seen a bit of this war maybe you'll be glad of the odd village dance.'

'I doubt it.' They drank their beer. 'Do you realise I'd got to twenty and I'd hardly been to London.'

'Some people around here have never been,' said Unsworth. 'And they're eighty.'

'Well, I don't want to be like that. There's all sorts on my deck, only as old as me but they've *done* things. There's one chap been to New York, another been to South Africa by airliner.'

'It's all exciting, this war,' said Unsworth. 'And it hasn't started yet.'

'I was thinking about those German sailors on the *Graf*

Spee. They get holed up in Montevideo harbour with our navy waiting for them outside. Christ, can you imagine what a shore leave that must have been? They're in a neutral port, safe for a while, and they're on the loose – the last leave – until they have to sail out to fight.'

'Never thought of it like that,' said Unsworth. 'Mind, they didn't fight, they scuttled the ship.'

'I know, I know. And they're with the señoritas in Uruguay for the rest of the war.'

They had two pints each by which time the bar began to fill. Alan, in his jaunty uniform, became a centre of attention. Some of his friends arrived in khaki or air-force blue but most were still in civilian clothes. 'The same as they've always been,' he said as they walked back home. 'Same jackets, same beer, same girlfriends, same jobs.'

'The Germans may arrive and change it all.'

'I doubt it,' said Alan. 'Don't tell Mum, but I'm going to volunteer for the Fleet Air Arm. For your training they send you to America.'

'It might just cheer your mother up,' said Unsworth. 'She thinks you'll end up in a submarine.'

'I am pregnant,' said Penelope.

Lady Violet had been out on the Boxing Day hunt with the New Forest Otterhounds. It had been a sharp, exhilarating morning hunting through the frosty streams and icy ponds, among the naked willows, although they had failed to kill an otter. Now, still in her riding habit with its green coat, she sprawled in her big red chair while she awaited a glass of Madeira and assistance with her boots. Her eyes came up slowly to fix her daughter. 'What does that mean?'

'Well, since it's Christmas I suppose I could say: "I am with child." I have conceived. I'm in the pudding club.'

'Christ Almighty,' said Lady Violet.

She sat stiffly upright. Terson, the butler, who hummed quietly but almost continuously, brought her the Madeira in a decanter and poured a liberal glass. His wrinkled eyes went to her boots but hers ushered him away. 'How did you manage that?' she said to her daughter.

Penelope said: 'The usual way.'

'Well, who is the father?'

'He is a friend.'

'I should bloody well hope he is.' Lady Violet took a heavy swig of the wine and choked. Penelope advanced and patted her firmly on the back until her mother spluttered: 'Enough, enough.'

Then she said, 'And are you going to marry this friend?'

'I doubt it, Mother. He has a wife. She is a senior officer in the ATS.'

'Oh, that's all right then,' said Lady Violet scornfully. 'It's part of the war effort, is it?' She regarded her daughter. 'Aren't you even going to cry?'

'No, I've done the bit of crying I had to do. He's a civil servant.'

Her mother regarded her over the rim of the sticky glass. 'This . . . friend . . . didn't he use any pro . . . didn't he take any . . . well, measures?'

'No. It was passion, Mother.'

'For God's sake, Penelope, how can you be passionate with a civilian in these times? You don't even have the excuse of him wearing a uniform.' She renewed her scowl. 'Or anything else apparently.'

'*Thank you*, Mother.'

'Passion or not it would have been prudent to take precautions. We almost called you Prudence. I'm glad we didn't now.'

'I did use a Rendell's tablet.'

'Rendell's!' Her ladyship spilt her Madeira and wiped

the splash from her lap in a single movement. 'Rendell's! Rendell's are no damned use even when they're fresh – and they *do* go off, you know. The world is full of Rendell's babies. Come to think of it you were one yourself.'

'Well, it didn't work.'

'Gin,' said her mother decisively. 'You must drink lots of gin. As much as you can get down you. And try falling down some stairs.'

The younger woman shook her head. 'I'm not drinking gin and I'm not going to fall down any stairs.'

'You *won't* have the baby, will you?'

'I don't know any backstreet abortionists.'

Her mother drank the remainder of the glass and hurriedly poured herself another from the decanter. 'They don't have to be in backstreets,' she reproved. 'There are several well qualified in Harley Street.'

'I'm not sure I want to do that. I may have the baby. I may want to keep a baby.'

'You mean *we'll* have to keep it.'

'No, Mother, I'll keep it.'

'Christ Almighty,' said her mother. 'What a damned fine way to spend Boxing Day.'

On New Year's Eve there was a '1940 Victory Dance' at the Southampton Pier Ballroom. There were sporadic outbreaks of fighting among servicemen and civilians, and between allies of different nationalities. Military police were on hand to fling the combatants out on to the freezing pavements or to take them to the army lock-up at the railway station. The band had played 'We're Going to Hang Out the Washing on the Seigfried Line' and everyone had joined hands to celebrate the coming of 1940 with 'Auld Lang Syne'.

'Don't you think they're being a bit optimistic?' asked Molly as Bairnsfather walked her home. They were comfortable together. He felt that he had known her a long time. She was muffled deeply into an imitation fox-fur coat her mother had owned since the 1920s.

'Calling it a Victory Dance,' he nodded crouching low inside the collar of his army greatcoat. Their arms were so thickly clothed that they could scarcely feel each other's waist. 'It's chancing it. Unless everybody packs up the war and goes home nice and quiet, I can't see it stopping this year.'

'You could be fighting,' she said sorrowfully. 'Against the Germans.'

He gave her swaddled waist a hug. 'Who else is there?'

'I don't want you to fight.'

'I'm not all that keen.' He grinned within his collar. 'I'll hide.'

'Or run away, Harry. We'll hide you.'

'Your old man would turn me in.'

'It's all right for him. He won't have to go and get killed.'

'He might have done once.'

'Then we wouldn't have been walking along like this,' she said. She turned her face up to the faintly luminous sky. All around them the blackout enshrouded the city. Some of the dancers from the Pier were in the vicinity. They could hear them but not see them. 'I think it's snowing,' she said.

Bairnsfather turned his face up. 'It is.'

'I'm glad you don't have to go back tonight.'

'I was on duty over Christmas,' he said. 'I can stay out as long as I like.'

It was not far to her house. Three dark streets and two carefully negotiated corners. He held her up when she slipped. Then she supported him. They laughed. Then they both slid and, crying out, fell on top of each other on the ice. A window went up. 'Will you shut up!' shouted a man's voice. 'Some of us have to get up.'

'Get up yourself,' answered Bairnsfather but not unkindly. Molly giggled. They were still lying all over each other, their coats insulating them from the sharp pavement. He called to the window: 'Put that light out!'

A curse floated out into the night and the window closed with a slam. Laughing, they began to try and pick each other up. He got to his feet unsteadily but, as he attempted to pull her upright, his balance went again and he landed against a frost-laden privet hedge, showering himself with white. Still on the pavement, Molly held the fur sleeves over her mouth. 'We seem like we're drunk,' she said.

He levered himself upright and extended his hands towards her. Her pretty face, pale in the fur, looked up appealingly. 'You look nice down there,' he said.

'Well, I'm not staying down here,' she giggled. 'This cold is seeping through.'

It was snowing more thickly. Tenderly, he managed to get her to her feet. Once she was there and they were holding each other for support, they remained in coated embrace. 'I love you, Harry,' she said. 'You're not married or anything, are you?'

The question surprised him. 'Married? Me? Not yet.'

'Promise?'

Bairnsfather swallowed deeply. Her face was veiled in snow. It was already lying in a small drift across the imitation fox. 'Promise,' he said. 'I'd have to save up.'

She laughed and they carefully walked the last stretch of the street. He knew by now not to open the gate because it squeaked. She did not think it would wake her father because he wore earplugs to minimise the sound if a high-explosive bomb should fall, but Ronnie was easily woken and would catcall to them from the window.

They went to the small garden gate at the side of the house. Ronnie had been known to booby-trap it but not this time. Bairnsfather opened the front of her fur coat and then his own. Under a whitened laurel they held each other's bodies, feeling the enclosed heat, and they kissed as the snow fell. 'You don't play football or cricket, do you, Harry?' she whispered. 'Regularly?'

'No, but I could learn.'

'No, don't. I wouldn't want a husband who was always out playing sport.'

'I won't, I promise. I'll collect stamps.'

He touched, then stroked her breasts under the woolly she wore over her dance dress.

'Shall we go into the air-raid shelter?' she whispered. 'It's cosy in there.'

He waited, then said: 'You want to?'

Now the hesitation was hers. Then she said: 'Yes, I want to.'

She put her finger to her lips. He could only faintly see it. She caught him by the hand and led him through the gate. The air-raid shelter door was closed over the entrance. The corrugated metal had a dull glow, like a reflection of the sky. A cat appeared over the earth-covered roof and Molly caught her breath as she saw its deep green eyes. Bairnsfather waved and it disappeared. She was easing the door open. He took it from her and continued to pull it wide. Again she put her finger to her lips. Then it was open enough for them to climb in. It was like going into a black, rectangular hole, but the buried humidity welcomed them. Both looked back at the house only yards away, undisturbed, dark walled, windows covered and roof now becoming clothed white with new-year snow.

Bairnsfather made to pull the door closed behind them but she intervened. 'I'll do it. I know how.'

Carefully she eased it into the aperture. Immediately they were in the darkest place Bairnsfather had ever known, a blackout within a blackout. 'Christ,' he said.

'I know,' she said close to him. 'If you can't see me, you'll have to feel.' She pressed her body to him in the dark and he responded. 'There *is* a torch,' she said. 'He hides it somewhere because of the battery. If I can find the cabinet thing I expect it will be in there, or near anyway.'

She left him standing against the bunks, one pressing against the side of his shin and the other at his shoulder, his points of reference in the dark. He heard her edging away towards the end of the Anderson and then feeling for the cabinet. It was getting stuffy. 'I've got it,' she whispered. 'He must have left it out by mistake. It's not often he'd do that.'

'Maybe he knew we'd come down here,' he joked.

Flicking on the narrow beam of the torch, scarcely more than the width of a pencil, she came back towards him. 'It's getting warm,' she said. She took off her coat and her cardigan and put them on the bottom bunk behind her. 'You hold the torch,' she said handing it to him.

Easing off his military greatcoat she pushed that behind her too. 'Don't crease it,' he joked nervously. He held her in the dark. 'You're sure?'

She had made up her mind. He felt her nod against his chest.

'We can't get on the bunk,' she said. 'It's not wide enough for two.' She shone the pinpoint of the torch on his anxious face. The light was so narrow that she had to move it from place to place, chin to mouth, to nose, to eyes, and eventually to his extensive forehead. 'I like your hair, well, your head,' she said.

'There's not much hair,' he said.

'That's all right. It makes you look sort of wise.' She handed the torch to him. 'You look at me now.'

He took it from her and made the same small journey across her face. Her lips were just parted, her nose still pink from the outside cold, the torchlight reflecting in her earrings. He put his hand over the light to soften it so that he could look into her eyes. They kissed and she began to undo the buttons on her dress. 'Would you like to see some more of me?' she said. Her voice was nervous.

'Yes . . . yes, anything.'

'I'm not showing you just *anything*,' she said softly. She had unbuttoned the dress to the waist and now she pulled it away. His eyes were now used to the dark and with the small light of the torch which he had placed on the bunk behind he could see the white glow of her shoulders. She only had a small brassière. 'It doesn't have much to hold,' she said.

'I like it,' he said. 'Honest. Big brassières always frightened me when I was a kid.' He was talking to cover his anxiety.

'Where did you see big brassières?' She was too.

'In the shops and in my mum's catalogue.'

'Naughty boy,' she said. 'Undo it at the back.'

His hands found the hook and he undid it. The garment fell away. He stared at her breasts in the dimness. Molly's hand went up for the torch. She handed it to him and he played the narrow light across her pale, clean skin, each slope, the easy cleft at the centre and then each nipple. 'God, you're lovely, Molly,' said Bairnsfather. 'Really lovely.'

'I'll hold the torch,' she offered.

She took it from him and his hands caressed the small mounds. He moved his lips over them while she angled the torchlight from place to place. 'Now you,' she said.

'I've got hairs on my chest.'

She stopped herself laughing. 'I didn't mean your chest,' she said.

He had never felt so happy. He undid the hard fly buttons and then opened the top of his rough trousers, attempting to keep them up by spreading his legs. 'What are these, for goodness' sake?' she asked.

'Underpants. Army drawers cellular,' he said.

'The things they do to you,' she sighed. Then she did something to him. Her pale, warm hand went inside the ungainly drawers and emerged holding his erection. He saw her eyes open in the half-light. She handed him the torch and he shone it on himself. Now both soft hands went to him. 'That's ever so nice, Harry,' she breathed. 'And by torchlight.'

'Children,' said Renée, 'do not cry as much as we think they do. They are not sentimental and they are very resilient.'

It was almost midnight on New Year's Eve. Bevan listened to her across the table, the lamp shining against her skin. Around them in the restaurant people sat in slightly desperate paper hats, doggedly cheery. They wore their hats also but they had forgotten them. They had spent the afternoon at Jerusalem House. There had been a great fire, tea and cakes and sandwiches, and Bevan had led the children in singing 'Underneath the Spreading Chestnut Tree', and had shown them how to perform the hokey-cokey.

'They loved that,' she said. She sang it softly across the table. 'You put your right arm in and you shake it all about.' She laughed. 'And seeing Mr MacFarlane doing the "Lambeth Walk" – that was the best.'

'Franz liked it,' said Bevan. 'He even left his homework.'

'Probably trying to learn new English words from the

songs,' she said. 'He is a serious boy.' She became thoughtful. 'Playing is everything to them. In Europe, in China, in the newsreels, you see them playing in the ruins of their homes, don't you. When you see those poor, destroyed people in the photographs, even then, when they've lost everything, the children can't help but smile for the camera.'

'They must miss their homes and their parents, your children,' he said.

Sadly she said: 'I hear them crying at night sometimes. They miss their cats and dogs too and their friends and their schools. But in the morning they have forgotten it. This is a big adventure for them. Because they are children.'

'I knew it myself,' he said.

She was puzzled. 'How was that?'

'When my mother died, just at the beginning of the Great War, I was fourteen. My sister was twelve. Nobody would, or could, take us. There were relatives, but nobody really wanted us. The men were going away to war. God knows where our father was. We went into an institution, an orphanage.'

She touched him across the table. 'I always knew there was something solitary about you.'

4

Nothing had been heard of their father for two years since the receipt of a phantom message which accompanied a parcel bursting from its string and containing his frowsy clothes. It read: 'Keep these as a memory.'

Their mother's response to her absent husband's heart-pulling request had been to cry all day and several hours into the following night but, after making some vague, vain attempt to trace the geographical source of the parcel (the decipherable part of the postmark said merely: 'Port . . .') she decided to cast him out of her mind and life for ever. The feckless Vincent Bevan had outstayed his absence; if it had not been for her violin lessons they would have been starving homeless.

He had only appeared on average once a year anyway, invariably seeking a meal, a bed and, often, a refuge, so that the final talisman came as a half-admitted relief and a release. As she sorted through the grubby shirt, peered down into the dangling underpants and levelled out the stiff socks, Vera tutted and sniffled but, after her twenty-four hours of weeping and in a burst of resolution, she dropped them all with disdainful ceremony into the dustbin. She stared at them in the bottom of the bin, the only tangible remains of her marriage, took them out, put them in a brown paper bag and dropped them in again. Love was done.

James and Agnes had watched from their window and

Vera had joined them at the same pane when, later that day, the Corporation of Southampton horse and dustcart, with its loudly vocal attendants, came grinding along the street, and their father's remnants were tossed in and anonymously borne away. Vera Bevan committed a single emotional hoot to her handkerchief, muttered: 'Goodbye, Vincent,' straightened her padded Edwardian shoulders, waggled her long skirts, and with a heaved final 'That's that' strode from the window to prepare for her next violin pupil.

James and his sister had learned to live without their father's presence but the finality of the dustcart grumbling off below the street's summer trees reduced them to a sad silence. They had always had a father somewhere; now, apparently they had not.

Mr Sullivan appeared in the early summer of 1914, so promptly, almost magically, that even two unquestioning children could not help the suspicion that he had been lurking in the wings. Now he was introduced at Sunday tea as 'Mummy's friend' and over the scones, they regarded him with suspicion and dislike. Their mother had few friends of either sex, so enclosed had been their lives at the top of the tall, overcast house. But now this rotund incomer had appeared and had actually *squeezed* their mother's waist in the middle of the afternoon. He spoke in a loudish voice and wore a loudish suit and had a loud sort of face, worn red at the cheeks, like someone who spent much of their time in the wind. Indeed Mr Sullivan was a bookmaker.

'He is a *very* kind friend,' Vera Bevan told them at one convenient bedtime while they were drinking their Horlicks. 'And he is going to *buy a motor car*.' She paused and studied their momentarily attentive faces over the top of the cups. 'And a piano. For me.'

'But you can't get a piano up the stairs,' James pointed out. 'They tried once.'

'It fell on a man's foot,' said Agnes.

'And what a fuss he made,' said their mother. 'But this piano is different. It's what they call a baby grand.' She laughed in a strange, wild way and exclaimed: 'I am going to have a baby . . . grand.'

Neither of the children responded because they did not fully understand the joke. 'It is a new German piano,' she informed their straight faces. 'A Bechstein.'

'Can they get it up the stairs?' asked James.

'I understand so.'

She regarded them fondly. 'Children, this means that I can give piano lessons instead of the violin.'

'Can you play the piano?' asked Agnes. They had never heard her. The enquiry made her flustered.

'Oh, yes. Well, I *could* once. I can soon pick it up again. You only need a full set of fingers. I'll play enough to give a few lessons. After all, they *are* beginners. I won't take anyone who is any good.' She looked suddenly sorrowful. 'I hate that violin.'

'So do we,' said Agnes.

Vera looked at her a touch sharply but then said: 'I hate it. It drove your dear father away.'

When Mr Sullivan who, to their embarrassment, was known to their mother as Sully, produced the promised motor car their reserve about him fell quickly, if only briefly, away. When he drove up the street people peered through their windows to see him because there were not many motor vehicles in the neighbourhood. Halfway down was a Model T Ford, and there was a fifteen-horsepower Crossley, and a two-seater Humbrette, and the people next door were sometimes visited by relatives who drove from Winchester in an Austin. The woman used to sweep the road where it would be parked. Mr Sullivan's car was impressively grey, the huge front lamps projecting like trumpets; the spokes of the wheels turned like a fairground and Mr Sullivan honked the bulbous rubber horn as soon as he had applied the handbrake.

From the top window Agnes and James witnessed the impressive arrival. 'Mummy,' called Agnes. 'Your Mr Sullivan has come in his car. It's beautiful.'

Their mother appeared from her bedroom dressed in long skirt, short jacket and frilly blouse, powdered and wearing a curly new hat on her carefully arranged hair. She put her arms around their shoulders, the boy tall beside his sister, and she gazed down into the street. Briefly, as if seeking approval or reassuring the children, she looked in to their faces but quickly returned her eyes below. The shape of the car was splintered by the branches of the ragged tree in the front garden but even as they watched Mr Sullivan moved it, not without a disconcerting series of small popping explosions, to where they could have a clearer view. He alighted wearing a leather helmet with big earflaps and with a long blue scarf wound around his throat. He waved his yellow gloves.

'Magnificent,' breathed Vera. Agnes frowned, unsure whether her mother meant the car or Mr Sullivan. His face added a blob of red to the scene.

'Will we be able to have a ride?' asked James.

Agnes, her hands on the sill, commenced jumping up and down by the window. 'We've never ridden in a motor.'

'I'm sure Mr Sullivan would be pleased,' said their mother but not very certainly. 'Even if it's not today.'

'Are you going to ride with him today?' asked James.

'Yes. That is why he's come.' She kissed them both fussily and whispered: 'The piano may be arriving this week.'

There came another disconcertingly insistent bleat of the horn from the street. People had come from their houses to look at the car.

Brother and sister stood in a sort of embarrassed silence until their mother appeared downstairs and hurried to Mr Sullivan and his motor. Face glowing he met her, and shaking off one yellow glove he opened the door and held out his hand to help her into the glistening leather seat. He then went around to the driving seat and vanished from their view. 'I hope it won't bloody start,' said Agnes. She had never sworn in her life. But the engine was already vibrating and Mr Sullivan released the brake and changed the grating gear lever. There were several more popping sounds but it moved away majestically and from their window they spotted the brief flutter of their mother's gloved hand. They supposed she must be waving to them and they dutifully but briefly waved back.

'Mr Sullivan must be very rich,' said Agnes. 'To have that thing.'

James did not turn from thc window. The neighbours were dispersing. 'He's taking our mother away from us,' he said.

Agnes regarded him sorrowfully but as though she already knew. 'He can't do that,' she said. 'She's ours.' Her small face became adult and sharp and she muttered: 'Sully.' They remained at the window, half hoping the car would return perhaps with the engine on fire, or their mother having second thoughts about leaving them. 'How long before they come back?' asked Agnes.

James said bitterly: 'I don't know.' He waved his hand. 'A drive in the country, a glass of sherry, a romantic tea, they could be hours.'

He thought she was going to cry. 'I don't want to play draughts for hours, James,' she said. 'You always win anyway. I can't be bothered with my books. And we don't like playing like we used to.' She regarded him hopefully but he said without looking at her: 'Mothers and fathers seems stupid now.'

'We'll have to do something.'

'It's draughts, I suppose,' Agnes sighed. She went to their toy cupboard and took out the wooden box. They set it down between them on the table. Neither had any close friends. It was as if living at the tall top of the forbidding house made them remote from other children. Sometimes they went to the homes of schoolmates but they could not ask them to theirs because of the violin lessons. They only rarely played in the street and the park was almost a mile away and their mother did not like them going there.

The heavy room was silent about them, almost protectively, as if it now had charge of them. It was still only late afternoon although the day was fitful and their lofty window was filled with dark, puffed clouds. They played draughts solemnly but without much skill or enthusiasm. James only lost when he wanted to lose and because she was so sad he allowed her to win now.

'You did that on purpose,' she said, only a little pleased.

'No, you played better.' She was setting the pieces on the board again when he leaned across, his eyes came up and he said: 'Do you want to go to the Bioscope?'

Agnes put her hands to her mouth. 'Oh, yes! Yes, James!' she squealed. 'I want to go! I want to!' Her expression dropped. 'We can't. We're not allowed.'

James gave her a small, swaggering grin. 'Why not? We won't tell her.'

She was so animated that she knocked over the board and the chequers as she scrambled from her knees. 'But . . . oh, James. Can we go? I've never been.'

'I've only been once. That time.' He regarded her trustingly.

She said: 'She didn't know. I didn't tell her.'

'I know you didn't.' He stood. 'Get your coat. I'll get mine.'

'Have you got any money? It's sixpence to get in. That's a shilling. I've got tuppence for the tram.'

'My savings,' he said solemnly. 'In the money box.'

Agnes said: 'She'll notice. She rattles it.'

'I'll put some washers in. She won't know.'

She was dancing on the spot. 'What will it be like? What will we see?' A thought stilled her. 'There'll be Lascars there, and Chinamen. She said that's why we couldn't go.'

'They're only Lascars and Chinamen,' he said. 'You see them all the time. They're from the docks.' But he was hesitating. 'Do you want to do it?'

'Yes! Yes!' she said. 'Let's go out from this room.'

She went into the hall and took her coat from the peg. Then she took his and tossed it to him. There was no going back now. He put a table knife into the mouth of the money box and took out six large pennies and a small silver sixpenny piece. They crept out locking the door behind them. Silently they descended the stairs. Mrs Colbourn was standing on the bottom landing holding her little sausage dog, Fritz, below her arm, its eyes like buttons. 'Going off out?' she said.

'For a walk,' said James quickly. 'Just for a walk.'

'I saw your mother go off in that lovely motor. She's lucky, isn't she.'

'Yes,' put in Agnes as though anxious to make a point. 'We're all lucky.'

'I'm not,' said Mrs Colbourn grumpily. 'My husband went and died and left me.'

'Yes, we know,' said James.

'I remember the coffin,' said Agnes brightly. 'It didn't seem very big.'

'He was average size,' said Mrs Colbourn. 'All I have now is my little Fritz.' She stroked the dog's head and it blinked.

They had to almost push past her to reach the door. The dog gave a farewell yap and the woman told them to enjoy their nice walk and avoid foreigners. 'There are so many,' she said.

When they had reached the end of the short path to the gate she opened the door again and called after them with a sort of desperation: 'They're not like proper people, you know.'

'Is she mad, James?' asked Agnes as they hurried away together below the trees.

'She seems to be. Crazy they call it.'

Agnes laughed: 'Crazy. What a funny word, crazy.'

There was a tram stopped at the foot of the street. Both children glanced guiltily around them before they climbed aboard. They sat on the slatted wooden seats on the upper deck while the tram clattered and shook along the Southampton streets. Agnes paid a halfpenny fare each. 'This tram is crazy,' she said to the conductor as they alighted.

As they reached the Bioscope Picture Palace their steps slowed. The crowd was just entering. The picture palace had only been open for a month and was the first in the city. 'There's a lot of Lascars,' said Agnes. 'We must never tell Mum.'

'Mum's not going to know,' he emphasised. 'And there's Arabs and Chinamen. Mrs Colbourn wouldn't like it. Around here is where they live. Near the docks.'

'Are we still going in?'

'Yes, silly. They're only from Southampton.'

The crowd which had been waiting for the doors to

open filed in eagerly and the two children moved towards the pay window. James was holding his sister's hand and he released it to fumble for the money. Slyly Agnes looked about her, up and down the road, as if she suspected Mr Sullivan's car might turn the corner.

'Two seats, please,' said James at the window. He deepened his voice and was glad he was tall. He put the sixpence and the six pennies on the brass plate and the man, wearing a uniform cap, behind the grille, passed them two tickets. 'Inside,' he said as though there was anywhere else.

They went through a curtain into a large, dim, fetid room. Heads were everywhere, rows of heads. There was an animated mumble. Another brass-buttoned man took their tickets and nodded towards the front with the peak of his cap. 'Down there,' he said. 'You won't be able to see over these sods. Sit by the piano.'

Agnes clutched James's hand tightly. They took their seats in the front row. There were some other children there, towards the end, crouched and staring up as if in fear at the drawn curtains. A bald man climbed a short ladder to a piano at the side of the stage. He gave a stiff bow to the audience, as if that was as much glory as he was likely to get, and began to plonk his fingers on the keys. Then another man in a bow-tie and frock-coat walked out from the wings and hushed the piano with a single flattening of his hand. 'He's the manager,' whispered James. Agnes had slipped far down in her seat. She stared at the figure upon the stage, the footlights shining up illuminating the wattles below his chin.

The manager took out a sheet of paper and read ponderously: 'It has come to the notice of the management that fleas and bugs have been brought into this picture palace.' He looked around threateningly. 'Those what have brought them in have got to take them out again.'

Rumbling voices sounded behind James and Agnes. Translations of the manager's ultimatum were being passed among the seats. The children looked around anxiously and James held his sister's hand as two men, one on each side of the auditorium, began shouting and pointing accusingly at each other. The manager bellowed imperiously: 'Don't blame each other. You've all got 'em!' He took a step to the front of the stage, the curtains opened and his shadow was projected large on the screen behind him. Agnes, thinking it might be part of the show, started to applaud, but stopped when the man shouted: 'Any noise and there'll be no pictures.'

That settled it. A mouse-like silence fell over the audience. 'Right,' the manager said. 'That's better. We have kiddies in the front, you know.' He gave a little bow in the direction of James and Agnes and some of the men in the seats behind stood and tried to see them. 'Sit down,' barked the manager. 'Otherwise no pictures.'

Then he took a piece of cardboard from his frock-coat and announced: 'The pictures today are called: *The Sheik of the Desert*' – a mutter of approval rose from the audience – '*The Kaiser Reviews the German Fleet*' – grunts and groans sounded – 'and *Tilly goes to Paris*.' This was greeted with hand clapping. 'There will be a comedy called *The Baker's Ball*.' There was louder applause. 'But first our National Anthem.'

He emphasised 'our' as though it were too good for the mob in the seats. Then he nodded brusquely towards the pianist who struck the resounding first chords. The Lascars, Chinese and Arabs stood and rendered various approximations of the words. James and Agnes sang self-consciously in the front row. It finished raggedly, the manager sniffed as if that was all that could be expected, and there was a clatter of seats as the men behind sat down and leaned back expectantly. The manager left the stage like a headmaster. A man went about dimming the gas lights. James felt his sister tense in the darkness beside him and he felt for her hand and held it. The screen darkened and then was vividly illuminated. Flickering figures appeared. Agnes shrank into her seat, her knees came up and she gave a squeak of amazement.

Towering immediately above their heads was the huge and handsome head of a sepia sheik. Arabs in the audience began to clap; Lascars and Chinese jeered. Agnes was staring unbelieving at the gigantic moving image. Then she cowered as a pounding horse charged across the desert. Words appeared on the screen: 'At the Oasis.' A dreamy girl appeared, sniffing a rose. Agnes sighed. She was captured.

'It was ever so lovely,' she said as they were on the homeward tram. 'And ever so huge. Big huge heads.' They had laughed helplessly at the comedy. In the darkness the whole place had hooted with different versions of mirth. When the projectionist changed the reels they could scarcely wait until the lights dimmed again. The pianist had thumped and tinkled as the action changed and changed again. At the end everybody clapped and again stood obediently for another playing of the National Anthem.

'I didn't like the look of those German battleships,' said James solemnly.

'The Kaiser man looked silly,' she said. 'Are they going to fight us, James?'

'*We're* going to fight *them*,' said James. 'Our guns are bigger.'

It was almost dusk when they left the tram. They had to turn two corners, below some municipal trees. Around the second corner they saw Mr Sullivan's majestic car stationary against the pavement. Both children halted. James thought to cross to the other side of the street but

Agnes began moving adventurously forward, at a crouch, like the sheik in the film. James followed.

When they reached the car they saw a shape they knew was their mother wrapped in an embrace, Mr Sullivan's big arms clutching her like a grizzly bear. The two children bent double and crept by the shining side of the vehicle. Once out at the front they ran quickly for the corner.

Agnes was crying a little when they went back into the house. 'Sully,' she muttered again. They went upstairs. They could hear Mrs Colbourn singing to Fritz. Inside their own door they waited another twenty minutes for their mother.

She fluttered in, her hat a little awry and the frills of her blouse flattened. She seemed to realise and straightened herself out. 'Have you been having a nice time?' she enquired.

'We went for a walk,' said James. It was probably the first time he had told her a direct lie. 'A long walk,' said Agnes.

'We must have some tea,' said Vera.

'Haven't you had tea or anything?' asked Agnes blatantly.

'We did stop for a while,' said her mother. She looked uncomfortable.

'It was a long ride, Mummy,' observed the little girl. James gave her a glance.

Vera Bevan looked as though she was unsure how to answer. 'It was a lovely ride,' she said eventually. 'It is the most beautiful motor.'

She went in the kitchen and emerged with a plate of scones and cake. 'The kettle is boiling,' she said. 'Or would you prefer milk?'

'I'd prefer a glass of wine,' said Agnes deliberately, adopting a little pose.

'Naughty,' said her mother but adding nothing. She sat in front of the children. Her face remained flushed. 'Mr Sullivan is a very nice gentleman,' she said like a reassurance to them all. She took a folded piece of paper from her handbag. 'He asked me to tell you about his motor car. So I wrote it down.' She put her nose near the paper. 'It is a Napier,' she told them. 'A six-cylinder noiseless Napier.'

'It banged when it went down the street,' said Agnes.

'Agnes, do you want to hear this or not?' Vera looked annoyed.

'Yes, Mummy.'

'Well, let me see, it has the power of many horses. I failed to write down how many. As you saw it is quite beautiful. All the best materials are used and the car workers are specially chosen. It can drive at up to *seventy miles an hour*. But Mr Sullivan is very safe.' She paused and studied her notes more closely. 'Oh, and it has Rudge-Whitworth wheels. They cost extra.'

After they had gone to bed and he heard that their mother had retired, James went into Agnes's room. He intended to admonish her for bating their mother but when he went through the door he found the small girl passionately kissing her pillow. 'I'm pretending it's the sheik,' she whispered. He sat on her bedside. 'James,' she said, 'I've never kissed anybody. Except Mother before that Sully came. Will you kiss me.'

He smiled at her, hesitated, and then gently kissed her. She clung to him.

When Mr Sullivan finally took them out in his Napier motor car they drove to the New Forest on a late July day with ponies, donkeys and cows bolting in fright from their approach. A man waved an angry hammer at them over a cottage gate. Their mother laughed too loudly above the engine and put her bonneted head on Mr Sullivan's shoulder. James and Agnes sat upright and unspeaking in the back seat. They stopped for tea and afterwards Vera said: 'Sully and I are just going for a stroll, dears. Wait in the car.' And the two walked away into a forest glade. As they walked the children saw the man put his puffy red hand around their mother's waist.

Clumsily he had tried to be fatherly to them, stretching his arm across James's shoulders, giving him unrequested advice, and treating Agnes to a series of jolly pats on her bottom. 'I don't like him,' said Agnes from her seat in the motor. 'He's got fat hands.'

'The piano is coming next week,' replied James. 'I don't like him either.'

'Just think. He's kissed her,' said the girl. 'With those great big lips of his.'

'I know,' said James.

'They're wet, his lips. I saw Mum wiping her face off afterwards.'

There was nothing they could say to their mother. The only information she provided was: 'Mr Sullivan is a close friend. The piano will soon be here.'

It arrived on a horse-drawn van and another crowd gathered in the street and encouraged the five puffing men who got it up the stairs. The leader of the gang was a rough and ruddy man with a coarse voice and an orange neckerchief. The instrument was much smaller than a grand piano but they still had to unscrew the legs. It took a long time to edge it up through the successive landings and it snapped the banister on one corner. Mr Whistler who lived in the flat between them and Mrs Colbourn called Mrs Colbourn to see. He had sometimes complained about the violin noises. They watched phlegmatically. Mr Whistler said to Mrs Colbourn: 'At least it won't make as much cat's noise.'

When the piano had reached the main room of the top floor the men opened wedges of sandwiches all wrapped in pages from *The Echo* and drank beer from bottles. One of them went downstairs to feed the horse, taking its bag of oats from a hook at the back of the van. After their lunch they heaved again at the baby grand and screwed the legs back on the corners. It sat looking neat and golden at one end of the room. Their mother brought her violin stool and sat behind it and, while the men watched, woodenly played a selection of tunes including 'Daisy, Daisy' which she sang. One of the men said sympathetically she would be better after a few lessons.

In the evening she played the piano for her children and much later for Mr Sullivan. After that she put her violin away in a cupboard and said she hoped she would never have to play it again.

August of 1914 was very hot. The two children seemed to be imprisoned in the top rooms of the house, the heat, smells and sounds of the street drifting up to their faces framed by the windows which, since the cessation of the violin tuition, they could open wide. Vera had advertised herself as a teacher of pianoforte but in that summer month it seemed that there were few pupils. She did not appear to worry. She was frequently absent in Sully's company leaving James to look after Agnes. On several evenings she appeared, face flushed apparently from the sun, telling of the exciting finishes at Epsom or Ascot.

James and Agnes sometimes went to the park but it was dusty and frequently populated by rough and robust children. James had promised his sister another clandestine visit to the Bioscope once he had secreted enough money. Their mother had become very careless about farthings, halfpennies and even pennies and both children quietly swept up the copper coins and put them in James's money box.

Each day they spent hours looking down into the street through the limp leaves. There were always comings and goings to partially observe, people emerging from neighbours' houses, gossiping on the pavement. They knew few of their names but now they became familiar by sight with some, more particularly the servants – for almost every proper house had a maid, sometimes two. They watched them going on errands and returning sometimes with hatboxes or parcels. The street sellers who came shouting with their horses and carts or hand barrows several times a day would go to the side doors.

The tradesmen could be recognised from the smells of their wares, although sometimes these were overpowered by the aromatic droppings of the horses. They knew the fishmonger by the waft of his haddock and kippers, the baker by the fresh scent of the bread; they knew the call of the man who pushed a cart with muddy vegetables along the street and they heard the solid chop of the travelling butcher's cleaver. Naming and observing the tradesmen provided a pastime for them as they stood, or sometimes brought chairs up and sat, at the lifted window during those hot days while they waited for their mother to come home.

One evening they went to the park. From their window they had heard the sounds of a band and they hurried down and let themselves out of the street door. Mrs Colbourn with the waddling dachshund Fritz was close behind them. They walked with her to the park. She was an incessantly chatty woman but they felt sorry for her because her husband had died and she had been unable to replace him. It was a military band and, in the evening light, the musicians looked fine in their red uniforms with the beaming brass of their buckles and instruments. Around the bandstand the park seats were already occupied and there was a growing crowd to hear the music, the ladies in their skirts sweeping the paths and the men in their best coats and straw or bowler hats. Some working-class men in caps or squashed hats stood with their women on the fringe of the crowd.

The band performed military music and music-hall songs like 'Two Little Girls in Blue' and 'The Old Kent Road' and the audience joined in and sang. The bandmaster seemed surprisingly small to be in charge. When he turned to bow to the applause they saw he had a moustache which curled around his cheeks. 'In these troubled times,' he announced, 'we are going to play a selection of marches, each one the march of a British regiment of the line.' Everyone cheered.

James and Agnes rarely saw a newspaper for their mother only read social magazines. On holiday from school they had no contact with other children who might have given them news. 'What's he mean by troubled times?' asked Agnes.

Mrs Colbourn who stood near them turned, her skirts erupting a little cloud of dust as she did so. 'The war, dear,' she said. 'The approaching war.'

Agnes glanced at James. A man with a cap standing nearby had a terrier on a lead which snarled at Fritz and Mrs Colbourn hastily manoeuvred her shortened dog to the other side of her skirts. 'You ought to 'ide 'im, all right,' said the man nastily. He had a woman with him who nodded as if threatening. 'That's a *German* dog,' said the man. 'There's going to be a war, you know, missus.'

'My dog is not going to war,' said Mrs Colbourn stiffly and with some courage. 'He was born in Sevenoaks.'

'Makes no difference. That dog is German. And we don't like Germans.'

For a frightening moment James and Agnes thought he was going to kick at Fritz. He levered back an uncouth boot but Mrs Colbourn swiftly tugged the dachshund out of range and then picked him up. 'The witless working class,' she sniffed.

'It's the working class what is going to have to fight this war,' snapped the woman. 'Not the likes of you or your husband.'

'My husband,' said Mrs Colbourn with an even deeper sniff, 'will not be able to fight. He died in the Boer War.'

James and Agnes stared at her with new respect. The dachshund looked up with its beady eyes as though the news was new. She turned and stalked away from the couple. The band was still playing lustily. The two children followed her out of the park and along the street. 'Low class,' she said, 'is low class.' She set the dog down and it waddled as if anxious to get behind closed doors.

'I'm sorry about Mr Colbourn,' said the puzzled James. 'We didn't know he died in the Boer War.'

'I thought I saw his coffin,' said Agnes.

'They weren't to know. So ignorant, these people.'

They parted at her door, each patting the dachshund sympathetically. Upstairs their mother was sitting moodily. 'We went to see the band,' said James. 'Mrs Colbourn was there with Fritz.'

'Was the band in tune?'

Agnes said: 'There's going to be a war.'

'With Germany,' said James in case she might have not heard.

'Nonsense,' said Vera but without conviction. 'The Germans are nice people. Quite nice. After all, the Kaiser is the King's kinsman.'

'He looks funny with that spike on his hat,' said Agnes.

Vera said: 'That's the fashion in Germany.' She regarded the children quizzically and said to James: 'Who told you such nonsense?'

'A man in the park. He said Mrs Colbourn shouldn't have a German dog like she has.'

'And the bandmaster said so,' put in Agnes. 'And he's a soldier.'

'It's all nonsense,' said Vera. 'There will not be any war. Mr Sullivan assured me so this afternoon.'

'That's a relief,' said James.

The next day Great Britain declared war on Germany.

There was an odd, tight atmosphere in the street the next morning which they could feel even up at the open window. Noises floated to them, people were gathered in groups under the trees, sometimes chattering, sometimes silent, as if waiting for something to happen. Vera still did not believe it. 'What nonsense,' she said. 'It's all a silly mistake.'

'There are some soldiers on horses coming,' reported Agnes without turning from the window. Her mother and James hurried to her side. The beat of the hooves resounded in the street. Neighbours began to clap in time with the clatter as the troops went by, their backs straight, their lances stiffly upright, their polished bandoliers rich in the August sun. Behind them came another four horses pulling a field gun. Vera took it in. 'James,' she said in a slow, defeated voice, 'you had better go and buy a newspaper.'

People were already out with buckets scooping up the steaming fresh horse droppings and carrying them in a patriotic hurry to their vegetable plots. In the main road a desolate-looking man was selling newspapers from behind a black, huge-lettered placard which displayed one word: 'War.' James paid a penny for a copy of the *Daily Mail.* The headline said: 'War Declared.'

'It's not a mistake, then?' James said to the vendor.

'Might be the biggest mistake ever made, son,' said the man. 'Anyway you won't have to fight. Too young, you are. For a few years anyway.'

James's mother was aghast. 'I wonder will the races still be held?' she muttered, staring at the front page. 'Sully was taking me today.'

'Sully may have to go and fight,' said Agnes hopefully.

Her mother regarded her with alarm. 'Never. Not a man like Mr Sullivan.'

'Won't he volunteer?' asked James reading the newspaper. 'It says that volunteers will be needed.'

'He's a man of substance,' said Vera. 'He has his wonderful motor car. He bought me my Bechstein. He's not some farmboy.'

By evening the crowds were thickening and becoming noisier. The public houses were open all day and the stench of beer hung over the streets. Drunkenness throughout the lower classes was rampant, endemic. The war was not very old before it would be illegal to buy a drink for anyone, even a man for his wife.

That night they could hear the excitement from the window. Further soldiers marched below, the khaki of their uniforms filtering through the trees, and people followed them shouting: 'God bless,' and cheering and urging them to go and kill the Huns. There were horses, too, with their bounty of manure. Somewhere a band trumped patriotic tunes. Girls danced with anybody. It was more like a festival than a war.

Their mother refused to allow them to investigate

further. 'Southampton is full of drunken clods,' she said. 'Let us hope they sober up in time to fight.'

But they knew that at some time she would make an excuse and go off to see Mr Sullivan. It came after tea when she told them she would only be gone for half an hour and repeated her warning that they were not to go out. Silently James and Agnes watched her leave. She waved and, remembering in time, came back to kiss them although the kiss was perfunctory, as were theirs.

From their vantage they watched her hurry along the street. 'Sully wouldn't drive his car with all these drunken clods about,' said Agnes. She turned challengingly to James. 'Let's go and see.'

They waited five minutes and then, as they had done so many times now, let themselves out secretly from the front door. Mrs Colbourn was walking anxiously along the garden hedges, Fritz waddling with her. 'They're after German dogs,' she said. 'They're not having my Fritz.'

She pulled at the low dog and hurried on.

'She's frightened,' said James.

Agnes said: 'They won't hurt her dog, will they?'

As though in answer there erupted a roar from the main road at the end of the street; the sound of the mob. James caught hold of his sister's wrist but she urged him on.

'Keep out of sight,' he said.

Agnes said: 'I want to see.'

More slowly they approached the main road. A Southampton Corporation tram was stationary, like an island in the middle of a milling horde of people. It had become a grandstand and people occupied both decks. Some men were hanging on the sides. From the unseen front of the crowd there came a sudden baying roar. Then another.

'They're doing something,' said James to Agnes. 'Wrecking something.'

All the street gaslights were burning and men and youths were hanging from the lamp standards. Others had lit flaming torches and waved them above the heads of the crowd. In one corner, away from the pagan uproar, a little man was playing a barrel-organ with a perched monkey holding a collecting tin. The man's face was oblivious to the crammed scene and the noise but the monkey stared out with bright and fearful eyes.

'Down with the Boche!' shouted a man. 'Kill the bloody Boche!' bawled a woman in a shawl. James edged Agnes away from the crowd. There was a sausage shop on the opposite side of the road which had been there ever since he could remember. 'They're attacking the sausage shop,' he said to Agnes.

'Why?'

'Because they're Germans.'

'But they're *here*. They *live* here. Elke Muller is in my class.'

There was an abrupt surge forward of the mob in front of them. They could hear the clang of police bells. Windows were breaking, the overwhelming smell of beer and burning filled the evening. A man fell from a lamppost, his fall broken by two others sprawled drunk below. A woman, her feathered hat tipped over her face, bottle in her fist, hung out of the side of the tramcar. Three policemen wearing tall helmets and on horseback appeared and shoved their way through the mob, truncheons held up. The space they made suddenly gave James and Agnes a view of what was going on ahead. 'Mr Muller is in the window,' said James.

'I can see him. He's shouting at them. And there is Mrs Muller. She's crying. I wonder where Elke is?'

More police arrived, this time in one of their new

motor charabancs. The crowd cheered derisively. The officers piled out and began pushing the people. Smoke was coming from inside the shop. The throng were shifting, some of them running away. Mr and Mrs Muller were no longer in the upstairs window.

'We'd better go,' said James. 'They might arrest us.'

As they began to move away towards their own street Agnes looked back and clutched James's shirt: 'It's on fire.' A flickering light came from the sausage shop, the hysterical shouts became screams and the police began to charge the crowd. One of their uniform helmets was being thrown about like a ball over all the heads. A column of yellow flame jumped up. 'Let's go back home,' said Agnes. 'I'm frightened.' Tightly holding hands they hurried away from the mob. Drunken men were lying on the pavement already like war casualties. A woman was being sick in a hedge and wiping her mouth on her feather boa. There were ranting people marching along the street bawling: 'Down with Kaiser Bill!' and 'Kill the Hun! Kill the Hun!'

They reached the house. James opened their door and pushed Agnes into the hall. Even as he did he heard a coarse shout: 'There! That's the bloody house!' The boy turned to face the man who was charging up the short path. Others followed. Agnes ran screaming up the stairs and James tried to hold the door but hopelessly. Mrs Colbourn came to her door, Fritz in her arms. 'There's that dog!' bellowed the leading man. He had an orange neckerchief and James had seen him before. 'Get the German dog!'

Even years later he could not believe what happened. The little, frightened, long dog was pulled from Mrs Colbourn's hold. James tried to grapple with the man shouting at him: 'You're drunk! You're drunk! Leave the dog alone!'

But the crush was too much. The man held on to the yapping Fritz and with a savage howl, only matched by that of the dog, threw it backwards to the mob behind him. Mrs Colbourn screamed and fell in a faint blocking the doorway. James saw the dog being tossed, wriggling like a worm, over the heads of the rabid crowd. It was flung high into the lamplight, writhing against the sky, and then dropped for the last time, vanishing into the crush.

James managed to keep his feet steady and, with the unexpected help of one of the men, lifted Mrs Colbourn to her feet. She was moaning for her dog. 'Fritz. Fritz. Where's my Fritzy?'

'Get her in the room,' said the man. James opened the door and they almost emptied her through it. 'No war against women,' the man slurred.

The man with the orange neckerchief pushed his way to the front again shouting: 'Upstairs! The German piano!' Then James remembered he was one of the gang who had delivered the Bechstein. 'No!' shouted James trying to block the stairs. Agnes was up there. 'My mother isn't home. You can't go up. I'm not letting you!'

They forced him aside and rushed, a dozen of them, frantically up the staircase. 'I'll get the police!' he shouted charging up the stairs among them. White faced Agnes came to the door on the landing. When she saw them coming she turned and ran. She went into the lavatory and bolted the door.

Breathless, weakening, James struggled through the arms and legs, fighting them, punching, kicking, but the men had already reached the top floor. He fell beaten on the stairs. 'No! No!' he shouted after them. 'That's my mother's piano!'

'There it is!' he heard the leader shout. 'Bloody German, that is!'

James tried to get up. He was weeping. 'Come on out!' he sobbed. 'This is where we live!'

It took them no time to unscrew the legs from the piano. They flung them aside so they bounced and banged on the carpet. James reached the landing and then the door. The room was full of men. 'Agnes!' he shouted wildly. 'Agnes!'

The lavatory door opened and Agnes stood watching calmly. The men had the piano on its side. They were sweating and swearing, urging each other. Two of them seized the discarded legs and using them as clubs smashed the window. Then with a concerted effort they picked up the baby grand and to the shouted instructions of the man in the orange neckerchief, tottered forwards with it. The night air was blowing in, flinging back the curtains. 'Stop! Stop!' pleaded James for the last time. 'It's not ours. It's Mr Sullivan's!'

'Let them do it,' said Agnes quietly. She was standing smiling.

With a great heave they did it. One of them bellowed: 'Watch out below here, boys!' Over the ledge it went.

Years later Bevan could still see it. 'The piano bounced off the tree at the front and ended up in the street with all the boozed-up mob cheering and laughing,' he said. 'The keys were hanging out like teeth.'

'What about the poor dog?' said Renée. They were sitting in the Running Hart in Lyndhurst. In a matter of days the raw weather that had lasted since the end of 1939 had miraculously melted away. Suddenly at the end of March the wind became warm, the air felt like spring and outside the window of the bar the churchyard was filled with sunlight.

'Fritz was never seen again,' said Bevan. 'One of

the war's first casualties, you could say. Along with the piano.'

'Your mother must have been shocked.'

Bevan grinned: 'Not so shocked as Mr Sullivan. It turned out he hadn't paid for the piano.'

She laughed. 'Poor Sully.' She echoed the nickname of a quarter of a century before as though she had known him.

'It got worse,' said Bevan. 'The authorities began requisitioning cars for the military. Cars and buses, lorries, horses.'

'And they took his beautiful motor car?'

'One of the first. Somebody must have had their eye on it. The cars were all lined up at the Southampton docks being sent with the troops to France. Mr Sullivan was told that if he wanted to drive his car again he would have to go with it, become a volunteer military driver. He couldn't be parted from it so he went. My mother was sobbing her heart out, but although he said he loved her he apparently loved the car more.'

'So in the end he was brave.'

'Well, it *was* the end as it turned out. He went over to the Western Front and somewhere or other got bogged down in mud. He was sploshing about for God knows how long – but he wouldn't leave the car. It did for him because he got pneumonia and died.'

Renée looked genuinely sad. 'Poor Sully,' she said. 'And your mother?'

'Went out the window,' he told her bluntly. She could see how bitterly he remembered. 'Jumped, hit the same tree and landed in more or less the identical place as the piano. My sister and I were both at school and the police came and called me out. I was the one who had to tell Agnes.'

They looked up as from the lobby of the hotel came

Lady Violet Foxley struggling with a scarred suitcase. She was not someone who could arrive unheralded. Bevan rose to help her and she puffed her thanks. 'Some people's war efforts,' she sighed, sitting and rearranging her hat, 'are more trouble than the war.'

They knew who she was. Bevan introduced himself and Renée. The barman, unasked, brought her a glass of Madeira which she sniffed and then minutely sipped. 'That's better,' she sighed as if the taste had greatly refreshed her. She regarded them from the upright armchair and said: '*Just* the people I need.' She leaned over the case and unlocked the discoloured hasps. 'My aunt's contribution to defeating the Nazi war machine,' she said producing bunches of thickly knitted socks. 'Years of wool ends went into knitting these. Unfortunately . . .' She picked up two socks rolled as a pair, one red and one yellow. '. . . Sometimes she ran out of wool.' Without comment she displayed another sock in which the colours changed at the ankle, then selected a white pair. 'For serving at tennis or serving in Finland.' They laughed. She leaned towards them conspiratorially. 'Will you take them off my hands?' She nodded at Bevan then transferred the nod to Renée. 'Your men or your little chaps at the school might find them useful.' She glanced towards the open window. 'Although, of course, the weather's changed now. It just would, wouldn't it?' She picked up a pair of heavy socks. 'They're rather thick.'

'Your aunt has been very busy,' said Renée. 'I am sure we could use them.'

'The sizes are a bit approximate, I'm afraid,' sighed Lady Foxley. 'Some of the feet are vastly different sizes in the same pair.' She picked up the socks gloomily. 'It depended on how long the wool lasted, I suppose. She's been all the winter knitting these. She can't get out much but it's a pity she couldn't have got someone to collect them from her from time to time.' Her hands plunged into the sock-full suitcase. 'I suppose the poor woman wanted to create an impression.'

Closing the lid and locking the hasps she said: 'Will you take them off my hands, if that is the right word?'

'We'll share them out,' said Bevan. They all laughed. Lady Foxley took another tiny sip of her Madeira and looked at the open window framing the showy new sunshine.

'Will the change in the weather mean the war will now get under way?' she asked. 'I'm afraid it will.'

'We'll soon see,' said Bevan.

'If Hitler is serious,' finished Renée. 'He has just been waiting for the snow to melt.'

'My daughter lives in London,' said the older woman. 'You know how they all chatter up there and she seems to detect an air of appeasement. There are still many people who want an accommodation with the Nazis. It's the easy way. But for how long, I ask. People feel this Government is weak kneed, we have an idiot for a Prime Minister. There's no stomach for a fight.'

Guiltily she looked about her and even glanced at the open window as if she suspected a crouching eavesdropper. 'I know one shouldn't talk like this,' she said lowering her tone and seeming a little ashamed. 'Casting gloom and despondency. What do you think will happen?' she asked Bevan.

'We're living in a fool's paradise,' he told her quietly. 'I think he'll go for the throat.'

Renée glanced at him as if he had said the unexpected. Lady Foxley's eyes became sad. 'I'm afraid this country will be engulfed,' she said. 'Those newsreels from Poland, and from Spain. We ought to have taken the warning then. We will be bombed. And invaded.'

Renée bit her lip. Bevan said: 'I think you're right.'

'It's no use at all relying on the French, or the Belgians for that matter,' said her ladyship with a touch of belligerence. 'Plucky enough, the Belgians, in the First War but I don't think they'll manage it a second time. You can run out of heroism.' She sniffed. 'And as for the French. They think it's all a bit of fun hiding behind their silly Maginot Line. Apparently most of their army goes home at the weekend.'

Bevan laughed though Renée looked as if she believed it. 'Some people are no good at war,' Renée said. 'The Germans are very good at it. They believe in it.'

'I've got a gun,' said Lady Foxley unexpectedly. 'And six rounds. My great-uncle used it in the Crimea and I'm sure it still works. I'd ask one of my sons, they're both officers, but I'm afraid it would be confiscated. Also I have a rook rifle.'

She looked speculatively at Bevan. 'I thought of giving a dinner party next week,' she said. 'One never knows when food is going to be rationed. Would you both like to come? I'm not sure what the rest of the company will be, but Penelope, my daughter, will probably be down from London, and one of my sons may be home. I think Saturday. Would you come?'

They said they would be delighted.

'One never knows how long one will be able to enjoy social life,' said her ladyship.

As though providing an answer the barman, who had gone into the main hotel, came back and said: 'It's just on the wireless, they say that the Jerries have killed the first British civilian, some poor crofter taking a stroll up on an island in Scotland.'

The weather had turned, within these March days, from bone-bare winter to almost summer. Along the southern coast the new sun warmed the land and the beaches, the sea looked almost blue, birds sang on roofs and trees and fresh-looking gulls swooped over the bright waves. 'Christ,' said Bairnsfather. 'I almost feel like taking my shirt off.'

'Get sunstroke and you'll be on a charge,' said Bombardier Hignet who had come unhurriedly from the orderly room. He turned his unhealthily pale face to the rays. 'I may just have a quick bask.'

'On a charge?' Bairnsfather and Brown were preparing to give the grass in front of the big house its first cutting. They were in shirtsleeve order, their heavy battledress blouses discarded.

'Sunstroke counts as a self-inflicted wound,' recited Hignet. 'Read King's Regulations, son.' He retrieved his third cup of coffee that morning from his niche in the orderly room and, still with his face canted towards the sun, drank it casually. 'Like wanking,' suggested Brown.

'That's not against King's Regulations,' said Hignet haughtily. 'Only if it impairs the soldier's ability to fight.'

'Nobody's told us to fight yet, so we don't know,' said Bairnsfather. 'Anyway . . .' He paused to regard Brown. 'Wanking can send you blind. Or mad.'

'Medical discharge?' suggested Brown.

Bairnsfather sniffed the unexpected air. 'I hope it keeps like this. Won't be too bad having a nice summer down here, the beach and the pub near.'

'And your girlfriend,' added Hignet with a hint of jealousy. 'You're all fixed for the duration, you are, son. Some of us have better things to do. We've got to get on with our lives. If we're not going to have a *proper* war then let's go home, I say.'

'You've been reading that bloody *Daily Worker* again.'

'*Daily Herald*, if you don't mind. My reading is very wide but I don't need to read the likes of the *Daily Worker*. Not being a member of the proletariat.'

As he said it some young men appeared, civilians, and began to kick a football about on the beach. The soldiers watched a little enviously. 'Nothing better to do,' said Brown. 'On the dole.'

'Here's some more,' said Bairnsfather. Hignet came from the step of the hut and peered around its side. A casual procession was heading for the sands. 'They've come from New Milton station,' he said. 'And there's some charabancs coming down the road.'

'Never mind the war,' said Bairnsfather. 'They still like to be beside the seaside. You'd think they'd have more to do.'

'Like us,' said Brown.

They knew he spoke the truth. 'Well, we might be doing something important quite soon,' sniffed Hignet. 'Confronting the enemy.' He took his cup back towards the hut door. Sergeant Runciman was striding, but none too purposefully, towards them. 'How many blades of grass have you cut?' he asked Bairnsfather. Hignet went back through the hut door and shouted: 'Want a cuppa, sarge?'

'Just one,' Runciman called back. 'Have to get on with hostilities.' He looked down at the lawnmower. 'Won't it work?'

'Don't seem to, sarge,' said Brown.

'Try pushing it,' said Runciman. He spotted the crowds invading the beach. 'Blimey, what's this, Blackpool?'

'Easter, sarge,' said Bairnsfather. 'They'll be diving in the sea next.' Ugson, who was on guard at the beach gate, with fixed bayonet, his fat face layered with sweat, glanced towards the waves.

'There's an okey-pokey man,' said Brown. 'I could do with an ice-cream.'

'Get on with the mowing,' said Runciman. Brown gave a token push at the mower and grimaced. It chewed up six inches of grass. 'Needs servicing,' suggested Bairnsfather. 'We could take it down to the Ordnance Corps shed.'

'And sit with your bums on the sands while they do it,' said Runciman. The beach was now sprinkled with people who had taken off their coats and sat on shawls and towels. Some had erected deck-chairs and were now enfolded in them looking at the light, incoming waves. A queue formed at the Italian ice-cream van. Children were splashing and shouting through the shallows and carrying buckets and spades down to the wet sand. 'They're treading all over our Maginot Line,' said Brown.

'There's nothing to prevent them,' said Hignet in his mock-educated manner. 'After all, it's a free country. That's what we're fighting for. Supposed to be.'

Runciman regarded him sceptically. 'Some people might think . . . well, that they'd have a bit more respect for the war,' he said. 'More things to keep them busy than eating ice-cream cornets and staring at the Channel.'

'This is not going to ackle,' said Brown.

Runciman regarded the lawnmower and then Brown. 'Not in a thousand years,' sighed Bairnsfather. 'It's buggered.'

'All right, take it to the Ordnance Corps blokes. But don't stay in the pub all day while they do it.'

He was about to turn, quite briskly considering the lassitude of the day, when three thick-necked youths approached the perimeter fence. Two of them carried quart-sized flagons of beer. The leader wiped his big mouth. 'Oi, we want to join the army!' One of the others poked a finger at Ugson's bayonet and mocked: 'That's made of ruddy rubber.' Ugson rolled his eyes. The sun shone on the bayonet.

'Fuck off!' said Runciman.

'And you,' grunted the youth. They were wearing heavy trousers, belts with threatening-looking buckles and cheap open-necked shirts. Bairnsfather and Brown watched uncertainly and when Hignet appeared again from the hut and saw the confrontation he vanished quickly.

An army lorry drew up in the compound and began to disgorge soldiers. Purcell shouted from the main gate. 'Trainee gun crew,' said Runciman looking over his shoulder. 'Come to learn the Bofors.'

''E tells us to fuck off,' mimicked one of the civilians outside the perimeter fence. 'All we wanted was to join 'is army.' He turned and did a pretended march, raising his beer flagon like a trumpet. The beer tipped out over his mouth and shirt. His companions roared with mirth then poked out their tongues like children and followed him. Runciman stomped off towards the lorry and the newly arrived soldiers with a half-glance at the retreating ruffians.

'Cunts,' he said below his breath. 'We *need* a bloody war.'

Bairnsfather took the fifteen-hundredweight platoon truck to transport the lawnmower to the workshop of the Royal Army Ordnance Corps, half a mile away. Brown and Hignet went with him, Hignet because, he said, he wanted to see a corporal at the workshop who was interested in starting a discussion group. He assumed the role of spokesman for the party.

'We've brought our unit grasscutter to be mended,' he said to the sergeant sitting at the opened door of the workshop behind a greasy desk strewn with oil-streaked army forms. There was an ugly pre-war tank being dismantled on the floor, one of the squadron which the engineers had been trying to make good since the previous October. 'Got it working yet, sergeant?' Bairnsfather asked.

'Yes. Like your lawnmower works,' grunted the sergeant. 'Murdoch!' He had purple bags below his eyes. A sad-browed man in greasy dungarees came across the cluttered floor with no show of enthusiasm. Hignet had to examine him closely before he could detect his corporal's stripes.

'S'arnt?' the man said. The Scots voice was apparent even in the single truncated word.

'These gunners have brought their very own lawnmower to be repaired.' The sergeant pretended to beam. 'Entrusted it to the Ordnance Corps.'

'Is it very heavy?' asked Murdoch sourly.

'Try pushing it,' said Hignet.

Murdoch took the mower. 'Shall I mend this first, sarge, or the tank?'

The sergeant ignored him. 'Come back in an hour, lads,' he said. 'We probably won't need the tank before then.'

Hignet overlooked the corporal he had said he wanted to see. They walked in the unaccustomed sunshine towards the pub. 'That was a Jock got himself killed by the Germans yesterday,' said Bairnsfather. He used his flat hand to imitate a diving aeroplane. 'Just out for a stroll in the heather.'

'Might have been that bloke's dad,' suggested Brown. 'He was miserable enough.'

Hignet said: 'When you think that the first civilian casualty, after nine months of this war, has to be some chap minding his own business, on some Scottish island you've never heard of. Over comes the Messerschmitt . . . sees Jock . . . bang, bang, bang.'

'Hit and run,' said Brown. 'Couldn't have been a planned attack – not on one bloke.'

Bairnsfather grimaced at him and said: 'Maybe he was playing the bagpipes.'

The pub stood in broad noon light. There were half a dozen dusty children standing outside looking lost, drinking Corona cherry drink from a bottle which they passed quarrelsomely from one to another. Two were trying to peep through the door into the noisy bar. One tiny, grubby-cheeked girl was squatting as if abandoned. A woman shouted at her coarsely from an open window and flung a slice of bread and jam. Almost contemptuously the child picked it up from the grit of the yard and bit into it but never looked towards the window.

The three soldiers had to duck below the door's crooked lintel, even Brown who was short. Inside it was dim and crowded and hung with the smell of bodies and beer. Brown pushed his way through the crush. 'Typical of the British, the moment the sun comes out they cram into a hole like this,' observed Hignet.

'The army's here!' mocked a man with a grubby handkerchief, knotted at the corners, fixed against his head like a skullcap. 'Why ain't you buggers guarding the country?'

'Fighting men require refreshment,' said Hignet disdainfully.

'Christ, listen to 'im. Posh sod,' said another voice. It was one of the three youths who had earlier taunted them from outside the wire. 'What you orderin', mate, a pink bloody gin?' The others laughed.

There were more of them now. Bairnsfather sniffed, detecting trouble, and estimated the distance and the route to the door. Brown had manoeuvred his way to the bar and was ordering two and a half pints, the half for Hignet. The three youths, their faces blowsy with unaccustomed sun and excess beer, confronted Bairnsfather and Hignet. Half a dozen more formed up, tactically, oddly in a military way, to their rear. 'You lot 'aving a nice 'oliday then?' asked the youth who had done all the talking. 'Got yer bucket and spade?'

'We're preventing the enemy from killing you,' said Hignet eyeing him.

There was a gust of ribaldry. 'Stone the bloody crows!' bawled a baggy woman. 'You're 'aving a lovely bloody time down here. It's your sort who *start* wars, you do, the soddin' army. You're as bad as those lazy sods in the fire brigade and those potty air-raid wardens.'

Hignet blinked at the logic. Bairnsfather said: 'Just wait till Jerry gets here.'

'You'll be the first to run,' said another man.

'What about what you *cost* us,' insisted the woman. She pushed her sturdy, ugly way forward. 'My old man pays income tax for you.' She looked around quite proudly. 'When he's in work.'

'So you can sit on your arses,' said the man in the handkerchief skullcap. 'I'd send the whole bloody lot of you packin'.'

Hignet was about to make some lofty retort when Brown, who was carrying the tankards from the bar, was blatantly nudged and sent staggering sideways against the crowd, the beer splashing and spilling as he stumbled. There were shouts and swearing and he swore back. Bairnsfather tried to pull him out of the ruck but in a moment they were in the middle of a fight. Brown, brandishing one of the tankards like a knuckleduster, threatened his way through the mob. Bairnsfather was exchanging clumsy punches with the leader of the original trio and Hignet was standing ashen and upright, his hands flattened before him in what he hoped was an Oriental fashion. 'I'm black belt!' His voice was shrill. 'I can kill!'

But the drunks had surrounded them and they were only rescued by the intervention of the barman, a massive

Irishman, who forced himself through the crowd, barging and bellowing: 'No fists in here! No use of fists! This is a peaceful pub.'

Then three men from the RAOC unit appeared in the door and with some joy and shouts of: 'Reinforcements!' plunged into the struggle, attempting to join up with the other soldiers. The civilians began falling back, the two sets of combatants separated by the peace-loving Irishman. Hignet was next to Bairnsfather. 'Sound the retreat,' he said from the edge of his mouth. All six servicemen made a final and fortuitously co-ordinated counter-attack and then turned for the door. The Irishman covered their retirement by blocking the aperture and shouting threats that he was going to shut the bar. The civilians fell back.

Outside the scruffy children were cheering ecstatically and jumping on the spot. The tot with the glass Corona bottle flung it, hitting Hignet on the knee. All the soldiers went at the double towards the platoon truck, Hignet limping. 'Your mower's in the back,' puffed one of the Ordnance men. 'You'd better clear off, mate.'

Bairnsfather, Brown and Hignet clambered aboard the fifteen-hundredweight and the other soldiers bolted towards the neighbouring gates of the Ordnance compound. Bairnsfather attempted to start the engine which spluttered and stopped. Quickly he looked over his shoulder towards the pub. The door had somehow been closed and the gigantic Irishman was shut outside, banging on it wildly to get in and surrounded by excited, screeching children. Bairnsfather tried the engine again. Again it only coughed. 'Brownie,' he muttered. 'Give it a swing.'

Brown jumped down, Bairnsfather threw him the starting handle, he hurried to the front of the vehicle and turned it heftily. The engine hardly stirred. He swung it again. It coughed politely. They heard the pub door bursting open. 'At the double,' said Hignet quietly as though it were merely a suggestion. All three abandoned the platoon truck and the lawnmower and began to run back towards their own compound, half a mile away.

They heard the crash as the pub door finally gave way and a drunken crowd of civilians burst out into the brash sunlight and began heading in their direction. 'Don't worry,' Hignet said as he trotted with an oddly amateur high-kneed action. 'They're just not fit. We are.'

Bairnsfather could not spare the breath to answer. Over his shoulder he could see that the baying men, followed by some women and children, were closing on them. The army boots slowed the soldiers. Gratefully they reached the perimeter fence and charged through the gate. Ugson, still on guard duty, slid prudently behind his sentry-box.

Sergeant Runciman observed the mob as he was supervising the drill of the visiting gunners around the Bofors. 'What the . . . ?' He soon realised. The civilians were now at the fence. Two drunken youths began to attempt to climb it. Another wedge of men were pushing their shoulders against the gate. 'Jesus,' said Runciman. He was not a regular soldier for nothing. He turned and shouted staccato orders to the trainees on the two guns. Bairnsfather and Brown watched astounded, Hignet with interest.

Ominously the tulip-shaped barrels of the twin Bofors began to descend. The mob at the wire stopped shouting. They watched as the barrels reached the horizontal. There was a brief muttering, then profound silence penetrated only by the snapping instructions of the sergeant. The guns slowly gyrated and pointed conclusively towards the crowd; the crowd began to back away, slowly, then at a quick walk, at a healthy trot, and finally a full, frenzied run. When they were at a distance they began to bawl and wave their fists but then they turned and ran again leaving some of the children behind.

Bairnsfather and Brown stared in awe at the sergeant. Hignet stood on the step of the orderly room hut shaking his head. Runciman did not even glance their way. He shouted another series of orders to the trainees and the guns slowly revolved towards the sea. 'Stand down!' he shouted to the trainee gunners. They left their positions around the weapons and, looking pleased, formed up in two ranks. 'At ease!' ordered Runciman. He took a deep breath. 'And that,' he said, 'is the basic movement drill for the Bofors forty-millimetre, dual-purpose, rapid-firing gun.' Then, like an afterthought: 'Mark one.'

He turned on his heel: 'Squa . . . ad! Att-ention! Squad . . . dismissss!'

Bairnsfather regarded him with something near admiration. 'You certainly put the wind up those civvies, sarge.'

Runciman appeared surprised. 'Civvies? What civvies? I didn't see any civvies.' He regarded Bairnsfather solidly. 'Where's the unit lawnmower?'

In Lyndhurst the courtroom windows were open for the first time in months and the fresh sunshine streaked in like two searchlight beams, by chance one alighting on the dock and the other on the elevated magistrates on their bench. The first accused of the morning blinked in the unaccustomed illumination. 'Guilty, sir,' he said as though anxious to quit the limelight.

'You haven't been charged yet,' Lady Violet, the chairman, pointed out. She was having trouble with the sun. It burned on one side of her face; she could feel her ear getting hot. There were blinds which could be tugged down but she was reluctant to order it after such a long time of dark weather.

Mr Deemster, the clerk, was sitting below the bench and in its shade surveyed the accused sourly. 'William Martin, drunk and indecent.'

'Guilty, sir. Both, sir.'

'Haven't you got anything to say for yourself?' asked Lady Violet.

'Guilty, missus.'

'Surely you have some explanation? Urinating in the churchyard. I wouldn't be surprised if you haven't opened yourself to a charge of sacrilege.' The clerk turned the leaves of his law books as if there might be a possibility. William Martin began to look concerned. 'It was my grandad's grave, lady. I allus do it. *He* used to do it to *'is* father. *My* dad reckons it makes the grass grow.'

'A way of paying your respects,' Lady Violet murmured.

'Like dogs do, your honour. Our family got people in that graveyard goin' on two 'undred years.'

'Fined five shillings,' said her ladyship.

Unsworth sat in his usual police seat. Jim Thurston, the local reporter, his brown saggy overcoat unbuttoned for the first time that year, was still writing laborious shorthand; he had never learned to write it swiftly. It seemed that the slow scene never changed, nor ever would. The figures remained in their proper positions, the magistrates, the clerk, the accused, the press and the police officer. Him. It was one of the crannies of England, a niche and a bastion; it was odd to think that they were fighting for, were prepared to die for, the freedom of the Lyndhurst magistrates' court.

Not that there was any visible sign of local institutions being changed, let alone threatened. The rugby club, kept in shackles by the long weeks of snow, had played its first game of the year at the weekend and there had been shouts of joyous relief from the recreation ground, and some casualties. There was a notice on the parish board announcing that practice for the approaching cricket season would take place on the following Saturday morning. The summer promised the usual long hours. Farmers could be in the fields until the ten o'clock dusk. Day-shift workers in the factories would emerge into light evenings. The parks would be open late.

From his seat in the court Unsworth read down the charge list. William Martin was the last of the weekend drunks and now an angry-faced stranger replaced him in the dock. He wore a London suit and an importantly striped tie. 'Henry Philip Newington,' he answered when asked to confirm his name, adding loftily: 'And I have to protest immediately about my presence here.'

Without hurry Mr Deemster examined him over his glasses and Lady Violet glanced questioningly at Mrs Manners and Mr Tomset, her fellow magistrates. 'Time enough for that,' said the clerk. Then, as if the man came from a remote country: 'We have procedures here as well, you know.'

Henry Newington was charged with an offence against the blackout regulations. Unsworth, the rural detective, was not alone in doubting the wisdom of the blackout, for two hundred and fifty people every week were being killed in the sightless streets and blind country roads, knocked down by cars and unseen buses, walking into other people, into lampposts, rivers and canals, falling down holes and off railway bridges. A patriotic police constable had been killed after climbing an unsafe drainpipe to extinguish a light left on in an office; four beery soldiers had met their ends, singing hymns while sitting in the middle of a remote night-time road unaware of an approaching bus. They, in their way, were war casualties.

It was humanly impossible for Britain to be extinguished every night, blotted from the maps. A song, performed in four-ale bars and music-halls, chorused the obvious: 'They can't blackout the moon.' On bright nights the coast was neatly and clearly outlined to any flier; the Isle of Wight, with its helpful Needles lighthouse, was plain as a jigsaw piece, the Solent shone and the River Thames wriggled like a silver streamer through the heart of anonymous London. Blast furnaces, railway yards and, curiously, floodlit detention camps for aliens and enemy prisoners, were luminously apparent to even the highest plane but there was a deadpan warning that groups of people should not look at the sky simultaneously since their white faces could be seen by the enemy. Across the Irish Sea, Dublin was wilfully illuminated and the neutral Irish Republic twinkled brightly right up to the black curtain that was the Ulster border.

'This blackout business is madness,' said Henry Newington.

'There's a war on,' recited Lady Violet. 'There are regulations.'

'It's doing more damage than the Germans.'

'At the moment I am inclined to agree with you,' said the chairman. Her fellow magistrates nodded. Mrs Manners had crashed into a dark perambulator, containing an unseen baby, while riding her blacked-out bicycle. 'But these rules are meant to be obeyed. The police have orders.'

'I was merely striking a match to find the light switch,' said Mr Newington haughtily. 'I hardly think *that* was going to bring on a mass bomber raid.'

'If you had switched on the *light* without any blackout blinds in place then you would really have been for it,' said Mr Deemster. 'Don't you know where your own light switches are?'

The accused looked peeved. 'I had only moved in that day. My wife would not leave the removals van because it was so dark and she doesn't trust people down here. We only came here because it's supposed to be a safe area.'

Heads were raised. 'Who told you that?' asked Lady Violet.

'The estate agent,' said the man in the dock. 'He advertised the house as in a designated safe area, immune from attack.'

'Who told the estate agent?' asked the chairman. 'Hitler?'

The man left the court with a fine of two pounds ten shillings. Unsworth's case was next. 'Wladyslaw Tyssowski!' the clerk called with some pride in the achievement. The Pole came heavily up from the cells below. Once again he was charged with stealing petrol.

The Pole turned his high-cheeked face towards Unsworth as though acknowledging a friend. 'Is he selling this petrol on the black market?' asked the chairman.

'I understand not, Your Worship,' said Unsworth. 'He has shown me two fifty-gallon tanks he has buried in a field close to his lodgings. He puts the petrol he siphons in these tanks.'

'Hoarding,' sniffed the clerk.

The accused nodded at Unsworth as if giving him a cue. Unsworth said to the magistrates: 'The tanks are almost full, Your Worships. He has a pump and a hose attachment. He says that when the Germans land he intends to spray them with petrol and throw a match to set them alight.'

The Pole stood proudly to attention. 'The Tyssowski Plan!' he shouted.

The firelight, and the pleasure of the occasion, touched her ladyship's face as she sat at the head of her fine and extended dining table. 'How long we will be able to go on doing this, I don't know,' she said. 'In a year's time we may be eating horse meat.'

'In the First War, of course, we *did* eat it,' said a big grey man at the other extreme of the table. 'It had a sort of yellowy tinge. Once the fat was cut off it wasn't unpleasant, as I recall.'

Bevan and Renée smiled at them. The room was panelled, warm and dim. It had probably been like that since 1918. Lady Violet confirmed Bevan's thought. 'We had dinner here to celebrate the Armistice,' she said. 'Exactly as now. The war was over but there were a few absent faces. I had two brothers and a cousin who never came back.'

'Won't happen again,' said Sir Nigel Donald, the grey man, confidently. 'They won't die like that.' Once he had been a colonel but, unlike most, he had discarded the rank when he retired. Sir Nigel had kept his uniform, however; it was hanging sprucely in his wardrobe in case it were ever needed. It still fitted. 'The young officers of the First War are the staff men now,' he said. 'They won't allow their men, or themselves, to be slaughtered. One third of the commissioned officers died.' He glanced at Lady Violet's uniformed son Arthur. Horace was in France.

'All's quiet on the Western Front,' Arthur said. 'Horace has been put in charge of cricket.'

Sir Nigel took in Bevan. 'You just missed it, I suppose, captain?'

'I just caught it. The last year. I was seventeen.'

'No age to fight a war,' sniffed Lady Violet.

Renée looked exotic in the soft light of the old and traditional room. She wore a beautiful long dark dress from pre-war Paris. Her perfume came to Bevan and he was conscious of the closeness of her bare shoulder. He wondered how long it would last. They had finished the soup and the salmon. Two maids, firmly supervised by Mrs Light the housekeeper, served pheasant. The humming butler Terson, his white gloves fluttering over the cloth, poured the wine. Renée smiled towards Bevan but the others were long accustomed to the humming. It was as it had been for twenty years.

'If he's going to make a move it will be soon,' said Arthur. He glanced at Sir Nigel as though they might have a shared secret. The big grey man nodded. 'I think he will,' he said. 'He must or we must, and frankly we're not capable of it. Otherwise everybody might as well go home. There are still people, politicians, as we all know, who think he is valuable as a bulwark against those they see as the real danger, the Russians.'

Renée said: 'I have seen what he has done in Austria. And now many other places. If he is protecting England from the Russians he is doing it in a strange way.'

'Why,' asked Lady Violet impatiently, 'does *everyone*, everyone in the land it seems, keep referring to this man Hitler as "He"? He does this, He is going to do that, what is He thinking? *He*. Who do we think He is? I thought only Jesus and God were supposed to have a capital H. He will be here, He will be there. It makes Him sound like a mixture of Christ and the Scarlet Pimpernel.'

Everyone laughed. Bevan said: 'Somehow it seems too friendly to call him Adolf.'

'But people do,' said Renée. 'It is like he is a joke.'

'They call the Kaiser 'Kaiser Bill',' pointed out Sir Nigel. 'Same thing. Bonaparte was always 'Boney'.'

'I knew an Adolf,' said a voice from the door. Penelope, Lady Violet's daughter, walked in. 'Not the same one. This one was nice. Loved walking through the German woods.'

The men rose. Penelope's coat hid her pregnancy. She looked warmly beautiful. Terson fussily appeared and took the coat from her and she sat down quickly. 'The trains,' she said. 'Packed. Perhaps it's the last chance, the last holiday.'

'The beach in Bournemouth was more crammed than before the war,' said Arthur. 'Children, donkey rides, any more for the Skylark, ice-cream, fish and chips.'

Penelope was introduced to Bevan and Renée. 'We have met before,' she said to Bevan. 'On Southampton station. I almost knocked you over.' Years later he would remember that evening moment. The outstretched hand, it seemed reaching for him, the warm dark eyes, the serious face just slightly changed by a smile. How strange it was when you first touched the fingers of the woman you would one day marry.

5

On 9 April 1940 the waiting ended. The pretence, the hopes of peace, the doubts of war, the indifference, the bravado and the jokes were all finished in a few moments as the German Army entered Denmark and overran the country in just under four hours. The Danish Army suffered thirteen men dead and twenty-three wounded and the German casualties amounted to twenty. In Norway, on the same day, Nazi troops concealed in merchant ships walked ashore.

'That's torn it,' said Bairnsfather solemnly as they grouped around the hut wireless set. Hignet had been interrupted by the news as he was attempting to interest them in a lecture he was organising in the canteen that evening. The speaker was travelling from Portsmouth. 'Human Aspects of the Industrial Revolution,' said Hignet. 'It's important to everybody.'

The bulletin continued serenely, the war communiqué over, the announcer's BBC tones reciting the racing results from the Epsom Spring Meeting. Hignet produced a pad and pen and attempted to gather names for his lecture. Nothing must be allowed to shake the solid British, certainly not some frightened Danish customs official hurriedly lifting a barrier for the Nazis. 'Lectures? We've got to play football, 'aven't we,' said Ugson, his customary Woodbine bouncing at the corner of his lips. 'We'll be shagged out after that.'

'Football! Football!' exploded Hignet. 'You'd put football above your intellect?' He studied Ugson and knew that he would. 'Come on, some of you.'

Bairnsfather sighed and signed. 'The world's going up in flames and you want to talk about the . . . What was it?'

'Human Aspects of the Industrial Revolution.' Hignet repeated it firmly and regarded the group with scorn. 'In any case, you're only going to kick around with those refugee kids. *That's* not football.'

'You know all about football then, do you, Hignet?' asked Cartwright. 'You've played?'

Hignet sniffed. 'Hockey was my game.'

'It would be,' said Cartwright. 'I tell you what, you come over to our football and we'll come to your whatsit revolution. How's that?'

'Right,' said Hignet. 'I'll be referee. I hope Ugson's not playing with that fag stuck in his face.'

'I expect I will,' said Ugson.

Once more it was a pleasant day, with Norway and Denmark out of sight across the springtime sea. 'It's not like they seem like real places, sir,' said Gunner Purcell as he tied his plimsolls. The football would be played on the school's tarred playground. 'They're like . . . well, just names in the news.'

'They're real enough,' said Bevan. 'And not that far.' He was not entirely sure how far.

Bairnsfather's shorts were lower than his ashen knees. 'I've got knobbly knees through delivering bread,' he said.

Ugson, his legs like slugs, had opened a packet of Woodbines with something of a flourish and offered them around so swiftly that no one had a chance to take one before he put them in the back pocket of his bulging shorts.

Bevan saw Renée coming from the school among a dozen boys. She was wearing trousers and the soldiers were intrigued. 'You playing, miss?' asked Bairnsfather. Her trousers were dark blue and she wore a short grey coat. Her face was rosy.

'I am the spectator.'

'I'll see fair play,' said Bevan. He had not played football since his schooldays and he had been inept then. He remembered that Unsworth, now the policeman, had been captain of the team. Renée had brought Franz out into the air. 'I had to pull him away from his books,' she said. 'And that stuffy room.'

Franz sniffed the air suspiciously and blinked at the sunlight. His stick-like legs protruded from what appeared to be a pair of women's bloomers but he was not embarrassed. 'I cannot kick,' he said to Bevan.

Bairnsfather said: 'Let's see if you can.' The scarred ball was being hacked inexpertly about the playground by the soldiers and the boys. Bairnsfather called for it and it was toe-punted towards him.

He said to Franz: 'Stand there, where you are, and I'll roll the ball past you from this side. You kick it.'

The boy's dark-ringed eyes were intense. Awkwardly he picked up the ball and studied it as if attempting to read it, then handed it to Bairnsfather. The others grouped to watch, the men and the boys, with their ugly shorts, their various unhealthy legs, their heights and breadths, their array of used faces, their sharp eyes. Ugson was still puffing smoke. 'Right, son,' said Bairnsfather. He held the football in one hand, resting against his forearm. 'Ready?'

'I am ready,' said Franz very seriously. He set himself rigidly. Renée smiled encouragement.

Bairnsfather rolled the ball slowly from the side. Franz kicked out frantically and missed. 'Watch it, watch the ball,' said Bairnsfather quietly. There was no co-ordination. He took the ball back and rolled it a second time. Franz again kicked wildly, just caught the spinning edge and tipped backwards on to the tarred playground. A shout of laughter went up but at once stopped. Franz slowly got to his feet; his eyes were hurt, almost haunted, cornered. 'Nearly,' said Bevan. 'Try again.'

'For you, I will,' said Franz. 'Once only.'

Bairnsfather rolled the ball, again slowly. This time Franz caught it with his toe end and sent it slithering along the playground surface, but only for a few feet. He turned to Bairnsfather and said: 'See, I can play.'

Hignet picked up the ball and holding a small book before his face, paced out eight steps along the playground wall. He took some chalk from his pocket and marked the extremes. 'The goal,' he announced. 'Eight yards . . .' He glanced towards Renée. 'Do they work in yards?'

'Metres. They have things to learn.'

'Just under eight metres,' he said holding up eight fingers. 'Now who will play in goal?'

'I'll do that,' said Ugson striding heavily forward, the smoke from his Woodbine emitting puffs like a railway engine. He took up a belligerent position between the chalk marks.

'Nobody's going to score against you, Ugly,' said Bairnsfather. 'You take up most of the fu . . . perishing goal.'

'I've had professional trials,' boasted Ugson. 'They called me the new Frank Swift.'

'All right,' said Cartwright. 'Hang on to this then.' He placed the ball and took three paces back. He kicked it powerfully and it hit Ugson in his broad stomach. Ugson collapsed with a gurgle and finally a groan. The soldiers hooted and after a moment the children did too. Renée's hands covered her laughter and she turned away. Cartwright snorted but then helped Ugson heavily to his feet.

'All right, Ugson?' asked Bevan.

'All right, sir,' said Ugson rubbing his belly. The cigarette remained in his mouth. 'I weren't ready.'

Bairnsfather picked up the ball. 'All right, two teams.' He pointed at random to each of the boys and the soldiers and quickly divided them. He pointed to Franz. 'You go in goal the other end.'

'There is no goal,' said Franz surveying the wall of the building.

Hignet strode to the wall, holding the piece of chalk, paced out eight strides and marked them. 'Now there is,' he said.

Franz went between the chalk marks and began ineptly jumping. 'I am a goalkeeper,' he called excitedly to Renée. 'I am a famous goalkeeper for Austria.'

Hignet produced a whistle and blew. The scrambled game began, men and boys scuffling after the ball, chasing it wherever it went, falling, shouting, laughing, puffing and dodging. Herr Rohm, the Scoutmaster, appeared from the school in his usual shorts and viewed the scrimmage with growing delight. 'I play!' he called and strode out on his spindly legs. 'Me, I can kick!'

He thrust himself into the mêlée and within a moment had floored Brown with a scything foot. Brown howled and lay holding his shin. Herr Rohm stood over him with frank enthusiasm. 'I have kicked a soldier!' The game continued. Ugson jumped one way, then the other, his thick arms wide, his cigarette puffing. 'Come on! Come on!' he bellowed. 'Come on! Come on!' echoed Franz's reedy voice from the other end.

Suddenly Cartwright's bulk and skill gained him space. He was three yards from Ugson's goal. The entire game froze. Ugson spread his arms. Smoke spurted from his lips. Cartwright kicked the ball. This time it hit Ugson full in the face. He collapsed groaning against the wall.

Everyone rushed forward. 'He's swallowed his fag,' said Hignet.

They dragged him to the doorway. ''E's like a volcano,' said Brown. They poured water into Ugson's mouth. 'I need a cup of tea,' he groaned. They went back into the school and sat at the long wooden tables while women in aprons served them with mugs of tea and wedges of bread and strawberry jam. 'I am a goalkeeper,' Franz told Mr MacFarlane when he came in.

Bevan sat at one end of the long, rough table. He felt suddenly isolated. The smell of the tea and the jam, the very feel of the place, the echoing shouts of children from corridors. He had been there before.

Mrs Colbourn from downstairs had come to fetch him from school. It was his fourteenth birthday. Mrs Colbourn now had a new dog, a Scottie called Jock, and she brought that with her. She told him only that his mother had suffered a fall and at first he thought she meant in the kitchen or while she was shopping, or toppling from a chair while reaching to wind the clock. It did not occur to him that she might be dead until he was in the street and he saw the ominously open window, a broken branch, and the area of the street below roped off with a set-faced policeman standing there. James remained calm; he could feel the hardening of his face, but Mrs Colbourn and the policeman both became agitated and asked him about any relatives and who should go back to the school to meet Agnes to tell her. James told them that they had an aunt and uncle in Bournemouth, although they hardly knew them, and that he would return for Agnes.

His sister was pleased but not surprised to see him for he sometimes went to meet her so they could walk home together. Now he held her hand. Their rapport was so tuned that she glanced at his expression and asked: 'What's happened to our mother?'

'She's had a fall.' He waited, then added: 'From the window.'

'Is she alive?' Her voice was steady, almost casual.

'She's dead,' he said keeping his gaze straight along the street as if watching for someone. He could feel the tears now. They rolled on his cheeks and Agnes gave him her handkerchief to wipe them. He was crying for both of them. She remained dry eyed but walked with exaggerated steadiness. 'What's going to happen to us?' she asked.

As they approached the house and she saw the open window she did begin to cry and he took her to her room where she held on to him and sobbed. 'It was that Sully's fault.'

Mrs Colbourn told the policeman that she would stay with them that night but she turned out to be a dangerous cook, almost exploding the kitchen because she could not work the gas jets. She was used to her coal stove. 'One emergency is enough in one day,' she philosophised. Her new dog groaned and cocked its leg in a corner and in the end Agnes told her they could look after themselves. Mrs Colbourn left guiltily but gratefully.

It was a misty evening, dark by seven. James went to the window, agape like a scream, and soberly closed it. Agnes said: 'Let's go to the Bioscope.'

He saw she meant it. 'I don't want to sit in here,' she said.

'I don't either.' He emptied the money box and found some extra pennies in their mother's dressing-table, left like a legacy. They got their coats and crept past Mrs Colbourn's door into the folding fog of the street. Now that they were out they felt their spirits lift and they were almost happy when they boarded the tram. Agnes held on to his arm and they sat close together, the only passengers on the open-top deck as the tram grumbled through the drear evening.

She continued to hold him while they sat engulfed in the warmth and dimness of the picture house. They hardly moved, their faces scarcely altered, as the reels changed and the giant characters moved above them on the screen. It was nine o'clock when they went out into the gaslight of the street, then sat silently on the home-going tram both wondering what was to become of them.

Mrs Colbourn was waiting at the door. 'You should have said.' It was half relief, half annoyance. 'I was going to call the police. I thought you had run away.'

'We went to pray,' said Agnes.

'You were gone a long time.'

'We prayed a lot.'

James felt sorry for Mrs Colbourn. It was not her fault.

They trod nervously up the stairs and inched the door open as though they thought Vera might be sitting there after all. But she was not. The room that had heard a hundred excruciating violins was lost in silence.

James made them some Cadbury's and then they played draughts. 'We won't have to go to school tomorrow,' he said trying to look on the bright side. Their hearts were not in the game.

His sister went slowly into her small bedroom. He turned down the jets of the gas lamps, then went to the bare window and stared down into the ghostly street. The broken branch was showing like a white scar. He turned away, extinguished the last lamp and climbed into his bed.

He was lying awake. He suddenly remembered it had

been his birthday. Agnes came into the room in her nightdress. Without a word she moved into the bed with him. He made room for her and they held each other all through the night.

From Bournemouth the following morning came their Uncle Eustace, a confused and pessimistic man who they had not seen for years but had not missed. 'I have been to the hospital,' he said. 'Your mother is rather poorly.' They were dressed in their best clothes. They had discussed this before the uncle's arrival and decided that whatever the day was going to bring ought to be met tidily; James was wearing his brown suit with long trousers and Agnes was in her velvet dress.

'Our mother's dead,' Agnes told him.

Eustace seemed to be capable of taking the solecism in his stride, merely adding it to his overall confusion. 'I was going to break it to you later,' he said. 'Or get somebody else to mention it. God knows I've had enough bad news recently for any man.'

'Sorry about that,' said James.

'What sort of bad news?' asked Agnes hopefully.

The children were close together on the sofa and their uncle sat uncomfortably on an upright chair. 'My wife, your aunt, has become most strange,' he said. 'She stands singing on the beach in this weather. She thinks she is Dame Nellie Melba. I had to give up work because of my coughing and we have very little money. My son has been wounded on the Western Front – a bullet through his toe – and there seems to be some suspicion that he shot himself in order to be repatriated in which case he will be court-martialled and could face a firing squad. We have a very small house and two Irish lodgers who fight and are sick. One of them was sick on our cat.'

The bereaved children sat listening to the summary

of his woes with quiet amazement. Then his reason arrived in one stark sentence. 'You cannot come and live with us.'

He sat wringing his hat, grinding his knees, apparently attempting to ascertain the effect of this news on them. Relief was fixed on both young faces. 'I hope you're not too upset,' he said. 'They are coming to see you this morning.'

'Who is?' Agnes asked.

'The Board. At least I think they are called the Board.'

A slow horror dawned on James. He looked sideways and saw Agnes staring at him. 'We can look after ourselves,' he said to the distraught man. 'We don't need the Board. We're not going to any orphanage.'

'No, we're *not*,' said Agnes angrily. 'Our mother taught the violin.'

'So I understand,' said the uncle weakly. 'You have no idea of the whereabouts of your father, do you?'

'None,' said James. 'He disappeared. His clothes came back. Mother told us he was probably dead.'

'It really is an unfortunate family,' sighed Eustace. 'I don't know what we shall do with you.'

The children looked as if they wanted to help him. 'We could stay here,' said Agnes waving her small hand around the flat. 'We could look after each other.'

Eustace brightened as if he thought they quite easily could. But then he shook his head. 'Your mother owed rent,' he said. 'The landlords . . .' He spread his hands and closed his eyes in the same movement: '. . . want you out.'

It had never occurred to either that anyone could remove them from the only home they had ever known. He regarded them bleakly.

'What will they do?' asked James. 'The Board.'

'We want to stay together,' said Agnes.

Their uncle clenched his hands again, so tightly this time that his knuckles seemed likely to burst through the drawn skin. 'I really don't know,' he said. Agnes thought that she had never met anyone who did not know so many things. 'We will tell them,' she said. She listened. A motor car was stopping outside. 'Here they are,' she said. She leaned towards her brother. 'Let's run. Let's make a dash for it.' The words came from the picture captions at the Bioscope.

Uncle Eustace surveyed them miserably, as if he wished they would. But there was no time. Mrs Colbourn was at the street entrance and fussily directing the visitors up the stairs. Her dog was barking. Eustace went to the door. It was a man and a woman, the woman looking severe, the man ill at ease. She had a dark hat, a black lace blouse and long sombre skirt; her face, embellished with a trace of moustache, was set in a frown. The man was round and pink; he had a winged collar and a watch-chain which he stroked nervously.

'You will be accompanying us,' said the woman. 'Since your mother made no provision for you.' She glanced scathingly at their uncle. 'And your relatives appear unable to look after you.'

'We can look after ourselves,' said James. 'We often have.'

The man laughed tentatively. 'But you need money to live,' he said. 'To pay rent and for food.'

'I am fourteen,' said James. 'I was fourteen yesterday. I can go out to work. We don't have to live *here*.' Agnes was watching him admiringly but the woman said: 'That may be in the future. But for the moment you must come with us.'

'We want to stay together,' said James. Agnes was beginning to cry. Tears bounced from her cheeks to her small hands as she nodded.

'It will be arranged,' said the Board man. He looked miserable. 'If it is possible.'

'There are girls' schools and there are boys' schools,' corrected the Board woman. 'You must get some clothes together and anything you want to take with you. But not too much. Only the things you can carry.'

'I'm off!' exclaimed Agnes. 'Come on, James!'

She made a rush for the door and the stairs. James went after her, whether to stop her or to join her he did not know. She reached the first landing, then, looking back, tripped and fell down the next flight. She was not hurt. She had often tobogganed down on a tin tray. Now, at the bottom, she rolled against the door. Mrs Colbourn and her Scottie came out and, weeping vigorously, their neighbour picked the girl up. 'All right,' said Agnes, unhurt and mounting the stairs stoically. 'I'll come. But I'm not *staying* anywhere, not without James.'

The two people from the Board had watched the performance with amazement. Uncle Eustace had covered his face and was now peering over the crest of his hands. 'I'll go to London,' announced Agnes when she had regained the top landing. 'I'll become a fancy woman.'

Vera's funeral was men only. James just qualified. He stood beside the grave, sore eyed, alongside his uncle and Mr Whistler from the middle floor who had scarcely spoken to their mother when she was alive but who now muttered incantations over her coffin. When he was taken to the big, stale, Victorian house in Winchester where they had been temporarily sent, Agnes met him in the threadbare hall. 'What was it like?'

'I don't know,' James answered. 'I've never been to one before. Mr Whistler from downstairs was there.'

Agnes said: 'Him! Why was *he* there when I wasn't allowed?'

'It was just for men. No women.'

'Only our mum,' she said glumly. She seemed to have something more pressing to tell him. 'They're going to send me to this girls' place,' she said. She was angry more than sad. 'And you're going somewhere else. Shall we run now?'

He held her forearms. 'Not now,' he said. 'I've thought it all out.'

Hope and confidence flooded her eyes. 'What have you thought?'

'Let them take us where they want,' he said. 'Just for the time being. Then we'll do something.'

Her expression clouded. 'What?'

'I'll get a job. I'm old enough. And we'll find a room together.'

'And not tell anybody where we are.' She cheered a little.

'Nobody.'

'We used to play living together, didn't we,' she said. She looked directly at him. 'Don't forget, will you.'

'I won't.'

'And don't lose me, James. I don't want you to lose me.'

'I won't,' he promised. He put his hands around her fair hair and kissed her forehead. 'I'll come and find you.'

In the end they had taken very little from their former home for neither could think of much they wanted; only the clothes they needed and the draughts in their wooden box. 'We won't be able to play now,' said Agnes on the day they were to be parted. 'Who's going to look after them?'

'You had better,' he said. Then, with some bravado: 'I may end up going to the war.'

She was shocked. 'But they're getting *killed*. Hundreds and hundreds. And you're only fourteen.'

'We don't know how long it's going on.'

The Board people came into the room. Agnes was very pale. She stood close against her brother's side. 'We have been very fortunate,' said the man who was the kindlier of the two. The woman seemed to have had more experience.

'James, you have been accepted for a place at the Thorncliffe Army School,' said the man. Agnes's face hardened. 'I told you so. You'll be killed, James, wiped out.'

He put his hand on her forearm. The man smiled just a little and said: 'It is only a school. The boys have lessons and are taught the basics of military training. It has produced several officers.'

Agnes appeared to be going to say something further but she was swiftly interrupted by the woman. 'And you, Agnes, are going to the Inverness Girls' Institute.'

'Inverness,' said Agnes. 'That's in Scotland.'

'It is.'

'Where's Thorncliffe?' asked James.

'In Kent. Near Dover,' said the man.

Agnes let out a howl and advanced truculently on the pair. James put his arms around her, half protection, half restraint. 'Agnes will be in Scotland and I'm right the other end of England,' he said.

'We've seen each other every day since I was born,' said Agnes savagely.

The man quietly forestalled the woman adding anything: 'But these are the best places for you that are available. Perhaps later things may change and you can be nearer.' They watched him intently now as if he were to be trusted. 'You must make sure you keep in touch.'

'Writing paper and envelopes will be available,' said the woman.

'What about stamps?' asked Agnes.

'Children get pocket money.'

'How much?'

'I really don't know,' sighed the woman.

James put his arm around his sister's waist. Her dress felt flimsy. 'It will be all right, Agnes,' he said. 'It won't be long.'

'Time flies,' said the man a little hopelessly. 'You'd be surprised.'

Abruptly they realised that this was the moment of parting. They stood close to each other. The woman rose first and took Agnes by the hand. She was gentler now. Agnes seemed to have surrendered. 'We must be on our way,' said the woman. 'It is a long journey.'

Agnes turned to James and buried her face silently in his shirt. He put his arms about her. They were both dry eyed now. The woman touched both of them and they parted. 'Don't forget the draughts,' said James.

They did not see each other for two years.

The man from the Board went with James on the train. It was a broken journey across country from Southampton and once they were seated in the carriage the man, curiously, since he had just been present during the most private and emotional moments of James's life, coughed and introduced himself. 'I should have mentioned it before,' he said, 'but my name is Harold Brilling. I'm known as Vice-Admiral Brilling, retired unfortunately, but you need not bother about that. Just call me Mr Brilling.'

Sitting opposite each other they solemnly shook hands. Their journey took them to Portsmouth, then in slow stages to Brighton, and from there into Kent and eventually back towards the Channel coast. They said very little on the way. When they changed at Brighton, and Mr Brilling bought some sandwiches, he told James that his own son had been lost at sea only a month before. 'He was nineteen,' he said. 'I was in the navy for forty years and came through without a scratch. Before this war there has not been any action at sea for a long time, you know. Sailors had to fight on land in the Boer War.'

As they approached Dover on the last stage of the journey he said: 'I wish it could have been a naval school but they're full up until the next consignment go off to sea. You are a good type of lad. It might have suited you.'

It was dark by that time. They had to take an omnibus and then walk half a mile. At the gate of the Thorncliffe Army School were two sentries, both small and about fourteen, who had difficulty in shouldering their rifles. A sergeant appeared, a man with a scar on his face and a limp, and escorted them to the front of the building. It loomed over James, its windows dimly lit. It had a tower at its centre. They went into the hall and the bleakness of the place closed about him. A big staircase, its walls lined with shields and crests and crowded, faded photographs, diminished into the tower. Agnes must still be on her journey.

'Hungry, lad?' asked the sergeant.

'I expect he is,' answered Mr Brilling. 'We haven't had much today.'

'In time for mess. Just,' said the sergeant.

'I must be off,' said Mr Brilling. He and James solemnly shook hands again. The man handed him a card. 'Please write and tell me how you are getting on. I would like to keep in touch.'

'Yes, I will,' said James.

'Sir,' said the sergeant sharply. 'Say "Sir" to the gentleman, lad.'

Mr Brilling smiled and put his hand up in protest but

James said: 'Yes, sir,' took the card and put it in his pocket. He felt as though he were parting from his only visible friend.

The sergeant appeared impressed and jumped to attention as Mr Brilling went out into the darkness. 'Fine gentleman,' he said to James. 'Good army type.'

'Vice-Admiral,' said James. The man merely said: 'Mess. Come on, lad. There'll be none left.'

He ushered him in through some khaki-painted doors and immediately into a huge and desolate room with long tables lined with boys in army shirts. Their noise and activity stopped at once as James entered. Two hundred pairs of eyes fixed on him. 'At the end, front rank,' said the sergeant pointing to a vacant place at the extreme of the first wooden table. A metal mug was already in position, and a woman in a big, splashed apron came and filled it with tea. James, watching the boys around him, sat down carefully. He picked up the mug and drank. The milk and sugar were already in the tea. The woman returned and put a plate in front of him, on which sat three thick slices of bread smeared with beef dripping. The boys around the table stared at it like runners-up at a prize-giving. Others slowly stood and gathered around. 'Why's 'e got extra rations, sarge?' asked a boy with ginger freckles.

'Three slices,' said another.

James looked guiltily at the bread and dripping. 'We only get two,' the boy sitting next to James confided. 'Unless it's our birthday. Then we get three.'

'And an egg,' said a cross-eyed boy.

'Well, it's not your birthday, Prosser,' said the sergeant sharply. 'This recruit has been travelling. You've stuffed yourselves. Now dismiss!'

The crowd broke up. Grumbling as they went they began to disperse from the mess hall. They wore rough and ill-fitting trousers with their khaki shirts; they looked like small soldiers. 'Dush day tomorrer,' announced Prosser. ''Ow old are you?'

'Fourteen,' said James. It was the first word he had spoken.

The boy wiped his nose with the back of his hand. He glanced towards the sergeant but the man was talking to the woman in the apron. 'You'll get tuppence,' forecast the boy. 'Over fourteen you get tuppence.'

James continued to eat his way through the bread and dripping. Prosser watched every mouthful intently. After two slices James nodded at the one remaining. Before he could say anything the other boy was cramming it into his mouth. He brushed the crumbs from the table and put them in too. He had swallowed the lot before the sergeant returned. 'Bring your kit,' said the man to James.

'There's a bed next to mine,' said Prosser. 'In 3-BB.'

'All right, you take him,' said the sergeant. 'And no pinching stuff from him just because he's new.'

James followed the boy up the back staircase. 'It's a good barrack room, this is,' said Prosser. 'And my bed's at the end. You can't smell the ones what piss their pits.'

'What's your name?' asked James. 'Mine's Bevan.' He decided not to call himself James. 'Jim Bevan.'

'Any good at football?'

'Not much.'

'Nor me 'cause of my eyes not being straight. They reckon I'll never be a sniper.'

The dormitory was long and bleak, its windows high against the ceiling, its brick walls painted dark green. There were two ranks of beds, one against each of the side walls. Army kit was arranged on metal lockers beside each bed. The boys were stripping to vests and sagging drawers. 'Lights out at twenty-one thirty,' said Prosser. The other boys stared across at James but they were hurrying. 'You're on a charge if you're not in your charpoy,' called one. James wearily got undressed.

'What's your charpoy?' he said to Prosser.

'Yer pit, yer bed.' He banged his mattress. 'This.'

James kept his shirt on and climbed between the bedclothes. There was only a bottom sheet and two blankets. He lay trying to get warm. A bugle sounded and all the lights went out. He lay crushed and deeply sad, wondering about Agnes. There were no sounds other than breathing. Then he heard a distant but distinct rumble. 'What's that?' he whispered across to Prosser.

'The guns,' whispered the other boy. 'The guns across in France.'

6

Captain Bevan, sitting in his office at the beginning of another domestic April day at the camp, still, like most of the population, service and civilian, only knew of the war from the newspapers and the wireless. From London came the encouragement that the Prime Minister and the War Cabinet were highly confident of victory. But the news from Norway was worse, much worse; everywhere the invading Germans and their shrieking Stuka dive-bombers were winning battles. British forces landed and found themselves foolishly marooned on islands without boats to reach the mainland. French Alpine troops arrived but the straps to their skis were still stored in Chamonix. Although the BBC now frequently played records of the music of Edvard Grieg, Norway remained remote, a country of snows and mountains and frozen fjords where few people had been.

The telephone rattled. Its jangle had recently been reduced to a choke but due to what were called wartime pressures, they would have to wait a week for a Royal Signals Engineer. Bevan picked up the earpiece from its pedestal and spoke into the bell-shaped mouthpiece. Through the open door he could see the resting Bofors gun. He listened grimly, but with an abrupt sense of excitement. They were going to do something.

He called Runciman. 'Anything up, sir?' Bevan motioned him to close the door.

'We're going to see some action, sergeant.'

'Oh, God,' said Runciman. '*This* lot.'

Bevan understood. But there were going to be many lots like this. They were going to have to learn to be soldiers the only way. By fighting. His heart fell when he thought of Ugson.

He briefed Runciman and the sergeant said: 'Right, sir, I'd better stir them up.' He almost flung open the door and marched off with a new intensity. Bevan felt glad he was around.

Runciman stamped into the orderly room where Hignet slightly lowered his newspaper.

'This traitor chap, this Norwegian called Quisling, Vidkun Quisling . . .' said Hignet. 'There are some interesting letters in *The Times*. See this one: "How many other famous or notorious people, or characters, are there with names beginning with a Q?"'

Runciman stood stiffly, his eyes hardening. But Hignet had gone behind the paper again. 'Quasimodo,' he read. 'Not the hunchback necessarily but Quasimodo, the Italian poet. Then there's Quiller-Couch, our writer, and I suppose you could include . . .'

'Queen Vic . . . sodding . . . toria!' bellowed Runciman.

Hignet came from the other side of the paper. 'Sergeant . . . ?'

Runciman was standing like iron, his hands clenched to his sides. 'I said Queen . . .'

Hignet finished it: 'Vic . . . sodding . . . toria.' He studied Runciman. 'You're upset, sergeant.'

'Upset! I'm not upset, Bombardier. I am de . . . bloody . . . lighted! *We* are going into action, Hignet. Action!' Then, in case Hignet would not guess, he added: 'Against the *Germans*.'

Hignet placed the newspaper on the desk and, pale now, rose: 'We are, sergeant?'

'*You* are, Hignet.'

'Oh, God. When? Where?'

'Where the High Command decrees. When? *Now*, Hignet, *now*.'

'All of us?'

'One gun crew. Ten men.'

'That many?' He looked around the harmless wooden hut. 'But I have to be here, sergeant. I look after the orderly room . . . the nerve centre. Nobody else can do this job.'

'We'll be asking for volunteers,' said Runciman. 'And *you're* going to be one of them, Hignet. We'll try and get *The Times* delivered to the battle front.'

Sharply he turned and stumped outside. The twenty-eight men of the troop were already falling in on the square in front of the two Bofors. 'Something's up,' whispered Bairnsfather. 'And it's not the rates of pay.'

Runciman snapped them to attention. He performed a short, stiff march along the ranks. 'Right, lads, we're going into action.'

There was a clatter in the back rank. 'Ugly's fainted,' said Cartwright. Runciman strode to the rear of the squad. 'Pick him up,' he grunted. Ugson was on his knees but rising. 'Haven't been well, sarge,' he said.

'Report sick then.'

'No, I'll be all right.'

'I want *fighting* men, Ugson. Does that include you?' There was a silence. Then Ugson said: 'I 'spose, sarge.'

'I want ten volunteers,' said Runciman returning to the front of the squad. 'You, you, you and you.' He continued to point. 'One pace forward, volunteers. March!'

'Brave lads.' Runciman displayed a chilled smile. 'Bairnsfather, Brown, Cartwright, Ugson . . . and you, Purcell . . . and even Bombardier Hignet.' He repeated the names as though memorising them. 'Report to

Barrack Hut A after you're dismissed.' He paused and then said cheerily: 'Then you can go on embarkation leave.' Uncertain smiles lit the faces of the soldiers. Others, not selected, grimaced as though they had been tricked. But some did not want to go, wherever it was. 'Twelve hours' leave,' said the sergeant. The smiles dropped.

He dismissed the parade. 'You coming, sarge?' asked Brown. They were heading for the huts.

Runciman halted as if amazed. 'Me? Coming? Of course I'm coming, lad. I wouldn't miss this for the world!'

'A chance to hit the Hun where it hurts most,' recited Bairnsfather woodenly.

Quietly Cartwright said to him: 'Which one am I going to spend my leave with?'

'Five hours each one,' suggested Bairnsfather. 'Couple of hours between to get your breath back. I was taking Molly to the pictures tonight. The film's called *Tomorrow We Die*.'

They went into the huts and sat on the beds until Bevan appeared. Runciman called them to attention. Bevan said: 'Stand easy.' They sat down again. He perched on the end of Ugson's bed like an uncle telling a bedtime story.

'Well done, chaps,' said Bevan. 'This is going to be interesting.' He dropped his voice as though he feared someone might be listening outside the hut. Runciman went to the door, opened it, scanned the surroundings, and closed it again.

Bevan said: 'I'll put you in the picture as far as I can. We are taking one of the guns – gun B, don't you think, sergeant?'

'It's easier to move,' nodded the sergeant. 'The other one's rusted in.' He glanced apprehensively at Bevan. 'In a way of joking, sir.'

'Right, gun B, it is,' decided Bevan. 'We move off at six hundred hours tomorrow. Breakfast at four thirty. Twelve hours' disembarkation leave from twelve hundred today.'

'Can we know where we're going, sir?' asked Cartwright.

Bevan glanced at Runciman. 'At the moment it's supposed to be a secret, although it's not difficult to guess,' he said. 'If any of you have skis then maybe you ought to bring them.'

'South of France,' sighed Ugson. 'I knew it.'

By now the weather had dulled and chilled to that of a normal English spring. It began to rain as Bairnsfather got off the bus and walked towards the Southampton public library. Molly was rearranging the top row of a shelf when he found her. Her legs looked shapely on the ladder. She looked down at him with alarm. 'They're sending you somewhere,' she said. Slowly, her face never leaving his, she descended the steps.

He grinned and, sharply looking in both directions along the bookshelves first, kissed her. 'You ought to be a spy,' he said.

'Where are they sending you? When is it?'

'They haven't let us in on that,' he said. 'I could have a good guess but I won't in here. Books have ears. I've got twelve hours' leave. Got to be back at midnight.'

She folded the ladder adroitly and while he was holding his hands out to help carried it to a corner. 'I'll get the afternoon off,' she said. 'They owe me some time.' She made a quick mental decision. 'Wait outside for me by the bus-stop. I'll only be a couple of minutes.'

He went out again and sheltered from the rain under the concrete plinth of a surface air-raid shelter, a piece of everyday wartime street furniture, built like a brick blockhouse, its doorway awash with rubbish, its walls scrawled in chalk and with a smell like a rotten pond coming from within. He saw her come down the steps from the library and peer along the road. She hurried towards him.

'Do you want to go the pictures now instead of tonight?' he asked.

She regarded him oddly. 'If you want to. On the other hand, nobody is at home. Dad's at work, Mum's gone to see my auntie in Winchester, my sister has taken her kids to London, and that little swine Ronnie's at school.'

They got on the bus and sat close against each other on the top deck.

'I'm going to start at the Voluntary Aid nursing place tomorrow,' she said. 'That will help me take my mind off you being away.'

'If I come back shot up you can nurse me better,' said Bairnsfather.

'I said I was just starting.' She squeezed his arm. 'Anyway, don't joke about it.'

They reached her front door.

'Have you had anything to eat?' she said as she unlocked it.

'Plenty,' said Bairnsfather. 'Big breakfast.'

'We'll have some fruit cake later,' shc said. She kissed him deeply when they were in the hallway. 'My mum's just made one.'

Then they hcard a voice. He glanced at her and she swore quietly. 'If that Ronnie is playing hookey . . .' she threatened. She went the few paces along the passageway and opened the door. 'It's all right,' she said. 'Somebody left the wireless on.'

He walked in behind her and put his arms around her waist from the back. The news was on. 'Where are you going?' she whispered. 'I won't say a word.'

'Captain Bevan says skiers might be useful.'

'Norway,' she sighed. 'It's all bad news from there. Be careful, Harry, won't you.'

'I'll dig an igloo.'

They looked into each other's decent faces and kissed again. 'Come upstairs,' she said. 'For once we'll be cosy.' She turned and went back towards the front door. 'I'll put the latch down.'

In the bedroom she drew the curtains, diminishing the grey afternoon light. Her mother and father's room had an odd air of disuse, like a place kept for special purposes, everything neatly in place: the alarm clock, the cough-mixture bottle, a prayer-book.

'I didn't realise your mum was one for praying,' said Bairnsfather. Casually she was starting to take her clothes off on the opposite side of the bed. He unfastened and unbuttoned his battledress blouse. 'It's Dad's,' she said. 'He reads a prayer every night.'

'Your dad? And I thought he was just conscientious.'

'He prays just to annoy Mum. He reads aloud every night. "Oh God, bless this woman" and that sort of nonsense. She doesn't take any notice.'

They were talking to cover their mutual shyness. It was the first time they had undressed in front of each other in daylight. 'At least we don't need the torch,' she said. She freed her breasts, pale and soft and shapely. He went across the bed on his stomach like a trained soldier and eased her down on to the quilt. 'Let's take this bedcover off,' she whispered as he petted her. 'She'll know.'

He slid from the bed and she took the pink quilt and folded it with care alongside the dressing-table. She was still wearing her skirt. He tried to undo the clasp at the side for her, but fumbled and she did it. Her half-petticoat went down with it. 'Sorry about the stockings,' she said. 'I've got a ladder at the top. I'll use them for when I'm doing this emergency nursing. You have to climb into the bomb craters and that.'

His eyes remained lovingly on her. She pulled her stockings away and stood, suddenly awkward as a young girl, naked, apart from her wrist-watch. 'Fold your trousers,' she advised pointing at them but keeping her eyes on his face. 'You can't go off to war all creased.' He thought she was going to cry. He pulled the bedclothes back and they rolled into the bed holding each other.

'I don't want you to go, Harry,' she whispered.

'I'm not that keen myself,' he said but still lightly. 'It won't be long. By the look of things we'll be in and out of Norway in no time.' Suddenly it occurred to him why they were being sent.

She was in his arms and wanting him. For a girl who worked in a library she was passionate. They moved below the bedclothes, now at ease with each other. When they had finished Bairnsfather said: 'At this rate we're going to have a baby.'

'Darling,' she said. 'I don't care.'

They were lying, resting, 'What if . . .' he began. 'Well, there *is* a war on. And they're just sending me off to it.'

'I'd still have the baby,' she said. They laughed quietly.

'She'll know we've been in here,' she said sliding from the bed. 'She's got a nose like a ferret.' She picked up her petticoat and began waving it around.

'I'll open the window,' said Bairnsfather. They got dressed, straightened the bed and went downstairs.

'Thank God that Ronnie didn't come home,' said Molly. 'Dad says it's a shame he's not in the army.' She went into the kitchen to put the kettle on the gas. He followed her. 'He's twelve,' said Bairnsfather only half joking: 'He might be in before it's finished.'

She looked concerned. 'You think so? It's not going to go on that long, is it?'

'It might be finished quicker than we think,' he said.
'With us the losers.'

'Well, we're not winning. Norway's the first time we've had a chance to fight the Germans properly and they've bloody near walloped us. It looks like they're the better team.'

Her face deeply sad she put her arms about his neck. 'I'm scared of what might happen to you,' she said.

He kissed her and attempted reassurance. 'I reckon we're going to get the others out,' he said. 'We're going to evacuate them. Otherwise there wouldn't be any point in sending us. It's a lost ruddy cause.'

She poured the tea, handed him a cup and made to cut him a slice of fruit cake. 'Light the fire, will you, Harry,' she said. 'Mum will be in soon.'

It was already laid; it was like a small altar to the room, the carefully screwed-up newspaper, the bare chopped sticks, the pieces of coal placed above them and another shovelful ready to be put on the flames as soon as they took hold. Smoke would go in a steady spiral up the chimney and join that rising from other chimney-pots in the street, signals ascending one after the other to show that people had come home.

Bairnsfather took the box of matches from beside the brass fender and lit the paper in three places. It was the *Daily Mirror* and he was able to see the crumpled drawing of the half-naked 'Jane' in the cartoon. The brown edge of the flame moved over it. He thought himself lucky. Girls like Molly did not sleep with anyone unless it was serious. There were plenty that did, but not girls like her.

'Come and sit on the settee,' Molly said. 'We may not be doing this for a bit.'

He sat against her and they cuddled before the growing blaze of the fire in the small grate, the flames reflecting on both faces. 'I couldn't stand it without a fire,' she said. 'I think I'd rather starve than be cold.' She regarded him anxiously. 'You will wrap up in Norway, won't you.'

He grinned. 'I don't even know I'm going to Norway yet. It's only a guess. I can't think of anywhere else they'd send us. They wouldn't be in such a rush to post us to France because there's nothing happening there. They've even sent some French troops to Norway.' He glanced at her warningly. 'Anyway, don't mention it, will you. Especially not to your father.'

'It would be all over Southampton in a couple of hours,' she nodded. There was a sound from the door. 'Here's Mum now. My auntie and her run out of gossip by four o'clock.'

Her mother, red and round and flustered, came along the passage. She looked a little shocked to see Bairnsfather. 'You haven't run off from the army, have you, Harry?' She got out of her coat and her daughter took it from her.

'Wish I could,' he laughed.

'He's going away, abroad,' said Molly.

Her mother went up the stairs. They sat and waited guiltily for her return. Then Molly called up to her: 'Cup of tea, Mum?'

'Yes, that would be nice.' She came downstairs. 'Funny smell up there,' she mentioned. 'The window's open. And I forgot to pull back the curtains this morning. Fancy me doing that.'

It was evening before Bevan could get away from the camp. His temporary replacement, a young lieutenant called Chance who had bright and startled eyes behind rimless spectacles, had just arrived. Bevan wondered how anyone with eyesight deficiency could be a gunnery officer. He and Renée walked along the chilly shore.

The sea and the air were grey, a low and solitary gull sounded. 'I've been posted,' Bevan said.

'You sound like a letter,' she laughed. 'Posted.' Then she realised. 'Oh, Bevan, they're sending you away?' She caught his arm. 'Where is this?'

'Don't know,' he said. 'I can guess but I won't bother you with it. I don't think I'll be gone long.'

She walked silently beside him looking down at the sandy grass. The bird still cried like a solitary warning over the sea. 'I, too, may be posted,' she said.

'Oh?'

'I must be going away. Not yet, but perhaps not too long, either. There is talk of taking the school out of this area, perhaps to the north of Wales. Tonight some people are coming to look at us. We are on our good behaviour. The boys are going to sing for them. They will decide whether they can give us a big building. Mr MacFarlane and the governors think that it will soon become dangerous down here.'

'That's possible,' said Bevan. He realised with a falling heart what she was trying to say. 'So you'll be going with the boys.'

'This is so,' she said soberly. She turned against him and hugged him to her. His arm went around her back as though to give her support. She kissed him on the cheek. 'I have to be with them,' she said. 'At least until they are settled in their new place.'

'And then?'

'I cannot think. But I will probably join in the war, somehow.'

'You're in the war already.'

'I know. We all are. But maybe I will do something else closer to the war. I don't know.' She was saying goodbye.

* * *

The fire had settled to a mumble in the grate; the room was homely within the cosy safety of its blackout curtains which seemed to keep danger out as well as light in. Molly's mother had spread the table with the food she had intended for the following Sunday tea: set symbolically at the centre were a big pork pie, round as a millstone, and a piece of ham, surrounded by salmon and shrimp-paste sandwiches, and tinned pineapple chunks. Now they were finishing with tea and chocolate cake.

'Have you ever wondered what these blokes who grow beards will do with them in the event of a gas attack?' said Molly's father as though it had occupied his mind all day.

Ronnie, taking a piece of cake from near his mouth and replacing it temporarily on his plate, said: 'Shave 'em off quick, I s'pose.'

'Very funny,' said Mr Warner. He grimaced at his son.

'I thought it was,' said his wife.

'What do they do then?' asked Molly anxious to get the matter out of the way. She was only grateful that her sister and the small children were not around the table. Mr Warner drained his teacup noisily. 'Them Jews and Sikhs,' he said eventually. 'They *can't* shave them off. They're not allowed.' He looked around triumphantly. 'They have to *fold* them.'

Bairnsfather, like an outsider, was looking from one to the other. Ronnie had returned the piece of mashed cake to his mouth. 'Neatly,' he said with his cheeks swollen.

'They do, actually,' reluctantly conceded his father. 'Fold them neat and tight. Then they can tuck them into their gas masks.'

'A big beard could smother you,' mentioned Ronnie. 'Worse than gas.'

His father consulted his watch and announced: 'Time for our practice.'

'No. No, you don't,' said Molly. 'We're not having that peformance tonight, Dad. Sorry, but Harry is going overseas.'

'All the more reason to test his respirator,' argued Mr Warner looking towards the khaki pack with something like envy. 'Hitler's bound to use gas soon.'

'*Not* tonight. No practice tonight,' said his wife as firmly as his daughter.

'Well, I'm going to,' said her husband testily finishing his cake crumbs. 'When you're all swollen and yellow, who'll have the last laugh then?'

He went from the room and they sat grinning around the table. They had some more chocolate cake and tea. After five minutes Mr Warner returned wearing his gas mask. Almost ceremoniously, with a certain high-minded defiance, he took it off in front of them. Around his face was a ring of purple dye. Ronnie looked as if he had suddenly remembered something and quickly left the table muttering about his homework. The others remained straight faced until Molly could stand it no longer. Pointing to her father's stained face she described an oval with her finger. 'You seem . . . Dad, you've got some sort of . . . dye . . .' She and her mother collapsed laughing. Bairnsfather clenched his teeth. Mr Warner put his hand to his forehead and strode to the mirror over the fireplace. 'I'll kill that little swine,' he sobbed beginning to wipe it off with a paper doily from the table. 'I'll swing for him.'

Bairnsfather got the last bus back to camp and he was there at ten thirty. Molly had walked to the stop with him and they had stood unspeaking and holding on to each other. As the bus, with its yellow slatted lights, came like a cat along the street, he kissed her finally. She tried not to cry. 'Look after yourself, love,' she said. 'And remember to wrap up.'

He got on to the bus and stood on the platform to blow her a kiss while it moved away.

He sat moodily on the journey back thinking what a bastard it was that now, of all times, he was going to have to go to the real war.

At the camp the sentry said: 'They've hooked up the gun.' Through the shadows he could see it attached to the back of its truck. 'Good luck, mate,' said the sentry. 'You'll probably come back all right.'

'Thanks,' muttered Bairnsfather. He went into the hut. He had already assembled his equipment – his field-service marching order, packs and ammunition pouches, his bayonet in its scabbard and his steel helmet – and now it all waited at the bottom of his bed. He added his gas mask to the pile. The others had prepared their encumbrances also. Before first light they would draw their rifles and ammunition from the armoury.

Cartwright stirred in the next bed. 'I've had a sod of a time,' he said.

'Making up your mind which one?'

'Wasn't a case of that. *Neither* of them was in. I went all the way on the train to Bristol and the wife was out – I thought I ought to go and see her first – and then the other one was too.'

'So you had to come back again.'

'Right. All I had tonight was a pie and a cuppa on Temple Meads station. There was a bloody RAF dance on. I bet that's where they'd gone, the pair of 'em. Sodding women.'

Ugson said from his bed: 'It's Egypt.'

Bairnsfather looked across. 'Egypt? Blimey, Ugly, what makes you think that?'

‘I met this bloke in the pub who’s got contacts with ’igh-ups in intelligence. He says we’re going to Egypt because they’re afraid Mussolini is going to come into the war, pull a fast one, and get the Suez Canal.’

‘Least we’ll get some sun,’ said Cartwright.

Ugson eased himself up in his bed, pleased to have an audience. ‘We won’t even have to go by sea. They’ll take us across to France and put us on the train to the south somewhere and then through the Med. That won’t be too bad, will it?’

They agreed it would not be bad at all. Bairnsfather rolled tiredly into his bed. It seemed only minutes later when Runciman came through the door to rouse them. ‘You’ve got to study these,’ he said. He flung around some small books.

‘Prayer-books,’ guessed Ugson before he had caught his. It was a Norwegian phrase book.

‘Lot of bloody good these are going to be,’ said Bairnsfather. ‘In Egypt.’

The Bofors they were leaving behind looked oddly bereft, its neck sticking out in the early light like a solitary swan. Bevan was going in the car with Bairnsfather, and the other men were travelling with Runciman in the truck which carried the ammunition and towed the gun. In the early hours a signal had been received cutting the party to eight men with one NCO and an officer. Shipping space would be tight. As they paraded, Hignet had been summoned to the orderly room by the insistently ringing telephone; in his prolonged absence they had decided to leave him. When he reappeared the party had already gone leaving Gunner Brown with his kit beside the remaining gun.

‘They’ve dumped us,’ said Brown trying to look sorry. ‘Two had to stand down.’

Relief flew over Hignet's face. He dropped his kit heavily and said: 'I was so looking forward to it.'

Bevan had made sure the men were loaded. Runciman had checked the gun and its coupling to the lorry. The roofs of the huts were clear against the pale sky by the time they drove away and the windows of Southerly had an opaque gaze, like the eyes of a blind man. Josef came out on his exterior stairway and waved them a single goodbye. It was almost as if they were leaving home.

Bairnsfather automatically turned the boxy military car towards Southampton. 'Docks road, sir?' he asked.

'Felixstowe docks,' said Bevan.

Bairnsfather almost stalled the engine. 'Felixstowe? . . . Christ . . . I mean, blimey, sir, I don't know where it is.'

'East coast,' said Bevan. 'Winchester, Basingstoke, Newbury, North Circular Road, out into Essex.'

Bairnsfather cheered. 'Ah well, that's a change,' he said. 'North Circular Road. Always wanted to go on that. Soon shoot around London that way.' They were travelling across the dawning forest. Cuticles of smoke were drifting from cottage chimneys. Two upright ladies on horseback approached the road like shadows from the trees and Bairnsfather pulled up to allow them to cross the road. They heard the lorry brake heavily behind.

'It's only manners,' said Bairnsfather.

Bevan grinned. 'I wouldn't do it too often. You could cause more damage than the Germans.'

He sensed Bairnsfather's anxious reaction. 'Do you reckon we'll be for it, sir?' he asked as the car moved forward again. 'Right in it?'

'We're not going to exchange compliments with them,' said Bevan. 'But nobody's told me what the plan is.'

'It's evacuation, I expect, sir.'

Bevan nodded. 'I imagine so. There doesn't seem a lot of sense in sending more troops to Norway. It looks like a lost cause. Mind you, someone in the War Office might be thinking differently.'

'No idea, have they, sir,' said Bairnsfather. 'Winchester Bypass?'

Bevan said yes. The road was new, innovative as the North Circular, but wriggling through the countryside like a river.

The tower of Winchester Cathedral rose through distant, indistinct trees, the city lying in early mist around it. A peaceful bell sounded. There was little traffic: a few lorries coming from Southampton docks, a line of straggling military vehicles and once an army car which urgently overtook them, the driver giving them the comradely thumbs up. They passed an air-force transporter carrying a Spitfire in broken pieces, the propeller bent like petals. 'Somebody didn't stop in time,' said Bairnsfather. Later they passed two naval lorries at the side of the road. In the mirror Bairnsfather watched the sailors pointing and mocking the skinny Bofors.

'Bell-bottomed buggers,' he muttered.

Before they reached Basingstoke Bevan told him to pull in and the driver projected the long, pointed, orange indicator. Bevan got out and went briskly around to the truck.

'Everything all right, sergeant?' he called up over the tailboard.

'All present and correct, sir,' said Runciman. The faces of the men turned towards Bevan, pale in the shadowed interior. 'They want to know where we're going.'

'East coast.' He could tell them that much.

'My bum's gone dead,' complained one of the men quietly from the front of the truck. They were sitting on metal seats, their equipment piled about them.

Bevan glanced at the gun and then banged on the tailboard of the lorry before going back to the car.

Runciman had tried to get the soldiers to sing but they had said it was too early. Now the man who had complained about his bum began to do so and they all joined in. Wherever he was going the British soldier – Tommy Atkins as he was so patronisingly known – could always be relied upon to sing:

We don't know where we're going till we're there,
There's lots and lots of rumours in the air.

The song echoed from below the tarpaulin of the truck, across the main road and over the fields, villages and cottages of an England as peaceful then, for a while, as it had ever been.

Basingstoke, although it had a big railway station, remained much the crowded-roofed market town it had been since the Middle Ages. By steam train from Waterloo on the Southern Railway it was an hour and a quarter from London and the expresses to the south-west also called there. The lorry towing the flimsy-looking gun trailed the camouflaged staff car through the old streets, Bairnsfather seeking the main road to Newbury. People going to work stopped briefly to look at them and children in the playground of a school rushed to the railings as they went by. As they picked their way through the streets Bevan became convinced that they were lost. Suddenly they were in a street full of cows. 'We've found the cattle market, sir,' said Bairnsfather. He stopped, snorted and looked in the mirror. Behind them the lorry was besieged by jostling cows. Bevan cursed and opened his door, pushing a heifer's nose away. He could hear Runciman's voice bellowing above the voices of the animals. 'Bugger it,' muttered Bairnsfather. He slammed the door and they started forward again, the brown hot bodies of the animals bumping and bulging against the sides of the small mottled vehicle. They could hear the farmers and market men shouting and eventually a space opened in front. They pushed forward and waited for the truck to catch up. A man standing on the pavement, rustic faced, tapped on the window with a thick stave. 'Where d'you think you're going?' he asked Bairnsfather. He gave a glance at the officer but then returned to the driver.

'The war,' said Bairnsfather.

'You'll need to do better'n this or it'll be over afore you get there.'

They reached Newbury and turned on to the Great West Road towards London. The lorry, fully laden, could not achieve more than twenty-five miles an hour and Bairnsfather, at the wheel of the striving Ford, had to contain himself.

'This is the sort of road for a good spin,' he said. They were driving past cabbage fields, among which was an RAF aerodrome near the ancient village of Heath Row. 'And that North Circular.' He crouched against the wheel. 'I'd like to zoom along here in my baker's van.' Bevan smiled at his boyishness. 'They've got first-rate roads in Germany, those autobahns,' continued Bairnsfather. The Great West Road carried little traffic. The petrol ration was stringent. 'I'd like to give it a go on an autobahn.' He glanced uncertainly at the officer. 'After the war, of course. When I get a car one day.' He checked in his mirror as if urging the following lorry to hurry up.

When they reached Chiswick his eyes glowed at the large sign which read: 'North Circular Road. To the North and East.' He turned the clumsy car in the direction of the arrow with what he hoped was panache. 'If the war hadn't stopped it they'd have started on the South Circular by now,' he told Bevan. 'Just think, a whole road around London, sir. That would move things. You could just keep zooming in a big circle.'

Bevan was checking some papers. 'We take a break at Chingford, on the Essex side. They're going to feed us at the drill hall.'

There was still another hour and a half to go. They turned from the highway and into the verges of Epping Forest. Chingford's tidy suburban houses set along its ordered streets glimmered in the April day.

They saw the drill hall, square and school-like, its flag flying sturdily from the white mast in front of its parade ground. An officer in full uniform with Sam Browne belt and medals was awaiting them on the front step, accompanied by a motherly-looking woman, standing a pace back and carrying a tray of steaming mugs.

Bevan climbed from the car, replaced his cap, quickly straightened his uniform and saluted. The other officer returned the salute with such ferocity that the younger man thought he heard the crack of his back. 'Welcome, welcome,' enthused the man. He was beyond military age, upright and steel headed, with an alert face and bright eyes. 'I am Major Hartley, the adjutant.'

The gunners were tumbling stiffly from the following truck and Runciman called them to attention. Hartley saluted again, in response to Runciman, this time not so violently.

The men's eyes were on the diffidently smiling woman with the tray of coffee. 'Our personal NAAFI,' said the adjutant waving his hand as an introduction. 'Mrs Firebrace, the vicar's wife.'

They all acknowledged her and gladly relieved her of the mugs. 'Lunch is served when you are ready, boys,' she said.

'Never had *lunch*,' said Ugson to Cartwright. 'Nosh, yes.'

They trooped into the drill hall. A trestle table had been set out and was spread with sandwiches and sausage rolls, a ham bone and two huge currant cakes. 'The stuff to give the troops,' enthused Major Hartley. 'No use going to war on an empty stomach.'

'Can we please say grace,' suggested Mrs Firebrace. 'My husband asked me to. He's conducting a funeral.'

Bevan held up his hand and the soldiers, already reaching for the food, reluctantly withdrew theirs. 'Stand to attention for grace!' grunted Runciman.

'Att . . . ention!' His glance went along the lines each side of the table. 'Eyes closed, Gunner Cartwright.' Cartwright dutifully closed them.

There was an ornamental artillery piece at one end of the cavernous drill hall. 'Still in good order,' said Major Hartley to Bevan. 'But it's Indian Mutiny. We're trying to locate some ammunition. We may need to press it into service.'

'You think that may be necessary?'

The older man straightened his head. 'I'm *sure* it will, captain. When you've got a lot of nincompoops as service chiefs and cowards as a Government, what can you expect? Frankly I'd like to stage a *coup d'état*, and I'm not alone. Turf them out at gunpoint. You're heading for Norway, I take it.'

'That direction.'

'What a mess that is. An utter folly. Churchill, who everybody thinks is so wonderful, is as guilty as any of them. You'd have thought he of all people would have learned his lesson about landing the British soldier on a mud bank – like he did in the First War, the Dardanelles. But oh, no. It's the same old business, lions led by donkeys.' Suddenly he laughed. 'I'll be shot at dawn,' he said. He then regarded Bevan almost fiercely.

'But if something's not done soon, we'll be finished.' Bevan saw that his eyes were wet. 'This great country, finished.' Then he said: 'Come and have a look at our battle honours.'

The men were still finishing off their cake, hanging on until the last minute, so Bevan followed the adjutant towards a door arched by a pair of spears. 'I retired two years ago,' said Hartley. 'I came back as adjutant here when war broke out. Territorial Army, of course, but most of them have gone off to be regulars.'

Bevan indicated the spears: 'South African War?'

'Chelmsford Market probably,' said Hartley. He opened the door to another extensive room. It was set out like an unused library, with armchairs, sofas and tables, but around the walls were long lists of names in gold on dark wood. 'I almost know them by heart,' said the older man. 'I knew some of them in life.'

He led Bevan to the end of the room and switched on a light. '*That's* the South African War,' he said nodding at one of the long panels. 'There's one of our two Victorian Crosses, Sergeant Taylor at Spion Kop.'

Bevan looked down the names of the dead. Not for the first time he wondered if they would now feel it had been worthwhile. 'Great days,' said Hartley quietly. 'Great men, even if you do have to turn on a light in Chingford to know who they were.'

Bevan could hear Runciman ushering the men out to the truck. 'South Africa,' said the adjutant almost to himself. 'In those days, captain, wars were fought by professionals. Not by lads off the streets.'

Bevan was pleased to see that the gun crew were lined up in front of the Bofors. They looked quite military. Runciman called them to attention and saluted. Hartley returned it. 'My lads off the streets are likely to be under fire in a few hours,' Bevan said quietly. He saluted and shook hands with the adjutant. 'Let's see how they get on.'

Hartley remained at attention on the front steps and threw up another salute as they turned from the gate. He looked quaint and solitary. 'He does a lot of arm-up-and-down, doesn't he, sir,' said Bairnsfather. 'Saluting.'

Bevan smiled. 'He's keen to do something. Given half the chance, he would have come with us.'

Bairnsfather laughed: 'Funny to think that here we are, driving along in good old England, dead peaceful, and tomorrow or the next day we're likely to be right in it.'

'How are you getting on with your girlfriend?'

Bairnsfather seemed only briefly surprised. 'Oh, Molly. Fine, she's good. We'd get married, I reckon, if I asked her nicely. But you never know at the moment, do you.'

Bevan nodded. He wondered where Renée would go; *why* she was going. Women seemed to walk away from him.

They were now out into the Essex countryside. In Epping Forest they saw an encampment of gypsies below the trees and a horse and cart in front of them meant they had to slow down. A one-toothed gypsy woman suddenly appeared at Bevan's window, trotting beside the car. 'Want any clothes pegs?' she bawled through the glass. Politely Bevan wound down the window. 'No, thank you,' he said. Bairnsfather leaned towards her as if he could deal better with the situation. 'We've done our washing this week, love,' he said.

'Fortunes told,' tried the gypsy. 'I tell a good future.'

Bevan waved a gentle hand at her and Bairnsfather called: 'Not today.' They overtook the horse and cart. 'Not much cop having your fortune told today, sir.'

'Waste of money,' agreed Bevan.

Beyond the trees, the countryside became flat and long. Towers of churches could easily be seen miles away on the straight horizon. It had been like that in Flanders, Bevan recalled. Church towers were always the first to be bombarded; nobody ever volunteered to climb one as a gunnery observer. Essex became Suffolk; waterways like strips of metal under the spring sky, reeds and miles of bright green. Horses were working the fields and pulling carts in the towns and villages. The war had made them useful again. In one place they saw a knife grinder and a soot-faced chimney sweep on a bike, his brushes standing up like trees.

'Could have used that bloke sharpening knives,' said Runciman when they had halted by a copse and the soldiers were lined up, urinating together. Bevan and Runciman had gone around to the other side of the truck, although they each wondered why. 'Might have been useful for the bayonets.'

They reached Felixstowe at the beginning of the evening. The townspeople had become used to soldiers coming through their streets on the way to the docks and Norway, and they came out to wave and shout blessings and throw cigarettes, chocolate and apples. Girls appeared laughing, making suggestive calls, and blowing kisses. 'They reckon we're going to die,' said Cartwright. 'Like heroes.' Ugson, trying to catch a flying packet of Park Drive, was struck by a bag of apples.

At the dock gates a military policeman directed them around a long shed, on the far side of which was a scraggy merchant ship. 'That,' said Bevan, 'looks like it's for us.'

'Norway here we come,' muttered Bairnsfather.

The ship's name, barely visible on her bow, was *Mary Anne Davies*. 'How far is Norway, sir?' Purcell asked looking up at it.

'Couple of days and nights,' said Bevan. He could

see the rust along the rails. The lifeboats were full of junk. Ropes sagged. A casual-looking man leaned over, surveying them, and dropping the ash from his cigarette carefully over the side. 'I can't swim,' said Ugson.

'Swimming's no good,' Runciman said. 'It's freezing.'

'Better getting drownded,' sniffed Purcell.

A massive military police sergeant approached and threw up a heavy salute at Bevan. 'You can get your men aboard, sir. I hope the Bofors will be all right. These dockers here are a bolshie lot.'

'Let's get on the ship,' said Bevan. 'There's supposed to be a truck with extra ammunition.'

'Arrived ten minutes ago, sir. You'll have enough ammo to fight a whole war.'

He went to direct a staff car which had just driven on to the dock but he called back to Bevan: 'Not many going, sir. They need all the space for them that's coming back.'

From the military car came two army padres, one tall, one short, like a comedy act, their white dog-collars gaping, and a third officer a little apart. The policeman strode over and flung up his salute again. He returned to the gun crew as they were taking up their equipment and preparing to climb the steep and swaying gangway to the deck. Runciman was already negotiating it with the uncertainty of a novice scaling a mountain. 'I s'pose they send the padres to explain things,' said the policeman to Bevan. 'The other officer is an embalmer.'

'Thank you for letting me know,' said Bevan.

He led the rest of the men towards the gangway.

'Two at a time,' bawled the man who had been watching from the rail. He placed a scruffy braided cap on the front of his head. 'That gangway can't take more than two.' The voice was wildly Irish. He gave a huge suck on his cigarette, finally threw it into the dock and came towards them. Bevan waited at the top of the gangway. Four of his men, loaded with equipment, were attempting to back down on to the quay again.

'How can you fight the Boche, all piled up with stuff?' asked the Irishman mildly.

Bevan did not know. 'We can only try,' he said.

'I take it you're in charge of these boys. Well, I'm in charge of this ship and it's a lot older than any of them.' He extended a hard hand. 'Captain Moore.'

'I'm James Bevan.'

'Welcome aboard.' Bevan felt the whiff of whiskey from his breath. Bairnsfather, who was at the top of the gangway, sniffed.

Moore looked challengingly at officer and men as if anticipating a rude comment. When none came he half turned and blinked his lid over a dull glass eye.

The clerical group on the quay were assembling their suitcases. Moore's eye blinked. 'Jesus, but it's unlucky to have a man of God on board, d'you know, and I've got two, although one's a Catholic.' He studied the third arrival who was carrying what looked like a large medical bag. 'And who is he? A doctor, maybe?'

'An embalmer,' said Bevan quietly.

'Oh, shit and sugar,' said Moore in almost a whisper. 'What will they think of next?'

The three men were trudging up the gangplank. The Catholic was fat as well as short and puffed before he reached the top. Four dockers were on the quay staring without commitment at the Bofors. Their attention was caught by the exertions of the clergyman and they openly laughed at him. He made the sign of the cross towards them. 'I'll get my sergeant down there with those dockers,' said Bevan. 'I don't want them dropping the gun.'

'No, that would indeed fuck it,' said Captain Moore. 'And we might be needing the gun.'

Bevan waited until the three army officers were on deck and shook hands with them after the captain had done so. They moved off with a dwarfish man in a steward's coat to find their quarters. 'Did you feel his hand?' whispered Moore to Bevan. 'The embalmer fella. Terrible soft.'

Bevan nodded to Runciman who was already moving back towards the head of the gangway and followed him down on to the dockside. He approached the man who appeared to be the foreman of the stevedores. 'Good evening,' he said politely. 'We might be able to help you with that gun.'

'It's cargo,' said the man. The three others stood and nodded. 'Touch it and we walk out.'

Runciman glared at the men. 'Maybe up here they haven't heard there's a war on.'

'We've got jobs to think about,' said the foreman, less belligerently. 'Once the army comes in and tries to do the loading, we'll be on the dole.'

'You could always join the army,' suggested Runciman. Bevan eyed him and they turned away and mounted the gangplank again, each watching the gun over his shoulder. 'If it ends up in this dock I'm going to chuck those twerps in after it,' sniffed Runciman. 'Them and their jobs.'

Captain Moore had watched and was waiting for them. 'Don't upset the bastards,' he advised. 'They'll bring the whole port to a standstill.' He indicated that Bevan should follow him down a companionway. 'Come and have a jar before we sail,' he said. 'The Godly men are at their prayers.'

Bevan followed him through a pungent hatchway into a wooden cabin, tight as a box, hot and alcoholic. There was a long-dead plant in a pot and a photograph of a ship which might have been the *Mary Anne Davies* in better times. 'I was going to get the place cleaned up, you understand,' Moore said reaching for the whiskey bottle. 'And I thought this tropic bloom might come back to life.' He gave the dried leaves of the plant a flick. 'But events caught up with me.'

A small green, white and orange flag stood on a shelf behind his table which also served as a desk. It had raised edges and, as though they were on a rolling sea, he placed the two glasses firmly against the sides while he poured. 'It's just habit,' he said.

He saw Bevan's glance towards the flag. 'I'm a neutral,' he said swigging his whiskey in one swallow and pouring another. 'Coming from the Republic, I take more sides than this table's got.' He swallowed again, this time more thoughtfully. 'It's just I don't like this twister Hitler.'

Bevan laughed and raising his glass said: 'You're not alone.'

'I worry what he might do to holy Ireland.'

The porthole was open a fraction, letting in a shaft of decent evening air; the sound of voices came from the quay. 'Maybe they've dropped your gun after all,' said Moore. He went to the aperture but then held up a reassuring hand. 'No, no, fair play. It's my crew coming aboard, off the train. And there's Mr Stead, the mate, arriving in his little car.' He waited as though watching a drama unfold. 'His wifc is driving him and thcy'rc having a kiss. He keeps sober and he's a good navigator. Good at getting around corners, you understand. He's got a memory for rocks and suchlike.'

Bevan finished his drink. 'I'll see that my chaps are all right,' he said. 'There'll be some more navy men here soon.'

'Not very many, I think,' said Moore. 'We need all the space we can get. But this crib is going to be uncomfortable going out empty. She sails better in ballast. Not much, but some.'

Bevan made to go to the door but the Irishman beckoned him to the porthole. 'Just take a glance at my boys, will you now. It makes you want to weep, doesn't it. And when you look at me and I'm the captain, well . . .'

He made room at the window. The crew, a dozen of them, were shuffling towards the gangway like men going to the scaffold. The mate remained standing near the boxy Austin in which his wife was apparently crying. Bevan could see that her face was pressed against the steering-wheel. 'In peacetime half of them would not be appearing at all,' said Moore. 'They'd be too boozed or wrapped up in some poxy woman's bed and they wouldn't get here. But wartime they could be shot, or worse, if they miss the ship. That's in theory.'

A fragile youth was first up the gangway, the brass buttons on his jacket reflecting the last of the evening light. 'My third officer, Mr Allen,' said Captain Moore almost despondently. 'He's hardly out of short trousers. And there's Yardly, the apprentice, and he's still in them. Sixteen if he's a day.'

A group of four, slower men were moving towards the ship. 'The stokehold gang,' said Moore. 'It's the only time you'll see their faces. But at least they're warm down there with the coal.' He became reflective and gazed into the eye of whiskey left in the glass. 'They've no idea where they're sailing,' he said as if it saddened him. 'Where the ship is going. They never do and they don't care either.'

'How many troops do you think we can evacuate?' asked Bevan. 'How many will the ship take?'

Moore shook his head. 'She'll take plenty if she stays afloat. But where we find them and how we get them off, don't ask me. They'll need to wave.'

They shook hands rather solemnly before Bevan left.

He found his route along the tight companionways aided by the dwarfish steward in his pure white jacket who pointed the way. Then a grumbling group of crewmen shuffled towards him and he opened a door and stepped in to let them pass. Some nodded, some grimaced. Two were coughing.

He found his men in a wedge of a cabin with three tiers of wooden bunks. They had managed to stow most of their equipment. Runciman seemed glad to see him. 'The gun is on deck, sir. I've sent three men to secure it. It's just in front of the bridge, or whatever they call that old shed up there.'

'Good field of fire?'

'Terrible. Nowhere is any good. Half the time you'd be blowing the masts, or the bridge even, to bits. But it's the best there is.'

Gunner Ugson tapped the rough steel bulkhead. 'D'you reckon this is waterproof, sir?'

'I hope so, Ugson.'

'So do I. I scraped it a bit and a great big rusty lump came off.'

'Don't do it again.'

'No, sir.'

Bairnsfather appeared at the door. He said to Bevan: 'There's some navy bods turned up. They're on land, just getting on.'

Bevan thanked him. 'I'll check the gun in a minute, sergeant,' he said to Runciman. 'I'd better make myself known to the navy.'

He sidled through the corridor again. On the deck it was now almost dark. Torches were waving on the quay below. A naval officer was coming up the gangway. 'Don't fall over, lads,' he called behind him. 'It's wet.'

Bevan saluted and introduced himself. 'You're our secret weapon against those Stukas, then,' said the man.

His sailors looked smarter, leaner, than Bevan's soldiers. 'I'm Verity. John Verity. We've got to try and rescue all the brown jobs, so I gather.'

'That's the general idea,' said Bevan. 'Whatever brown jobs we can find.'

They felt the ship shift at midnight. Those who were asleep woke at the jolt and heard rough sounds from the quay as she cast off. The engine made the vessel tremble in every rivet. Someone was coughing in the fetid darkness. 'Feel sick yet, Ugly?' called Cartwright.

'No, but I don't trust this bloody thing, I can tell you,' said Ugson. 'I didn't join the army to get drowned at fucking sea.'

Bairnsfather was thinking of Molly, deep in her peaceful Southampton bed. How long would all this last? The ship gave another jerk, like an old horse trying to wake up for work, and a small shower of paint and rust scattered across his blanket. He brushed it away and on to Purcell below who shouted for him to quit.

'I bet even those navy blokes don't fancy going to sea in this tin can,' said Cartwright.

'They like them big safe ships with them big guns,' said Ugson.

'You wait till they see us on the bloody Bofors.'

'Bouncing up and down on the waves.'

Only minutes after the vessel had sailed they felt the first nudge of the North Sea. 'We've hit something,' muttered someone.

'A U-boat, I bet,' said another.

'Balls, lad, balls.' Sergeant Runciman appeared at the end of the cabin and turned on the almost dead bulkhead light. He had been trying to sleep in what looked like a locker at the end. There was scarcely room to lie down on the mattress on the hard floor and his feet projected through the door. Men had been stepping over them on their way to the latrine. 'The sea will lull you to sleep,' he said. 'Like a ruddy cradle.'

'I'd rather be at home,' said Cartwright. 'Whichever one it's with.'

The ship gave a more pronounced heave and then rolled and righted herself. 'You're *not* home, Cartwright. The same as the rest of us,' said Runciman. 'We're here, wherever it is.' His face was yellow in the low lamp. 'Try and get some sleep.'

'How far is it, sarge?' said Ugson. 'How long?'

'Normally, I reckon it takes about two days,' said Runciman. There was another lurch and his face tightened as he clutched the door frame. 'But in this thing you can't tell. We'll get there when we do.'

'And then get out as quick as we can, eh sarge,' said Cartwright.

'No promises,' said Runciman.

That night Bevan dreamed of his wife again. Eve was naked apart from his white mess jacket, as she had been on that first night. She was laughing and jangling the medals too, but this time she was tempting Gunner Ugson. Ugson had his arms held out helplessly to her as she danced in front of him but he kept looking over his shoulder and calling: 'Is this all right, sir? Is it all right?'

She had returned after two years in America, as she had said she would, timing her arrival carefully for the night of the county ball. He had heard she was back and hoped she would be there. She was with her family and friends but when the master of ceremonies called: 'Ladies' invitation waltz,' she walked over to him smiling. 'When are we going to get married?' she said. 'You promised you would ask me.'

Everyone said it was a lovely wedding. Her brother

had been killed in France and she was her father's only child now. She looked magically beautiful that day three months later and people told him how lucky he was. His new father-in-law gave him a promotion and a rise in salary to fifteen hundred pounds a year.

On their wedding night he fell in love with her. He had been hoping it would happen but he had not expected it to be so soon. As they lay together through the hours of the spring darkness he thought that he had found the right one, or that she had found him.

The opposite, unfortunately, was true of Eve. As he went about his normal life in the weeks that followed, she seemed to lose interest in him, to change her mind, to realise there had been a mistake. She became quiet, then sullen. A few months after their marriage she left for another trip to America and she was away for seven weeks. He said he was willing to wait if that was what she wanted.

On her return Eve seemed to be glad but decided that they should spend more time in London. Her father rented an apartment in Kensington for them but James was never content there. The confinements of the streets, even superior streets, were too much for him. Often he was in the country and she remained in the city.

A year after their marriage her father died, making her a wealthy woman. Summarily she announced that she would be going back to the United States to promote a vacation resort. Her kiss at the station was perfunctory. Her mind seemed elsewhere. James shrugged and stayed behind. She was away six months and on her return she said that she intended to sell the estate and use the funds in her American business enterprise. 'Does that mean you're sacking me?' he asked. There was little left between them.

'I suppose you could say so,' said Eve. She had an

annoying trace of an American accent. 'You can't be a manager if there's nothing to manage. Perhaps the new owners will keep you on.' She laughed in her sharp way: 'Perhaps you could be part of the sale, James.'

For two years they lived apart, he in Hampshire where he became a farm manager, and she in the United States. When she returned for the last time she was almost bankrupt and she was also pregnant. 'Remember, they always called me Lumpy,' she had said defiantly. 'Now I am.'

Early morning found the *Mary Anne Davies* wallowing in a world of velvet grey with long, sullen waves. Its bow lifted and fell like a steady axe head. Wilson, the embalming officer, lay pallid on his bunk, looking a likely candidate for his own skills. Bevan left him in their shared cabin and went to check on his men. As he climbed crookedly on to the outer deck he was stabbed by the sea-cold air which went up his nostrils and cleared his head. Spray hit him like hail. Holding the rail he blinked around the gaunt horizon. There was another ship in the distance, ploughing on the same course, and there was the smudge of a third further away. He wondered where the British Navy was.

As though in answer he found two sailors around the corner of the deck, jammed against each other in an alcove next to a pile of elderly lifebelts. They were wearing blue balaclavas and layers of navy clothes. Both were groaning and a pair of ashen faces peered out at him like those of prisoners from cell windows.

'All right, chaps?' he enquired.

'No, sir,' moaned one. He made some attempt to stand up but his companion made none. Bevan beckoned both to stay.

'Not too good then.'

'First time we've been to sea, sir,' said the first.

'It's 'orrible,' mumbled the other. 'Wish I was in the army.'

Bevan went down to the galley and was pleased to see that Bairnsfather and Ugson were eating their breakfasts. Runciman, looking taut, came in from another door. 'Everyone surviving, sergeant?' asked Bevan.

'As far as I can tell, sir,' said Runciman. 'Some of them may have died in the night for all I know.'

Bairnsfather was gamely sticking a fork into a sausage. His plate was awash with fat; eggs, bacon and fried bread were lying around like flotsam. Ugson muttered: 'There's a bloke over there putting marmalade on his kippers.'

'Don't look,' said Runciman as if it were an order. He got a mug of coffee for Bevan and one for himself. Bevan took a slice of toast, folded a rasher in it and sat down with the men.

'Gun drill in half an hour, sir?' suggested Runciman.

The men regarded him with horrified disbelief. 'Sarge . . .' began Bairnsfather.

'That's fine,' said Bevan eyeing the sergeant. The ship plunged again and gave a metallic groan.

'Right lads,' said Runciman having difficulty with the two words. He drank his coffee, lifting it stiffly, but closed his eyes when the ship rose. 'Breakfast, then gun drill. Do us all good, a bit of fresh air.'

The sailors had been dragged into two ranks on the deck. A petty officer was haranguing them. Without pity he surveyed the yellowy complexions lined in front of him. Lieutenant Verity was watching, pale faced and trying not to grasp the rail. Captain Moore observed with wry interest from the wing bridge. 'Mr Stead,' he said. 'What chance have those poor Germans got against men like this?'

'No chance at all, captain,' replied the mate. It was not his watch – he had been on the bridge most of the night – but he had come out because he could not sleep. His wife had given him a note to be opened only at sea and he had kept the pact. The note said that she was going to leave him unless he got a job ashore. She could not stand the anxiety, the nights and the waiting. The war would have to do without him.

They watched the soldiers stagger out into the brisk wind. 'Ah, here's the army,' said Captain Moore. 'Now we're all going to be safe.'

Bevan watched Runciman harry the gun crew into the open. Ugson came out in a rush and went straight to the rail. He hung over it. 'Not into the wind!' bellowed the captain.

Ugson pulled himself away and, after a twisted look towards Moore, stumbled after the others around the gun on the forward deck. Runciman had them drawn up and soon the jagged wind in their noses made them feel better. Bevan felt pleased. He glanced along the deck towards Verity's sailors, then looked beyond the ship to see that the two merchant vessels he had seen that morning were keeping the same dogged course, dipping, rising, dipping.

The soldiers took the tarpaulin wrap from the Bofors and went through loading drill; the ammunition crates were piled against the bulkhead under waterproof sheets. Runciman shouted his commands against the wind. They all knew what was coming next. The sergeant bellowed: 'Fire!' and, as they always had done, the men shouted: 'Bang!' 'Bang!' and 'Bang!'

'Fuck me gently,' said Captain Moore from the bridge. He fell on his folded arms. The mate grinned, the man on the wheel looked amazed, and the sailors along the deck began to snigger. 'Bang . . . bang . . . bang . . .' repeated the captain to himself. 'Well, I never.'

Suddenly an isolated, floating call echoed above them. The gun crew looked up in surprise to see a man's head projecting from the crow's nest almost at the top of the foremast. 'Poor bugger,' said Cartwright. Then they heard him shout: 'Aircraft at six o'clock!'

'The bastard!' responded Captain Moore as if it were a personal affront. 'Where are ye? Where are ye, ye bastard?'

The gun crew remained like a tableau. The plane was over them before they could react, black crosses showing starkly on its wings. Runciman almost choked. The soldiers stared speechless at their first live enemy. 'Action stations!' Bevan's voice was strangulated. Moore was bellowing from the bridge. He was so loud, so angry, so Irish, that for a moment the whole gun crew turned towards him. They saw him waving a rifle at the aircraft. 'Keep away from my ship, ye Nartzie bastard!'

The plane banked over the sea and came back as they scrambled to get the gun into position. Runciman kept decreasing the elevation. They swung it in the direction of the aircraft. 'Dornier!' shouted the man from the crow's nest as though they needed the information. The shadow of the raider fell across them like a hand. 'Fire!' bawled Runciman. Bairnsfather, for the first time, pressed the pedal in earnest. The gun let rip in a hammering staccato, deafening them all and filling the air with choking smoke and cordite. They missed the plane completely and saw it swoop round mockingly and come in on the other side of the vessel. Runciman swung the gun and they let loose again, firing as they had been taught, trying to keep calm.

'Missed him!' cursed Bevan. He had his field-glasses trained on the aircraft and imagined he could see the pilot laughing. The Dornier came back again. Very low this time. They banged off another shattering volley but got nowhere near it. As the plane turned for the last time over the ship something dropped. Everyone ducked. It landed on a canvas cover, bounced and slithered on to the deck. The gun crew stared at it. A large German sausage.

From the bridge Moore was cursing everybody, the Germans, the gun crew, his own impotence. His blank eye seemed to blaze more fiercely than the good one. He waved the rifle wrathfully. 'Didn't even scrape the bastard!' he bawled at the soldiers. The plane was now droning safely away to the north. On deck a loud crack sounded and every man looked to see the forward mast tipping slowly and breaking as it toppled like a trunk of a slim tree. The man in the crow's nest howled as his pod swung sideways and then turned upside down; the mast, held only by its ropes, waved like a pendulum. The unhurt man was strapped into a harness and now hung from it. 'Get him out, for Christ's sake,' bellowed Moore. He glared accusingly at Bevan. 'The only thing your gun hit, mister officer, was my fucking rigging.'

'There now, anyway, you can say you've seen action.'

They were sitting morosely around the galley table, the gun crew, Runciman and Bevan, when Captain Moore came in. Like a father he put his heavy hands on the shoulders of Ugson and Bairnsfather. 'And you've *heard* action as well. It's bloody noisy, is it not?'

No one did anything more than nod as though, still deafened, they were unsure what he was saying. Bevan nodded towards him gratefully. It was Cartwright who spoke: 'Not one ruddy hit, captain. Except your mast.'

'Ach, he was too low, the crafty bugger,' said Moore. 'A daredevil if you like, a mad Nartzie, come to take a look at us. You'd have needed a torpedo to hit that one.' He studied them as if wondering whether to tell them the truth. 'The fact is,' he said, 'guns are never much use at all, not at all, against aeroplanes. You can loose off as much stuff as you like, send tons of metal into the sky and you'll be lucky to touch them. Not unless the flier's a fool. All it does is make a lot of noise, a racket like a battle is going on, what they call in the fillums sound effects, don't they.'

The gunners looked crestfallen. 'They're all right on the ground, guns,' he said in an attempt to reassure them. 'Bigger the better. I bet that little thing you've got there, the Bofors . . . I'll wager with a nice fat tank in the sights you'd have a good chance but it's better to fight a plane with another plane.'

Bevan asked: 'What was that rifle you were using, captain?'

Moore now looked abashed. 'Ah, it was only a token, ye'll understand. That wouldn't make a moth hole in a Dornier. It's an Italian carbine. The police, the *carabiniere*, in Italy have them. It belonged to my father although God knows where he came by it. He used it in 1916.'

'So where was . . . ?'

Moore held up a rough hand. 'It was not in the general war, not the Great War, but in the Dublin Rising of 1916. My father was in O'Connell Street. He used it against the British. They shot his ear off for his trouble.'

No one said anything. Then Moore said: 'I took it to Spain for the Civil War. I used it against Franco.'

'Did you kill anybody?' asked Ugson.

'No, no. No chance of that. I was on board ship then, running the blockade you know, and I wasted a bit of time and ammunition firing the thing at those Stukas. The Germans were trying them out in Spain. Didn't hit anything of consequence but it made me feel better.'

He stood and waved to the small attentive steward.

'Let's have a few drinks here,' he said. He glanced towards Bevan. 'If that's all right, mister officer.'

'Fine,' said Bevan. 'Thanks.'

'A few beers and whatnot,' said Moore. He grinned towards Bevan. 'At least our friend the embalming officer didn't find any business,' he said.

Runciman said: 'He could have practised on that sausage.'

They all laughed.

By night-time they knew they were nearing the place. As the light diminished they realised that they were only one of many ships, merchant vessels and warships, lolling on the neighbouring sea. Eventually each one vanished, enfolded in the advancing darkness. From the deck Bevan watched the pinprick blinking of a signal lamp. The wind was low but the air cold. The unknown coast and all its dangers lay ahead.

At ten o'clock he advised his men to bunk down and get as much sleep as they could. 'There's nowhere else to go, is there,' grumbled Cartwright.

'There's a dance at the back of the ship,' Purcell told him. 'You can dance with those hairy-arsed stokers.'

Bairnsfather had pulled the rough blanket over his head. His mouth and nose emerged for a moment. 'Cheer up, Carty. At least you've got two women to dream about. I've only got one.'

Bevan and the naval lieutenant Verity were called to Captain Moore's cabin at eleven. They sat down at the wooden table in the dim lamplight. He had the whiskey bottle out and poured out three measures.

'They've just sent us the signal,' said Captain Moore. 'All the orders are scrapped, which is no surprise. I've now been given a new position for the ship to anchor. We'll be a mile offshore and the land you'll see is Norway.

We'll be taking the soldiers off the beach in boats. They've got the boats at long last so they won't have to use ours which is just as well because mostly they're painted into the davits.' He regarded them confidingly. 'Just incidentally, if we should have to abandon ship at any time the boats on the stern are more or less watertight and we have one or two life-rafts with no holes.'

The younger men nodded solemnly. 'Your orders are more or less as you know,' said Moore. 'You, captain, must shoot down the Germans and you, lieutenant, must get your sailors organised to help those poor castaway soldiers off the shore. I will do my best to keep the ship afloat.'

He paused as if trying to remember anything he had forgotten. 'The two holy men will get their guidance from God, I suppose. How they sort out the Prods from the Romans in the heat of battle, I don't know, myself. They were having a Bible game – you know, questions and answers – with the tame embalmer today and he won. It was very interesting. Quotations, you understand. Like the one about man being born to trouble as the sparks fly upwards . . . Things you'd never dream.'

'You mentioned the heat of battle,' mentioned the naval officer diffidently.

'A figure of speech,' said Moore. 'I've no means of knowing how hot it will be.'

'But you think there will be one.'

'Oh, I don't know that either. Nobody's told me, a poor bloody captain, how far or how near the Germans are. I know one place they'll be and that's up in the sky. There'll be a battle of some sort.'

At dawn Bevan was on deck. His men were sitting down to a hot but silent breakfast. He had slept little; the sea was easier now and he had felt the ship slow and, twenty minutes later, grunt to a stop. The anchor chain went down with a rusty clatter.

As the night cleared the land ahead thickened in silhouette. There was a small harbour with smoke drifting from it. Through his field-glasses he could see activity on the quay: human figures, vehicles. A dozen merchant ships were grouped impassively around the bay, like them, waiting. Behind the scene shadowy mountains gradually solidified. He realised that what he had thought were the summits were only the snowlines. The very air seemed grey.

'Is that not the most God-abandoned country you ever saw, mister officer?' called Moore from the bridge. He was standing with the mate and Yardly the apprentice, one flat faced, the other with a nervous twitch.

Bevan's gun crew came on deck, helmeted, apprehensive. Runciman had told them to leave their gas respirators below. 'You can't get gassed at sea,' he said.

'There's a lot of smoke over there, sarge,' pointed Cartwright. 'Is that from bombing?'

'People cooking their breakfasts, I expect,' replied Runciman without looking. They were ranged around the gun which was stripped for action, its wide nozzle seeming to sniff the air. Ugson, whose job was to sweep the hot, used shell cases overboard, held his broom like a weapon. Along the rail the young sailors were lowering nets. The petty officer fussed. 'Come on, lads, get that net over. You might catch a fish.' Verity watched them doubtfully.

'Boats leaving the shore!' shouted Stead the mate.

'Boats leaving the shore!' piped the apprentice.

Half a dozen small craft could be seen making their way clumsily through the dim morning water, low as though crouching. As they neared the ship, first their heads came into view, then their stark faces.

'No sign of Jerry,' sniffed the Catholic padre. He and the Anglican and the embalmer were walking in circles on the deck as though waiting for something to do. He called up to Captain Moore on the bridge, repeating cheerfully: 'No sign of Jerry, captain.'

'The man has no gift of prophecy,' muttered Moore. He was looking high above. 'Jerry's up there,' he said quietly to himself. Then he bawled: 'Take cover on deck!'

It was a Stuka dive-bomber. It fell straight out of the sky as though plunging into the waves, and dropped a stick of bombs into the sea among the approaching small boats. It had pulled out and was turning away before Bevan's men could swing the gun to Runciman's bellowed orders. The bombs flung up columns of water and the boats disappeared behind them but then emerged, still advancing, through the smoke and the spray. From the ship's deck came cheers. The young sailors were at the sides, manning nets hanging to the water, as the gun crew impotently searched the sky. Alongside the ship the retreating soldiers scrambled from their boats. They were soaked with oil and water, their eyes gaped like the eyes of blind, shocked men. Spider fashion they climbed aboard, throwing themselves over the rail from the nets. Bevan reached down to help one man to his knees. The soldier was shivering, his face was black and there was blood on his mouth. 'Fuck this for a game of soldiers,' he said, adding: 'Sir.'

All day men were ferried from the harbour and the beach, their heads projecting from the small boats like cut-out targets in a shooting gallery. The German planes came back in shifts and by afternoon the land was palled with smoke. The attacks had been concentrated on the shore and the men aboard the ship began to feel lucky. Food and tea and beer were brought out to the dumb-faced soldiers beginning to pack the main deck. The lower decks were full. 'There goes our privacy,' said Bairnsfather.

They were eager to use the Bofors; protectively they ranged around it as though it were a prize animal, a metal giraffe. But only three times did German planes approach them and then it was so abruptly, coming low out of the smoke drifting from the land, that they had no time even to shout or swing the gun before the target was gone. Now the planes were all fighter aircraft, Messerschmitts. None of them opened fire; they seemed to be pulling away from their previous targets, turning off almost disdainfully as though the ship were of no consequence. 'Scared,' said Cartwright. 'Yellow.'

'Leaving us till later,' sniffed Runciman. 'They've got more important things than us, lad. They'll come back when they've done over there.'

'When we're out in the bloody sea,' said Ugson, clutching his broom and looking sideways at the cold waves.

'It can't be long before we clear off out of here,' said Bairnsfather hopefully. 'This tub is full to bursting. And it'll be dark by then.'

There seemed to be no more space. Disconsolate soldiers sat silently, shoulder to shoulder on the open deck. Two hundred huddled men, saying nothing, exhausted, defeated. One man or another did make a faint attempt to sing but they faltered and were silenced by the eyes of others. 'No sign of the old thumbs-up spirit among this lot,' said the embalmer to Bevan.

Some of the wounded were being treated below decks by two medical officers who had come from the shore with them. Men were still being helped aboard. Two sailors went around with bars of chocolate. 'Anyone want some nutty? Nutty anybody?'

The soldiers grunted as they accepted the chocolate

bars. 'We're the ones who are nutty,' said one man to Bevan. His face was smeared with oil and he had a dressing around his head. 'We've got to be.' Bevan nodded but said nothing. Encouraged, the man continued. 'It's not going to last much longer anyway. Not at this sodding rate.'

By the last strands of daylight the ship was full. Captain Moore was holding his Italian carbine as he had been all day. The planes which had skimmed the tops of the masts had been too brief and sudden for him as well as for the army gunners. 'Bang,' he had muttered after the final Messerschmitt had gone.

Night had joined the smoke, solidifying the darkness, by the time the ship began to move. An echo of its groan sounded from the soldiers. 'At least we're getting away from here in one piece,' said the Anglican priest. 'God has answered our prayers.'

'Perhaps He's only postponed a decision,' said the Catholic. 'Or changed His mind. He's been known to change his mind.'

There was a young lieutenant propped against one of the useless lifeboats like a man with time on his hands. He listened to their conversation. 'While you're at it, you might like to ask your God if he's seen our air force anywhere,' he said. He was so weary that he seemed to have difficulty in reaching the end of the sentence. His eyes were intense, his face drained. Each of the padres waited for the other to speak.

'The glamour boys failed to turn up,' said the officer. 'Maybe they couldn't find Norway.'

'Perhaps nobody told them,' suggested the Protestant lamely.

'All I know,' the lieutenant said closing his eyes, 'is that the Luftwaffe were bombing and strafing my men as they pleased. We never saw our famous, fucking air force.'

He opened his eyes briefly and closed them again as if he did not expect an answer.

The ship made turgid progress through the black sea although it was now calm. The sailors went around the deck throwing blankets and tarpaulins over the crushed troops. 'She'll not do more than four knots with this cargo,' said Captain Moore. 'She's not the *Queen Mary*.'

He had invited Bevan to the bridge and offered him a whiskey which the officer accepted gratefully. Stead had gone to get some rest. The apprentice was sitting in a corner, on the deck boards, apparently asleep. 'Look at him,' said Moore compassionately. 'He ought to have his nanny to tuck him up.'

'Never had a nanny, sir,' said the youth without opening his eyes. 'We couldn't afford it.'

As they laughed, guns began to fire beyond the horizon. Bevan had seen to it that his gun crew had been fed in relays and four of them now lay around the gun covered by their greatcoats. 'They won't be woken yet,' said Moore. 'That's not our fight over there with the big guns. We'll be able to watch it.' He grinned seriously. 'Thank God you've got a navy, mister officer.'

They could see that the battle beyond the horizon was growing, the flashes intensifying and flaring more frequently. The rumble of the guns rolled over the intense night and the black water like the echoes of a distant storm. 'It's good that you can have a fight at sea without the interference of aeroplanes,' said Moore. 'Like it was in the olden days. Aeroplanes spoil war, don't you think?'

Bevan replied: 'There's a man down on the deck, a lieutenant, asking where our air force was when they needed it.'

Moore did not respond but instead imitated a dive-bomber with his free hand. 'In Spain,' he said, 'they learned quick, the gunners. Learned to wait until the Stuka had pulled out of the dive. They might come down fast and like a banshee but it's a different job for them to climb out of it again. That's when they can be picked off. I'm sure the fighter boys know. Crash.' The end of his finger went into his whiskey glass.

Now there was a frieze of pulsating illumination all along the horizon. Some of the men on deck had gone to the rail to watch but most of them stayed where they were as if it were no concern of theirs. Then a great onion-shaped explosion rose, red and expanding, accompanied by a deep, travelling roar. 'Some poor bastard's been hit in the guts,' said the captain. He looked intensely sad. 'God rest their souls.'

Bevan said he was turning in and the two men shook hands before he left the bridge. 'Thanks for all you've done for my gun crew,' said Bevan. 'And for the whiskey.' Allen, the third officer, appeared on the bridge. The apprentice was deep asleep against the bulkhead.

'Twas nothing,' said Moore. 'For a neutral.'

'I'll tell the boys how to shoot down the Stukas your way.'

'Like I told them, guns against planes are not much bloody good. But you can try.'

Bevan went below. The embalmer and the two padres were now occupying the cabin. The clerics were sleeping on the floor, head to toe, between the bunks, the Catholic wearing a blissful smile. The tall Anglican stirred and apologised. 'There are eight soldiers in the cabin we had,' he said. 'We did not feel disposed to argue about it.'

'Thanks for saving the bunk for me,' said Bevan, and climbing over them he rolled into it and tipped into an exhausted sleep. All four men woke in simultaneous confusion with the blaring of the ship's Klaxon. The clerics moved aside as best they could to let Bevan scramble out. He opened the door and the Klaxon's blast intensified. 'Like Balaam's ass,' said the Catholic.

Putting on his steel helmet as he went Bevan gained the deck. His mouth was dry, his heart jumping. The gun crew were already swivelling the Bofors to Runciman's sharp orders as he scanned the morning sky. The rescued soldiers on the deck were rolled against each other, some wearing helmets, most putting their hands fatalistically and pointlessly on their heads. The Klaxon stopped. Bevan saw that Moore was on the bridge. Then everyone froze as the sound of the dive-bomber screamed from above them. Runciman shouted but could not make himself heard above the noise. The gun layers wound their handles madly and Ugson, clutching his broom like a charwoman, lifted apprehensive eyes.

'Hold your fire!' Bevan called to Runciman. 'Wait till he pulls out!'

'Holding fire!' bawled Runciman.

The Stuka was directly above them like a descending hand. From that angle it seemed oddly slow and they watched, riveted, as it dropped on its crooked wings. Its scream intensified. 'Yer fearful bastard!' Moore shouted from the bridge, his voice somehow above the din of the plane. He had the carbine ready. They watched the bombs fall away as if the Stuka were laying eggs. There seemed no way that they could miss the ship but miraculously they hit the water thirty feet to the starboard side, violently tipping the hull as they exploded. Men were flung and rolled across the decks. Runciman waited, agonisingly, then gave the order to fire as the plane pulled out of the dive and began its ungainly upward stagger, its terrible menace in descent transformed in a moment to an elderly feebleness, almost comic. They missed. Their field of fire was restricted by the bridge and the rigging. All Runciman could do was shout: 'Ugly-looking sod!'

They waited for it to come back but it turned away as if in embarrassment and made for the east. The ship plodded on. All of a sudden there was a commotion from the bow and Bevan, clambering across those lying on the deck as though on stepping stones, saw that they were changing course. Moore was giving orders from the bridge. There were men in the sea a mile off.

It was a lifeboat, crammed with men and with others clinging to its sides. As they drew near someone shouted: 'It's Jerries! It's fucking Jerries!' and all the soldiers began to laugh hysterically, their pent-up fear and frustration released. They pointed and yelled derisively. Then one of the men near Bevan muttered in amazement: 'Christ, he's going to rescue the buggers.'

The jeers turned to shouts. 'Bloody Irish!' someone bawled towards the bridge. Resolutely Bevan went forward and ordered the men back from the rail. 'You're doin' right, mister officer,' bellowed Moore. 'Make room to get these survivors aboard.'

He had slowed the engines and the vessel hove to, sluggish in the sea only a hundred yards from the lifeboat. The Germans looked up with collective fear. One of those in the water, clinging to the side of the craft, let go and slipped out of sight. The shipboard sailors began throwing nets over the side while the merchant seamen launched one of the usable boats. Others were flinging lifebelts. After a hesitant moment the soldiers stopped their jeering and began to help, calling instead: 'Here y'are, Jerry!' and 'Swim for it, Fritz!' It was like a game. While they were playing the Stuka came back. Runciman had been watching for it and he shouted as the plane dipped.

This time the bombs were even closer. One shaved the hull and blew up in the water below, another fell twenty feet away and a third almost directly on to the lifeboat carrying the German survivors. 'Hold fire!' Runciman shouted almost at himself. 'Hold fire!' Once the flurry of bombs had fallen the dive-bomber began its slow and inelegant climb, the swooping bird of prey become a chicken. 'Get the bugger now!' shouted a soldier, a spectator flat out on the deck.

The shadow lifted and the plane was at last a clear outline against the sullen sky. The gun crew knew they had it this time. They swung the Bofors. Bevan stood like stone. Runciman waited, and waited, then yelled, triumphantly: 'Fire!' Bairnsfather pressed the pedal. The gun barked and shuddered. Some smoke puffed from the Stuka, quite a small puff, and then came an orange explosion. The tail fin flew into pieces and with an almost clownish dive the bomber banked noisily and fell into the sea. All on the deck were stunned until they realised what they had done. 'Got him!' howled Bairnsfather. 'Got the bastard!' Bevan waved his hands exultantly, speechless. Runciman stood grinning, but as though it were only something to be expected. He patted the Bofors. It was still hot and he cursed and blew on his palm. Then they all went mad, dancing and cheering around the gun. Bevan hugged his sergeant. The soldiers on the deck turned away from the scenes in the sea and celebrated with them. Then with a swift and frightening roar a German fighter plane came in at just above sea level, its guns sparking, raking the deck in a single act of fury and revenge. Men were flung everywhere. They lay across each other, some untouched, some wounded, some dead. Runciman, knowing they had been caught out, swore more at himself than the attacker. Cries and screams went up all along the deck. 'Stay with the gun,' Bevan ordered. 'He might be back.'

He saw the embalmer hurrying towards him, stepping over prostrate men. 'The skipper's been hit,' he said. 'And the mate.'

Bevan felt sick. 'Right, I'll come,' he said. The bridge was in chaos. The helmsman was lying dead and Allen had taken the wheel, his face stark. The apprentice was trying to put out a fire with a bucket of water, throwing it with odd, petty carefulness, a little at the time. Captain Moore was lying on the deck of the wing bridge. The Anglican padre was with him. 'For the sake of the good Christ,' said Moore as Bevan got to the deck, 'can I not have my own Roman man?'

'He's been injured,' said the Anglican.

'Typical. Never there when you need them.' Moore scrutinised the padre's face as if it had become suddenly and intensely interesting. Bevan could see that his stomach was hanging out. 'You don't do last rites in your church, I suppose?' asked the captain.

'I could try,' said the padre.

Moore's eyes were drooping as though he were very tired. 'Your boys did fine, mister officer,' he said to Bevan. 'Got the first fucker. Mr Stead will get you safe home.'

In one corner Mr Stead sat as though taking a break, his face coated with blood, his eyes staring beyond belief.

The captain died without fuss. Bevan, sick inside, took a step towards him and the padre moved aside. Bevan picked up Moore's big warm hand and held it for an instant, then he turned away and went back towards his own men and the gun.

Only two of the men in the German lifeboat survived. After that the enemy left them alone. Towards midnight there was another naval engagement beyond the horizon. Yardly the apprentice and the naval officer were on the bridge. 'I hope we're going the right way,' said the boy.

Bevan stood half of the gun crew down and told Runciman to get some sleep. When the sergeant came back after three hours Bevan was leaning against the gun, almost asleep himself. He mumbled apologies. 'You're better off up here, sir,' said Runciman. 'It's not nice down below.' He picked up a blanket lying near the gun and handed it to the officer. Bevan nodded gratefully and wrapped it around him. He leaned against the rail and went to sleep with the guns grunting beyond the skyline.

7

It was the remote guns that used to lull him to sleep when he was in the army school; lull him to sleep, or sometimes wake him, and at other times were the sounds of his dreams. The boys would listen to the barrage in the dark of the dormitory and guess whose artillery it was, for there were distinctly different sounds. 'That's the big German gun,' whispered Prosser from the next bed. 'Big Bertha, I expect.'

'That can fire twenty-five miles or even more,' said James. 'If it was right on the French coast it could reach your bed.'

'What about yours?' Prosser said.

James received a few tearful notes from his sister in the early days. He had written telling her to be brave and when the guns were keeping him awake, he would imagine the Flying Scotsman rushing his letters north. After a few weeks she wrote a longer letter telling him things about the school and the girls there and her unhappiness seemed to have evaporated. She even finished in a hurry because she had something else to do. After that, although he wrote to her six times, he heard nothing for twelve months. He was angry with her briefly, then sad that he could no longer see her talk and laugh with her and finally glad that she had apparently found another life. They were parted.

The boy-soldier's life at Thorncliffe had taken over his

days. He enjoyed the brisk activity, the rough company and the primitive surroundings. The irrepressible Prosser became his firm friend, the best he had ever had; Prosser the Tosser the boys called him.

Lessons occupied half their day and the other half was taken up with military training and lectures. The school was almost on the cliffs above the English Channel – its red roofs could be seen far out to sea – and James took a boy's pleasure in the drills, the mock battles and manoeuvres in the airy fields. Here at last was security; the knowledge that if you obeyed orders you would find order. He had no fears and now few memories. When winter came the rooms in the school were bleak, sometimes so cold that the boys would huddle in groups in the corners keeping each other's bodies warm, a lesson in comradeship.

But when the seasons changed the sea shone and the edge of England was bright green above the white cliffs. James was promoted to boy corporal and then to sergeant the following autumn. As he grew taller, so the physical life broadened him. He became a sure shot in the target range with the heavy Lee Enfield rifle. 'Bull, inner . . . Bull, bull . . . inner,' the marker used to shout. 'Watch out, Bevan,' warned the limping sergeant. 'Snipers never last long.'

He was surprised, as the second Christmas at Thorncliffe neared, to receive a conscience-stricken letter from his uncle in Bournemouth. His aunt had been taken away; his uncle said Christmas would not be the same without her. A shilling postal order was enclosed. James bought Agnes a diary for Christmas but her careless greetings card did not arrive until late January. It said merely: 'I'm all right. Hope you are all right too. Love for 1916 from your sister Agnes.'

She would be fourteen that year and he wanted to see

her. In the late summer she wrote and said that she was leaving the school. 'I am going into service in the town,' she said. 'Earning four shillings a week and my keep. Very excited.'

Anxiously he sent a letter so that it would reach her before she left, asking her to promise to send her new address, but there was no reply. He wrote twice more with the same result. He decided to go and find her.

He had no idea how he would get to Scotland. If he simply went absent they would be looking for him and he would have to hide all the way. Prosser sounded doubts. 'Some kids have got a long way when they've bunked off,' he said. 'But most get caught easy. Scotland's miles away. How're you going to get that far?'

James knew that without money he would soon be picked up. But he had to go and he lay awake plotting. He tried to imagine what Agnes looked like now, how grown-up she was, if she needed help. On her own, away from the safety and discipline of the school, what would she do? Unless she had changed, unless they had squashed her spirit – and he doubted that – she was going to find trouble.

Thinking about her, he smiled to himself in the narrow privacy of his bed: Agnes sliding down the stairs on the tin tray; her wide-eyed face lit by the flickering images of the Bioscope screen. Headstrong Agnes the cheeky, the funny, the brave. He had to find her.

It was almost as if God agreed. The following day he was called from bayonet practice. 'A visitor, Sergeant Bevan,' said the instructor. 'A vice-admiral, so it reckons on his card, I believe. You might be seconded to the navy.'

Mr Brilling was waiting in the ante-room of the main lobby. He looked quite small, dented in a way, standing in the room with its sparse furniture and its portraits of King George and Queen Mary. He shook hands gravely. 'I have been studying the medals and awards the King is wearing,' he said.

'You'd have to have served a long time to get all those,' said James.

The elderly man smiled solemnly. 'Or be extremely courageous.'

Mr Brilling said that he happened to be passing but James realised that to get to Thorncliffe he must have had to make a diversion from wherever he was going. James realised how sad and shy he was and felt suddenly sorry for him. The man seemed to want to say something to him, something to have between them. Instead, he said: 'How is your sister?'

'She's left that school, sir,' said James. 'I don't know where she is.'

His visitor said he would try to find out and write to him. He left, giving James a gold half-guinea at the door before the sergeant arrived to show him out.

The boy clutched the small, heavy coin deeply in his palm. All money was supposed to be handed in to the school orderly room, recorded in a book, and doled out in small portions on Saturday afternoons when the boys were permitted to go into Dover. But he had no intention of surrendering the half-guinea. It was enough to start him on his way.

'Saturday's the best,' said Prosser. James did not confide in anyone else. 'I'll answer for you at roll-call and church parade so they won't know you've buggered off absent without leave till Sunday night earliest.'

The boy soldiers had to parade for inspection before being dismissed to go into Dover for their free afternoon. As boy sergeant it was James's duty to accompany the officer along the lines as the inspection was carried out.

From the front rank Prosser winked at him. He kept a calm face.

'Half a guinea's not going to get you to Scotland,' Prosser whispered as they waited with the others, a long rank at the bus-stop. 'You'll need grub.'

'It will get me as far as London,' said James. They were standing apart from the others but he kept his voice low. 'I'll have to think of something else when I get there.'

'You'll be a deserter,' said Prosser as if he did not like to mention it.

'I know,' said James.

'Deserters get shot by firing squad.'

'I'm not old enough to be shot.'

The bus went first to the harbour station. It slowed as it approached and the boys could see the activity on the quayside. Those on the wrong side of the bus moved across to crowd the windows and the driver called back to them not to do it because he said they could tip the bus over. 'There's enough wounded soldiers as it is.'

At the harbourside a ferry was discharging men in unkempt uniforms, some creeping down the gangways, others carried on stretchers towards a waiting train with big red crosses on its sides. A line of blinded soldiers, each with his hand on the shoulder of the man in front, shuffled along as a sergeant gently recited: 'Left, right, left, right.' Two men were sitting on boxes, weeping, one touching the ground with his hands, patting it. All around their bandaged and broken comrades waited for someone to tell them what to do. There were long-skirted, big-bloused nurses helping them on to the train and a bluff warrant officer with a clipboard giving directions. The boys in their ill-fitting khaki watched from the bus.

'This is where I'm getting off,' whispered James to Prosser.

He made for the open platform of the bus, now

almost stationary behind some plodding horse-drawn ambulances, and dropped to the ground unnoticed by the driver who was watching the scene and shaking his head. In uniform, and carrying nothing but the coins in his pocket, he slipped easily among the soldiers.

One of the men was calling for a nurse. His companion was lying on the ground, his head on his pack, apparently sleeping. 'I reckon he's gone,' said the soldier as the nurse came through the crowd.

James stared in horror as the woman opened the young man's eye and then felt for his pulse. 'Poor soul,' she said. The soldier handed her a blanket from a pile beside him and she put it around his companion as though tucking him into bed. ''E managed to get to England,' said the soldier.

They were ushering the wounded on to the train. James scarcely hesitated. There were half a dozen crutches against one of the carriages and he picked one up and putting it below his armpit lifted a leg and stumped towards the nearest train door. At the top of the steps was a medical orderly. 'Come on, mate,' he encouraged. 'Let's give you a hand.' James avoided looking directly at him. 'Thanks,' he muttered.

He handed up the crutch and the orderly helped him to reach the top step. 'Ain't a proper ambulance train, this one,' said the man. 'They just painted red crosses on it.' He jerked his thumb along the corridor. 'Walking cases right down the front.'

James quickly began to feel a deep sense of shame. The compartments of the train and the corridors were full of wounded; the guard's van had stretchers all over the floor. Some men were singing 'It's a Long Way to Tipperary', the brash marching song that had encouraged them to go to war in the first place, and to which, even now, for all the sacrifices, they still haplessly clung.

But most were incapable of singing, even of speaking. Even as recruits the general health and physique of the British soldiers had been pathetically poor; they had gone undernourished into the trenches from civilian slums and village poverty. Now they sat wedged together in their bandages, staring straight ahead, uncomprehending; men and boys, thrust into a world beyond their imaginations. The soldiers by the windows did not seem to want to look out at what was happening on the quay. One with his face pressed hard against the glass had his eyes shut. For the sixteen-year-old James in the grown-up uniform the vision was like a nightmare.

He decided to stand in the corridor resting his bogus crutch against the polished wood at the end. But a door swung open and a cracked, shaky voice called: 'Room in 'ere for one, Tommy.' He was afraid they might see his face, see how unused he was, how he had never known a battle let alone a wound, but they hardly spared him a glance. He was just another soldier. The man who had called to him still had mud on his tunic and his face was bruised. 'You got a wash then,' he said as James sat down nervously. 'A swill.' His half-scrutiny took in the boy's uniform. 'And a change.'

James deepened his voice and said: 'Yes, that's right.'

'Only the leg, is it?'

'Just the leg.'

He remained sitting stiffly. There was a thick smell of iodine in the compartment. Four men were opposite him, their shoulders crooked, and there were another three on his side. Most had their eyes closed. A whistle was blown outside and every man came to, filled with instant apprehension. Then they realised where they were. 'Christ, I thought it was over the bloody top again,' breathed one. 'The bloody whistle.'

'No more over the top for you, mate, or me,' said the

man who had called James into the compartment. 'We're back in Blighty.' He began to sing in a low, thin, voice: 'Take me back to dear old Blighty, Put me on the train for London Town.'

'Shut up,' grumbled one of the men. 'Shut yer face,' said another.

The train was soon beyond Dover and into the Kentish countryside. As the fields appeared, bright and innocent, a few of the soldiers began to take notice. 'It's just the same,' said a man near the window. 'Like we never been away.'

Another laughed idiotically: 'It's been 'ere all the time.'

The door was opened and a warrant officer who had been directing operations on the platform stood with his clipboard. James dropped his head as if he were asleep but all the man asked was: 'All right, boys?'

'All present,' responded the man next to James. 'Nobody's going to desert now.'

The sergeant major laughed uneasily. His brasses gleamed, his tunic was pressed and he had no medal ribbons. He seemed embarrassed. 'Couple of hours, that's all,' he said. 'Get you into hospital.'

He shut the door again softly, as if in apology. The train rolled on through villages with oast-houses by hop fields; farm men worked in unscarred meadows, there were tidy cottages and ordered towns. People stood on the stations and woodenly waved Union Jacks at them as they went by. Few of the soldiers responded. 'I can't believe I don't 'ave to run any more,' said the man next to James. 'What's your name, mate?'

'Bevan,' said James. 'Jim.'

'Reg Palmer, that's me.'

Awkwardly they shook hands. 'Running,' said Palmer. 'Every day we was running. Running at the Boche or running away from him. I expect he was doing the same, running at us and running away. Just like a dance. Where did you get yours?'

Bevan almost panicked. 'Down a hole,' he said desperately. 'Fell down a shell hole. Right down.'

'Safest place to be,' said Palmer. 'Unless another big bugger of a shell lands in the same 'ole. Well, it's all finished for us now, thank Christ.' He wagged a warning finger. 'Don't let them get you better too quick or they'll ship you out again.' He glanced sideways. 'You never want to see France again, do you? I bloody don't.'

'No, never,' said James.

As they neared London, going past the towns that had started to grow on its outskirts in the early part of the century, some of the men began to stir and to point from the window. 'Look, that's a good pub on the corner.' . . . 'All them people in the street, look at them. My missus will want me to go shopping.' . . . 'Look, a football match! Playing football.'

'It's Saturday afternoon,' remembered someone.

Silence fell over them as outside the window it began to get dark. James wondered how he could get out of the train undetected and how he would find another to Scotland. He had only been to London once, when his mother, before she met Mr Sullivan, had taken them to the zoo and Agnes had cried over the captive animals.

Now the train was running by brick walls and the street lights were coming on, dimly because of the threat of Zeppelin bombing. 'Victoria,' said one of the soldiers as if remembering an old acquaintance. 'Victoria station.'

Most of them were peering out now. The platform seemed clear except for some military personnel. 'They don't want anybody to see us buggered up like this,' said Reg Palmer. 'They'd think we've gone and lost their war.'

They left the train, a long, difficult and agonising business. Nurses and orderlies with stretchers appeared on the platform. The downcast mumbling men followed them, forming themselves into rough columns to shuffle out into the station. James joined in the ranks, terrified he would be discovered. He hobbled on his crutch. An orderly asked if he wanted help but he shook his head and pointed to the injuries of others. He was frightened and ashamed.

As they entered the concourse the soldiers were confronted by a blatant throng of sightseers: men and women, in hats and coats, standing four deep, kept in check by fussy policemen. Some waved flags and some cheered. 'God 'elp us,' said Palmer shuffling beside James. 'The toffs 'ave come to stare at us.'

The wounded men stared blankly at the civilians; the bloodied, muddied soldiers faced by the washed and clothed who had safely stayed at home. 'Sod off, the lot of you!' bawled a bandaged man. 'We're not a flamin' circus.' A woman tossed a packet of cigarettes and it was kicked away.

An order was called and the wounded column stumbled to a halt. The crammed onlookers now became as silent as the sullen troops. Motor and horse-drawn ambulances were waiting at the entrance. Then, like a scene from a farce, a column of German prisoners, some still wearing their spiked helmets, marched from another platform. They too were dirty and defeated and kept in line by the bayonets of their guards. The men of the two armies stood and confronted each other only a hundred yards apart. Then one of the British suddenly shouted: 'Good old Fritz! Good luck, Fritz!' and his injured comrades began to cheer and wave as best they could. The Germans reacted with a shout and held up their helmets and their arms. 'Tommy! *Guten Tag*, Tommy!'

The Londoners who had gone to stare were hushed; their expressions fixed and the silly flags they carried drooped. 'Keep smiling, Jerry!' shouted Palmer and the straggling troops cheered again. 'It'll soon be over.'

James's escape was simple. Daylight was fading in the station and gas lamps were being lit by a man with a long pole who travelled through the platforms on a bicycle, pulling down levers as he went. Groups of soldiers were traipsing towards the ambulances and to motor buses parked alongside, and there was the distraction of the noisy German prisoners and their bewildered guards. One young man abandoning a crutch and slipping away was not noticed. He even had time to stop at the canteen set up outside and have a cheese sandwich and a cup of tea for nothing. Then he made his cautious way out into the evening.

The map of London he had studied at Thorncliffe now seemed remote. The reality outside was of thronged people, walking in all directions, with buses and cars and horse-drawn vehicles wedged in the streets. Standing on the pavement he knew he would have to move quickly before he was spotted, before he was asked for his papers or someone patriotic offered him help. Miraculously a bus with 'King's Cross' painted across its destination board appeared and trotting between the pedestrians he jumped on to its platform. On the lower deck there was an empty seat and he took it, moving furtively against the window.

He had not seen a woman conductor before but now one bustled along the bus in her ample skirt. 'How much to King's Cross?' he asked. She was the only human being that day to notice how young he was. She looked over his face and then his uniform and smiled with kindness. 'Nothing to you, son.'

He returned her smile.

'Catching a train?' she asked. 'Going home to your mum?'

He said that he was and she shook her bonneted head and passed on. The journey took almost an hour. He kept his face to the window and watched the wartime sights of London travel by. It was amazing, a world of lights and activity, noise and traffic. People were going into theatres in the West End, above which the names of shows and plays were spelled out in electric light bulbs. On the pavements were groups of singers and musicians. The public houses were lit and full of customers. The guns of France had never been heard there.

At the end of the journey the conductress wished him good luck. She leaned towards him and for a moment he thought she was going to kiss his face but she merely patted his cheek and said: 'You keep away from them trenches, my lad.'

He went into the cavern of King's Cross station. It echoed with whistles, hooters and the heavy roaring of locomotives, and steam was gushing and hanging like clouds against the high roof. Crowds were hurrying to and from the trains, some men in uniform, women porters wheeling barrows of luggage, noise and movement everywhere. He moved cautiously but kept walking because he did not want to appear conspicuous in all the activity. There was a sign advertising the forces canteen, below which some lively Salvation Army girls were serving cups of tea and slices of cake to servicemen. He paid a penny for tea and cake and stood frowning at the departure boards. The Glasgow train would be leaving at nine o'clock. He had half an hour to wait.

He decided to delay getting on the train until the last moment and in the meantime to keep shifting so that he did not arouse the suspicions of any military or civil police. He felt the unspent half-guinea in his pocket like a reassurance although he knew that it would not get him far.

The two fresh-cheeked Salvation Army girls were observing him from their canteen on the platform. Their clean, pert faces were framed by their purple-ribboned bonnets and their hair – one was dark, the other fair – which curled beneath the brims. The dark girl laughed and whispered to her companion. Hurriedly James looked away.

First one, then the other, left the cakes and the tea urns to the other helpers and advanced on him from either side.

'You look a lonely chappie,' said the dark girl.

'Are you lost?' asked the other. They were skittish.

'No, I'm well, thank you,' he said.

'What a gentleman,' giggled the blonde. Together, as though they had practised it, they leaned forward and kissed him, one on each cheek. Their breasts, puffy under the stiffness of their uniforms, pushed against his chest and arms. 'God bless you,' said the dark one smiling as she stepped away.

'Yes, God bless you, soldier,' said the blonde with a glance at her friend as if she wished she had blessed him first. They hid their giggles behind their hands and went back to the cakes and tea. James felt an unknown glow. He went towards the train.

At the barrier there was a man clipping tickets. Briefly he was distracted by the Salvation Army girls who were calling to James and waving; thinking they were doing it for him the ticket collector jovially returned their waves. James walked unstopped, unspotted, on to the platform.

He decided that the inspector on the train would start work from the guard's van at the rear, so he went into the furthest carriage forward, which was empty, and sat wondering how far he would get. It was five hundred miles to Inverness. Then he began to think about the two girls, what the soft rounded pressure of their breasts had been like.

Often he had wished for a girl, a woman, to teach him about herself. His ambitions were more chivalrous, even knightly, than carnal and he composed his dreams with care. On his pillow he rescued lovely girls from the foul intentions of sordid German soldiers, often while he was on horseback.

Waiting for the train to move he wondered why the Salvation Army girls, who he could still see serving at their wooden canteen, had been so forthcoming. Perhaps they imagined he was a fighting soldier just back from Flanders. A young woman came into the compartment with a small sleepy child and she smiled at James. 'Soon be over,' she said.

'I hope so,' said James again feeling like a cheat. 'I haven't been to the trenches yet. I'm only a . . .' He baulked at saying he was a boy soldier. 'I'm still training.'

'Don't go if you can help it,' she said. 'My old man's come back with 'orrible trench mouth. Ulcers.' James was relieved when another woman got in and then two men who disappeared behind their newspapers. The small child grizzled and the women began to talk.

The train pulled away. James half closed his eyes, but kept a watch out for the ticket collector from underneath the peak of his cap. He had already made a plan. He would search for his ticket, say it was lost, and offer to get out at the next stop. There he would wait for another train and try the same procedure. It would take a long time to reach Scotland and Agnes like that.

He dozed despite himself and when he woke he heard the voice of the ticket collector moving down the corridor. He got up, smiled clumsily at the other passengers and left the compartment, looking to left and right as if searching for the lavatory.

The ticket collector came out of one compartment and sturdily opened the door to the next. At the same time the train's speed began to lessen. James looked out and saw lit windows going by, more and more slowly, until the engine with a blast of steam and the scraping of iron on iron, came to a stop.

Quickly James got to the end of the corridor where he could not be seen from any of the compartments. He lowered the window, feeling the night air rush in, turned the brass handle and, closing his eyes, jumped.

He landed heavily on an embankment and looked up to see the train ten feet above him. Winded, and fearful that he might be seen, he covered his face with his sleeves. Then the engine flung out another roar of vapour and the steel wheels began revolving and squealing above his head. The opened door was banging loosely.

The long train rumbled by above him. When it was gone it left a deep stillness. Misty rain was falling, and he could see lights in the distance, back the way the train had come, but around him all was dark and damp. As far as he could judge about twenty feet of the embankment remained below him. Cautiously he stood and stumbled down the decline. There was a fence at the bottom and he climbed it and dropped into a wet, narrow road. A few yards away was an adjoining lane, and he could see the obscure white finger of a signpost. He walked to it. It read: 'No Through Road.'

James looked all three ways. He seemed to have landed at the most empty spot in middle England. Then he heard the jog of a pony and the wheels of a trap, and saw a lantern bouncing. His first thought was to drop into the hedge but instead he stood at the verge of the lane and the pony neighed as it went by, as if it knew him. He heard a woman's hearty voice shout first to the horse and then back at him. The trap stopped with a scrape of wheels. The lantern ceased swinging. Then a firm enquiry came through the darkness: 'Are you all right back there?'

'Yes, thank you,' he called.

'Let's take a look at you then.'

Slowly James walked towards her. She was half turned in her seat. She wore an enveloping coat and a jaunty hat, below the brim of which the lantern showed a soft, well-curved face. 'Good evening,' she said. Her voice was melodious now that she was not shouting. 'Are you lost?'

'Yes, I am a bit,' said James. 'I fell from the train.'

'Oh, my heavens! Are you injured?' She leaned over to look. 'You seem to be in one piece.'

'Yes, I'm all right,' said James. 'It was stopped. I was just shaken.'

'You'd better climb up here. I'm going home.'

'Thank you,' he said. Gratefully and uncertainly he climbed alongside her. Her smile was encouraging. 'No night to be abroad,' she said. 'However did you come to tumble out of the train?'

'I leaned on the door and it opened,' he said. 'The train had almost stopped anyway, but by the time I'd got my breath it had started up again. I don't even know where I am.'

'Pickersby,' she said as if he was sure to recognise it. 'Northern Hertfordshire. I am Mary Antonia Franklyn.'

Smiling roundly in the lantern light she held her gloved hand towards him and he shook it awkwardly. 'And your name?' she prompted.

'Oh, yes, sorry. James . . . James Bevan.'

She flicked the reins and the horse moved forward. 'Which regiment?' she asked. She glanced sideways to see his cap badge. 'None, actually,' he said. 'I'm a boy soldier. I'm at an army school in Kent.'

'That's a good distance,' she said.

'I was going north to find . . . to see my sister.'

Oddly, they seemed to run out of conversation. The pony clipped along and the wheels sounded. 'My house has electricity,' she said suddenly. 'It's the first in this area. You must see it.'

'I'd like to,' said James. He had the sensation that something strange and important was about to happen to him.

Her house lay in a small valley set among trees that rustled in the dark. Against the night sky James could see the shoulders of low hills that surrounded it. There were some lights in windows both downstairs and upstairs. 'Oil-lamps,' said Mrs Franklyn with some regret. 'We cannot have electricity when only the servants are at home. Runs the juice down, you know.'

'I expect it does,' said James. He was looking at the substantial house. 'Eight hundred and twenty-three acres in all,' she told him. 'Mainly let, of course. I could never manage it on my own.'

She had halted the trap in the curved drive. The little horse gave a snort of achievement. James climbed down and hurried around to the other side of the vehicle to give her his hand. She fluttered a little and thanked him. 'One is not used to such courtesies now,' she said. 'Something to do with being at war.'

She led him towards an impressive porch. Lights glimmered behind windows of coloured leaded glass. She pulled a bell which sounded gravely within. The door was opened without any sound of locks and a butler with showy side whiskers stood bowing almost before it was fully opened. 'Trenchard,' announced Mrs Franklyn. 'We have a young guest.'

'Exactly,' said Trenchard as if nothing was ever news. 'Welcome, sir.'

'Mr Bevan,' she said. She studied James and noted his stripes. 'Sergeant Bevan.' They were in a handsome hall with the head of a wild boar projecting from the wall and a fine longcase clock opposite. A magnificent staircase with carved balustrade ascended into the dimness.

'Sergeant Bevan fell out of the train,' said Mrs Franklyn. The butler, taking her coat, murmured: 'Exactly.'

'We must look after him until morning. I think he might like a drink.'

'Exactly, madam. And what would you like, sir? Colonel Franklyn left some fine whiskies.'

'A fine whisky would be excellent,' said James. They laughed and Trenchard said: 'Exactly.'

The butler retreated. The house was warm about them. She led him into a drawing-room larger than he had ever seen. There was a carved fireplace and a great and hairy Irish wolfhound sprawled in front of the flames. 'That's McColl,' said Mrs Franklyn pushing the dog with her foot. 'He doesn't often get up.' She indicated a deep sofa. 'Please sit down, James.'

'My uniform's a bit messy from that embankment,' he said.

She smiled directly at him and motioned him to sit anyway. Now she was without her coat he could see she was a comfortably sized woman. Her face and her smile were sweet. He lowered himself into the cushions. He was concious of the hugeness of his boots on the white rug. 'You poor boy,' she said surveying him carefully. 'What a thing to happen.'

'Is your husband serving?' asked James tentatively.

Her big eyes rolled to the ceiling. 'He was. The Turks shot him. He was in command of Indian troops and they had to shoot *him* – the only white man for a hundred miles.'

'Dead, Mrs Franklyn?'

'Dead, I'm afraid.'

She leaned sideways and flicked an ornate brass switch. A lamp beside her went on. 'There,' she said proudly. 'Throughout the house. Even on the landings. My husband had the electricity established just before he embarked for Mesopotamia. It's like a memorial to him.'

James said he was very sorry and she nodded as if it were she who was sympathising with him. Trenchard appeared at the door with a tray of drinks. He handed a tumbler containing a rich red liquid to his mistress and another containing an amber measure to James. 'Water with it, sir? Or straight?'

'Oh, either,' said James. 'Straight or water.'

Trenchard arched his eyebrows which were bushy ginger although his hair and side whiskers were grey. He said: 'Exactly,' again, bowed and left the room.

Mrs Franklyn was smiling. 'You are a nice young man, James,' she said.

'Thank you, Mrs Franklyn,' said James. 'You seem a nice lady.' She raised her glass and then put it to her lips, her eyes shining over its rim. 'Rum,' she said. 'Demerara.' James lifted his glass likewise, took the first sip of Scotch of his life and exploded in choking and coughing. She was immediately all concern, hurrying across the room to take his glass and strike him none too gently between the shoulders. Trenchard reappeared, strode diffidently towards him, took the whisky glass and sniffed at it. 'Exactly,' he said. 'Must have been a bad batch.' His hair and whiskers shook. 'It's the war.'

When James had recovered, apologised and said he would like a Bovril instead, Mrs Franklyn suggested that he should have a bath and change his clothes. 'Ossie was about your size,' she said wistfully. 'There's a full wardrobe upstairs.'

'Is it convenient for me to stay?'

'Of course, James,' Mrs Franklyn said. 'We don't often have anyone who has fallen from a train. We must see that you are bathed, clothed and fed. Tomorrow you can continue on your journey.'

She showed him to an upstairs bathroom. It had a hot-water geyser bigger than the one at Thorncliffe which served a whole dormitory. There was a bedroom next door with a carefully made double bed. 'This will be yours,' she said. 'Where is your mother, by the way?'

'She's dead,' said James. 'Nearly three years ago. I don't know where my father is. I think he may be dead too.'

Her huge eyes became magnified with tears. 'You poor young soul,' she mumbled stretching the pauses between the words. 'There's so much sadness in the world now.' She went to the wardrobe, opened it and began to select clothes, glancing at him over her shoulder at intervals to size him up. 'You're almost the same size as Ossie. As he was,' she repeated. 'You're quite big for your age. How old are you, did you say?'

'Sixteen,' said James who had not said. 'I'll be seventeen soon.'

'As old as the century.'

'Exactly,' said James realising he was sounding like Trenchard.

She laid an expensive-looking shirt, a pair of tailored trousers, some long underpants and a waistcoat on the bed. She added a pair of woollen socks and produced a pair of black brogues. 'Lift up your foot, dear,' she said. He sat on the bed as she measured the sole of the brogue against his army boot. 'I thought so,' she nodded. 'Just right.'

She left the room and he heard the water running in the bath, after a muted explosion from the geyser. He did not dare to imagine what might happen. Perhaps lonely war widows often took in young soldiers who had fallen from trains. His mind whirled, his body tingled.

Mrs Franklyn returned with an opulent dressing-gown. 'There,' she said handing it to him. 'I'm afraid Ossie did not have good taste when it came to robes, although he looked very dashing when dressed as an inhabitant of the Ottoman Empire. I have a photograph which I must show you.' She waved to him coyly as she went out again. He locked the door after her. As he took his clothes off, he caught sight of himself in a long mirror. His reflection filled it.

After he had put on the robe he took another look, turning around in front of the glass to admire its extravagance. He projected his heavy knee from the folds and struck a pose, grinning to himself. He was disturbed by an attempt to open the door and then a timid knock. 'Your bath is ready, James.'

Breathing deeply he went towards the door. 'I didn't mean to lock it,' he apologised. 'It's just habit. If you don't lock it at school they come in and play tricks.'

She led him into the steam of the bathroom. 'It will soon clear,' she said. 'Make sure the water is not too hot.' Then she vanished through the vapour.

James closed the door silently and went towards the bath. It was half full. Quickly he removed the dressing-gown and climbed in. There was a bar of Pears soap, oval, in an enamel dish and he took it and rubbed it frantically with his hands over the surface of the water to make a patina of suds. Mrs Franklyn came back.

'I would love to wash your hair,' she said. 'I always washed Ossie's hair in the bath and I miss doing that.'

He sat like a child in the warm sudsy water. She took the soap and, rolling up her sleeves like a washerwoman, rubbed it into a froth. Then she worked her hands over his head, gently circling, and beginning to sing below her breath like someone who has found happiness in their work. Her palms went down over his shoulders. He sat stiff and straight, his inside in turmoil. Then she rubbed the suds into his chest. 'Oh, I miss my Ossie so much,' she sniffled. He saw that she was really crying.

'I expect you do,' he managed to say.

Without warning she plunged both hards below the water and caught him softly by the testicles. His half-shout was stifled to a groan and then another as her plump hands moved up and down and up again, rubbing him below the water. 'Oh, you are a big boy, Jimmy,' she murmured. No one had ever called him Jimmy before.

James was now lying stiff as wood against the back of the bath with his penis pointing pinkly from the water. She continued to be engrossed in soaping it. He had to put his hands somewhere so he reached up towards the top half of her dress. 'Hold hard a moment,' she said almost heartily. She released one hand but kept working with the other. Dexterously she unbuttoned her dress down to the waist, and unlaced a silk camisole. Her full breasts fell out spectacularly. 'Oh, Mrs Franklyn,' he said. 'Nothing like this has ever happened to me.'

'Nor me, Jimmy,' she breathed fervently. She was sweating in the steam. She tapped the head of his member, lightly as if testing it. Then she suddenly leaned and to his utter astonishment passionately kissed the swollen end. 'Oh, Mrs Franklyn,' was all he could say.

Her voice came up faintly: 'I'll get you some supper later, dear.'

'I was afraid you might think me a little flirtatious,' Mrs Franklyn said.

Again James groaned. It was well into the early hours. From the depths of her bed he could hear an owl hooting. It was the fourth time she had woken him with some chance remark accompanied by a heavy push of her bosom. For all he knew she might have been talking continuously while he slept only rousing him after an interval for rest. 'I must sleep, Mrs Franklyn,' he mumbled this time. 'I must sleep.'

'Of course you must,' she murmured hanging her tubby, naked body over him. 'You need sleep for your strength. So, just oncc more, Jimmy, just once.'

'I'm not experienced.'

He felt he had not even the power to raise himself on his elbows. 'Don't you worry, dear,' she said. Once more her hand, and then her hands, delved below. They were soft, full hands. 'There, look,' she said sweetly. 'There he is again. Come to visit Mrs Franklyn.'

'But I can't, Mrs Franklyn. I must sleep.'

'You lie there,' she soothed. 'Close your eyes if you so wish.'

He closed his eyes and, another surprise, felt her clambering above him. He did not realise it could be done like that. Her thighs clasped him and he felt her hang backwards, take his swaying member in her hand and feed it luxuriously into her body. His eyes half opened and he looked up at her, rotund and passionate, in the dim light of the electric lamp dangling from the ceiling. As she moved he thought the shade of the lamp began to sway. The bed springs creaked. God, but it felt lovely. She fixed him with her excessive eyes and he squinted up at her. Her face was set in a determined glare, as though nothing would stop her now. Exhausted as he was he began to move with her. 'That's right, Jimmy,' she purred. 'That's right. One, two, three and a big one, two, three and a big one.'

As he climaxed again he truly thought she had gone mad. Warnings that sex affected the brain rushed back.

She flung herself from side to side her hair swishing around her face, her mouth roundly open in a silent cry. He was amazed that he could come to it again but he did and she let out a long, seeping howl, threw herself back and then forwards on to him, her big breasts hitting his chest like boxing gloves, and knocking every last wheeze of breath from him. 'No more, Mrs Franklyn,' he managed to plead. 'No more.'

To his immense relief this time she nodded and said: 'Enough is quite enough when you aren't used to it.' She then rolled over, almost liquidly, like a large squid, and fell into the bed alongside him where she quickly let out a healthy and satisfied snore. He looked over cagily and decided that she would not be back for more that night. His eyes dropped and he slept.

It was bright morning when he woke. Winter birds were noisy in the garden and Mrs Franklyn was standing, glowing beside the bed, enveloped in a pink frilled dressing-gown from which her head projected like that of a big exotic bird. She carried a tray upon which were a teapot and a delicate cup and saucer. 'Have you rested, Jimmy?' she asked.

James eyed her apprehensively but her expression was composed, without intent. He gave her a careful smile and said: 'Good morning. Yes, I'm rested, thank you.'

Her round, pleasant face flushed and to his consternation she placed the tea tray on a small table and advanced on the bed. She only sat on it, however, and in a motherly way. 'You were sent to me by God, Jimmy,' she said. 'When I saw you standing in the dark I knew at once God had sent you.' She held his hand for a moment. 'I hope you didn't mind. My husband has died for his country. Perhaps you should consider it part of your war work.'

'I will,' he said.

She touched his bare chest but all the passion had gone

from her now. 'You don't have a ticket for the train, do you?' she asked.

He felt himself colour. 'No. I didn't have enough money. That is why I had to jump.'

'I thought that was so,' she said. 'Inverness is almost five hundred miles from here.'

'It's a long way, I know. But I want to find Agnes.' He pursed his lips. 'I'll have to do what I did before. Hide.'

'No, no,' she said laying her hand on his wrist. Her touch remained warm. '*And* you have to return.'

'I planned to give myself up,' he said. 'To the police or the army. Then *they'll* have to get me back.'

Consternation filled her face. 'But . . . what will they do? Can they court-martial a boy?'

It sounded odd hearing her call him a boy. He said: 'I don't think they can. But I'll get some sort of punishment. Demoted, confined to barracks, extra duties, drills. The only way to get out of that is to volunteer for France.'

Her hand went to her mouth. 'Oh, no,' she said. 'You're too young for those terrible trenches.'

'There are plenty there of my age,' he said.

'What a world,' was all she said. Then almost absently: 'Young fellows drowning in mud.' She went from the room and returned with a tin cash box. The key looked tiny in her fingers. She took two white five-pound notes from it. 'This will pay your fare and provide your rations,' she said. 'And your billets.'

Tears came to his eyes. He tried to wipe them away. 'But Mrs Franklyn . . . I can't . . . I wouldn't . . .'

'You must,' she said pressing the notes into his hand. His fingers closed around them.

She leaned towards him and kissed him on the chest, then on the face, her breasts rolling against him again but softly now. 'You must find your sister.'

* * *

She drove him to the station in the trap. He thought how much he had learned since he had last been aboard it. There was a train going north at eleven and they sat unspeaking, shyly holding hands below the rug. He was wearing her husband's handmade black brogues; his army boots were in a brown-paper bag. Eventually she said: 'On your return journey, Jimmy, you might consider calling on me.'

'I'll remember.'

'You ought to go now. The train is in five minutes and you must get your ticket.' She leaned over and, still in a motherly fashion, kissed him on the cheek. He climbed down from the trap. The pony turned and snorted gently at him. He walked towards the station and she turned the trap in the road. He made to wave to her but she was already on her way back towards her lonely, electricity-lit house, her gaze fixed between the horse's ears.

He reached Glasgow in the evening. The street outside the station seemed to be crammed with noise; the drunks and the tramcars staggering in the rain. Without looking around he picked his way into a side street, mean and dark. From the centre glimmered the gaslight of a pie shop and he went in, brought two meat pies and asked the woman where he could get lodgings. She was eating a pie herself, her mouth crowded with meat and pastry. She pointed to the left.

The next house in the terrace had a notice reading: 'Rooms.' He knocked on the door and a pop-eyed man let him in. They had a room; it was small but it only cost a shilling.

It took only a cupboard, a litter-like bed and a frail chair to fill the room. 'You'll ha' to go outside to do ya' business,' said the man. His eyes protruded alarmingly and when he blinked the lids failed to cover them. 'Ta ha' a piss, ya' understan'.'

James said he understood. ''Tis roon the back. If ye need to shit, get there quick. Afore the others.'

The man went, muttering to himself as he stumbled down the stairs. James followed and he obligingly led him out of a rear door and into a yard, wet and foul, with a shaky shed leaning against the wall. 'There's na light,' said the man. 'Some bastard has took it. So don't fall doon.'

James avoided doing so and crept back along the yard and into the house. 'Will ye take a dram?' asked the man now sitting at a table piled with a pyramid of bottles, crockery and the remains of food, shadowed by a dull oil-lamp. 'I was thinking o' clearin' up,' he said.

Politely James refused the whisky. 'I had enough last night,' he said not untruthfully, recalling Trenchard's scotch. He went up the gritty stairs again. There was no heat in the room and he climbed into bed among the matted blankets. The pillow was filled with paper. He kept his uniform on, taking off only Mrs Franklyn's late husband's shoes and putting them with his boots, still in the brown-paper bag, under the bed. He heard the sounds of the street and remembered the comfort of last night's mattress and her plump embrace. He did not know how long he had been asleep when he was woken by drunken shouts, then a woman's screeching. He got up and put the rickety chair under the doorknob and, lying fearfully, waited for someone to burst in. Nobody did. He heard snoring and a man cursing in his sleep. He closed his eyes again.

James was still afraid of being spotted and asked for his papers and leave pass by the police or the military patrols at the stations, but there were many soldiers travelling and he remained cautious. The Inverness train was at ten in the morning. He kept himself concealed, boarding it only as it was about to leave and finding a seat in a front compartment of the crowded carriage.

The great engine pulled out of Glasgow. The other seats were occupied by women, one with a small boy in a sailor suit, and one elderly man who gazed apparently without seeing over the silvered handle of his walking-stick.

The journey took all day. At a small station a young woman in black got on and took a seat vacated by one of the others. She had been crying and the sight of the sailor suit made her cry again. The boy's mother and the other women tried to comfort her but in the end she left and stood in the corridor, staring out into the sullen country and weeping with the rain against the window. The old man remained blank eyed over his stick.

At six in the evening the engine steamed into Inverness. James, keeping an eye out for the police, went with the crowds. There was a motor bus outside the station and he asked the conductor for the location of St Ursula's School for Girls. It was outside the town, said the man, but the bus would be going past. 'It's late though,' he warned. 'They lock the lasses awa' at night.'

The bus rattled out into the country. It was almost dark and outside the window there was only a void. He felt elated that he was at the end of his journey, that he had succeeded so far. Now how would he find Agnes? 'St Ursula's,' called the conductor. 'The saint of virgins.'

Some of the passengers laughed. James got off and watched the vehicle trundle away. He was outside the gates of the school, its pointed roofs against the sky. There were few lights showing and he tried the gates but they were locked. On the stone column was a huge bell-pull. He tugged it. Nothing happened and he tried again. Eventually a bleak little light appeared and then came a lantern travelling through the dark towards him. A long face, stark white and unpleased, appeared through the ornate bars of the gate. 'And what would ye be seeking at this time o' the night?' she asked.

'My sister,' he said bluntly. 'Agnes Bevan. Is she still here?'

'Enquiries must wait fa' tomorrow,' she grunted. 'Away with ye or I'll call the constabulary.'

She turned and the lantern retreated into the darkness towards the open door. James almost called after her but he thought of the police. He watched the door close, shutting off both lights. Emptily he walked away from the gate in the direction of the town. He was going below the heavy wall of the school, dragging his feet with disappointment, when he saw the white of a face in a single window above him. He stared up and the face moved away but almost at once returned. He waved. There was the fluttering of a hand and he remained standing below. There came a scraping noise, and some grit fell. The window was opened no more than an inch. It was a girl. 'Who do you want?' she whispered.

'Agnes Bevan,' he called up softly. 'Do you know where she is?'

'She's awa'. She's in the town working for Mr Sheldon.'

'Where? Where does he live?'

'By the market-place. I've got to go. They're coming.' The window was shut quickly and the face vanished. James waited for a moment and then set off on the comfortless road.

It took him half an hour to walk back to the middle of the town. The rain thickened. His khaki tunic was becoming heavy with it; the drops trickled from the peak of his cap. Colonel Franklyn's shoes were getting damp. No vehicle passed in either direction and there was scarcely a light on any side.

Eventually some cottages materialised and then what appeared to be the main way into the town centre. Five minutes later he found two boys standing under a gas lamp as though it might give them shelter from the rain; hands in pockets, they were conversing deeply. He asked where the market-place was and, pointing to the ground, one boy said: 'Ye'r treadin' on it.'

They pointed out Mr Sheldon's house, more imposing than the rest, set at the corner of the square next to a shop with the sign: 'Sheldon. Builder and Undertaker.' James went to the door, shook the rain from his cap and knocked. It was some time before a light flickered in the fanlight. The action of opening the door was irritable and the face that protruded through the gap no less so.

'Who'll be dead?' asked the woman. 'Is it the funeral business ye want?' Her hair was pulled back and her eye sockets were deep so that her face looked like a lantern. The clock in the market square sounded.

'Sorry,' said James. 'I believe Agnes Bevan works here. She's my sister.'

The face sniffed. 'Yer sister she may be, but she doesna' work here no longer.'

The door was uncompromisingly slammed in his face. He knocked again. The light fluttered behind the fanlight. 'Begone,' said the woman through the narrowest of apertures. 'I dinna ken where she'll be.'

Once more the door was thrust home and he turned away, wet and disconsolate. He turned and walked along the pavement where the gas lamps reflected in the wet. The two boys were still talking earnestly but they saw him walking away and called to him. 'Who is it ye'r seekin'?' asked one.

He told them. They did not know but the first one

said he would ask his sister. He trotted across the square, his legs stiffly protruding from his short trousers. A door opened and closed. The remaining boy studied James's uniform. 'Ha' ye been scrappin' the Germans?'

'Not yet,' said James. 'Soon I'll be going.'

'Ah, I'd like to be scrappin' them. So would Wullie, there. We want the war to go on until we get there. Another three years.'

The door opened again and the boy came out with a skinny girl who had an apron over her head in the rain. 'Is that Aggie?' she asked. 'That was workin' for Mr Sheldon at the house.'

He had never thought of Agnes as Aggie. 'Aggie? Oh, yes, that will be her.'

'She's flitted from there. She works in the laundry. Now, this time o' night, she'll be at the Craigie.'

She turned and, sheltering below the apron, trotted back to the door. 'What's the Craigie?' he asked the boys.

'The Craigie?' they repeated as though astonished he did not know. 'It's a wee pub.'

They both pointed to the opposite corner of the square. 'Along the way there,' said Wullie.

James thanked them and went across the cobbled square. 'Guid luck wi' the Germans,' called one of the boys. 'Aye, guid luck,' said the other. They were envious. He waved with what he hoped was assurance and took the tight lane. It was in darkness except for one house, low as a cowshed, halfway down. There were lights in the windows and he could hear the sounds of voices. Above the door an inn sign creaked although there was no wind, only rain. He could not see what it said.

He attempted to look through the window but it was steamed up. There was a small pane above the door and he peered through that into a packed room. There were harsh voices and gruff laughter. Through the tight window he looked as best he could around the room, above the heads. Then a man pushed his way out of a crowd carrying two tankards. In the moment that the people parted he saw her standing, laughing, as only she laughed, looking straight towards him. Agnes.

She went from sight again. He pressed down the latch on the door and walked into the smoke and smells. Several people turned to look at him and a woman with rotten teeth grinned as he went down the single step. He eased his way towards the bar.

There she was, her back to him now, with two tiny children in grubby clothes, with smeared faces and golden curly hair. One was standing on the bar and the other was trying to stand, Agnes supporting it with one hand. The onlookers cheered at the child's attempts to remain upright. The older one spotted James and stared at him through the crowd. Then Agnes turned and saw him.

'Oh, God. James.'

Impulsively she moved towards him leaving the infant balancing on the bar. It fell into a sitting position and then tripped over the back of the counter with a shriek.

'The bairn's in the sink!' cried an old woman hurrying behind the counter.

'Dougal's in the slops!' shouted a man.

Agnes spun away from James and rushed back. The baby was being retrieved, howling and coughing, soaked in beer. Held upright it spat a mouthful of ale over the old woman. The other child, arms spread, was proudly keeping its balance. A woman rushed from a room behind the bar and hooted with laughter when she saw the baby. She picked it up and hugged it wetly to her. Agnes lifted the other child in her arms and turned again towards James.

'Hello, James,' she said soberly.

He leaned and kissed her around the grubby toddler. 'Hello, Agnes.' His smile filled his face and she smiled back: 'You don't seem to have changed very much,' he said.

She lived in a narrow room on the edge of the town. They walked back, eating eels and bread they had been given at the pub. She sat on the bed and he on the only chair. 'Why did you leave Mr Sheldon's?' he asked.

'Mr Sheldon,' she said simply.

'He was making advances?'

'I had to lock my door, but sooner or later he was going to get it open. I didn't mind Hamish but not Mr Sheldon.'

'Hamish?'

'Och, the son. He was bonnie, as they say.' Her voice now had an edge of accent. 'For an undertaker's son.'

'How bonnie?'

'Really grand. He looked fine going off to war in his uniform and his plaid.' She regarded him challengingly. 'I don't think it's such a terrible thing to lose your virginity to a man going off to war in a kilt.'

'Agnes, you're only fourteen.'

'I'm fifteen before too long. Anyway, what does that matter? He came to my bed one night in full uniform. It's as easy for a man as for a woman when the man's wearing a kilt. He just lifts it up. Then he went off to fight.' She appeared doubtful. 'At least I think he did. I heard he only got as far as Fort William.' She regarded him challengingly. 'James, have you lost your virginity yet?'

There was only a low light in the room but she saw his blush. 'You have!' she said. She squeezed him with a sort of excitement. 'Who was she? Was she beautiful?'

'In a way, she was,' he said. 'It only happened two nights ago.'

'Ah! I beat you to it.'

They sat talking long into the night. 'I'm not staying here,' said Agnes. 'I slave in the steam of the laundry all day and then I go the Craigie to look after the children. When they're not falling in the slops.'

Her laugh was infectious. They hugged each other. 'Where will you go?' he asked.

'To London.'

'It's no place for a young girl.'

'Don't be silly. I can look after myself. Being up here has taught me that. Down south there are good jobs in the munitions factories.'

'Girls have been blown up.'

'Or I could work on the trams. Do *something*, anyway. At least women can work now. I'll manage.' She hesitated, then said: 'I'd like to sing and dance, you know, James. I mean on the stage. At that school I was always in the concerts and many a time I've sung in the Craigie, standing on the bar. I'm really good. They like me to sing.' Abruptly she appeared concerned. 'Will you be punished for what you've done?'

'Going absent? I'll volunteer for the real army,' he said.

'And get yourself killed. I warned you a long time ago.'

'I remember,' he smiled. He looked about the room.

'You need some place to sleep,' she said. 'You must stay here, James.'

He surveyed the close room with its solitary bed and desolate fireplace. 'If I put my head in the grate I could stretch myself across the floor.'

Agnes stood and said: 'Better than that.' She opened a cupboard where a few clothes hung. 'See what I've got.' She pulled out a long roll of canvas with cords at each end. 'A hammock. Like they used in India.'

'You are still amazing.'

'Old Ma Sheldon was throwing it out so I snaffled it. I even got the man downstairs to put some hooks in the wall.' She pointed. 'In case of visitors.' She picked up the hammock and James helped her hook it up. Doubtfully he tested it. 'Will it take my weight?'

'Not yours, mine. If you fell out you'd bring the house down.'

She kissed him and he held her tightly to him. 'You get into bed. You must be tired out.' She opened the door. 'The lav is on the landing. I'll get myself ready.'

She went out. James sat on the bed and realised how deeply weary he was. He took off the brogues, got out of his jacket and trousers and lifting the blankets on the bed rolled beneath them. Agnes appeared in a long white nightdress, her breasts slightly swelling it. 'I'll need some help, James.'

He climbed from the bed and held the hammock while attempting to help her into it with his other hand. She got in but at once slid out the other side. She began to laugh. They tried again. This time she hung on, balancing herself for a moment, but then tipped out. Laughing too, he caught her. 'Once more,' she giggled. 'We'll be waking the house.' He was conscious of how light, even bony, she was. 'Push my bum, James,' she said breathlessly hanging across the hammock. He did. She managed to get herself into it and tentatively stretched the full length of it. 'That's going to be grand,' she said. 'Good night, James.'

Holding the hammock steady he kissed her again. He backed away towards the bed and crept under the blankets. His eyes closed at once. There was a creak and the hammock swung. Agnes clung on with one hand but then slid to the floor. 'It's no good,' she sighed. 'I'll break my neck in this contraption.'

Without another word, and without looking at him,

she stepped towards the bed. James moved over and she slid her slight frame below the blankets. They were tightly against each other, her back to him, his arms encircling her. 'It doesn't matter,' she whispered. 'It's like it was before, remember? After all, we are brother and sister.'

8

In early May 1940 a high and solitary German plane dropped a single bomb in a field in Kent, turned and went home. There were no casualties and the only damage was the hole in the field. It was the first bomb on English soil. The following weeks were to see the massive sweep of the German armies through Europe only halted by the grey waters of the English Channel. British police were issued with revolvers.

'What is *that*, if I might ask?'

Unsworth had laid the gun in its shiny leather case on the kitchen table. 'It's a six shooter. Like Hopalong Cassidy's in the films.'

'Why have *you* got it?'

'To shoot Germans.'

'I don't like you having a gun. Somebody might shoot you back.'

Ellen had the week's washing piled around her feet. She had lit the boiler early that morning and when the cauldron above the coal fire was bubbling she dropped in the Reckitt's blue bag. 'You're supposed to be in charge of civilians,' she grumbled giving the first load of washing a stir with her whitened boiler stick worn thin by a thousand Mondays. 'Not having guns to shoot at parachutists.' She sniffed and wiped her eyes. 'I don't know what things are coming to. We've got an army, haven't we? Why give the police force guns?'

He turned her gently. 'It's only the steam,' she said wiping her eyes with the pudgy back of her hand. She regarded him sorrowfully. 'But you know what I mean, Alf.'

'I doubt if you'd hit a parachutist with this thing,' said Unsworth patting the revolver with a touch of sympathy. 'Not if he was coming down at any velocity.' He laughed. 'It's got a kick like a cow. You should have seen the practice. Bullets flying everywhere. The station dog took off and hasn't been seen since.'

Catcher heard the word 'dog' and came into the kitchen. 'Let's see how he likes it,' said Unsworth.

'No, you don't,' said Ellen firmly. 'We don't want any bullets around here. Not until the proper time comes.'

'I wasn't going to fire the thing. It's not loaded anyway. I've only got six rounds of ammunition, that's all they could give us.' He reached for the shiny holster, unbuttoned it and took out the huge revolver. 'Weighs a ton,' he said. Ellen was staring at it, repelled. 'Let's see what Catcher thinks,' repeated Unsworth. He proffered the gun, butt first, to the dog who smelled it and backed away with an uncertain whine.

'I don't blame him either,' said Ellen. To his surprise she reached for the revolver and took it in both hands, lifting it with difficulty but then pointing it around the room. Unsworth gently diverted it. 'Not at my chest,' he said. 'Or anybody else's.'

'Unless it's necessary,' she said. 'If a German came into my kitchen I'd blow his head off.'

The telephone jangled. It seemed to Ellen that it sounded different if it was police business. Her husband came back from answering the call. 'You know the war memorial in Brockenhurst?' he said. 'The one with the field gun on it.'

She had to think. 'These war memorials all look the

same. Even if you can remember them at all. I think I know what you mean. What about it?'

'The field gun that was on it, isn't any more. Somebody's pinched it.'

Ugson and Cartwright walked like veterans into the weekly dance at Lyndhurst public hall. 'Let any bugger try to tell me what war is all about,' sniffed Cartwright, 'and I'll tell *them.*' He looked sideways at Ugson: 'Won't we?'

Ugson had doubts. 'We can't say we've been to Norway, it's against orders.'

Cartwright was scrutinising the available girls and the rival males, civilian and servicemen, ranged around the dance floor. The band was almost lost in cigarette smoke. 'What do this lot know about *action*?' he said. 'Sod all.'

'Sod all,' agreed Ugson.

'I bet none of those blokes, army, RAF or whatever, have been in any. As for the civvies . . . well, a couple of pints and a feel of some girl's drawers is about all the action they know.'

'I wouldn't mind that,' said Ugson. 'A feel of drawers.'

Cartwright went to get the beer. 'There's two girls over there, by the bar,' he reported when he returned. 'Yours is not much good.'

'She'll be all right for me, Carty. I'm not proud.'

'That's what I thought. We'll drink these and move in on them. Can't leave your beer lying around in here.'

They drank quickly and Cartwright led the way. The nondescript girls were still there. 'Want a dance then?' asked Cartwright.

'Port and lemon, please,' said one of the girls. 'My name's Peggy.'

'I said a dance, not a drink.' He looked at Ugson. 'Didn't I, Ugly?'

'We'll have a drink after,' suggested Ugson apologetically.

'Oh, all right,' sniffed Peggy. 'As long as we do.' She examined both soldiers and chose Cartwright. Her friend, a whispy blonde, regarded Ugson with no sign of enthusiasm. He extended his arms and with a sniff she stepped sulkily on to the dance floor. The band stopped almost at once and she looked as if she was going to walk off. 'What's your name?' he asked to stall her.

'Shirley. You're Ugly.'

'I can't help it. Oh, you mean my name. How d'you know?'

'Your mate called you it.'

The master of ceremonies, a bald men in a huntsman's coat, announced from the misty location of the band: 'Waltz. Waltz, ladies and gentlemen.'

Shirley sighed, turned her eyes to the ceiling and held out her thin arms. Ugson moved close but she eased him away. 'We've seen action,' he mentioned as they began to dance. Cartwright came alongside with the other girl. 'We've seen action, haven't we, Carty?' he repeated, attempting the look of a veteran.

'I was just saying,' said Cartwright. 'To Peggy.'

'*We've* seen action,' said Peggy. 'On the pictures.'

Both girls screeched with laughter at the joke. Ugson looked painfully at Cartwright. The girls took their hands from their faces and, seeing the men's reaction, grumpily continued to waltz. 'I don't care about the bloody war,' sniffed Shirley. 'Neither does Peg. We're not interested. Only if the Yankees come in.'

The lugubrious dance went on. 'We nearly got killed,' said Cartwright.

'Oh, all right,' sighed Peggy. 'Tell us where.'

‘Can’t,’ said Ugson leaning towards the other couple. ‘It’s secret.’

For a moment both women looked faintly more impressed. ‘You can tell us.’

‘Can’t,’ said Cartwright. ‘We had casualties.’

‘Blokes dead,’ said Ugson.

‘We won’t tell the Germans,’ giggled Peggy. ‘*Spell* it out.’

Ugson glanced at Cartwright. ‘All right,’ he said.

‘It starts with N . . . then O . . .’

‘I know!’ exploded Shirley. ‘NOWHERE!’

Both girls collapsed with mirth, holding their cheap dresses at the hips. They fell away from the soldiers and staggered to the side of the dance floor, leaving Ugson and Cartwright at the centre. They stared towards the hysterically laughing females.

‘Fuck ’em,’ sniffed Cartwright.

‘That’s what I say,’ said Ugson sadly.

‘At least we don’t ’ave to buy them drinks.’

The early summer skies remained unruffled. The two Bofors, noses to the air, waited, but still no raiders came. The bad news became more threatening every day but in the south the English coast was as placid as a backwater. It was only erratically that barbed-wire entanglements began to appear on the beaches and service officers drove up in batches to briefly sweep the Channel with their outsized field-glasses like explorers surveying a recent discovery.

The sentry at the camp gate, under orders to remain alert, saw the boy on his bicycle from a good distance. The coastal road was straight. Franz pedalled maniacally, the wind buffeting his glasses, his fair hair flying, shouting like the Valkyrie he was pretending to be. He braked and pulled up in front of the army gate. The bicycle was a novel experience to him, as was the open air, but he took to it with his customary enthusiasm. 'Halt!' challenged the sentry, Gunner Purcell. 'Who goes there?'

Franz, astonished by the officiality of it, answered: 'I am Franz.'

'What d'you want?' demanded the lanky Purcell. He felt stupid with the bayonet extended towards the thin boy in glasses.

'I have a letter. Do not shoot me. Or stick me with that spike.' He fumbled in his pocket and took out a folded envelope which he handed to Purcell. From the guardhouse, twenty yards from the gate, came Gunner Cartwright. 'What's he want, Persil?'

'He's from the school.'

'I played football with you,' Franz reminded them. He pointed at Purcell. 'You were not good.'

'Shall I shoot him?' asked Purcell over his shoulder.

'It would make trouble for you,' forecast Franz.

'He's got a letter. It's for Captain Bevan.'

'I'll take it,' said Cartwright assuming responsibility quickly. He took the envelope. 'Have you played any more?' he asked Franz.

'No more, the ball has broken.'

'We'll have to come and pump it up.'

Franz threw up a salute, Purcell lifted his bayonet, and the boy turned the bicycle and pedalled furiously away shouting like a warrior. 'They're odd, those kids,' said Purcell. 'They're not like our kids.'

Cartwright took the letter. Bevan was in his office filling in a Whitehall form about the religious denominations in the unit. 'What are you, Cartwright?' he asked. 'What religion?'

'My dad always reckoned he was Philadelphiancala-thumpian,' said Cartwright. 'Put down C of E, sir.'

He handed the letter across. 'The odd kid from the Jerusalem place brought this.'

Bevan took it and thanked him. He had just said goodbye to Lieutenant Chance, who had temporarily replaced him during the Norway expedition. 'All right, was it?' the short-sighted officer had asked as if Bevan had only been to the dentist. Bevan wondered if, behind those glasses, he had any notion of what was happening. Without waiting for an answer Chance said: 'All quiet here.' Bevan, glad to see him go, muttered: 'So was it on the Western Front.' Now he waited until Cartwright had gone before opening the letter. It was only one line long. 'Darling Bevan, I would like to see you tonight.'

Lady Violet Foxley eased her horse through the trees; they were in no hurry and the horse took time to slyly nibble at the greenest of the new leaves. It was a morning ride she had made many times. She wanted to enjoy it to the utmost now because she felt profoundly that the life she knew would soon be altered, that nothing would be the same again. A deep drone in the sky made her pause and she and the horse, who had heard it too, looked up through the screening branches to see a tiny, lofty aeroplane, moving through pale clouds. It was remote, unthreatening. 'One of ours,' she said.

There was scarcely any need to touch the reins for the animal knew the ride intimately. It even knew where to pause by the forest brook where once her father, furiously leading the hunt, had come tumbling off and ended sitting and swearing in the water. She never failed to smile at the place. It was her first hunt and he had been trying to impress.

Penelope was to have joined Lady Violet that morning. She was down from London but her pregnancy was more pronounced and she had decided to stay off horseback.

She was going to have and keep the baby. There had been some difficult scenes. 'Why don't you produce this fecund person?' her ladyship had demanded. 'Does he have other children? Does his wife know about *all* of them?'

'There is no point in me producing him, even if I could,' Penelope had argued. 'His department is being moved somewhere distant. I doubt if I will see him again.'

'Let's hope to God he's handsome,' her mother had said bitterly. 'I couldn't stand an ugly grandchild.' She sniffed. 'We'll soon know.'

Now she rode through the sylvan shadows, wondering, worrying about her family. Both her sons were now in France. Everyone, apart from the High Command apparently, knew that France was about to be invaded and would probably crumble like a cheese. She often prayed when on horseback and she prayed now.

'Take 'er easy,' came a voice through the screen of trees. 'Bring 'er round, Catcher. No, not like that. Round bit, pointing.'

The horse cocked its ears and Lady Violet listened, leaning over its head. They had halted in good cover. She put out her arm and pushed away overhanging branches. In the glade before her were four men tugging at a small artillery piece. 'Push 'un, push 'un, Catcher.'

She eased her mount forward through the cover. Little Catcher saw her first and his face drained. He came to a sort of attention, rolling his eyes at the others. They turned and saw Lady Violet.

'Good heavens,' she said. 'Whatever do you have here?'

Catcher, still at his version of attention, said: ''Tis a gun, m'lady.'

'We found 'un,' said Tom Dibben. He pointed to the ground. 'Right 'ere, didn' we, boys.'

'We're goin' to hand 'un in,' said Rob who she knew was landlord of the Birchwood Hut. 'To the police.'

They were relieved at her smile. 'Well, I wonder who left it lying about?' she said. 'It looks just like the one that used to be on the war memorial in Brockenhurst.'

'That's it!' said Rob smacking his forehead with his hand. 'That's where we'd seen 'un. Brockenhurst!' He looked at them as though horrified. 'Somebody must 'ave took it.'

'It wasn't doing much good there,' said Lady Violet. 'And it looks quite businesslike. Do you have any ammo?'

'No, m'lady,' said Catcher. 'Ain't none. But we thought it would look . . . well, like froitening.'

'Froitening,' confirmed Tom Dibben. 'Scare they Germans, t'wud.'

'Splendid notion,' said her ladyship. 'We must be prepared. But you can't leave it out here in the forest. It will get wet. Why don't you take it up to the manor and put it in the stables.' She put her finger to her lips. 'And tell no one. It will be our secret weapon.'

It was seven o'clock when Bevan walked along the beach towards Jerusalem House. The sand was wet. It was a fretful evening; the waves were choppy and the sky was like stone. Workmen who had been putting up the barbed-wire coils all day had gone home promptly at five just as they would have done in peacetime. Bevan had wondered why they could not employ soldiers since there were plenty sitting around. He had even put an enquiry through to divisional headquarters in Winchester offering his men as labour but the suggestion had been declined. 'Too difficult, old boy,' said the colonel at Winchester. 'Gives the civvies a job, in any case. Never do to take the bread out of a working man's mouth, you know. Too many unemployed.'

As Bevan walked three Hurricane fighters appeared with a noisy snort, flying low over the sea, keeping in triangular formation. They looked confident, reassuring. He wondered how many were ready. How many Spitfires, how many guns and tanks. Soon they would be needing them. But for the present the scene remained peacefully grey. Gulls tried balancing on the glinting barbed wire.

Renée was watching from her high window. They had met in the evening. She waved a red scarf as she always did. He wondered how long it would be before some busybody reported her as another alien signalling to a U-boat. They had laughed about it and he had said that perhaps she should wave a Union Jack. Still she waved the scarf.

On fine evenings it was their habit to walk towards Lymington. Sometimes they stopped at a pub along the coast, sometimes at a small restaurant. Afterwards they would return secretly into the sleeping school building and she would lead him up the stairs to her room.

Tonight there was something different about her. She had sent him the note and when they met she embraced him fiercely. Their walk was only short and they returned to Jerusalem House when there was still a trace of daylight. There was no need for rectitude at that time of the evening. Some of the boys were still playing in the yard and the staff had just finished their supper as they entered the big stuffy kitchen. They all knew Bevan by now. Herr Rohm, in his customary Scouting clothes, strode through, greeting Bevan with a firm pumping handshake and a hearty pat on the back before departing.

They sat down to cold meat and potatoes with baked beans. 'The boys love baked beans,' said Renée. 'Franz says it is because Heinz is an Austrian name.' She took a bottle of white wine from a cupboard, eyeing a mark on its side which indicated its level.

When they were seated at the huge scrubbed table, one each side, she said solemnly: 'There are going to be changes, Bevan. To begin, Herr Rohm is to go to London. He speaks five languages, you know.' She leaned closer. 'Some hush-hush job.'

Bevan grinned. 'Herr Rohm, hush-hush?'

She nodded. 'You cannot imagine him as a secret agent.'

'It's difficult.'

He knew she was going to tell him something but he did not prompt her. Near midnight when they were lying, familiarly now, in her tumbled bed under the eaves, she said: 'Do you remember the first time you made love to anyone, Bevan?'

'Very well,' he replied. 'I don't think anyone forgets.'

'My time,' she said quietly, 'was with a friend of my father.' She was lying on her back. She closed her eyes for a moment. Nothing she said surprised him now.

'Was he your father's age?'

'A little younger, but only a little. Perhaps five years. But it did not matter. It was right for me. In Vienna I had one or two student boyfriends but nothing exciting ever happened with them. They were . . . How is it said? – love lorn – but they never *did* anything. One used to kiss my *hand*. They were too much like gentlemen. Then this business friend of my father stayed at our house. He was attractive. I was seventeen. We went to bed together one afternoon. I can remember the sound of the traffic in the street below. And we went other times after that.' She laughed but with a hint of regret. 'Sometimes I think my father arranged it.'

'You mean that?'

'Well, maybe not *arranged* it. But he took care not to notice. To leave us in the house together. Perhaps I was part of a good business deal.'

'Didn't that upset you?'

'No. I didn't realise it then. I was very young. And, in any case, it was good for me too. It is not something I am sorry about.' She half turned. 'And you . . . when was your first time?'

He smiled at the ceiling. 'Also with someone older. Probably as different in age as your father's friend. It was when I went absent from the army school at Thorncliffe to go and see my sister Agnes in Scotland.'

Lying against her he related his adventure with Mrs Franklyn. Renée was entranced. She put the sheets between her teeth. 'It is a wonderful story,' she breathed. 'It makes me feel I want you again.'

They turned to each other. 'Four times?' she whispered, her eyes mockingly wide. 'You did it *four* entire times?'

Bevan said: 'At least. I was young and strong.'

By now they were very accustomed to each other. As he lay moving into her he sensed sadly that this would be the last time.

'Was that better than Mrs Franklyn?' she teased.

He kissed her. 'It was different.' He paused. He did not want her to tell him yet. 'I went back to see her. On the return journey from Scotland.'

Her expression warmed. 'But of course you would. And was she pleased?'

'Not at all. Her husband, the dead Ossie, was there.'

Renée put her hands across her mouth. 'He was not dead after all!'

'There he was, large as life, and I turned up with a bunch of flowers.'

'Oh God, this is too much.'

'You can only guess at my motives in going back.'

Renée giggled: 'Now that you were rested.'

'I stood outside the door and rang the bell. I heard a man's voice. For a moment I thought it was the butler but then I heard him laughing uproariously and I realised. I just had time to put the flowers behind my back. He opened the door, tanned, alive, in civvies. Words failed me. My mouth just opened. "Hello!" he said. "Who are you?"

'Behind him I got a brief glimpse of Mrs Franklyn dancing about like fury, trying to make signs to me. It was incredible. Fortunately I thought of something to say. I said: "I'm lost. Can you tell me the way to the station, please."

'"Of course, of course. You poor chap," he said. "Come on in. Have some tea. I've just got back from Mesopotamia. My wife thought I was dead! What do you think of that?"

'I just had time to throw the flowers behind some shrubs by the door. "Come on in lad," he said, "come on in." Then I realised I was *wearing his shoes*. Thank God, he didn't seem to notice.'

Renée tried to subdue her mirth. 'So then you had to go into the house and pretend . . .'

'. . . That I didn't know Mrs Franklyn. Exactly. God, what an ordeal. He made me stay for tea. She was sitting right opposite me, trying not to look at me. He told me how he had been posted as killed in action by mistake. I was terrified he'd recognise his brogues. It was so outlandish, I can't tell you. Eventually it was Mrs Franklyn who drove me to the station in the pony and trap. Just like the first time but neither of us said a word. Not a word. At the station I got down and thanked her and we shook hands and I went in and I never saw her again.'

'How amazing,' said Renée. Her eyes were wet but not from her laughter. 'You took her flowers,' she said in a subdued voice. 'Always a gentleman. Perhaps you are still too much of a gentleman, Bevan.'

Eve his wife had said that. Renée held his hand in the bed. 'Tomorrow,' she said not looking at him, 'I am leaving here.'

He had known she was going to say it. 'How long?' he said.

'Who knows? The school is going to be evacuated to North Wales. I told you before. They fear this place will be too dangerous. I am going ahead to organise the accommodation in the new place, then the boys will come as soon as possible.'

They lay silently for a while. He stroked her naked breasts tenderly. 'I'll miss you,' he said.

'And I will miss you.' They kissed again. It was for the last time. 'We have been good company.'

On 10 May Winston Churchill became Prime Minister. In sunny Bournemouth the opposition Labour Party at its Annual Congress, held as usual despite the dire war situation, agreed to serve in a coalition government with the man who had been its implacable opponent.

The funereal Neville Chamberlain was sent into political oblivion by Leo Amery, usually a dull speaker, who rose in the House of Commons and for once to the occasion, using the echoing words with which Oliver Cromwell had dismissed Parliament almost three centuries before: 'You have sat too long here for any good you have been doing. Depart, I say, and let us have done with you. In the name of God, go!' On the same day the German Army invaded Holland and Belgium.

'Had to happen,' shrugged Bombardier Hignet as they

heard about Churchill on the barrack-room wireless. 'But he won't make any difference.'

'They should send for you, Higgie,' suggested Bairnsfather. 'You'd sort the bloody war out.'

'They could do worse.'

Churchill told Parliament he could promise nothing but blood, toil, tears and sweat. His words, impersonated by a BBC actor because the new leader said he was too busy, were broadcast to the British people. He had begun his leadership with a deceit. 'Well, now we know what we've got to do,' said Hignet. 'Sweat.'

The hard, sombre but counterfeit voice had offered no respite, no easy way out; no promises were made. All over the land early summer basked, the fields were full, the roofs of the towns glowed, pretty villages sat safe as ever. There was horse racing and the first cricket of the fresh season was being played in English meadows. In London people sunned themselves in Hyde Park serenaded by a choir of unemployed miners, and a brass band of workless shipbuilders.

The German armoured thrust into Holland and Belgium caused Hignet to pin up a map of Europe in the orderly room. 'Thought you wouldn't mind, sir,' he said when Bevan saw it. 'Give the lads some idea of what is going on.'

'What *is* going on, bombardier?' asked Sergeant Runciman who had come in with Bevan to check the ration inventory. 'Tell us.'

'They're doing just as I said they would,' said Hignet. 'Pushing through the soft, neutral countries. The trouble is we think everybody keeps to the rules. We forget the Huns don't play cricket.'

'You don't have to be Napoleon to have realised that,' said Runciman putting his nose near the map. 'About the neutrals.'

'Our War Cabinet didn't,' said Hignet.

Bevan said: 'Well, Hignet, have you done your blood, toil, tears and sweat this morning?'

'I thought I'd leave it until I'd finished the guard roster, sir.'

'Right, but don't forget.'

'I want to see you bleeding, tearful and sweating,' said Runciman. 'Toiling might be beyond you.' Bevan laughed and went out. Runciman narrowed his eyes and leaned from the waist again stiffly towards the map. 'Where are we anyway?'

Hignet, surprised, pointed: 'There's Southampton, sergeant. We're just west. About here.'

Runciman regarded him spitefully. 'Not *us*, bombardier. Not this troop of the Royal Artillery. I'm quite aware of *our* location. I wouldn't be a sergeant otherwise, would I?' He pressed the reprimand. '*Would I, Hignet?*'

'No, sergeant, you wouldn't.'

'I meant the army on the Continent. The British Bloody Expeditionary Force. Have you been informed of its location?'

Hignet became flustered. 'Round about here, sarge,' he said pointing towards north-eastern France. 'It said on the news that British troops had entered Belgium for the first time since the First War and were moving to engage the Germans. In Bren-gun carriers. As you probably know, we have a treaty with the Belgians going back to the early 1800s.'

'Good. I'm glad you told me that. I'd forgotten.' He paused thoughtfully, then said: 'Have you ever seen a Bren-gun carrier, Hignet? Of course you have. It's a little metal box on tracks, isn't it. But have you ever seen a German Tiger tank, Hignet?'

'No, sarge. No, I haven't actually.'

'They're big, Hignet. They're fucking huge.'

* * *

There was no sign of an official general emergency although a National Day of Prayer had been proclaimed for the Sunday. Saturday morning was undisturbed when Lady Violet Foxley and her daughter Penelope walked from their house into the May air. Mainprice opened the door of the Rolls Royce and Penelope boarded the car awkwardly.

'I feel a little embarrassed using the Rolls with the war situation as it is,' said her mother. 'But we've always gone to the village fête in it and I think the locals expect it. So we're helping the cause. And what a topping day.'

Penelope, sitting heavily, said: 'What is the good cause this year, mother?'

'Oh, something. Gas masks for Abyssinia, I think.'

'It's too late for that. The Italians have already gassed them.'

'No, you're right, dear, that was last year. It's probably the church fabric. They try to use the takings for something overseas and something closer to home each alternative year. It amounted to thirty pounds, twelve and threepence last year, after expenses, rather good, I thought.' She scarcely paused. 'What will you have to say to the vicar?'

'Oh, probably: "Good afternoon, vicar." Or does he now prefer to be called padre?'

'Penelope, don't be facetious.'

'About getting myself pregnant without bothering him, you mean. I'll tell him to mind his own business. He didn't do it.'

Lady Violet allowed herself a grim grin. 'It would be something if he *had* done it. Now that really *would* be a miracle.'

Noiselessly they rolled through the village, the sole motor vehicle. People on their way to the fête, couples and children, older people, women in groups, turned, stared and then waved shyly. 'She's carrying a lump,' said Annie Dibben. 'I saw 'er getting in the car at the station. She needs a wheelbarrow.'

Her husband hushed her. 'So did you.'

'I was wed.'

'Don't I know it.'

From the car Lady Violet elongated her neck to survey the trek to the fête. 'I wonder what sort of refugees the British would make?' she remarked. 'Those poor people, thousands clogging the roads in Holland.'

Penelope took in the traipsing villagers with their prams and their dawdling infants. 'In this country there wouldn't be far enough to run,' she said. 'At least on the Continent you can keep going for a while. Here you'd be faced by the sea.'

An army vehicle loaded with soldiers was waiting at the junction, the driver with his hand thrust out indicating a right turn. 'Stop, Mainprice,' Lady Violet said to the chauffeur. 'Let them go ahead. They may be off to stem the invasion.'

'I think they're going to the fête, m'lady,' said the chauffeur. 'They've been helping to put up the tents and that. And they're going to run the shooting stall.'

'Ah, perhaps we'll be able to shoot people, that sounds like tip-top fun,' smiled her ladyship. 'I can think of one or two. It would be worth a penny of anybody's money.' Her daughter sighed.

Lady Violet nodded. 'There's that nice officer – a captain, wasn't he? He came to dinner with that exotic girl.' Bevan waved to them as the platoon truck turned into the main road. 'Besotted, I thought, didn't you?'

'No, I didn't actually,' said Penelope. She remembered Bevan's look.

Her mother glanced at her. 'Jerusalem House, that

refugee school, is moving to North Wales. She's probably going with them.'

'She's gone. I saw her at the station with her baggage. We waved.'

They had reached the gate to the green. The fête had been held in the field for longer than anyone could recall. Village memories were all the same, of early summer under an indefinite blue sky or rain cascading from the overhang of the tea tent. There would be a dog show, a pony show, a flower show, coconut shies, a roll-a-penny stall, a shooting gallery, a brass band from Lymington, and the village May Queen. The older women could remember when they as girls had danced around the pagan maypole, while a hurdy-gurdy played its tinny tune. Grandmothers still looked wistfully at sepia photographs of themselves; laughing innocence, capering in a circle of silk streamers.

Today the sky was washy blue, the clouds swollen yellow. There was no weather forecast but the village soothsayers, including Madame Lily Smith, who had once worked her magic on Bournemouth pier, were confident that it would stay fine until sunset. She had a tiny coloured tent emblazoned with her name in silver where she told fortunes for threepence. Penelope surveyed the languid sky above the fresh elms and green beeches, and wondered that it was still so unchanged, so peaceful.

'It is very sobering,' said the Reverend Goodenough, 'to think that an hour in an aeroplane would carry you over the most terrible scenes of war and destruction. Did you see the sad pictures in the *Manchester Guardian* this morning?'

'I saw them in the *Daily Telegraph*,' said Lady Violet.

Penelope was helping with the tea tent. Her mother and the vicar walked along the stalls, he with his hands feeling without co-ordination for each other behind his back, she with a rolled parasol sloping over her shoulder like a rifle. Three soldiers were in charge of the shooting gallery. Instead of the usual bull's-eye targets they had set up a row of Hitler faces drawn on cardboard, the oblong moustache and lick of hair done in boot blacking. Joined on to the left ear was Hitler's hand open in a Nazi salute. 'Shoot old Adolf. Penny a go!' invited Gunner Ugson. 'Padre, have a pot-shot at the Nastie?'

Lady Violet nudged Goodenough. 'Do have a try. One day you might be called on.'

Reluctantly the vicar took the air rifle, sniffing at it suspiciously. 'Penny a shot, sir,' Ugson reminded him respectfully. Goodenough fumbled in his coat, brought out a purse and from that produced a coin which he handed edge-on to the soldier. ''Ave a shot at Hitler!' shouted Ugson. The field was filling up now and people gathered around. Bevan walked to the stall. 'The vicar is practising to be an assassin,' Lady Violet said.

The Reverend Goodenough winced and pointed the light weapon in the direction of the target. Without aiming, without even putting the butt to his shoulder, he clenched his eyes and pressed the trigger. The pellet went unerringly through Hitler's moustache. 'Christ,' said Ugson.

'Christ indeed,' muttered the clergyman and turned away. 'I have an aversion to killing. Even Hitler,' he said to Lady Violet as they walked off. 'I did offer myself for military service, after you . . . well, encouraged me to do so at Christmas. But I have indifferent eyesight and – it turns out – one flat foot.'

'Only one?'

'Just one. The army doctor said I would not be able to march. Perhaps limp.'

'You'll probably be more use as a cleric than a soldier.

Who knows what is in store. You may have to mediate for people's very lives.' She became hearty. 'Offer yourself as a hostage.'

'I pray not.'

'Well, the Germans are Christians, nominally so anyway,' her ladyship said. 'You wouldn't realise it by what they're up to at present, but they have their churches. Cologne Cathedral is quite beautiful. What would happen if they took over here? Would you allow them into your church?'

As though to shut off the thought, Goodenough closed his eyes as he walked and almost toppled on to a child in a pushchair. The child cried out, the vicar apologised, the mother said it was her fault for not looking where she was pushing. She told the child to shut up. 'I don't see how I could stop them coming into the church,' he said to Lady Violet as they continued. 'Entire armies are finding it difficult stopping them.'

'And you would conduct evensong service as usual?'

'I think I would. I would have to.'

She nodded a touch grimly. 'It might improve the singing,' she sniffed. 'Not to mention the collection.'

Unsworth had brought a copy of *Mein Kampf* by Adolf Hitler as a prize on the raffle stall. 'Any good, is it?' asked Mirabelle Hurrock, Catcher's wife, who was in charge.

'Haven't read it,' said Unsworth. 'It's all in German. Somebody handed it in at the police station because they thought it looked suspicious in their house.'

Mirabelle riffled the pages of the book. 'Well, I'll take it,' she said dubiously. 'Whoever wins it could always put it on the fire.'

Unsworth saw his wife coming across the field with their dog. She was hurrying with excitement, tugging at the lead. He smiled and waited. 'Alf,' she said, 'Alan's coming this afternoon. He managed to telephone, but he'd already sent a telegram.' She took the orange envelope from her handbag. 'It gave me a turn, I can tell you. I could see the telegram boy coming up the street and I thought something must have happened to him. I couldn't bear it. But . . . but . . .'

She handed him the piece of paper with its strips of wording. 'He's bringing a girl,' smiled Unsworth as he read. 'Well, well.'

'I hope she's nice,' she said. 'I'm sure she will be. I told him it was the fête and he's coming straight here. It's a pity he – they – can't stay, although how we would sleep them, I don't know. They're going to Bournemouth for a wedding and he has to be back on duty tomorrow.'

At one side of the meadow, below the newly green elms, the Lymington band, in their scarlet tunics, began to play. The music, familiar down the years, floated over the bright scene, and then came the newer songs: 'There'll Always be an England' and 'This is Worth Fighting For'. Terry Lawrence, the bandmaster, was also a customs officer at Lymington harbour. He owned a boat in partnership with two other players, Jed Railton on the tuba, and the teenager Will Peters who played the drums. In less than a month they would be transported from that village field to a fate they could not then imagine.

'It's lovely,' said Molly as she and Bairnsfather strolled along by the trees, sedately arm in arm at first but, once they were away from the stalls and the people, with his khaki sleeve firmly around her smooth waist. 'I never thought I'd be able to wear a summer dress this early.'

'It's so ruddy peaceful,' said Bairnsfather. 'Just like it's always been, I expect. I bet this place has hardly changed since the First War. Look at it . . .' They halted and cast around the scene. There was the pony show in the distance from where they could now hear Lady

Violet's authoritative voice over the megaphone: 'Best turned out now. Come on everybody, let's get the best turned out started.' The dog show was in the centre of the field. They were judging the champion tail wagger. Tom Dibben was wagging his mongrel's tail by hand and saying: ''E generally does it by hisself, but 'e's nervous.' There was a toffee-apple seller, a home-made cakes counter, hoop-la and cries from the coconut shy; queues formed outside the fortune teller's tent and the ladies' lavatory. A fan-shaped group of children sat entranced by the Punch and Judy show where Punch was beating his wife with a stick. The May Queen, a rounded blonde of sixteen, had just blushingly arrived on a horse-drawn hay cart; there were cheers, she waved a pink arm and her crown fell over her face.

'I wonder if we'll have a fête next year?' said Penelope Foxley.

'I hope so,' said Bevan. 'But you never can tell.' She was so pregnant that he wanted to ask after her husband. She wore no wedding ring.

'I don't have one,' she said.

'What was that?' He smiled apologetically. 'What don't you have?'

'A wedding ring,' she said cheerfully. 'I could see you looking. I don't have a husband for that matter. It's very daring, I know, but I am going to do without one.'

Bevan did not know what to say.

'Oddly enough,' she said 'the last time I saw the father was the first day I saw you, at Southampton station.'

'I saw you both on the platform,' he told her.

She smiled. 'Oh, did you now?' With a touch of mischief she said: 'Your lady friend . . .'

'Renée,' he said. 'She's gone to Wales. The school is moving.'

'Yes, I saw her at the station the other day. She had some very stylish luggage.'

There was a throng around the shooting gallery. 'That was a good idea of Hignet's, drawing those Hitler faces,' said Bairnsfather to Molly below the trees. 'Everyone wants to take a pot-shot at Adolf.' The snap of the air rifles echoed over the field and smoke issued above the heads of the watchers. 'All that smoke,' said Molly. 'That anti-aircraft gun of yours doesn't make as much as that, does it?'

'It's Ugly,' said Bairnsfather. 'He's always got a fag on. Pure horse dung.'

Molly, the shadows of beech leaves over her young face, turned her attention to Penelope. 'I hope I don't get too big.'

Bairnsfather scanned the field. 'Too big?'

'That lady. The one that's expecting. Talking to your officer.'

'Oh, yes . . . Well, no. I see what you mean.' He turned slowly to face her. 'What *do* you mean . . . anyway . . . ?'

She had gone scarlet and on her cheeks sudden tears glistened. 'Harry,' she sniffed. 'I'm pregnant. It's our baby.'

'Blimey,' he said blankly. 'Are you sure?'

Molly looked affronted. 'Of course I'm sure. I don't go around with anyone, you know.'

He put his arm out to her. 'I didn't mean it like that. I meant are you sure you're . . . like that?'

'I've only missed a month,' she sniffed. 'But I've got a feeling.' She clutched him. 'My dad and mum will go mad, my dad will, anyway. What are we going to do?'

Bairnsfather hugged her and pushing his face into her hair he said: 'We're going to get married. It saves me asking you.'

He put his arms around her waist to the back and she

leaned against him. 'Oh, Harry, I wondered what you'd say. I'd . . . you know . . . lose it if you wanted to. But I can't stand gin.' She began to sniffle and giggle at the same time. 'You're sure you don't mind?'

'I'm glad,' he said uncertainly. 'Honest, Molly. I'm glad. It's the first thing I've ever *done*.'

'When will we be married then? It'll have to be soon. I want to be brazen and wear white.'

He squeezed her. 'It'll have to be soon, anyway. Otherwise this ruddy war is going to . . . Well, the sooner the better.'

Close together they walked towards the band and stood, her hand on his shoulder, listening on the fringe of the other people. Unsworth had taken the dog's lead from Ellen who was scanning the horizon saying: 'He ought to be here soon, any time now. I hope she's a nice girl.'

'Now look at that,' said Catcher Hurrock. He stroked the dog and lifted its face as if to make sure, then looked at Unsworth. 'You went and kept 'un.'

Unsworth said: 'We had room for a spare dog.'

'He be growan. What d'you call 'un?'

'Catcher,' said Ellen over her shoulder.

Catcher grinned with pleasure. 'That's the first toime I ever did 'ave a 'ound named after me. Or anything else.'

'Sometimes we call him Scratcher,' mentioned Unsworth.

'Same thing. I been called that a few toimes.'

'Alf,' said Ellen. 'He's arrived. I can see him. Look by the gate.'

Unsworth could see the dark blue of the navy uniform at the entrance. 'Yes, that's Alan. Has he got someone with him?'

'He has. It's his lady friend. Alf, I feel so nervous.'

At that moment a silence dropped on both of them.

They could see the couple advancing through the crowds. 'Oh, God,' breathed Ellen eventually. 'She's a darkie.'

Catcher was still standing by the dog. He looked in the same direction as they were. 'Don't see many o' them around 'ere,' he said. 'Not proper darkies.'

'All right, where have the enemy got to today?' Runciman strode behind Bevan into the orderly room and fatalistically threw his cap on the desk. It was strange for an officer and a sergeant to receive a briefing from a bombardier but Hignet listened to the wireless, read the newspapers minutely and studied the maps. Bevan wondered if he knew more of the disastrous situation on the Continent than the generals and politicians.

'They've got across the Albert Canal.' Hignet sighed with disappointment. He had fashioned some cardboard arrows pierced with drawing-pins, those representing the German Army coloured with boot blacking, the British whitened with toothpaste and the French and Belgians the bare cardboard.

'I thought you said they'd never do that,' said Runciman as if it were Hignet's fault. 'Get across.'

'I only know what I read and hear, sergeant,' said Hignet loftily. 'The Belgians said they'd never get over the Albert Canal. For a start they'd got that massive fort thing there.'

'Eben Emael,' said Bevan. 'Impregnable.'

'Not impregnable enough,' sniffed Hignet.

'How did they get across the canal then?' asked Runciman standing close and staring at the map as if he could see the enemy. 'Swim?'

'Looks like it. Or maybe somebody forgot to blow up the bridges.'

Runciman said to Bevan: 'And we're sitting here doing Sweet Fanny Adams, sir.'

'Waiting for orders,' said Bevan. 'The Belgian Army is supposed to have half a million men. The French have more than a million.'

'Most of them off duty by the look of it,' said Hignet.

There was a knock at the door. Since hostilities had taken a turn for the worse Hignet had decided to tighten security and the orderly room door was often now kept closed. 'Come in,' called the bombardier. Gunner Purcell was outside and, leaning to look from his chair, Bevan saw that the man with him was Alf Unsworth. He called him in.

Unsworth glanced at the map. 'Looking for loopholes?'

'Feeling a bit useless,' said Bevan.

Unsworth studied the situation on the wall. 'You get like that, don't you. Never mind, we may be able to fight the war our way soon. We'll be all that's left.'

'Good job too,' said Runciman. 'We'll know where we stand. Us and them.'

'Could I have a word?' said Unsworth to Bevan.

'Got time for a cup of coffee?'

'I'll make the time.'

They left the room and walked towards Southerly. Unsworth eyed the Bofors. 'Are they any good?'

'Not bad. We bagged a Stuka, you know. Off Norway.'

'I heard. Congratulations. News gets around. For all these Careless Talk posters people can't help talking. The British talk now more than they ever did, even to their neighbours.'

They went into the house. Josef served the coffee, eyeing Unsworth apprehensively. 'Was that your son at the fête on Saturday?' asked Bevan. 'The lad in the navy.'

'With the black girlfriend,' sighed Unsworth. 'That was him. Ellen had a fit. She was nice, the girl, but my wife doesn't think God meant it that way. She was from the Gold Coast and she works at the Colonial Office. As soon as she'd gone, even before the tea things were cleared away, Ellen was at the home encyclopedia looking up Gold Coast. She came back, like a sheet, and said it was known as the White Man's Grave.'

Bevan laughed and said: 'Most mothers would have been the same. This war is going to change a lot of attitudes.'

'It's never going to be the same again,' said Unsworth. He leaned forward confidingly. 'I've come about your chap here . . .' He half looked across his shoulder. Josef was serving two officers in a distant corner. 'I'm afraid I've got to take him in. That's what my orders are. He's to be detained under the Defence Regulations.'

Bevan breathed heavily. 'Christ, the Germans are halfway across Europe, the country's going to be fighting for its very life, and all we can concern ourselves with is a harmless mess waiter.'

'I know. But I'm only a lowly copper.'

'He's stopped listening to German radio stations,' said Bevan. 'He told me so the other day. He listens to Radio Paris now.'

'How long before that's a Boche station?' said Unsworth. He stood. 'I've got to go. We're still trying to find the gun somebody pinched from the Brockenhurst war memorial. Silly, isn't it.'

'It is, a bit,' said Bevan. 'When will you come for him?'

'About nine thirty tonight. I thought I'd give him a chance to get a few things together and wait until it's getting dark. Save him some embarrassment anyway. He'll go off to the Isle of Man, I expect. They're sending them all there, the aliens. May be quite nice up there now the summer's coming on.' He glanced at Bevan. 'I'll tell him now if you like.'

'No,' said Bevan. 'Leave it to me.'

* * *

Molly's father had just come in and was eating his tea. 'What's this?' he asked holding up a slice of tart. 'Tastes of carrots.'

'It is carrots,' his wife said flatly. 'Carrot flan. I got the recipe from the wireless, that *Kitchen Front* programme. It's supposed to help you see in the blackout.'

Mr Warner pushed the plate away. 'I can see in the dark all right as it is,' he said. 'I'm not starting having carrots for my tea.'

'You might be glad of them.'

Ronnie came down the stairs and without speaking settled in a corner chair reading the *Wizard*. Eventually he said: 'It says here that astronomers like the blackout because they can see the stars better.'

'It was them who said there wasn't going to be any war and there was,' retorted Mrs Warner. 'That Edward Lyndoe in the *People* said it on the very day war was declared.'

'*Astrologers*, that is,' sighed Ronnie. 'They *read* the stars, not look at them.'

His mother took no notice. 'The spiritualists were the same. They said it was because the messages from heaven, or wherever they're in touch with, had got mixed up.'

'I'm not eating carrot flan,' said her husband.

'All right. I'll get some fruit cake. I thought being patriotic, like you say you are, you'd like it.'

'Being patriotic has nothing to do with eating carrots.'

She went into the kitchen and almost at once the front door opened and Molly came in from the library. She looked flustered but it went unnoticed. She was going to her voluntary nursing training that evening. Glancing at her father and brother she said: 'Hello,' then went into the kitchen.

'Have some nice carrot flan,' her father called after her.

'You'll see what Harry is doing in the dark,' shouted Ronnie.

Mr Warner picked up the *Evening Echo* with disgust. 'Six pages,' he grumbled. 'How can you read six pages?'

'The *Wizard's* only every fortnight and the *Knock Out*'s only got twelve little pages,' pointed out Ronnie. 'But it's funnier than the *Echo*.'

The women were some time. Mr Warner began to fret and called: 'Where's my cake?'

'And mine,' shouted Ronnie.

The women came in, Molly behind her mother. 'There's your cake,' Mrs Warner said putting it in front of her husband. He glanced up suspiciously. It was a small house and few feelings went unnoticed. 'And here's your daughter,' said his wife. 'She wants to get married. She's having a baby.'

'Christ!' said Mr Warner screwing up the newspaper.

'I knew it,' said Ronnie.

Unhappily Bevan climbed the iron staircase to Josef's room. He could hear dance music. Josef was ready, his one suitcase, scarred but sturdy with two leather straps around it, standing inside the door. 'That's Radio Paris,' he said with a sort of hope. 'I don't play any of the German stations now.'

'I know,' said Bevan. 'You told me.'

'Mind you, they're fiddling while Rome burns.' He saw nothing incongruous in the analogy. He looked damply at Bevan. 'I'm ready to go, sir.'

Bevan nodded. 'I want to tell you this is beyond me, Josef,' he said. 'I've spent all the afternoon telephoning to try and get it changed. But it's no use. War gives some people a chance to glory in damned regulations.'

'I know it's not your fault, sir. You've always been very decent to me. I might quite like the Isle of Man. The camps are reasonably comfortable, I'm told. A lot of the people they've sent there are Jewish so it will probably be quite artistic. I could try my hand at painting. It's something I've often thought of doing if I had the time. Funny how everybody puts Jews in camps.'

'It's probably because they're afraid of them,' said Bevan. 'Because they're clever.' He picked up the case, touching Josef's hand aside. Unsworth was waiting outside in the police car.

'Jews always seem to be herded together somewhere or other,' said Josef. The swing music was following them out of the room and he turned and stepped back to turn off the radio set. 'Pity I can't take it with me,' he said.

'As I told you I'll look after it,' said Bevan. 'I'll keep the room locked up as long as I'm here.' Then, wryly: 'Perhaps I'll come up for a bit of peace and quiet during the invasion.'

A constable got out of the car and opened the rear doors. Unsworth, sitting at the front, said an apologetic 'Good evening', and handed a single sheet of paper to Josef. 'That's your travel arrangements,' he said. 'I'm afraid you'll have to have an escort.'

'I've never had an escort before,' said Josef. 'Makes me feel quite important.'

The uniformed policeman had put the suitcase in the boot. Bevan climbed into the back seat. 'They're not interning you, are they, sir?' asked Josef with a shaky laugh.

'I might be next, the way things are going,' said Bevan. 'I'll just come as far as the gate.'

They drove the two hundred yards. 'I've been reading up about the Isle of Man,' said Josef. 'They believe in fairies there, you know.'

'In the police force you have to believe in fairies,' grunted Unsworth. 'And ghosts. All those things.' At the gate Bevan left the car. He shook hands with Josef and then climbed out and shut the door. Bairnsfather, who was coming tipsily from the bus-stop, saw Bevan throw up a salute and wondered who was in the car.

Gunner Brown came out of the guardhouse. The sentry challenged Bairnsfather, saw who it was and lowered his bayonet. 'Don't run me through with that thing,' said Bairnsfather. 'I'm getting married.'

'In pod, is she?' said Brown. 'You wicked bugger. I bet she'll look great in her nurse's uniform.'

'I'm getting married,' said Bairnsfather stiffly but swaying on his feet. 'That's all you need to know, Brownie. I've just got a bit boozed with my future father-in-law.'

'How did he take it? About the baby?'

'Quite well after the first shock. I wasn't there then. Molly wouldn't let me. She said it would be better if she and her mum broke the news. The old man ranted on a bit but by the time I turned up he'd calmed down and was looking forward to being a grandfather. They've already got one of those pump-up baby gas masks in the house and I reckon he liked the idea of another. He could pump one with each hand. Anyway he took me down the pub and we had a few. Who was in the car?'

'Which . . . ?'

'The one Captain Bevan was saluting. Was it a general or something?'

'No, it was just that old bloke from the officers' mess. They're taking him off to be shot as a spy.'

Hignet moved the arrows emphatically across his map. 'There, there and there,' he said. He regarded Runciman and said: 'We're buggered.'

The elongated Gunner Purcell limped through the door. 'I want to report sick, sarge.'

'What's wrong with you, lad?'

'Ingrowing toenail, sarge.'

Runciman turned to Hignet and Hignet turned from his map. 'Let's see it,' said the sergeant.

Purcell sat on the other chair, unbuckled his gaiters, unlaced his boot and pulled off his thick grey sock. The big toe glowed red. 'Why can't you have outgrowing toenails like everybody else?' demanded Runciman. He sighed and turned to Hignet. 'All right. Give him a chitty.'

'Is that where the Germans are?' asked Purcell looking from his toe to Europe. 'They're getting closer, ain't they.' He struggled with his sock still looking at the arrows.

Hignet said almost proudly: 'Closer every day. This lot . . .' He tapped the black arrow. 'Are halfway through the Ardennes.'

'What's that?'

'The Ardennes, Persil, are about the only hills there are in Belgium. They reckoned tanks could never get through them. But they are.'

'It's getting dangerous,' said Purcell.

Runciman said grimly: 'Get your toe better, if you want my advice, lad. Otherwise, when it comes to it, you won't be able to run.'

Bevan came in. They stood up including Gunner Purcell, still without his boot. 'Ingrowing toenail, sir,' he said.

'I hope it won't stop you going on manoeuvres,' said Bevan. 'Because that's what we're doing.'

'Manoeuvres, sir?' said Hignet. The very word suggested mobility. Runciman gave him a sharp look because he had spoken out of turn. Bevan took no notice.

'Yes, they're going to run us around the countryside a bit,' he said. 'Good idea. Keep us fit for the invasion, if it comes. We've got to leave two skeleton crews for the guns and everybody else gets in some infantry training. All the odds and sods in the camps around here have to send a contingent. We're going to rendezvous with them tomorrow and, by some magic, we are going to be formed into a fighting force.'

Whatever they thought neither Runciman nor Hignet said anything. Purcell, lifting his swollen toe from the ground and squeezing his face, said: 'Will I have to do it, sir?'

'You can be a casualty,' said Bevan.

Although they knew it was only a pretence, a game even, the men had the uncomfortable feeling that before long it might become a reality. They assembled on a battlefield sort of morning: low, grey rain, trees obscure on the horizon, and the drifting smoke from a forester's garden rubbish lending an accidental authenticity.

'Seems mad to me,' grumbled Cartwright. 'They get you into the artillery, teach you how to use an anti-aircraft gun, then send you out to crawl through the ruddy undergrowth. I'm right, ain't I?'

'The only thing right about you, Cartwright, is the last bit of your name,' sniffed Runciman. 'You're a soldier first and foremost and you do as you're told.' They were in the lorry bouncing towards the assembly area. Hignet, appearing as though he were wearing somebody else's ill-fitting equipment, said: 'I'm more of a strategist, a planner.'

The sergeant regarded him scornfully. 'Mostly planning to keep out of military activity or anything resembling it.' He surveyed the faces in the back of the lorry, jolting as it left the main road and went among the trees on the forest tracks. 'All of you ought to get it into you brains that you could be in the real war in a couple of weeks. It's not going to take long for Jerry to get here once he's rattled through France. So if you can learn anything today you ought to make sure you learn it properly. It might save your lives.'

A sombre silence fell. They were wearing steel helmets which sometimes clanged against each other as they moved. 'On the other hand,' continued Runciman, 'it might be a help when you're on the offensive, killing Germans, maybe with your bare hands.'

'Is there a NAAFI?' asked Ugson.

'Are there toilet facilities?' asked Hignet.

Runciman sighed. 'All of that,' he said. 'And a hairdresser, a dry cleaner, hot baths and a free beer tent.'

They halted after half an hour. Bevan, in the car leading the way with Bairnsfather at the wheel, looked ahead towards the groups of soldiers standing and sitting in the forest clearing. They were smoking and drinking tea provided by the NAAFI mobile canteen parked below the trees. 'This lot look ready for anything,' he said. 'Almost.' A thin rain fell.

A military policeman, the only businesslike figure in sight, directed them to an area on the flank of the clearing. They pulled up below a line of spruce trees. 'Always make use of the maximum cover,' Runciman instructed as the men dropped from the lorry. 'Then you'll only get bombed or machine-gunned by bad luck.' He saw Bevan and saluted. 'Won't they, sir?'

An officer's voice called through a megaphone: 'Right, gather around chaps, under the trees. We don't want you getting wet before battle.'

There were about two hundred steel-helmeted men, all from scattered units along that part of the coast. 'Christ,' said Bairnsfather. 'They've got the Pay Corps here. Those blokes with glasses.'

'Maybe we're getting more money,' said Purcell. 'Danger money.'

Led by Bevan and ushered by Runciman the artillerymen moved below the trees. They handled the rifles awkwardly and Ugson dropped his. Runciman swiftly looked around to see if he had been noticed by men from the other units. 'Hold it with both hands if you can't manage with one,' he almost snarled. 'Get a grip, Ugson.'

The troops were now formed below the collar of trees around the clearing. The drizzle thickened. The colonel who had called through the megaphone walked to the centre of the semicircle followed by his batman who unleashed an umbrella and held it above his officer's head. 'Right, chaps, I hope you can all hear me,' the colonel blared through the megaphone. 'I'm Colonel Roger Bentley-Fry.' He was red faced and rotund in a taut way, bent like a bow at his belt. 'But you can call me "sir".'

A few laughed. 'Only a joke, chaps,' bellowed the colonel. 'To put you at ease. But I don't want the joke to continue through this exercise. In no time at all the Hun may be on our doorstep and this will be the real thing.' He jerked and turned his pink face as if he expected someone to contradict him and seemed disappointed when no one did. 'The object of the exercise today . . .' he said. 'Exercise Flushout we're going to call it. The object is to imagine that enemy paratroops, numbers unknown, have landed in the forest between here and Fordingbridge. I would show you on the map but it's got wet in the rain. The Jerries are awaiting a supply drop and are holed up until it arrives. It's our job to flush them out before they get it.' His face jerked about questioningly again but no comment came. 'Will the officers in command of each unit come forward now and I will go into the details on the map, if we've managed to wipe it dry. Otherwise, chaps, stand easy, take a NAAFI break.'

As the officers moved forward the rest of the men crowded towards the NAAFI van, engineers, sappers, cooks, clerks and the gunners. They stood below the trees drinking tea from their mess tins, their rifles hooked in reverse over their shoulders to prevent the rain going down the barrels, single drops dripping from the rims of their helmets. Some wore rubber rain capes. 'You know,' said Hignet, 'For the first time since I joined up I feel like a real soldier.'

'You would,' said Cartwright. 'You wasn't in Norway like us.'

'In action,' said Ugson.

'Don't go shooting anybody,' said Bairnsfather. 'It's only pretend, you know, Higgie.'

Bevan returned. Runciman went to meet him halfway, eagerly and with a bit of professional bounce.

'Right, lads,' said Bevan. 'Let's show them that gunners make good all-round soldiers. We're to sweep the area directly north-west of here, towards the villages of Hyde and Gorley, just short of Fordingbridge. The Pay Corps will be on our left flank and the Army Catering Corps on our right.'

They flung the dregs of the tea from their mess tins and pushed them back into their packs. Runciman told them: 'You are going to be issued with live ammunition. Five rounds each only. Do not load these into your weapon until you get orders to do so. We don't want you wiping out the Pay Corps.'

Under his direction they moved off in single rank towards the curtain of trees, Bevan in the lead. Other columns were entering the forest at different angles. 'Pen-pushers on the left, cooks on the right and with five rounds of ammo we can't load,' grunted Cartwright. 'This would make the Germans shit their trousers.'

The rain was stopping. The plodding file passed a pair of cottages with a damp curl of smoke coming from a central chimney-pot; two forest men wearing waistcoats and collarless flannel shirts leaned on adjoining wooden gates, each puffing a pipe. They watched the soldiers tramp towards the heather-covered hill ahead. 'Makes you laugh, don't it, Charlie,' said one.

'That's 'ow I was thinkin'. Look at 'e at the back. Lame as a donkey.'

Gunner Purcell heard the remark and grimaced as he limped on his ingrowing toenail. He was falling further behind and eventually had to sit like a tall gnome on a stone. 'Persil, who gave you permission to fall out?' Sergeant Runciman ordered the rest to halt and they turned and regarded the seated gunner.

'Can't march any more, s'arnt,' said Purcell. 'It's agony.'

The two foresters leaned over their gates, their mirth transformed into irregular puffs of smoke from their pipes. Runciman glared towards them muttering: 'Daft old sods.' He surveyed Purcell. 'All right, Captain Bevan said you can be a casualty. Now you are. We'll send a stretcher party back for you. Don't go away.'

'I can't,' said the gunner causing the two onlookers to emit more puffs of laughter.

Runciman told the file to march on and they began to mount the gorse-clad rise ahead. At the top the sergeant looked back and saw the distant seated Purcell drinking from a beer mug. The foresters had been joined by a woman who was handing him some food. Runciman swore. After another mile they reached an enclosure in the trees and found a Royal Army Medical Corps ambulance with its crew grouped disconsolately around a vacant stretcher. 'We've got a customer for you,' said Runciman. Eagerly they looked up. 'Over the hill there. By two cottages. He's got an ingrowing toenail.'

A corporal said: 'Well, it's a start.' They picked up the stretcher and began going towards the hill, trotting in formation, the stretcher between them as they went through the heather. A rabbit loped unhurriedly for cover.

The unit pushed on. The shower had eased but every step was damp. They reached another row of cottages and Bevan, at the front, called a halt. He consulted his map. Runciman, like a confidant, came to his side and examined the route with him. 'This is where we fan out,' said Bevan. 'Each man to keep in touch with the man on either side. No more than fifty feet apart. I'll take one flank and you take the other, sergeant. We move down into this wooded area and contact at the bottom of this hill.'

Runciman, like a busy schoolmaster organising a cross-country run, positioned the men and Bevan, feeling slightly theatrical, called: 'Squad, forward!' Raggedly they moved down the hill and into the trees.

It felt real. Bairnsfather found he was dry mouthed, his eyes switching from side to side, keeping in touch with Ugson on his left and Cartwright on his right and watching for the enemy. The .303 felt warmer, less clumsy now and he held it like a friend. He realised he was enjoying this. The odd fragment of rain still dripped from his steel helmet and his face was damp. They tramped on for half an hour through the trees, then into clearings and then through trees again. He had not realised there was so much room in the forest. Once they had to cross a stream, running rapidly over stones. The men all appeared on the bank together and looked towards Runciman first and then Bevan for instructions. 'There's a bridge further up,' said

Bevan checking his map. 'No point in everybody getting wet feet.'

Runciman, with some reluctance, nodded. They formed into a file again, went upstream and crossed the humped stone bridge before fanning out into their previous formation. They had only progressed another quarter of a mile when Bairnsfather heard voices. German voices. He almost dropped his rifle. 'Ugly . . . Ugly . . .' he whispered.

'I 'eard,' said Ugson. 'Who is it?'

'Jerries,' said Cartwright appearing through the trees on the other side. His eyes were wide under the rim of his helmet. 'I can hear them clear.'

The three soldiers crouched together, faces fixed, ears straining. They were startled by the sudden appearance of Runciman behind them. His expression was taut. 'Germans, sarge,' Ugson whispered and pointed.

'Stay here. Don't move,' ordered Runciman quietly. 'Captain Bevan is coming in from the other side. So watch your fire.'

He moved off, carefully but swiftly, through the screen of trees. 'Fire . . .' muttered Ugson. 'He said "fire". We're going to have to shoot. I don't like the look of this.'

'Shut up,' muttered Cartwright. 'They'll hear you.'

'Maybe they don't speak English,' grumbled Ugson stupidly. Bairnsfather clenched his teeth.

The voices came from a clearing by the stream. Bevan and Runciman approached from either side. Bevan, who could not believe it was a dangerous situation, had nevertheless taken his revolver from its holster.

Runciman minutely parted some low branches and saw the Germans. They had been working in the stream, for three of them wore waders and spades were piled under a tree. There were six, all wearing the pink-patched brown dungarees of prisoners of war. There were two British soldiers guarding them, although they had stacked their rifles with the spades. The whole group was standing around a vigorous wood fire under a metal griddle which supported a huge frying-pan throwing out smoke and smells. Runciman broke cover and advanced into the clearing, but still cautiously. He saw Bevan move in from the other side. The enemy prisoners looked up and grinned sheepishly. The two soldiers jumped to attention. 'What have you got there?' asked Bevan sniffing towards the pan.

'Eels, sir. Fresh eels.'

'They're ruddy lovely, sir,' said the other guard. 'Luscious.'

'Didn't know we'd taken so many prisoners,' said Runciman. He looked around the clearing and counted them. Bairnsfather and the rest of the section came through the trees. The two guards greeted them.

The first guard said: 'Sailors mostly, sarge. The bloke over there, the one with the bad arm, he's Luftwaffe, picked up out of the sea.'

'We're guarding them,' said the other soldier quite proudly.

'I can see that,' said Bevan. His men had finished surveying the Germans and were now studying the aromatic contents of the pan. Piles of potatoes and onions had been sliced and put in with the chopped eels.

'We're . . . well, *they're* doing a bit of dredging in the stream. With shovels,' said the first guard. 'It floods in the winter, so they reckon. Keeps the prisoners busy.'

'They're not bad blokes really,' said the second guard. 'Harmless.'

'At the moment,' observed Runciman, 'they're cushy.'

'Until all their mates turn up,' agreed the first guard gloomily.

Two of the prisoners approached the group, cheerful, even jolly-looking men, the clownish blodges of colour on their brown overalls adding to the illusion. 'Your men would like eels?' one asked Bevan. He had a Slavic face. 'We have many.'

'We found a lot of these fellows in the water,' said the other. 'Heinrich is a chef when there is no war.'

Bevan glanced around the now eager faces of the Englishmen. 'NAAFI break, I think, sergeant,' he said.

'Yes, sir. Ten minutes?'

Bevan sniffed the cooking pot: 'At least.'

The soldiers briefly cheered. The prisoner called Heinrich went behind some bushes and came back with a pail. It was half full of wriggling eels. 'Good to eat,' he said.

They ate the repast from their mess tins and washed it down with water from the stream. 'In Germany,' said Heinrich, 'We have good forests. More good than this place.' They rinsed the tins. Bevan, briefly glancing at the guards, shook hands with Heinrich and his men joined in, patting the prisoners on their shoulders and laughing at the unexpected pleasure of the morning. As they moved away the guards came to attention and the prisoners stood and grinned.

'Funny people,' said Runciman as they moved up through the gorse again.

'Germans, sergeant?'

'Prisoners, sir. Funny people. They're neither here nor there, are they.'

They found Purcell outside the two cottages where the forest men were still leaning on the gates. Purcell was lying bandaged all over, his long body strapped to a stretcher. His face was anguished. 'Those medic bastards did me up like this and sodded off,' he complained to Runciman. 'It started to rain and I could feel the bandages tightening. Another ruddy shower and I'd have been squeezed to death.'

'I reckon 'e would too,' nodded one of the foresters.

'Un wouldn't 'ave taken long about it neither,' said the other. 'When it came on to rain we thought 'un was going to strangle, di'n we, Ted.'

Hignet had grown into his role. His daily briefings in the orderly room on the progress of the war on the far side of the English Channel were attracting interest from a variety of ranks in the general military area and his personal appearance and attitude changed with the attention. His former demeanour of barrack-room lawyer, his vague glasses, his misshapen uniform and dulled belt brasses, had gone. There was a sharpness to the trouser creases and the folds of his battledress, and he now gave a frequent energetic polish to the metal on his belt and his cap badge and a nightly application of Blanco to the belt and gaiters which he wore with glimmering boots.

Rotterdam had been mercilessly dive-bombed, the Dutch had folded, the Belgian Army had capitulated, and battalions of French soldiers were heading for their homes, but Hignet was flourishing.

'The German infantry, heavily supported by armour,' he said pointing a recently acquired cane which gave him even more of an aura of authority, 'are sweeping west and north.' He tapped the map, now supplemented by several others drawn by himself to a greater scale and detail, an activity which kept him occupied in the afternoons when not much happened in the orderly room.

The modest hut became crowded. Hignet's lectures were timed for the morning NAAFI break and the soldiers stood right out to the door. Two earnest and young artillery lieutenants, one podgy, the other apparently half starved, began attending. They were known as Laurel and Hardy and they sometimes asked questions which Hignet was always able to answer in short snappy phrases.

The bombardier planted his cardboard arrows with emphasis. When one fell from the map nobody laughed and it was respectfully handed back. 'The British Expeditionary Force is being bottled up,' he announced. 'Here, here, and here. The French have caved in on a broad front. A tank commander called de Gaulle, I think . . .' He consulted *The Times*. '. . . Yes, de Gaulle, has tried a counter-attack but that, brave as it was, has failed. Our counter-attacks have also been blocked and our only chance, as I see it, is to fall back on the Channel ports, Calais, Boulogne, Dunkirk and so on, and somehow sail off out of it. Except that this morning I heard that Calais and Boulogne were both in German hands.' It was as if he had been told privately and not by the BBC news. 'That leaves Dunkirk and that is at the mercy of the Luftwaffe.'

'What do you suggest then, Higgie?' asked Bairnsfather from the back of the room.

'Me?' said Hignet as if amazed. 'Me? It's not up to me. If it had been we would not be in this mess in the first place.'

It was gone midnight when the telephone rang. Terry Lawrence, the Lymington customs officer, was only occasionally called late. He climbed from bed and his wife rolled over, wondering sleepily who could be ringing. He went into the little front hall of their house overlooking the harbour. Outside the blackout curtains he could hear small boats stirring at their dark moorings, rigging tinkling in the light wind. It was George Bentley, the coastguard. 'Terry, there's something big brewing. I've had orders to call out all the boats in our area as quick as I can.'

'What sort of boats, George?'

'Any sort. As long as they're seaworthy. As long as they can get across the Channel. I just heard from Southampton that they're getting the Isle of Wight ferries to sea.'

After five minutes Lawrence put down the phone. His wife called: 'Who was it?'

He went into the room and said: 'I've got to be going. It's an emergency.'

'Want a cup of tea?' she offered without questioning him further. He said he would and began to put on his clothes. He pulled a second thick sweater over the first and got out his oilskins. She eyed them. 'Out to sea, then,' she said. The kettle soon boiled and she made the tea.

'Yes. I don't know much about it yet. I've got to rouse the other lads, Jed and young Will. I'll go around and knock them up.' He looked up at her, rosy faced in the kitchen lamp. 'I don't know how long I'll be gone, love,' he said. 'It looks like we'll be going to France. Don't say anything.'

'I won't,' she promised. 'What about the band concert tomorrow? It was Boscombe, wasn't it?'

'That's right. Give them a bell, will you. Tell them some of the band won't be there.'

They drank the tea without saying anything else. Then, as he was about to go, she moved forward and leaned against him in her woolly dressing-gown, her face tight. 'Be careful, won't you, dear,' she said. 'You're a bit old for all this.'

9

For ten days at the end of May and the start of June 340,000 men were evacuated from the beaches and the bombed port of Dunkirk. They were taken back to Britain in a fleet of ships, 222 war vessels and 665 other volunteer craft including a fire float, dredgers and holiday paddle-steamers which days earlier had been plying on the Thames. German tanks and infantry, blocked bravely by a rearguard force short of Dunkirk, never made a concerted effort to attack the helpless British on the beach, the Luftwaffe attacks were not pressed home. Some believed it was God's assistance, others said it was a blunder by the German generals in diverting Panzer Division tanks, and there was even a whisper among politicians that Hitler did not want to embarrass Britain with a major defeat when he still felt he could make an armistice which would secure the west while he attacked Russia.

Hignet said he simply did not understand it. 'It occurs to me that there may be some incompetence in the German High Command,' he shrugged, 'but I am not in a position to know at present.'

'We're moving the guns to Southampton,' said Runciman coming in the door. 'They're bringing troops from France in there and they'd be a sitting target for Stukas.'

'Trying to make up for their missed chances,' agreed

Hignet. He unpinned the campaign map from the wall and folded it pedantically.

'You won't be needing that any more,' said Bairnsfather who had come into the orderly room to find Runciman. 'That battle's lost. You ought to get a map of England, mate.'

'When the time comes,' said Hignet wisely. 'At least we're getting the army back. Most of them. Pity they've had to leave everything else on the beach.'

'Worth being a French scrap-metal merchant,' said Cartwright joining Bairnsfather at the door. 'Lorries, guns, thousands of tons of the stuff.'

Runciman said: 'We're ready to move, are we?'

The two Bofors looked sprightly, even eager, their noses sharply in the air as though keen for the trip. Bevan arrived. Lieutenants Laurel and Hardy were to stay in charge. 'Good hunting,' said Laurel vaguely.

'Show them what for,' said Hardy.

'The repartee that flies around here is incredible,' grumbled Runciman under his breath as they marched away in a pair.

''Itler will be 'ere by the weekend,' said Ugson as they loaded the ammunition.

'Get on the ruddy truck,' sniffed Runciman. 'If I happen to see Winston Churchill I'll tell him what you said.'

Ugson climbed on the vehicle with the others already leaning against the ammunition boxes. They set off, towing the first Bofors on its four detachable wheels. The second followed. In the streets civilians looked pleased, even relieved, to see them. They waved and the soldiers waved back.

The weather remained fine, a peerless summer's morning stretched along the beaches, privately enjoyed by half-naked workmen who were building concrete pillboxes and uncoiling more barbed wire. Southampton's old waterfront basked in the warmth, and the city stones that the Pilgrim Fathers would have seen as they set sail for Plymouth and eventually America, glowed. Children in a public paddling pool stopped splashing to stare at the rolling guns. When they stopped at the edge of the park and were manoeuvred on to the grass, a charge of boys and girls in saggy woollen swimsuits advanced and stood in a wet, shivering circle.

'Back, back, back you go,' ordered Hignet.

The children were unimpressed and shuffled away only a few feet. As soon as Hignet had turned they shuffled forward, and continued to stare at the guns. 'Hey, Four Eyes, 'ow can you see the Jerries with those glasses?' called one of the boys and the others laughed but the chatter ceased as the guns were detached and swung on to the grass. A man serving in an ice-cream kiosk shouted: 'Can't you put them somewhere else? I've got to earn a living.'

'Are you an Eyetie?' shouted Cartwright.

The vendor angrily banged a notice on the side of the kiosk that read: 'Maltese Owned,' and shouted: 'British Empire, see!'

The children continued to watch the soldiers, fascinated when they came to remove the rubber-tyred wheels from the guns and set the weapons down in their firing positions, a leg stretched at each corner. The wheels were stacked next to the vehicles. Four men were erecting a tent. 'Them wheels will be pinched around 'ere,' called one of the boys.

Hignet was busily establishing an orderly room in a tent not much bigger than the adjacent ice-cream kiosk. He had a card table and two folding chairs, an 'In' tray and an 'Out'. He pictured himself in the South African War, on some kop or in a rift valley, pith helmeted, establishing the headquarters tent for a red-coated regiment easily visible to a Boer scout miles away. He whistled contentedly. Runciman approached: 'Where's the rations, bombardier?'

The whistle dwindled. 'They should be here, sarge?'

'They're not here, Hignet.'

'Damn it, I told that corporal in the cookhouse to get them across.'

'Well, that corporal's forgotten. The sun is high in the bleeding sky and these men are hungry and thirsty. They could turn nasty.'

'I'd better go back, sarge. I'll take Captain Bevan's car if he'll let me.'

'If you fell under Captain Bevan's car nobody would worry. Get going.'

Hignet, muttering threats against the cook corporal, made for the car. Runciman said to Bevan: 'He's going for the rations, sir, but it will take him two hours.'

'Everyone's starving,' said Bevan. 'I am.'

'Chips,' said Runciman. 'We'll get tons of chips.'

'Chips it is, sergeant.'

He saw Bairnsfather talking with a boy at the edge of the area. Bairnsfather had realised that the park chosen for the gun site was not far from Molly's house and the arrival of Ronnie had confirmed it. 'See that one with not much hair,' he had heard the familiar junior voice pipe. 'He's got my sister up the spout.'

Runciman approached. 'Do you know this lad, Bairnsfather?'

'Yes, sarge, worst luck. He's going to be my brother-in-law.'

'Does he know where the nearest fish-and-chip shop is?'

'I expect so. He knows everything else.'

'How much do I get for going?' Ronnie asked. 'Weepy

will come with me.' He nudged a sticky-eyed boy. 'We'll go, won't we, Weepy.'

'You might never see the chips,' warned Bairnsfather.

'Well, you go,' said Runciman. 'Take Cartwright with you. The boys can show you the way. We'll buy them a bag of chips.'

'How much do we need?'

'Enough for an officer, a senior NCO and fourteen men,' said Runciman. 'Two pennyworth each.'

'Any fish?'

'Chips only. The War Office can't afford fish.'

The sergeant handed him three shilling coins. 'Get plenty,' he said. 'Mess funds will have to stand it. And don't forget the salt and vinegar.' He was about to move away. 'Oh, yes, and get seven bottles of Tizer.' He handed over another two coins. 'That should be plenty.'

Ronnie and Weepy detached themselves from the other children and proudly marched, arms stiffly swinging, alongside Bairnsfather and Cartwright. 'You seen Molly this week?' asked Ronnie as they turned down a street.

'No,' said Bairnsfather. 'I've been on duty.'

'She's getting a lump.'

'Just show us the chip shop.'

Cartwright said to Weepy: 'What's the matter with your eyes?'

'I play with my plonker,' said the boy.

The pair led them into a third street with the chip shop at the end, white tiled inside and out with steam drifting from the door. A man in a sagging boater was shovelling coal into the fire beneath the deep-fat fryer. A big woman with a glistening face said: 'What will it be?'

'Thirty-two separate penn'orth of chips and one piece of fish,' said Bairnsfather. He whispered to Cartwright: 'We'll eat the fish.'

'What about ours?' demanded Ronnie.

'Thirty-four separate penn'orth,' corrected Bairnsfather. 'And one fish.'

The man looked up from stoking his fires. The edge of his boater was smouldering. Impatiently he snuffed it out with his fingers. 'What sort of fish?' he said. 'We've only got cod.'

They waited while he and the woman shovelled the chips into separate squares of newspaper.

'Salt and vinegar?' asked the woman.

'Some salt, plenty of vinegar,' said Bairnsfather. The woman gently shook the salt over the chips and then sprinkled the vinegar from the darkened bottle on the counter. She put the thirty-four packets into a grubby brown carrier bag and Bairnsfather handed two of them to Ronnie and Weepy who began busily picking at the chips with their fingers. 'One piece of cod,' said the shop man. He put it into a whole page of the *Daily Herald*. 'That will be thirty-four penn'orths and fourpence for the cod. Three and tuppence exactly.' He regarded them speculatively. 'How long will those guns be there?'

'Can't tell you, mate,' said Cartwright. 'Even if we knew. Careless talk.' He pointed to a wilting poster on the steamy, tiled wall which warned: 'Be like Dad, Keep Mum. Careless Talk Costs Lives.'

Bairnsfather said: 'And seven bottles of Tizer.'

'I was just thinking about the chips,' said the man putting the bottles of cherry-coloured drink on the counter. 'Whether to order more spuds.'

'We're open every night,' said the woman. 'Seven till ten or when the chips run out.'

The soldiers went into the sunlit street. They strode around the first corner and, with their backs turned, secretly divided the piece of fish and ate it while the boys loitered hopefully.

Then they turned another corner. The road was

strung with slow buses, army and navy lorries, each one crowded with dark-faced, hollow-eyed, glowering men. They sagged against the bus windows, some asleep, all looking exhausted. In the backs of the lorries they leaned against each other. Some were patched with field dressings. They were survivors of the greatest defeat the British Army had ever suffered: Dunkirk.

'Hide the chips,' said Cartwright and they did.

Sentries had been posted and after dusk some girls and women appeared outside the park and began shouting to the soldiers between the gaps in the iron railings. Ugson, his guard duty finished, found Bairnsfather in the tent, lying on a camp cot, blankets piled above him like the hump of a camel.

It was half past ten. Ugson shone a torch. 'Harry,' he said close to Bairnsfather's ear. 'Harry, can you lend me a couple of bob?'

Bairnsfather, roused from deep sleep, surveyed him from a cleft in the blankets. 'Tomorrow, Ugly,' he said eventually. 'Tomorrow, mate.'

'I need it now.' He put his face closer. 'One of those girls outside is only charging five shillings. And I've got three in small change.'

Bairnsfather levered himself up in the cot. 'Ugly, you're not going with one of them, are you? God knows what you'll get.' He glanced around the tent but they were surrounded by prostrate men.

'I'm *hoping* to get a shag,' whispered Ugson. He looked pitiful in the torchlight. 'I'm not like you, Harry, a bloke of the world. I haven't had many shags. In fact, I haven't had any, not proper ones.' He became pleading again. 'And it's only five bob because it's mid-week.'

Bairnsfather sighed and picked up his small pack from the floor. He rummaged and brought out a two-shilling piece. 'Don't put it around that I paid for you to get the pox,' he warned.

'I won't tell anybody,' said Ugson. 'You won't, will you?'

Bairnsfather sighed and pushed him away gently. 'Have a good time,' he said.

'Thanks, mucker, I'll give it back to you on pay day.' He vanished out into the night of the park and Bairnsfather pulled the blankets back around him. Somebody, Cartwright he thought, was snoring busily but it was regular and it lulled him to sleep. In what seemed mere minutes Ugson was back at his bedside again, his face emotional in his own torchlight.

'Harry, Harry, I've got to tell you.' Bairnsfather groaned. Brown sat up in the next cot and Purcell on one elbow.

'I've just had the most terrific shag,' Ugson said.

Bairnsfather tried to put his head back below the blankets but Brown said: 'Where?' and Purcell sat up expectantly like a tall, skinny boy awaiting a bedtime story. 'Go on, tell us,' he prompted. Sleepily Cartwright sat up and asked: 'Is it morning?'

'Ugly's going to tell us about his fuck,' said Brown.

'Fuck Ugly,' said Cartwright crouching back under his blanket.

'That's what we're waiting to hear about,' said Purcell. 'Go on, mate, spill the beans.'

'Christ, Persil, can't you chose your words a bit more carefully.' It was Hignet, the last to wake. Cartwright sat up again and sighed: 'All right, tell us.'

Bairnsfather said to Ugson: 'I thought you didn't want anyone to know.'

'That was before, but I've got to tell *somebody*,' said Ugson. They were waiting. He said: 'She was outside the gate. Luscious . . . well, fair . . . not too bad. It was only five bob because it's early closing, she said. We went down the road holding hands to a place where they put empty dustbins. And there was this cat making a terrible row, meowing like mad. It was just there, rubbing itself against her stockings . . .'

'Go on,' said Purcell.

'Do you know what she did? I couldn't believe it. She just got hold of the cat and stuck it in the dustbin. Then she closed the lid. It was howling inside.'

'Get to the fuck,' grumbled Cartwright.

'Well, I don't reckon you could call it that. Not technically. D'you know, she told me to sit on the bin, the same one as the cat was in, and then she opened my flies, took out my dick and *put it in her mouth*!'

There was an explosion of excited amazement. Eyes opened, jaws dropped. 'In her mouth?' repeated Brown slowly.

'Right in,' said Ugson. 'She just got hold of it and threaded it in.'

'It's called Fidelio,' said Hignet doubtfully. 'Or is that Beethoven?'

'This was Dotty,' said Ugson. 'Dustbin Dotty they call her.'

'What did it feel like?' asked Brown.

'Feel like? Well, it was bloody lush. Christ, I thought she was going to swallow me. I could feel her tonsils.'

They collectively groaned. 'And what about . . . You know . . . ejaculating?' blinked Hignet. Ugson looked at him as if he had changed the subject.

'Coming,' explained Bairnsfather patiently.

'Oh. In there as well!'

'Ahhhhh.' The lanky Purcell threw himself on his blankets and began to writhe. 'In *there* . . . ?' said Cartwright. 'Well, I know about gobbling. But coming . . .'

Their faces were enraptured in the torchlight. 'What happened then?' asked Hignet as though taking notes.

'She . . . she . . . swallowed it.'

They threw themselves on their beds and howled and moaned. 'You picked up a real bit of class there,' said Bairnsfather.

Eventually Brown said: 'What happened to the cat?'

'I let it out. She just left me sitting on the dustbin lid with my dick hanging out and went off.' He looked around for approval.

'There's no end to romance,' said Hignet.

Sergeant Runciman appeared at the tent flap. 'Glad you're all awake,' he said. 'Fall in at twenty-three thirty, that's in fifteen minutes. We're going to France.'

Even at that hour vessels in the port were unloading cargoes of weary soldiers from Dunkirk. As they towed the two Bofors through the city, ghostly convoys were rolling in the opposite direction, the slatted lights on the vehicles probing uncertainly through the blackout.

'How come we're going to France, sarge, when everybody else is trying to get out?' Brown asked Runciman. There was a hint of bitterness, a touch of tension.

'It's something called Orders, Brown. When you've been in the army as long as I have, lad, you'll know not to question Orders. Personally, I think it's bloody stupid.'

Nobody else in the lorry said anything. Those who had been to Norway remembered it again, the fear and the reality of it. They passed the railway station where vehicles were disgorging troops on to a train. There was hardly a sound, nothing beyond a widespread murmur from the mass of evacuated men, only the plod of their boots and somebody giving instructions, almost suggestions. 'At least we've got Hignet with us this time,' said Runciman. 'Not like Norway. He can tell us where we are. Got your maps, Hignet?'

'I'm a strategist, sergeant,' said Hignet from the dark back of the truck. 'I leave local details to those concerned with tactics.'

Nobody laughed. Ugson had fallen asleep against Bairnsfather's arm, lolling against him like a tired child. 'Somebody will tell us, I expect,' said Runciman. 'We're probably earmarked to take the brunt of the German advance.'

'I hope ruddy not.' There was a deep, apprehensive silence. Then Cartwright said: 'I've got two women to think of. If it gets nasty I'm going on the run.'

'The swim more like it,' replied Runciman.

They reached the dock gates. The men furthest into the lorry heard one of the guards laughing and saying they were going the wrong way and Runciman replying: 'We're a volunteer suicide squad.' Bairnsfather closed his eyes and wondered whether Molly's baby would be a boy. It would be a shame if in twenty years' time he had to be doing this.

At lcast Bcvan kncw somc of thc plan. Hc was waiting for them on the quay. They parked the guns neatly in the dark. 'In the absence of any air attacks on the disembarkation areas on this side,' he told them, 'It has been decided that we'd be more useful across the Channel. They're short of anti-aircraft guns, or anti-tank guns, I don't know which, both probably, at Dunkirk, so we're going to help to cover the last stages of the evacuation, one way or another.' He nodded to the strangely shaped silhouette of a ship lying in the harbour. 'I understand we're going over on that.'

They peered through the night. 'That . . . sir . . .' said Hignet, 'appears to be a paddle-steamer.'

'Well observed, bombardier. So it is.'

A gang of civilians approached. 'We're going to get your bang-bangs aboard, mate,' said one to Bevan. 'We won't drop 'em, promise.'

'I'm counting on you not to, mate,' replied Bevan quietly.

He led his men to the quayside. The paddle-steamer had begun churning water and moving against the jetty, awkward as a duck. 'If one of those paddles gets put out of action . . .' began Hignet studying it.

'. . . We'll be going around in circles,' finished Runciman.

No one said anything more as they waited until the ungainly vessel was against the quay. On its bow was its pretty name: *Maid of Marlow*. A gangway was pushed towards them and they trooped after Bevan on to the deck. Even in the dimness they could see it was brightly painted. Runciman ran his torch along reds and blues and yellows and eventually on to a bulkhead portraying the bulging figure of Popeye. Propped against Popeye was a black destination board with white lettering which read: 'Windsor Only.' 'I wish,' said Bevan.

They filed below, dropped their equipment and groaned as they stretched out on wooden seats. Once the guns were secured on deck Bevan and Runciman also went below. 'What about the wheels, sarge?' asked Bairnsfather tiredly.

'No need to take them off. We'll probably have to get them ashore as soon as we get there. Sleep tight, lads. Sweet dreams.'

Those who fell asleep were woken abruptly by the grind and rush of the paddle wheels. Bairnsfather sat up and Cartwright said: 'I wonder how fast this thing goes?'

'More like how slow,' said Bairnsfather.

'I'm glad I let that cat out of the dustbin, Harry,' said Ugson. 'I wouldn't like to think of it still shut in there.'

'You're a decent man,' said Bairnsfather. The cat and the dustbin seemed many miles away.

It was a placid night and the sky seemed to lighten once they were out to sea. Bevan and Runciman sat on two slatted seats next to the guns. Bevan said: 'Imagine having to get a whole huge army off a beach. I doubt if Napoleon could have done it.'

'The lads haven't had much anti-tank training,' said Runciman.

'I was worried about that myself.'

'I suppose once you see a Panzer division heading towards you there's not much you can do. You either shoot or run.'

'What a strange business this all is,' said Bevan.

'A fuck-up, I think it's called,' said Runciman bitterly. 'If you'll excuse the language, sir.'

'That describes it perfectly. Who got us in a situation where we have to get a damned paddle-steamer to take us to war?'

'There can't be that many men left on the beaches at Dunkirk now,' said Runciman. 'They've been pulling them out for ten days. It beats me why the Germans let them get away. You'd have thought they could have just moved in with a division and some armour and cleared up.'

'We've been blocking the roads to the coast,' said Bevan. 'But it's hard to believe that the Germans couldn't have burst through.'

'Perhaps Jerry's more sporting, or more stupid, than we think.'

The clumsy craft wallowed through the sea, her paddles churning a white fan on either side. They could see the outline of her captain on the bridge. 'He's got some job,' said Bevan. 'Trying to navigate this thing after being on the Thames. You can hardly go off course on a river.'

'I can't believe how close France is,' said Runciman. 'When you go straight across. All those little boats they sent.'

'The adventure of a lifetime,' muttered Bevan.

'Three chaps from Lymington are missing. One of the coppers told me. A customs officer and two others.'

They left the deck and went below where they stretched out on the wooden seats with the snoring soldiers. Bevan slept only fitfully before getting up. Runciman was lying on his back with his mouth wide open as if he were shouting orders. One of the gunners groaned and stirred. It was four thirty. It should be getting light.

Bevan went on deck. It was chill up there. The captain called from the bridge: 'Going to be a pleasant day.'

'Good,' said Bevan. 'A fine day for the beach, you think.'

'This'll be the last run the *Maid of Marlow* will be making. It's nearly over.'

Bevan said that by now he would believe anything. The captain laughed: 'There aren't very many vessels there now. It was like Henley Regatta last week.'

Unhurriedly he came down on deck, casting his eye around it as if wondering where the trippers had gone. 'I never thought I would sail further than Teddington, not now,' he said. He was a square man with a calm face and pale eyes. His name was Dimmock.

'I don't suppose the ship did,' said Bevan.

Dimmock laughed. 'I had my doubts, but she's seaworthy enough. Better than a lot of the coasters they've been using.'

'When will we get there?'

'Tomorrow morning,' said Dimmock to his surprise. 'I have orders to wait out here for an escort and a couple of other ships. Soon we'll be down to dead slow.'

Half an hour later they were scarcely moving, wallowing in the long sea. Bevan's men were stripped to the waist, outwardly jolly, inwardly tense, lying around the guns in the breezy sun, watching for planes and pretending they were not. The only aircraft they saw was a flight of ancient RAF Gloster Gladiators and a cruising Sunderland flying boat which labouriously dipped its wings to them.

Other ships began approaching from the opposite direction: freighters, tugs and the fire float lumbering towards them through the easy sea. 'At least they'd be able to squirt at the Germans,' said Cartwright.

It was only then that they began to realise the vast spread of the operation. The vessels were crammed with soldiers. Not one waved. 'It's been like this for ten days,' remarked Dimmock to Bevan and Runciman. 'God knows how they thought it would work. But it's worked.'

Two hours later, when the summer afternoon was diminishing, they heard the paddles start to wash through the sea again and the vessel began to make its way. 'All for nothing,' said Captain Dimmock. 'The escort's been diverted and the other ships aren't coming. We're on our own.'

Bevan kept the crews near the guns. 'We've spent all our active service at sea,' grumbled Ugson. 'I've even stopped being sick.' The early June evening was calm and lovely; there was a deepening purple sky in the warm sunset and seabirds were circling the masts. Darkness did not fall until almost eleven.

A steward opened the bar and each man was allowed to buy one bottle of Bass to go with the army rations. A lost case of army corned beef was discovered and opened by Cartwright with his bayonet. That night Bevan and

Runciman slept more comfortably in a double cabin and the men made mattresses of life-jackets.

The short hours of darkness passed without incident although Bevan, going on deck just before dawn, saw gun flickers like lightning over France, and as the light grew they were approaching the shore.

Off shore vessels began taking shape. The nearest were warships, lying reassuringly close. 'No sign of Jerry,' Bevan called to the captain standing on the wing of the bridge.

'He's been in and out,' Dimmock called back. 'But nothing like he should have been. Our boys were playing football on the sands.'

They passed by the warships. One of them sounded a greeting. Runciman came on deck. 'I've posted one gun crew,' he said. 'The rest are going to breakfast.' He sniffed at the air. 'Quite fresh for a battlefield.' Beyond the bow they could see most of the extensive beach now. It seemed bereft of humanity but great piles and pyramids of equipment were on the dunes, scattered, stacked abandoned under a smoke-hung sky. In the sea, with the tide flowing over them, the tops of half-submerged military trucks lay like rafts. 'That's a good notion,' said Bevan to Runciman. 'Drive them out at low tide and then put pontoons between them and out to the boats.'

'Not everybody can swim.'

'Can you, sergeant?'

'No, sir.'

Now that they were nearer they could see some men on the beach, moving about in the early grey among the stranded vehicles and stacks of equipment like figures in a ghostly town. 'We can get in alongside,' called the captain. 'At least, we did before. There's one bit of jetty that's still standing.'

'You'd think the Huns would have dive-bombed that,' said Runciman. 'I would have.'

Their men came on deck, blinking, rubbing their faces. 'Couldn't shave, sergeant, no hot water available,' said Hignet.

'It's total war, Hignet,' said Runciman.

They looked towards the beach with the dunes behind it draped in smoke. Ugson said: 'There's nobody left.'

'There's some blokes over there,' Purcell pointed as though his lankiness gave him an advantage. 'And a few more the other side.'

All about them the harbour was wrecked, the funnels and masts of ships projecting from the oily, debris-coated water. The paddle-steamer went in cautiously. Hignet sniffed at the acrid air. 'Wonder why he's left this one jetty?' he said to Runciman.

'I was wondering that myself.'

'Could be a trap. Get us in here and then send in a few Stukas.' With his hand he imitated a diving plane. 'Bang, bang, bang.'

Runciman surveyed him. 'You missed out when we went to Norway, Hignet. Enjoying your outing this time?'

'Yes, thank you, sergeant. So far. But it's not a particularly interesting part of France.'

As he said it there was a deep engine roar and a shadow flitted across the deck. The men on the gun opened fire. The others threw themselves on the deck. A stick of bombs straddled the harbour water sending up debris as though they had exploded on dry land. 'Was that the Stuka you were mentioning, sarge?' asked Hignet picking himself up.

'Dornier,' said Runciman. He went to the gun and punched Bairnsfather gently on the shoulder. 'You got a shot in anyway.'

'A few,' said Bairnsfather. 'None of them even close.'
'He might come back.'
'I hope the bugger does.'
Now the *Maid of Marlow* was edging closer. It was miraculous how the jetty had escaped destruction. There was even a working crane. A small car was driving along the cobbles. Bevan went to the gangway as it was lowered. A Royal Engineers colonel climbed from the car, younger than Bevan, brown faced as a holiday-maker. 'You're taking the last load,' he said. 'Odds and sods and a few prisoners.'
'Prisoners, sir?'
'Huns. We've got about twenty. Might as well take them back. It would be nice to have something to show for all this damned mess.' He jogged along the deck and up to the wheelhouse. He shook hands with the captain and swallowed a cup of coffee which was waiting for him, held by a neat steward with a silver tray. Then he went down to the deck again. 'My name is Henderson, by the way,' he said to Bevan.
'James Bevan.'
'Right, get one of your Bofors down to the end of this jetty, captain. Those wrecked trucks look like half-decent cover. If the Jerry advance party get there before we've finished loading the last man, they'll probably pop into the port area through that gate. They're pretty obvious sometimes, it's just that there are a lot of them. Your chaps can give them a warm-up and then clear off out of it as sharp as you can.' He glanced at the painting of Popeye. 'This floating funfair is not going to be here too long.'
Bevan saluted. 'I'll keep the other gun on board,' he said.
'Right, captain. They've been a bit casual with their air attacks lately, almost as though they can't be bothered.

The First Battalion Welsh Guards are dug in at St Omer, just up the road, and they've stopped the buggers getting any closer, for the time being anyway. But the rearguard is just about on its last legs. We only want to keep them at bay until we get this vessel out of here and a couple of others off the beach. Those grey jobs out at sea will provide support bombardment as necessary. I'm scared bloody rigid that the navy are going to clobber us in error, get the range wrong, but they've missed us so far.'

He said: 'All clear?' Bevan saluted and said: 'All clear, sir.' Henderson went ashore and got back into his car. Using a regulation hand signal, as if he were in a suburban street, the driver did a three-point turn and drove back the way he had come.

'Which gun, sir?' asked Runciman.

'B-gun, sergeant. Crew of four men.'

'The fewer that have to run the better,' said Runciman. He turned to the men on deck. 'Bairnsfather, Purcell, Cartwright, come with me.'

Bairnsfather thought of Molly and cursed quietly. Using the ramp they got the gun ashore and manhandled it into place on the quay. 'Give them a hand,' shouted Bevan. He went ashore himself and, with the exception of four men who remained on the other gun, every other member of the unit helped to push and pull the Bofors to the end of the jetty three hundred yards away. Once it was in position the men not detailed for its crew turned and ran, trying not to look anxious, back to the ship. Bevan stayed and watched Runciman organise the Bofors's position between two burned-out army lorries. 'I'll get the captain to give two toots on the ship's siren,' said Bevan. 'When you hear that retire at the double.'

'Leaving the gun?' said Runciman reluctantly.

'Leaving the gun. It's a pity but there it is. You're carrying the ammo, right?'

'Right,' said the sergeant. 'I doubt if we'll be here long enough to need much.' With a look over his shoulder, Bevan walked back to the ship.

A straggle of soldiers appeared like apparitions across the sand. Two men were kicking a football, passing it doggedly between them as they headed for the steamer. A few had their rifles but not many. They slogged along the jetty as though at the end of a long route march, their shoulders bent, their faces dark and almost without expression, as if not caring whether they went home or not. From the deck Brown gave them an optimistic thumbs up but no one responded. The group of German prisoners who followed half an hour later were cheerful by comparison. 'They know which side they're on,' observed Hignet.

It seemed that the long arch of beach was now all but clear of men, the end of a momentous operation. 'Over three hundred thousand, they say,' said Captain Dimmock to Bevan. 'Our fellows, French and Belgians. Pity we had to leave all this stuff behind.' His hand swept the breadth of the beach, piled and littered with vehicles and equipment. 'If the Germans follow us across sharply enough they're going to find an army with no arms.'

The enemy prisoners were ushered into a roped-off area in the bow. 'They'll jump over those ropes easy,' observed Ugson. He watched as the Germans sat quietly; some began to light cigarettes and one man puffed on an ornate meerschaum pipe. Speculatively Ugson glanced towards Bevan on the other side of the deck. 'If they can have snout, so can we probably,' he said to Hignet. He fumbled for a cigarette. 'Don't,' said Hignet also eyeing Bevan. 'You're on duty, they're not.'

On the shore, at the end of the jetty, the Bofors crew crouched and waited: Runciman the ammunition carrier, Bairnsfather the loader, Purcell and Cartwright in the gun layers' seats. The barrel was horizontal. Behind them the paddle-steamer was loading the last of the men from the beach. Nothing happened for half an hour. Then around the narrow corner into the harbour area a grey motorcycle and side-car appeared almost sedately. 'Hold fire,' Runciman ordered quietly. The combination was followed by a second, and then a third which had a machine-gun in the side-car. Silently the gun layers swung the Bofors. 'Fire!' ordered Runciman. They fired.

The men on the ship had a clear view. The leading vehicle flew up into the air as though it had sudden wings, the second slewed around and caught fire. They could see a German soldier running in flames, heading for the harbour. He jumped into the water. The third motorcycle was flung violently against a wall, but the driver resourcefully managed to pull it around and his companion in the side-car hung on and fired a wild burst from his machine-gun. Another salvo from the Bofors hit the building behind the enemy, sending masonry toppling. The surviving vehicle had somehow turned a full circle and roared away in the direction from which it had come. The British gunners cheered wildly and the men on the ship joined in the vivid excitement of killing and winning. The German prisoners watched but continued to smoke as though it was of no interest. Bevan looked towards the captain on the bridge. The captain waved at him and there was a double blast of the ship's siren.

At the end of the jetty Runciman shouted: 'Right, retire!'

They turned and ran. Before he followed them Runciman regretfully patted the gun.

Some of the troops aboard ship were cheering them as they bolted along the jetty. Cartwright was first aboard, Purcell loping after him like a giraffe and Bairnsfather behind him. Reaching the gangplank he slipped and as he recovered there came a brief, almost gentle crackle of small-arms fire from the shore. Purcell fell back on to the gangway and slid down into Bairnsfather's arms, knocking him backwards. Runciman, who was in the rear, staggered as the pair collided with him. Everybody cursed. It was almost funny. Then Bairnsfather saw that Purcell was prostrate with blood gushing from his neck.

Bevan had rushed to the side. 'Get him aboard,' he ordered. 'And quick.' He revolved and bawled across the deck: 'Medics! Medics here!'

Runciman took Purcell's arms and Bairnsfather took his boots. Purcell, eyes open wildly, was trembling, wriggling as they carried him. Cartwright hurried back down the gangplank and took the weight around the wounded man's middle. They were all sweating, gabbling, sobbing, all telling Purcell that it was going to be all right. Nobody wanted to look at the flowing blood. Even as they lifted him to the deck, with the other soldiers still crouching, fearful of another burst of gunfire, Captain Dimmock bellowed and the gangway was thrown back ashore. They had already cast off the mooring lines. Then, like a scene from an old silent movie comedy, the little army car appeared at the end of the jetty and bounced along it. The captain called out again. The car pulled up unhurriedly after the driver had pedantically flapped his arm in the slowing-down signal. Colonel Henderson unhurriedly got out of the vehicle and waving to the captain as if asking him to wait for a moment, he and his driver replaced the gangway and climbed up it. The paddles were rotating and the steamer backed in jerks out into the harbour.

'Oh, bad luck,' said the Colonel seeing Purcell. 'I bet we haven't got a doctor.'

'Two medics,' said Bevan. His face felt starched.

'They're just coming.' The two men came along the deck. 'Clear the area, please sir,' said one. 'We need room.'

They knelt beside Purcell. His comrades, their hands to their faces and mouths, stood back. Ugson was weeping like a child. Purcell opened his eyes. 'It's being so tall,' he said as if in apology. Bevan said to the medical corporal: 'How is he?' The man said nothing but looked up and shook his head. The other one said: 'We need a doctor.'

Bevan looked at Henderson. 'He's my first casualty.'

The young colonel looked at the shore. 'It must have been a freak burst. There's not a sign of them now.'

Bevan said: 'If we put him ashore the Germans will look after him. They'll have a doctor.'

'I'll go with him, sir,' said Ugson wiping his eyes. 'He's my mucker. I'll stay with him and tell them.'

Henderson said: 'Captain Dimmock won't take this thing back in now. He can't.'

The captain called from the wing bridge: 'We'll get him to one of the naval vessels.'

He had backed out of the harbour. There was no further fire from the shore. Under the mocking blue sky the coloured steamer turned without grace, her paddles churning the pale, calm sea, and began to head out. By that time Gunner Purcell had died.

Bevan sat eating with Henderson and Captain Dimmock around a table in the officers' quarters. They were on their second bottle of wine, already half finished. 'If the British started the war in a spirit of National Rat Week, which we certainly did,' said the colonel, 'then the French thought it was a non-stop Bastille Day. Just a bit of ooh, la, bloody la. One day, when all this is written down, it will read as a classic in lunatic planning and sloppy welfare.'

'Perhaps on their side too?' suggested Bevan.

'The missing killer punch,' nodded Henderson. 'It's amazing. They had us cold.'

'There was a National Day of Prayer,' said the captain unexpectedly.

Henderson said: 'I'd have swapped that for a battery of twenty-five-pounders when we needed them.' He sighed: 'The whole damn thing need not have happened. I was in the line west of the Ardennes. According to the French no armour could penetrate the Ardennes and then what do we see but all these blue lights snaking through the mountains. German tanks.'

'I understand that we've left forty thousand French troops behind,' said the captain. 'They'll be behind barbed wire by now.'

'The French could not organise their evacuation,' said Henderson. He drank almost a whole glass of wine in two gulps. 'Nothing goes right for them. The one moment when we could have counter-attacked with a good chance of turning their flank the French general capable of giving the order was killed in a road accident. An everyday careless driver. That corporal could have lost us the war.'

There was a knock on the door and the steward came in accompanied by a worried Sergeant Runciman who saluted. 'Pardon, sir,' he said to Bevan, 'but the prisoners have started to sing.' Henderson laughed silently, putting his head in his hands. 'Our boys are very upset,' said Runciman still addressing Bevan. 'With what happened to Gunner Purcell, they don't like the Germans singing.'

'There's nothing in the Geneva Convention about preventing singing,' said Henderson looking up.

'I could have the hoses turned on them,' suggested Dimmock.

'That *is* against the Geneva Convention.'

Bevan got up. 'Will you excuse me,' he said. 'I don't want trouble.'

Runciman led the way. He could hear the prisoners chorusing lustily in the dark. 'It's that "We'll March Against England",' said Runciman with disgust. 'I'm scared our blokes are going to wade into them and sod the Geneva Convention.'

The two men strode along the deck. By the time they had reached the prisoners' area in the bow another wave of songs had begun. This time it was from the British Army and led by Bairnsfather. His close comrades and then some of the other men around joined in, tiredly but with increasing vigour. The officer and the sergeant paused.

'When the Führer says "We are the master race"
We're going to *fart*, *fart* right in the Führer's face!'

The ludicrous song swelled from the deck. Bevan saw that Bairnsfather and Cartwright were leading the chorus. Some men were leaning provocatively over the prisoners' ropes to shout the words, thrusting out their buttocks and making farting noises. The enemy had been outsung.

Bevan stepped forward and the singing ceased. He confronted the square of blank-faced prisoners. 'Anybody here speak English?'

'I speak a bit of German, sir.' One of the medics who had attended Purcell stepped from the crowded soldiers behind Bevan. Hignet was right after him. 'I speak a bit more,' he said.

'I thought you might, bombardier,' said Bevan. 'Tell these men that they've got to stop singing.'

'Yes, sir. Shall I tell them what will happen if they don't?'

'I don't know what will happen.'

'I'll tell them.'

Hignet stood in front of the Germans and loosed off in a version of their own language. He flung his arms, he jabbed his finger at them, he shook his fist, he screamed. His comrades watched awestruck.

'He'd make a good storm-trooper,' grunted Runciman.

In the dimness the prisoners' eyes began to shift and they fidgeted in the confined space. Several nervously lit cigarettes. Hignet shouted at them to put them out and they did. They remained silent and with a final, fist-clenched harangue Hignet stumped away.

'They understand shouting, sir,' Hignet said to Bevan. 'That's why Hitler succeeded. I told them they'd have their balls shot off and they'd be chucked overboard.'

'The balls or the prisoners?'

'Both, sir.'

Bevan made his way back to the captain's quarters, shaking his head. Dimmock and the colonel had been listening to the BBC Home Service news. 'We were right,' said Dimmock. 'We were the last out of Dunkirk. The navy's pulled out.'

Bevan sat down and listened. All signposts were to be removed from the roads of Britain. Church bells would only be rung to warn of a paratroop landing. Another news item followed: 'The Ministry of Food has announced that from next week all children will be entitled to free milk at school. Each child will get a third of a pint per day . . .'

Colonel Henderson stood wearily. The captain turned off the radio. 'Fuck me,' sighed Henderson. 'Free milk.'

Their course was for Ramsgate and by first summer light they were in sight of the great wedges of cliff on the very corner of England, white and full of power as knights awaiting battle. 'You'll be thinking about having to write to your chap's parents,' said Henderson. They were on deck, the morning cool and calm as peace.

'Purcell. Yes,' said Bevan. 'I've been trying to think of something that's not banal.'

Henderson nodded. They were at the rail and two fishing boats were about their everyday work half a mile away, their crews waving. 'I've had to do it once or twice,' he said. 'When the action is finished you have to sit down and try to think of something comforting to say to them. My father, in the Great War, had to write so many letters like that, he began keeping a notebook of phrases so that he didn't use the same words over and over again, like a circular, as he used to say. He even lent it to other officers. There were bits of poetry, all sorts of things he'd pinched or memorised.'

'I hope to God I never get to that stage,' said Bevan.

'I wonder what will happen to this ship now? You can't always go to war painted like a circus.' Henderson paused. 'My father desperately wanted to get into this show. It's odd, isn't it. Christ, I'd like to have nothing more to do with it.'

'An old warhorse.'

'More apt than you think. He's sitting up in Northumberland writing a history of the horse in war. He's eighty.'

'The Germans still use a lot of horses.'

'They're the only European army that does, for all their Panzer divisions and parachute troops. One good dose of equine fever and we may not have lost in France.'

Captain Dimmock came steadily down from the bridge. He eyed England as if he had been away for years and it had changed in his absence. 'I'll be back on the Thames next week, I expect,' he said. 'Kids rushing around the deck, mums drinking cups of tea and dads with handkerchiefs tied around their heads. It will all be just the same. They're going to have a new river-bus service in London from Westminster to the City, you know. It's starting in August.'

The paddle-steamer rounded the rocky headland. There were people on the cliffs waving to them and as she ploughed slowly and thankfully into the harbour at Ramsgate, the shore was lined with cheering people. 'From now on,' said Captain Dimmock, 'The most difficult thing I want to do is to negotiate Maidenhead Bridge.'

Henderson and Bevan shook hands with him. 'I'm going to London,' said Henderson. 'Straight to bloody Westminster. I'm going to buttonhole somebody, even Churchill if I can, and tell them straight what a damned mess they're making of this war. It's got to change. I doubt if they'll listen, they're politicians, but I'm going anyway.'

Bevan got his men ashore. There were four vehicles waiting: a truck for them, two others for the German prisoners, and a military ambulance for the body of Purcell. The soldiers fell in and Runciman called them to attention as the stretcher was carried off with the blanket over Purcell's face. Ugson had to wipe his cheeks with his sleeve. The crowd appeared to think that the Germans were Continental allies brought back from Dunkirk. A woman threw an apple to one of them who took a bite and threw it back.

'Funny people, prisoners,' said Bevan quoting Runciman's own words to him. 'Neither one thing nor the other.'

Runciman did not seem to recognise the sentiments. 'You're right, sir. Funny people.'

When Bevan was seventeen he had to guard one hundred and two German prisoners. He knew the number exactly because every morning and every night it was his duty to count their heads. By that time, in the fading summer of 1918, it was not strictly necessary because the war, which had almost run its course, had drifted into the distance, there was nowhere for the captured Germans to go.

They were kept in a destroyed churchyard, the church itself only a stump. There was the remnant of a perimeter wall, bitten by shell fire, and this was lined with barbed wire. Some of the old graves were still visible among the bombardment craters and the bones which had been unearthed had been piled in the hollow of the church. After four years a few more bones made no difference.

It was near Hazebrouck, twenty kilometres from St Omer, inland from Calais and Dunkirk. Wellington had made the town his base before Waterloo, and a century later the British erected their headquarter tents in the same fields. From 1914 to 1918 the ponderous battles had rolled to and fro across the flat country, making it even flatter; there were cratered ridges, now naked of trees, and rivers polluted with blood. But the war had at last retreated. French peasants were selling produce in the streets. They handed fruit to the German prisoners in exchange for souvenirs, buttons, caps and boots. A spiked helmet could be bartered for a packet of tobacco.

When James arrived in France, aged seventeen, wondering what he would find now that he was heading for those gun flashes he had once seen from his dormitory bed at Thorncliffe, the final agonies of the conflict were being sombrely played out.

Above ground level September was beautiful, the days clement, acres of sky reflected in acres of battlefield mud that stretched across northern France. There was now a sense in the air that this time it was truly nearing the end. The acrid smoke began to clear. British and French artillery batteries contested by signal the honour of firing the final salvo, while the Germans calculated when to take cover for the last time.

James, together with the others of his draft – boys mostly but some veterans, alternately gloomy and full of a sort of jolly madness, who were returning to France after leave or recuperation – had expected to find himself in perilous trench but he was instead attached to a carrier-pigeon unit.

'They birds, most o' them anyhow, have come through with scarce a feather missing,' said the signaller Sergeant Barker, the keeper. They had a converted civilian motor bus for a mobile pigeon loft. 'They flies above the poison gas, they get so 'igh the gun blast passes under they bellies, and it would take a bloody fine German sniper to 'it one on the wing.'

James had been embarrassed at first that he should spend what remained of the war cleaning up pigeon droppings and learning the names and numbers of the birds. The lofts projected from both sides of the solid-wheeled bus like Spanish balconies. The bus had for years clumped across the rough hinterland of the Western Front but it was only in the final weeks, when James had just joined, that it came under fire. Sergeant Barker swore that a spy must have given away their location. The bus had taken a wrong turning on the changing battlefield tracks and, late in the evening, with the pigeons cooing in their boxes, the sniper had fired a single shot which sent the birds into a frenzy. Barker drove the ungainly vehicle madly away from danger while James lay on the floor, among the showering droppings and feathers. When they stopped eventually they found that the solitary bullet had gone right through one of the pigeons. 'Number 431,' said Barker tenderly.

They buried 431 by the roadside and the other pigeons soon forgot their ordeal for afterwards they were directed to Calais, where the birds delighted in the sea air, flying and fluttering in the breezy sunshine, and then later to headquarters at Hazebrouck. There they parked the strange bus. Nothing happened for days. There were no dispatches to send. 'It's these motor-bike messengers,' grumbled Sergeant Barker. 'Charging about makin' that nasty row. A pigeon's silent.'

One September morning Barker drove away in the direction of Calais and England. James was posted to a company who were putting barbed wire around the destroyed churchyard. 'It's to stop the ghosts getting out,' said an old soldier.

By the time of his eighteenth birthday the war had almost shuddered to a stop. The German armies having advanced for the last time, the final big fight, the Second Battle of the Marne, was waged to the standstill of exhaustion. The German front line was broken, their commander-in-chief Ludendorff resigned, the navy at Kiel mutinied and the Kaiser abdicated. The prisoners at Hazebrouck sat in silent batches as if nothing more was to be expected. British soldiers came out of the trenches, rat bitten and lice ridden, and soaked themselves in the hot water contained in the great beer vats of the local brewery. They had been promised a sure future, a land fit for heroes, and they were eagerly looking forward to it. Millions had died, but not them.

James thought about Agnes. Before being shipped to France he had been given forty-eight hours' embarkation leave and had gone to London, once more to seek her out. She had sent him a roughly scribbled note with an address where she hoped to be put up when she left Scotland but, although he had written to her there, he had heard no more. At four in the afternoon he left the training depot in Kent for his brief leave, and two hours later he was searching the East End streets of Stepney.

'Agnes Bevan?' said a woman at the scratched door of the address he had been given. 'She did come, but then she went, dear. I'm not familiar with where. You could ask at the pub.'

A woman there remembered her. 'She went up west, I think.' She turned to a man in big trousers behind the bar. 'Where did that Agnes go?' The man had smiled as though he knew something. 'West,' he said.

After another two hours, when it was almost dark, he had found his way to a lodging house in Hoxton. On the third floor, up a grim staircase, he knocked on a door. There was no reply but looking down he saw the envelope of the letter he had sent telling her he was coming. He edged it out a little with his toe. It had never been opened. He pushed it back.

'Sometimes she stays out,' said a young woman who came up the stairs. She had old lines on her face, her cheeks were unhealthily scarlet and her hair straggled from a flowered hat. She wore a daring skirt and boots which almost met it at the knee, with buttons to the top. 'My name is Audrey,' she said.

'Why would she be out all night?' asked James.

'Lodging with friends, I expect, dear.' She eyed him speculatively. 'Wait with me till she gets home?'

Her suggestion was lost on James. 'I've only got a few hours,' he said. 'I'm going to France.'

'I hope you don't go and get killed.'

'So do I. How can I find her?'

Audrey looked doubtful, then smiled a smile that was the only youthful thing about her. 'I'm going up west,' she said. 'I can show you where she might be.'

They sat together on the top of an omnibus. Audrey

insisted on paying both fares. 'If I can't help a soldier I'm not worth much,' she said.

'London's a strange place,' he ventured unhappily as the bus trundled along Piccadilly. 'Agnes is only fifteen.'

Audrey put her hand mockingly to her mouth. 'Fifteen! She says she's eighteen, the hussy.'

They left the bus and headed for the Bohemian Theatre. James's hopes rose. 'She always wanted to be on the stage,' he said. The girl took him by the hand. 'She's promenading,' she said. 'Walking around.'

'In a theatre?'

'There's lots do it. We don't have to pay either.'

He saw what she meant. A variety show was on the stage, a comedian staggering as though drunk, the audience bellowing with laughter. But in the side seats of the theatre, almost out of view of the stage, there were women wearing feather hats and tight dresses who kept getting up and down and sauntering along the side aisles, leaning over to haggle with men. James saw one man leave his seat, call another, and they both went out with two waggling women on their arms. The lights went up as the raucous audience applauded the comedian and the pit orchestra began to play shakily, the conductor's bald head bouncing like a balloon. Women were now strolling blatantly all over the theatre, swaying and laughing and adjusting their hats, boots and bodices and putting rouge on their cheeks. 'I can't see her here,' said Audrey. 'Let's try a teashop.'

She took his hand and almost tugged him from the theatre and out into the gaudy street. There were omnibuses whose drivers honked their rubber horns, jammed against spluttering cars and horse-drawn vehicles. A brewer's dray pulled by four shire-horses creaked under the lights of Regent Street.

'A teashop is open at this time of night?' he asked.

She laughed coarsely. 'This time of night is when they do business, dear.'

She seemed to enjoy pulling him around. Women in the street shouted to her and laughed, pointing at James. He felt like running. How was Agnes part of all this?

'London's a bit of fun if you're an officer,' she said. 'You should try and be one. People grumble because some of them only get the pox instead of going off to France and getting killed.'

She turned into an oil-lit street in Soho and took him through a door. 'Officers only,' said a man behind a cash desk inside.

'Aw, come on, Charlie. He's just off to France.'

'Officers only,' said Charlie.

Down a wide staircase behind the man stumbled a pair of giggling girls entwined with two young and drunken lieutenants whose peaked caps they were rakishly wearing. Bright red lipstick was smeared over their faces and on the mouths of the men. James backed away to let them go out into the garish street. 'He's looking for Agnes, his sister,' Audrey said to Charlie.

'She's not in here. Not seen her for a week.'

'She's fifteen,' said James bitterly. 'Do you realise that?'

'Wish her a happy birthday,' said the man.

James lunged forward and caught him by his lapels. 'My sister, where is she?'

'Wait a minute, wait a minute!' spluttered the man. 'Horace!' he called up the stairs. A youth appeared. 'Horace, call the bobbies.' James released him. 'We've got a telephone,' threatened Charlie. 'We can telephone them.' Audrey pulled James towards the door. Charlie followed them and pushed James between the shoulder-blades, propelling him into the street.

'Officers only,' he repeated.

* * *

He never did find Agnes that night. They went to several more gaudy places, including the Café Royal where people were engrossed in the new craze, the tango, a close and erotic dance from Argentina. There were groups of girls and women, simpering, giggling and some drunk and outrageous. To him they looked ugly. His sister was not to be seen. Audrey disappeared at the Café Royal after a whispered promise to be back soon. That was the last he saw of her.

Now he needed to sleep. He trudged his way to Charing Cross station, through the thronged streets. It was as though non-combatant civilians were celebrating the end of the war months too early, jostling along pavements, threading through traffic, pouring in and out of public bars, coming in pushing droves from theatres and shoving into the new cinemas. There was an elation in the air. The seventeen-year-old soldier wandered through it. When he asked directions he was thumped on the shoulders and wished all the best of luck; men offered to take him for drinks if they could find a bar that would accept other ranks. He thought that the trenches – their silences, their noises and their decent comradeship – would be better.

At Charing Cross he sat on a wooden seat, pulled his uniform collar up and began to doze. There was the hissing of trains, shouts, whistles and hoots, and it was not until after midnight that the station begun to subdue. A slow woman arrived with a broom and swept around his feet. Then another woman, much younger but just as weary, came and sat beside him. 'Want to do a trick for a shilling?' she asked.

He told her he did not have a shilling but if she knew a trick she wanted to show him then she was welcome. She laughed but remained close to him, finding comfort in his khaki shoulder. She went to sleep against him, dribbling on his sleeve. A man shuffled along the almost deserted platform, stopped in front of them and began to play the spoons. He had a rank of discoloured medals hanging on dirty ribbons on his chest and as he played, the medals jangled along with the click-clacking spoons. The woman woke up and said enviously: 'He's all right. He's got a skill.'

The man stopped playing as if he had reached the end of his repertoire, and regarded James and the girl longingly. She gave him a penny saying: 'Poor bleedin' soul.'

James's eyes were drooping. She rose from the bench and said she had just remembered an important appointment. When she had gone, limping he now saw, he stretched himself on the hard bench and went to sleep. When he woke it was light and he was being prodded by a railway porter. 'You'll be too late for the war, soldier, if you don't show a leg,' said the man laughing at his own wit. James sat up. There was a canteen at the end of the platform and they were just opening. He bought a cup of tea for a halfpenny, a special reduced price for servicemen. He decided to go back to Stepney.

Agnes was still not there, nor was Audrey. For an hour he sat on the interior stairs but the street door below was never opened. Going outside he walked up and down the pavement in the growing warmth of the day. There was an old stone square at the end of the street, a downcast place that had probably once been elegant. He sat there until noon, then went back to the pub where he had asked about his sister. 'Ain't you found her?' asked the man with the big trousers. He shook his head and smirked.

Outside was a man selling cockles and mussels and James bought a plateful with a square of bread and ate them in the street. He was feeling defeated, disconsolate.

Once more he went back to Agnes's lodgings, climbed the stairs and once more extracted his letter from below the door. He found a pencil in his pocket and wrote: 'I came to see you but you were never here. Love as always. James.'

Then he returned to Charing Cross by omnibus across busy and congested London, where apparently carefree people were sitting out in the sun. He was glad when he was aboard the puffing train taking him back to the army. To the war.

There were a hundred thousand Chinese working on the Western Front, small, labouring men who earned one French franc a day. They had their pigtails cut off and were given numbered wristbands to identify them. The pigtails were put into piles and burned, giving off an oily and exotic smell. Several hundred of the Chinamen died in the battlefields or from the sicknesses of an alien place. Nobody knew their names. When they were buried only their numbers were recorded.

A company of the Chinese Labour Corps arrived in Hazebrouck, moving in stoic lines, and began to rebuild some of the torn buildings so that they would be fit for the winter. They went about their work silently and expressionlessly as the days grew shorter and colder; it seemed that all they needed to do was eat and sleep a little. The German prisoners watched them with scorn. James attempted to ask them where their homes were and how they had ended up in France but they made no sign of understanding him.

On the morning of 11 November, the eleventh hour of the eleventh day of the eleventh month, the final guns sounded. Standing outside the barbed wire with his unused rifle slung on his shoulder, James listened as the last salvos died away. 'Be bad luck if you had your name on one of them shells,' said one of the other guards.

They trudged up and down. It did not seem like victory, but he felt he had become a soldier, even a veteran, during the weeks he had been in France. When the ultimate guns echoed, the sound of ragged cheering went up around the damaged town. James and the other guards outside the wire half enthusiastically raised their hats and joined in. Then, as one, all the Germans in the compound raised a huge hurrah.

'God only knows why they're cheering,' said the other guard. 'They've lost the war.'

'They'll be going home,' said James.

Eventually he would also be going home. Wherever home was. There was no place waiting for him and no one, except Agnes, that he knew. He had hopefully written to her from France and she contritely replied. 'I am so sorry, James, that you missed me when you came. I was away in the country with good friends. God bless. Please keep alive.'

Despite his own conscientious letters it was weeks before she wrote again. On the bottom of the single sheet was a pencil postscript: 'I mad her rite this. Luv. Audrey.'

'I have a very interesting life in London,' wrote Agnes. 'I have visited many places and I have a lot of friends. When you come home from France please come to see me at the above address. Your ever loving and ever faithful sister, Agnes.'

The brevity and carelessness of the letter hurt him but he kept it with his few possessions in his kitbag and read it several times. Once he was scanning it again, as if hoping to find a hidden meaning, and one of the bored Germans wandered to the wire and said: 'It is from your sweetheart?'

'Yes,' he answered. It was simpler to say that; you were not supposed to talk to the captives while guarding them.

'In a few months I will see my sweetheart in Dortmund,' said the young German. 'And all will be happy again. Also my auntie.' He looked quizzically through the wire. 'Auntie? That is right? Auntie?'

'That's right,' said James keeping his voice low.

'Do you have an auntie?'

'No. Not now.'

'My auntie is fat. But you have a sweetheart.'

James moved cautiously along the wire but the prisoner followed as though stalking him. 'Some men do not want to go home,' he whispered. 'They do not want their wives or their children. They do not want to go again to their work. They like it here.'

There were British soldiers like that, fearful of returning to the old, difficult, wearying life. They suspected, rightly, that the land fit for heroes might well be a land fit only for the unemployed.

It was almost miraculous the way the countryside of France had recovered by the summer of 1919. Away from the ravages of the front line, the flooded trenches, the abandoned redoubts where the scars would take much longer to heal, the meadows became green again and poppies blew among the fresh cornfields. Sun made the new leaves luminous and streams ran clear.

Gangs of soldiers were clearing the debris from the town. The German prisoners had gone home smiling thankfully, waving to the French people and kissing some of the local girls. The days were easy. No one seemed in a hurry to find the energy to rebuild the damaged place. It was almost as if they felt that the longer it took the less chance there would be for it to be destroyed again.

People were grateful to be warmed by another summer and to know that they had survived.

Late one afternoon when the soldiers were clearing some farm buildings an unexploded shell was unearthed and before the area could be evacuated it blew up. James was the only serious casualty, his injuries caused not by the explosion but by a bolting team of horses harnessed to an empty cart. He was thrown aside by the stampede but the cart struck him, breaking both his arms, injuring his ribs and knocking him unconscious.

When he woke in hospital a film was being projected on the white ceiling of the ward so that the injured and wounded soldiers could see it while lying in their beds. James lay, trying to resolve the situation, while Ben Turpin's antics made the patients laugh.

'You like the movies?' The voice was gentle and American and he imagined she was part of the film, but then he realised her question had come from behind his iron-railed bed. He had never heard an American speak except on the screen.

'My name is Norma,' she said precisely. 'I know you are James and you are English. How are you feeling, James?'

'Very confused,' he answered. 'Where am I?'

'At St Pol.' She had hair like corn and a bright, open face. She looked no more than twenty. 'You are one of the very few English patients. They are mostly American and some French.'

'Are you a nurse?'

'Well, no. I help. I came from the States a year ago, about the same time as you came from England.'

'I missed most of the war and now I get this.'

'You were lucky. You might have died.' The pictures were flickering silently on the ceiling. She sat familiarly on the side of his bed and he began to laugh with her at the comedy. The last time he had laughed like that was at the Bioscope with Agnes. When the projectionist was changing the reel Norma rose lightly and said: 'I will leave you to enjoy the rest of the picture show. I will come back tomorrow to see you, James. Perhaps we can be friends.'

'I hope so,' said James fervently.

Norma returned every day to sit at his bedside and they talked or she read to him from *The Last of the Mohicans*. She seemed disappointed to find him after five days in a chair on the balcony of the ward. 'They let you from your bed so soon?'

She was glowing, fresh faced, clean dressed, her eyes engulfing. He had never been in love before although he had often wondered about it. 'I asked if I could sit out here,' he said. 'Two broken arms is no reason to be in bed.'

'What about your other injuries? Those horses' hooves must have hurt.'

He smiled at her concern. 'It was the cart that hit me.'

'Details,' she said with a flick of her hand.

'Don't worry,' said James. 'I like it out here. There are a lot of badly injured men inside.'

'There are,' she agreed solemnly. 'Have you seen that poor boy from California, stitched all over. There's not an inch of him that isn't stitched. His face, everything. I've been told not to make him laugh.'

She said that she was going to make her rounds but would return. He told her truthfully that he would look forward to it and with his eyes followed her as she walked along the balcony, speaking to men lying in the morning sunshine. Her back was straight, her hair bright and her dress pale blue and starched. This, he told himself, was the answer to the mystery; how being in love felt.

Happily he lay back looking out over the coloured country. There had been battles there early in the war but the land had healed, and a farm man was leading a horse and cart along a lane. James began to think what he would do when he left the army. He must go and find Agnes again, make sure she was safe, and then settle somewhere and make a life. There was nobody to tell him where to go, what to do. He wondered if he would marry, and who his wife might be, and where they would live. He saw Norma returning.

'I have sister's permission,' she whispered, 'to give your back a rub. It must be very uncomfortable after lying in that bed.'

'It is,' he said. 'Very.' He felt her hands under his armpits although he was quite capable of standing unaided. The two slings cradling his arms were across his bare chest like the sails of a boat. He was wearing his hospital blue pyjama trousers with a red dressing-gown around his shoulders. 'We just need to go to that dinky room at the end,' said Norma.

Carefully she propelled him down the corridor to the white double door and guided him in. There were shutters at the window and the light was cool and muted. He wanted to put his arms about her, embrace her, romantically kiss her as a film star would. His love would be gallant; pure and true.

'The problem will be with those slings,' she said briefly frowning. There was a low bed. 'If you can lie down on your front and kinda put the slings in front of you, higher than your head, like a crab's claws, then I think we're in business, James.' She was so close he could smell her freshness. 'I'll try,' he said.

She helped him to manoeuvre face down on to the

bed and to project his bent arms. 'That seems to work pretty well,' she approved quietly, beginning to roll up her sleeves. 'Tell me, are you stiff?' His heart was hitting his ribs.

'A little,' he said.

'Close your eyes and relax.'

She sat on the side of the bed and surveyed his back. 'You're still bruised,' she whispered. 'You poor young guy.'

'Only across the shoulders,' he said bravely. 'Lower down I'm fine.' What was she going to do?

'Oh, that's good. Would you like me to tell you about myself?'

'I would, of course,' said James. 'Anything.'

He felt the extremes of her fingers moving lightly on his skin, reconnoitring. 'My papa owns this hospital,' she said. 'Well, I guess not *owns* it, but he paid for it. His war contribution. My mother and my aunt were here from 1917 until almost the end of the war and then my sister, Pansy, and me, we came over to carry on the work. We're not nurses, of course. We just . . . well, help.'

Her fingers caressed him. He imagined them in love, married.

'Pansy is twenty-five, five years older than me, and she concentrates on the doughboys, the Americans. I work with the Continental soldiers.' She flicked her hands across the top of his buttocks. 'French and Belgians mostly. You're my first Englishman.'

She worked softly into his back as if it was interesting territory. 'I'd like to use a little oil,' she said quietly. 'Would you like that?'

'Oh yes, I would.' His voice had become a squeak.

There was a moment when her hands were withdrawn. He wriggled, attempting to accommodate his erection between his body and the sheet. 'You comfortable?' she asked bending close to his ear. The starch of her dress collar touched his face and he felt the brush of her breast on his neck. She eased his pyjamas away from his buttocks and he felt the shock trickle of warm oil. 'We'll soon have you right,' she said.

For twenty minutes she massaged him luxuriously. They ceased speaking, James lost for words, the girl suddenly and softly whistling between her teeth. The oil ran between his buttocks and her fingers followed it. He wanted to move his hands to touch her. He wanted to tell her he loved her. Eventually a gong sounded, many miles away it seemed, and she said: 'Wow, lunch already.' She patted him fondly on the bottom and then wiped it with a gentle towel. He was terrified that she would see his erection but she turned to put the oil somewhere and he managed to lever himself up and manoeuvre his dressing-gown around him. She helped him pull up the pyjamas and she must have seen his penis. She continued to smile. He sat on the edge of the bed, his broken arms across his lap.

'You're all pink in the face,' she smiled.

So was she.

On the following day she did not appear, nor on the morning of the day after. Every moment he watched for her. In the afternoon a young woman came on to the balcony and said she was Norma's sister. 'You have become acquainted,' she said.

'Where is she today?' he asked. 'She wasn't here yesterday either.'

Pansy, who was taller and less pretty, put strong ringless fingers on the edge of his chair. 'She'll be back,' she said. 'I guess so anyway. She's gone to Le Havre. Her fiancé is coming in from the States.'

'Oh, I see. Her fiancé.'

'Bulwer,' said Pansy. 'She is going to break off the engagement. Her work is here.'

James prayed she would not leave now, not now he was deeply in love. He saw them sailing to America, being married in New York and living happily in the great country. He slept that night with the same dream. When he woke Norma was standing at the foot of his bed. 'I came back to you,' she smiled.

'I'm glad. I wish I could put my arms around you.'

'Don't worry,' she said. 'Soon they'll be better.'

As soon as he was allowed to go outside the hospital grounds they walked through fields shoulder high with poppies, talking and laughing. Now, at last, he knew what being young was like.

There was a disused barn where no one but other hospital lovers went. Someone had brought in sheets and laid them comfortably across the old, smelly hay. A shell had opened a hole in the roof leaving it gaping to the sun, the racing clouds or to the stars. She always wore a peasant straw hat and a light dress. To James, walking in his bright blue hospital uniform with the coat hung like a cloak over his shoulders, it seemed that, at last, he had found all the things he had dreamed of; no searching, no disappointments, no dangers, no fears. She was a gloriously simple young woman for a lost and wounded boy soldier. In the barn she was quick to arrange the mouldy bales of hay, covered with the convenient sheets, into a sweetly smelling couch. The accommodation of his broken arms required the shape of an armchair. He would sit naked on the draped sheet, his plaster encasements resting on each of the arms formed by the hay. She, her dress opened down the front with nothing below it, would climb carefully on to his lap, so that they were face to face, lip to lip, her breasts against his chest.

Despite her youth she could orchestrate their love-making; prolong, climax, when she chose. At the end she would hug him like a friend, often forgetting his broken arms until he shouted. She always wore a newly starched blue dress and carried a replacement in a cloth bag. He loved to lie in the hay armchair and see her peel the rumpled dress from her peachy body, watch her adjust her wide straw hat which she often wore throughout. There was always a light mischief in her eyes; her face was touched with sunshine coming through a hole in the roof. He delighted in her nakedness, the warm country-girl breasts, her muslin stomach. He loved her deeply and never wanted it to end and she promised, of course, that it never would. But it did.

'The trouble with you, James,' Agnes told him, 'is that you *like* women too much. You love them too much. You believe them too much. You never distrust anything a woman tells you. Just because we're women, you know, we don't always tell the truth, we're not always nice, decent. Sometimes we don't even realise that we're lying.'

It was London in the autumn of 1919. She was seventeen and wearing lipstick and rouge. The peace treaty had been signed at Versailles and they had seen the smudgy newsreels of the midget statesmen bobbing stiffly about in their tall hats and self-importance.

The café where James and Agnes sat was as big as a ballroom, and an orchestra played on a stage between palm trees. There were waitresses in black dresses, white caps and straight pinafores; they carried trays with teapots and cups. It was five o'clock in the afternoon and couples were dancing.

'Will you dance with me, James?' said Agnes. 'We've never danced.'

She smiled at him, like the Agnes who had been a girl. 'It's only a waltz. You can do a waltz.'

'Just about,' said James. He rose and offered her his arm.

They reached the floor and he set himself in place looking down at his feet. 'You are a great big handsome dope, James,' his sister laughed slipping her slight arms about him. He began to move woodenly. Agnes looked up into his face and saw he was silently counting. One-two-three, one-two-three.

'At least she sent you a letter.' They stiffly revolved at the first corner and set off in a straight unturning line towards the far side of the floor. Other dancers were whirling.

'Dearest James,' he recited as he placed his feet. 'I am going home to the States. My work here is finished. Thank you for your friendship.'

'And *you* were part of her work.'

'I suppose I was.'

When the band began playing a foxtrot James hurried her from the floor to the table. She was working in a millinery off Oxford Street although she was often out at night. He had a job as a clerk in a tobacco warehouse and a single-room lodging across the river. The streets were full of the unemployed, wandering, seeking shelter, hoping against hope.

'We should count ourselves lucky,' said Agnes. 'Here we are in London, with jobs and places to live, and we've got through the war and everything will go on famously.'

'And no family but each other,' said James taking her hand.

'How lucky we are.'

But it was only for a while.

It was 4 June 1940. An army lorry was waiting for them

on the quay at Ramsgate and Bevan climbed in the front. The *Maid of Marlow* was still unloading troops. The lorry driver, an acne-faced lance-corporal in the Royal Army Service Corps, asked: 'Where to, sir?'

'You don't know?'

'Not a clue, sir. Orders was just to come down and pick up some blokes from Dunkirk. What was it like?'

Bevan said: 'A picnic.'

'Could do with a few days on the beach myself.'

'We need to head for Southampton,' said Bevan impatiently.

'I don't know the way.'

'What's your name?'

'Thicknesse,' said the driver. Bevan was not surprised. 'Haven't you been provided with a map?'

'Somebody's half-inched it, sir. And all the signposts have gone. It's only just been announced but already they've been taken down. They're even digging the old milestones up. And you can't ring church bells neither.'

'I hadn't thought of ringing church bells,' said Bevan shortly. 'But we need to get back.' He saw a military policeman at the dock gate. 'Stop here.'

'Signposts have all gone,' the MP told him as if it were a personal achievement. 'If you weren't army I wouldn't even be able to point you in the right direction.' He added: 'Sir,' as an afterthought, then thrust out his red-banded arm and, concentrating on Thicknesse as though they would better understand each other, said: 'Take the first right, then left, and it brings you on to the main road to Dover.' He turned to the officer. 'Southampton did you say, sir?' Bevan nodded.

'Well, after Dover it's going to be a bit of a pickle. If I was you I'd just turn half-right at Dover and go on and on, keeping the sea on your left. You're bound to get there in the end.'

Thicknesse moved the lorry forward again. 'Right, didn't he say? Then left was it? Once we get to the sea we'll be all right, sir.' He half laughed. 'Or left.' Then he said: 'If I can find the sea.'

Outside the town Bevan told him to stop. He got from the cab and went around to the back. 'Ugson,' he called. The bashed face rose from the rear. 'Sir?'

'Ugson, ride up the front, will you. You can navigate.'

Ugson looked flattered but worried. 'I ain't got a clue where we are, sir.'

'Neither does the driver. Just remind him that when he gets to Dover he's got to find the sea and then keep it on his left.'

'Right sir, I'll tell 'im,' said Ugson. With some relief he clambered from the truck and Bevan climbed in. He told the men to shift so that he could sit in the centre of the group with Runciman opposite him. Their expressions were sombre. They were returning one man and one gun short.

'I'm writing to Purcell's mother,' Bevan told them. 'What if you each wrote something, just a couple of lines, and we'll send it all off together?'

'He was a good lad,' said Runciman. 'A bit on the lanky side. We ought to do it now, sir.' The men were all agreeing. 'Or when we stop for a pee break. It's difficult with this thing bouncing about.'

'I have a diary,' said Hignet. 'I'll take a few pages out. It's an archaeological diary my uncle gave to me.'

'It will do,' said Runciman. 'Let's have a page each, bombardier.'

Hignet produced the diary. 'It's meant for exploring prehistoric sites,' he said. 'But what with the war, I haven't had the time.'

'You're a prehistoric sight,' said Runciman distributing the pages.

The lorry eventually stopped. 'Dover, sir,' said Ugson coming to the tailboard. 'He thinks.'

Bevan climbed down first, back in the place where twenty-three years before he had joined the train with the wounded men from France. They were in a road bordering the sea. Barbed-wire rolls were strung along the promenade. Two brick pillboxes faced the Channel and concrete blocks, hopeful tank traps, stood readily on the pavement. Some soldiers were carrying an old Maxim machine-gun to the first pillbox. Above it the Channel gulls wheeled and cried in the summer wind. There was a woman behind the counter of a little tea bar, under a bright awning, smiling out expectantly at the soldiers from the lorry. 'Tea break,' said Bevan. He peered across the water. It was a clear day and the coastline of France was visible.

They sat on the toothy tank traps and drank their tea. Some had biscuits and Cartwright had a cheese sandwich. Then they passed Bevan's fountain pen and another owned by Hignet from hand to hand while they wrote their personal notes to Purcell's mother. 'Is it . . . was it . . . spelt like Persil?' asked Brown.

Hignet fixed him. 'P–U–R–C–E–L–L,' he recited. 'Like the composer, not the washing powder.'

A policeman came alongside them on a bicycle. 'Does this belong to you?' he asked Runciman. Between his fingers and thumb he held up a page from Hignet's diary. 'Found blowing along the road. It's a map.'

Hignet claimed it. The policeman said: 'Who's in charge?'

'I am,' answered Bevan. He was losing patience. 'You may have noticed that I am a commissioned officer. These men are engaged in writing notes to the mother of a lad we lost yesterday at Dunkirk.'

'Oh,' said the policeman as though he had difficulty

believing it. 'We have to check. This map has got the word "camp" underlined. It could be misunderstood. It's the sort of thing we have to watch for.'

Hignet advanced and the policeman haughtily showed him the map. 'See, it says "camp" and it's underlined. What am I supposed to think?'

'It's a special map, constable,' sighed Hignet. 'The camp mentioned is an archaeological site.'

'It's still underlined.'

'It's a Roman camp,' said Hignet.

The policeman mounted his bicycle. 'Well, it shouldn't be underlined,' he repeated as he pedalled away. 'There *is* a war on, you know.'

They watched him go. 'There *is* a war on, you know,' mimicked the woman from the tea bar, who had been watching. A copy of the *Daily Mirror* was draped across her counter. The front page carried a photograph of the evacuation of the Dunkirk beaches and the headline 'Bloody Marvellous'. Runciman walked over and looked at it. 'Fancy swearing like that in a paper,' said the woman.

They boarded the lorry again. The driver, Thicknesse, said to Runciman who had relieved Ugson in the cab: 'I could have written something on a bit of paper for that bloke's mum.'

Runciman looked at him sideways. 'You didn't even know him.'

'His mum wouldn't know that, would she?'

He started the truck and, checking where the sea was, began driving west. 'If it was a bit later you could follow the sun going down,' remarked Runciman.

From the tailboard, where he now sat, Bevan watched the coast drift by. Several times they had to make diversions because of defence works. Everybody seemed, at last, to be busy, alert, aware of the danger, although at midday they came upon a group of munching workmen stretched out in the sun, shirts off, facing the tangled wire and the bright beach, as if they did not believe a word of it.

Every stretch of sand was curled with entanglements and every promontory guarded by a new blockhouse, although few guns were to be seen. Some Bren-gun carriers were parked in a town square and they saw some fresh-looking Canadian troops marching in Brighton. Out to sea small, busy ships bobbed up and down, sowing mines, and a Spitfire flew over.

As they neared their destination the defences became more concentrated. At Portsmouth the grey superstructure of the waiting battle fleet hung over the small house tops, and at Southampton every crossroad, every bridge, every railway junction had a concrete pillbox.

They were only a mile from their camp when they were once more halted at a checkpoint and Bevan, looking from the back of the truck, saw a bus crowded with boyish faces. He knew at once what it was. Jumping from the tailboard he strode across the road. Mr MacFarlane was showing a sentry some papers. As he turned away towards the bus again he saw Bevan, smiled and held out his hand. 'Jerusalem is moving,' he said.

'So I see.'

'The sentry thought the boys might be juvenile enemy agents.'

'It's to North Wales then.'

'Yes, this is the last bus. We've been moving over the past month.'

'Indeed. Renée told me you were going. She's in Wales now, is she?'

'At the moment. I don't know for how long. Renée, as you have undoubtedly realised captain, is . . . well, a moveable feast, shall we say. Hasn't she written to you?'

'No, she hasn't. Remind her, will you.'

'I'll do that. She might even write. Thanks for everything, especially the coal.'

'Oh that, yes.'

He glanced up to the window of the bus to see the pale face of Franz. The boy waved a book he was reading, then got up and went towards the door. Bevan and he shook hands gravely. 'I know all the important towns of England,' he said.

'Good. And now you're going to Wales.'

'I have already started to learn the important towns of Wales.'

'Move on,' called the sentry.

'We're holding up the war,' said MacFarlane. He climbed aboard the bus and all the boys cheered as it moved away. Bevan knew he would never see her again. It would not matter. He had been just temporary. They reached the camp and Bevan went into his office. Among the official mail on his desk was an envelope marked 'personal'. It was from a solicitor to say that Eve wanted a divorce.

Bairnsfather got twelve hours' leave. 'What's he doing?' he asked Molly's mother when he arrived at the house. From the window he watched her husband march up the few yards of the back garden path, stiffly about turn and march back the other way.

'He's in this Local Defence Volunteers,' said Mrs Warner. 'He spent hours doing that yesterday. He could hardly move when he went to bed. I had to help him up the stairs.'

'The Germans have said they'll be shot when they're captured,' said Bairnsfather studying his future father-in-law.

'He'll find some excuse,' she shrugged. 'They won't

shoot him. They're all there every night at the drill hall, marching up and down. And then at the pub. He took the garden fork with him last time.' She giggled. 'He looked like he was digging for victory. They didn't have enough guns.'

Ronnie appeared. 'Is he still at it?' he said. 'He'll be worn out by the invasion.' He turned on the big wireless and squatted impatiently. 'It takes hours to warm up, this set. Music-hall is on.'

Molly was upstairs. Bairnsfather sat down to wait for her. Mrs Warner poured a cup of tea. The radio crackled and they heard Suzette Tarri singing 'Red Sails in the Sunset'. 'Who else is on?' asked Bairnsfather.

The boy looked surprised that he had asked. 'Arthur Askey is top of the bill. And there's G. H. Elliot, the Chocolate-coloured Coon. He's not really black. He just puts black on his face.'

'To go on the radio,' said Bairnsfather.

'The newsreaders always have evening dress,' sniffed Ronnie. 'That Frank Phillips, Alvar Liddell, Bruce Belfrage and the others.'

'Since they started saying their names,' said Mrs Warner with some pride, 'Ronnie knows them all.'

'I'll know if it's a Nazi making out he's a newsreader,' said the boy proudly.

Mr Warner came in from the garden. 'I'm ready for them,' he said. 'Let 'em come.' He nodded to Bairnsfather and turned off the wireless saying: 'That row.' He turned to Bairnsfather: 'How was it?'

'Not bad.'

Ronnie turned it on again. 'It's not a row, it's Suzette Tarri.'

'Suzette bloody Tarri,' said his father, nevertheless not attempting to turn the switch again. 'All you think about is the ruddy wireless.'

'Radio,' corrected Ronnie. 'Calling it the wireless is old-fashioned.'

'There's going to be an announcement of national importance,' pointed out Mrs Warner. 'Churchill is speaking tonight.'

Molly came down the stairs. She blushed as she embraced Bairnsfather. 'I was worried about you. They're going to say the banns next Sunday.'

Bairnsfather, watched by the three others in the family, hugged her and kissed her on the cheek. 'It was all right,' he said. 'Couple of hours on the beach in France. Like a day's outing.'

Everyone was waiting for Churchill to speak to the nation, and the Jolly Sailor was crowded. Men stood around and stared at the veneered radio set on the bar, huge and specially polished for the occasion. No sound was coming from it. 'It's Albert Sandler and his violin on the Home Service and *Ack-ack, Beer, Beer* on the Forces,' said George the landlord. 'Nobody wants to hear the fiddle and there's no anti-aircraft or barrage-balloon blokes in.'

'Yes, there is,' said Molly's father. He pointed at Bairnsfather. 'He's ack-ack. My son-in-law. Well, soon to be.' Bairnsfather failed to restrain him: 'Just back from Dunkirk.'

There was only brief attention. A lot of them were merchant seamen and were beyond being impressed. 'I don't want *Ack-ack, Beer, Beer* on,' groaned Bairnsfather waving his hand. 'I've suffered enough.'

Some of them laughed. There were three women, all together in one corner, and they coyly waved to him. A tiny man, hardly reaching the bar, was banging his tankard on the polished surface trying to get the landlord's attention. The landlord pretended not to notice.

'It wasn't really like a day-trip, was it, Dunkirk?'

Molly's father spoke from inside his glass, his lips almost touching the contents, and he looked something like he did in his gas mask. He seemed to make a sudden decision. 'I know you're not matched up with our Molly yet,' he said, 'but you can call me Dad if you like. Or Archie.'

'No, it wasn't a day-trip, Archie,' Bairnsfather said. 'We were only there a few hours but that was enough. I lost one of my mates. He fell on top of me. Knocked me over. Probably saved my life.'

They sat drinking in silence. Archie said he would get the next and he rose to go to the bar. Churchill would speak at nine. It was a quarter to. The landlord gave the radio set another polish. His wife came from the room at the back. 'Plenty in,' she approved. 'Winnie ought to be on every night.'

Archie returned, looked into his glass and after a pensive moment said: 'Harry, I don't mind what's happened. You know, about you and Molly. I think you'll make a good husband and she's my girl.' He patted Bairnsfather on his khaki knee. 'We're men of the world, you and me. So you got her pregnant. I did a few things in the Great War, believe me.'

'What did you do, Archie?'

Archie took a drink and said: 'I was going to tell you.' Then he had another mouthful. 'We used to have a brothel, a knocking shop, behind the lines and once we got out of the trenches that's where we'd creep off to. You had to have some light relief. A good bath, get rid of the lice, and a decent meal, a few beers and then down to the place. I even remember the name, though I don't speak French. It was called "La Repose".'

'Is that where you . . . where you . . . ?'

'Had it the first time? Of course it was, son. There was nowhere else in those days. I was a . . . well, all right, a beginner. But I soon learned the ropes, as it were.' He became lost in the memory. 'There was one girl there, and don't ever mention it to the wife, who I could have married if she hadn't been . . . you know . . . what she was. I really liked her and she liked me. She told me that she would not even have charged me but they used to issue us with a ticket as we went in so she had to.'

'Sounds romantic.'

'Oh, but it was. Well, to me it was, a lad out of the trenches. She had a great big bump in the middle of her forehead. Like a cyst, I suppose you'd call it, the size of a walnut. I didn't like to ask how she came by it. A lot of other blokes wouldn't go with her because of that bump. They reckoned you could hang your tin helmet on it. But I didn't mind. The rest of her was quite nice.'

He glanced at Bairnsfather as though fearing he had said too much. 'Not a word.'

'Not a word,' promised Bairnsfather. 'Like you said, we're men of the world.'

The clock above the bar showed five to nine. The landlord, with a final polish of the wooden case, turned on the switch of the radio. Albert Sandler was just coming to the end of 'Roses of Picardy', a song from the battlefields of the First War. The women in the corner began spontaneously and sentimentally singing it and some of the men joined in. The programme was faded out but they still sang the final words:

> There's one rose that's blooming in Picardy,
> And the rose I love best is you.

Silence fell over the bar. The tiny man, who had climbed on a stool, pushed his glass soundlessly towards the landlord who filled it without a word. Everyone turned towards the radio as though it would not speak until they gave it their undivided attention. Big Ben chimed nine o'clock. Some counted the chimes and looked towards the clock over the bar. It was right. 'This is London,' boomed the announcer. 'The Prime Minister, the Right Honourable Winston Churchill.'

Hardly a finger moved. Not a glass was lifted. Deep and rough, Churchill's voice filled the room. 'I speak to you tonight at a moment of great danger for our country . . .'

After a moment or two a few glasses were raised to mouths. One of the women wiped her eyes and a man who blew his nose was hushed. The deep words went on: 'We shall not flag or fail. . . . We shall fight on the beaches, we shall fight on the landing grounds, we shall fight in the fields and in the streets, we shall fight in the hills; we shall never surrender.'

The emphasis, the finality, the immovability of the word 'never' caused the men to nod. 'I'll never surrender,' said the tiny man at the bar.

He slid from the tall stool to stand, with everyone else, at attention while the National Anthem was played. Then one of the men called to some others. They had to get back to their cargo ship. They finished their drinks and said a quiet good night.

Bairnsfather and Archie went out into the void of the street. 'It's a shame you won't be able to have church bells at the wedding,' ruminated Archie. 'Molly would have liked a few bells.'

10

The weeks that followed were very strange. The German Army rolled easily through France and were in Paris by mid-June but, improbably, the French Air Force still bombed Berlin; the Italian dictator Mussolini, having awaited his moment, declared war and sent troops into the French Riviera only to be halted at the frontier by customs officers and repulsed by the small local garrison at Menton. In Britain, Italian-owned property was attacked by mobs, as German interests had been in the First World War. Italian waiters were thrown in the air.

After months of setbacks the hapless British and French troops in Norway were finally withdrawn and with a sigh of resignation the Norwegian Government surrendered. Nothing was going right.

But behind their growing defences – the pillboxes, some constructed facing the wrong way, the jagged wire along the beaches and plans for using mustard gas on an invading force and setting the sea aflame with petrol – the British were enjoying a fine June. Long, dry days, warm nights and fresh dawns, sunsets that seemed to beam out reassurance, and evenings stretched by an hour on the clocks.

The Local Defence Volunteers, now 350,000 strong, officially aged sixteen to sixty although one man had fought in the Indian Mutiny, paraded in every town and village, some brandishing ancient pikes from museums. Others went on route marches so ambitious that they were unfit for work for days.

The mood was optimistic, unworried as befitted a country which had not been occupied nor had known an invader for centuries, and whose army had the reputation of losing every battle but the last. Cheery deck-chairs were laid out in trim gardens and bands played in public parks; people queued for the cinema three times a week, race meetings were held and tennis, cricket and golf were played. Because of rationing some were eating better than before the war. There was, however, a shortage of onions.

'Won't be getting those nice Brittany onions any more,' said Mr Lampit, the Lyndhurst greengrocer, to Ellen Unsworth. 'The Huns will be eating them now.'

'Greedy so-and-so's,' sniffed Ellen. She had collected her weekly groceries, four ounces of butter, eight of bacon, one-shilling-and-sixpence-worth of meat and one ounce of cheese for each person. A pound of jam every month was also permitted. Unsworth had suggested that the one ounce of cheese should be kept for a mouse that sometimes appeared. Ellen recalled the Breton onion sellers, short, brown-faced men with handsome moustaches, Johnny Onions they were called, who once travelled the towns on bicycles strung with their wares, crying to the wives: '*Oignons! Oignons!*'

Lampit sighed. 'Soon no onions from the Channel Islands either.'

Ellen seemed alarmed. 'My sister's in Guernsey,' she said. 'She and her husband. They've got a tomato farm.'

'Won't be any more of those either.'

'They'll have to clear out, I suppose,' she said as if there might be something they could do about it. 'They're going to evacuate everyone who wants to leave. I had a letter from Kath yesterday.'

'I wouldn't worry,' said Lampit. 'In the *Express* it said that we'd bombed Turin, and the bombers refuelled in Jersey because they couldn't get to Italy in one hop. You never know, maybe we'll put up a fight.'

Lampit's small, red-haired son began running behind the counter, making aeroplane noises. 'Airy buzzers,' he said. 'These are airy buzzers.' He began dropping raw carrots. 'They're bombs,' he said. 'I'm bombing the Germans.'

'We've got some fresh radishes,' said the greengrocer. 'From Cornwall and very nice. At least the Germans haven't got there yet.'

Half an hour later at the police station, Alf Unsworth ran his finger down a list of names and stopped, thankfully, two-thirds of the way to the bottom. He picked up the desk telephone. 'Ellen, she's all right. She's landed at Weymouth.'

'What about Sam?' Ellen had just got in. She put her shopping on the table.

'Sam's not on the list.'

'He must have stayed to look after the tomatoes.'

Unsworth imagined Sam Fellowes, five feet two, tending his tomatoes working in his greenhouses while the armed enemy stamped along the lane. He would see their helmets above his stone wall. Doubtless he would look up briefly and then purposefully go on with his work. 'Kathleen was on a boat called *Channel Pride*,' he said down the phone. 'It was the last to leave Guernsey.'

'Thank God,' said Ellen but without emphasis. She and her sister had never been close. 'I'll wait for her.'

'I don't know what sort of formalities they have to go through at Weymouth,' said Unsworth. 'I expect there'll be plenty of paperwork, all the rigmarole about spies and so forth. But she's bound to turn up some time today. You'd better put the kettle on.'

'She'll want a cup of tea,' agreed Ellen. 'After escaping like that. I wonder where Sam is?'

Unsworth returned to the papers on his desk. Twenty ration books had been stolen from the Lyndhurst food office. He laboriously filled in a form. When he reached the heading 'Description', he wrote: 'Standard ration book. No name or particulars entered.' The stapled pages of the buff-covered booklet were drawn in squares representing fats, meat and sugar. It showed the owner's name and address and wartime registration number, identical to that on their identity card. On it were also a ringed crown, the words 'Ration Book' and 'Ministry of Food' and a serial number. There was not much more he could say about it.

That morning there had been a renewed warning to police to be on the lookout for IRA agents and saboteurs. They were infiltrating the country with the thousands of Southern Irishmen who were crossing to work for good money on airfields and in factories or, for a great deal less money, to join the British forces. The IRA men had their own war. They were planning to take advantage of the confused situation to carry out explosions in Britain.

'It's a swine having to watch out for the Irish at the same time as the Huns,' said Superintendent Plummer, Unsworth's superior. 'As though we haven't already got our hands full.'

'While we're watching for one enemy we might as well watch for two,' pointed out Unsworth. 'It's all good practice.'

Plummer nodded. 'It's just a bloody nuisance.' He put another slip of paper on the desk. 'A tip-off,' he said. 'Somebody thinks they know who pinched those ration books. He says he's being a nark because he's patriotic, but is there a reward?'

* * *

The Channel Islands, adjacent to the French coast and so distant from the British mainland that they were indefensible, had been abandoned to their fate. Jersey had given itself up to a lone German pilot; he landed his plane at the new airport, went to a telephone box and, with two pennies borrowed from a bystander, contacted the governor who promptly surrendered the island to him. Although Guernsey had capitulated, Stuka dive-bombers attacked the harbour almost as an afterthought, killing only civilians for there were no military left. On the isle of Sark the traditional ruler, the formidable Dame, received German officers in her official room as though it was they who had come to surrender, and on Herm, two miles across the water, the caretaker of the lone large house, owned by a British lord, sat in the sun and witnessed the islands around him being bombed and occupied, the only part of Britain to fall under German domination.

'Poor Sam,' said Ellen Unsworth when her sister arrived with her single suitcase. 'Being left behind with those Nazis.'

'Somebody had to look after the tomatoes,' said Kathleen. She began to sniffle. Ellen went to a drawer and got a handkerchief for her because she had left hers behind in the hurry to leave. 'It was Pip, Squeak and Wilfred.'

'The cats,' remembered Ellen. When she and Alf had gone to the house on Guernsey for a week during the last summer of peace the three cats, named after the characters in a newspaper cartoon, had each occupied a special upholstered chair, with an embroidered antimacassar on each bearing the name of the cat. Visitors had to sit on the hard kitchen chairs. Ellen had not enjoyed that, not for a week.

Kathleen's eyes streamed. 'Have another cup,' suggested Ellen.

Her sister snorted into the handkerchief, so overcome she could only nod. 'Everyone who left, their pets had to be destroyed,' she said eventually. 'They thought they would run amok. Can you imagine my cats amok?'

'But Sam *stayed*,' pointed out Ellen.

Her sister regarded her sulkily. 'He didn't say he was staying until the cats had gone. I could never understand it. If they'd killed a few Germans it would have been more to the point, but instead of that . . .' The tears engulfed her again.

'What a shame,' said Ellen.

Kath looked up as though she had just recalled a distant name. 'How is Alf?' she asked. 'Busy, I expect. There's a picture in the *News Chronicle* this morning of a policeman in Jersey chatting away to a Nazi soldier. I saw it in Weymouth.'

'We get the *News Chronicle*,' said Ellen. 'But I haven't looked at it. I've been trying to make a few pots of jam. It's not easy with the sugar ration.'

'I know. I suppose they'll give me a ration book. Is Alf all right?'

'Funnily enough, he's busy trying to find out who stole twenty ration books from the food office at the moment.'

'No decency, some people,' said Kathleen. 'Although I expect they fetch good money.' She drank her tea and wondered why she and her sister had never felt entirely comfortable together. She suspected it was because she had been prettier and had almost won a scholarship. 'If I write to Sam d'you think the Germans will deliver it? They must have a postman. I'll have to tell him where the insurances are and that sort of thing.'

'What a shame he had to stay behind. Very brave of him.'

'"Leave the tomatoes for a couple of days and they're

gone," as Sam said. I hope the Jerries pay for their food.'

'They'll just take them, I expect,' said Ellen. 'Like they take everything. After Poland, Holland and suchlike they won't worry about a few tomatoes.'

They heard the car arrive. 'He still gets petrol then,' said Kathleen.

'The police have to,' said Ellen patiently. 'They can't walk, can they. Not detectives anyway.' She leaned over confidingly. 'He's got a gun, you know. A great big thing. Don't say anything, but he has.'

'Oh, we'll be all right then.'

Ellen had already thought of the consequences of her sister's arrival. 'You'll stay as long as you like,' she said. 'You know that. Until you can get somewhere else.'

Unsworth came through the door and embraced his sister-in-law.

Ellen poured another cup of tea which she gave to her husband, then went to the kitchen dresser and took the *News Chronicle* from the drawer. Her face furrowed at the photograph on the front page.

Unsworth had already seen it. It had been passed around the station. The Jersey policeman, in his British helmet, was giving directions to a German officer. 'Look at that,' said Ellen. 'Even showing him the way, a British bobby.'

'What can he do?' shrugged Unsworth. It had already been argued among the policemen. 'He's under the control of the civil power and the civil power has given up, so that copper has no choice.'

'He's got to do what he's told,' agreed Kathleen lugubriously.

'A lot of people have. A lot of people are going to have to,' said Unsworth.

Ellen sniffed disdainfully over the newspaper. 'Well, I

think he ought to *look* as though he doesn't like doing it, giving directions to a Jerry.'

Unsworth drank his tea. 'Perhaps he directed him the wrong way.'

He sat on his usual polished bench in the Lyndhurst magistrates' court and thought, not for the first time, how unchanging things were. After the news that morning, as he was having his breakfast – now only half a rasher of bacon and one egg – Unsworth had heard the repeat of an American commentator's broadcast to New York from London: 'These people,' said the man in his drawl, 'are facing extermination and all they can do is sing dumb songs.'

'Singing whilst drunk,' said the constable in the witness-box.

'My sister and I,' the man in the dock helpfully added. Two other men stood nodding beside him. 'It's a song about German-occupied Holland.'

'I have heard the song,' put in Lady Violet quickly as though fearful he might sing it now. 'But you were drunk and incapable. With these other men.'

'Tactics,' said the man while the others again nodded. 'We'd been discussing the best places and methods to ambush enemy tanks around here. We're in the Local Defence Volunteers.'

'I suggest you remain sober during these ambushcades,' said her ladyship. 'Fined two shillings each.'

They were replaced in the dock by a concerned-looking youth. He wore a widely open-necked shirt and glasses, one eyepiece of which was blanked out with black tape. The policeman recited from his notebook: 'The accused was standing outside Brockenhurst station carrying a banner which I produce as evidence.'

He held up a large square of cardboard attached to

a broom handle. The three magistrates leaned forward. 'It's not very clear,' said Mr Deemster, the clerk. 'The paint has run.'

The constable said. 'It was raining, sir. But it says: "Stop this war now. Surrender to the . . ." I think it says "inevitable".'

'Inevitable,' confirmed the young man. 'It's what we've got to surrender to.'

'The Prime Minister doesn't think that,' pointed out Lady Violet.

'What's Churchill know? He caused Gallipoli in 1915.'

'Do you admit carrying this . . . device?'

'Alone,' nodded the accused.

Lady Violet turned to the constable. 'What was the effect on people who saw this man with his banner?'

'Not too good, ma'am. People coming out of the station were very upset. I had to arrest him for his own safety.'

Lady Violet leaned over and examined the youth. He blinked repeatedly. 'What if a storm trooper were assaulting your sister? What would you do about that?'

'I haven't got a sister.'

'All right. Your mother. I presume you have a mother, or had at some time.'

'I don't agree with violence or war wherever it comes from.'

Her ladyship glanced at the other magistrates; their heads came together and they whispered. Eventually she looked up. 'You will be fined twenty pounds.'

'I won't pay.'

'Or go to prison for a month.'

'I'd rather go to prison.'

'And so you shall. You'll be quite safe from the Germans in there.'

Unsworth was next in the witness-box. A small shifty man was in the dock. He could not keep his hands still.

He was charged with stealing twenty ration books, the property of HM Government, from the food office at Lyndhurst. 'I am applying for a week's remand,' said Unsworth. 'And in view of the seriousness of the offence, in custody.'

'Granted,' said Lady Violet. She eyed the accused as if trying to find some good in him but being unable to do so.

'I wonder if we will be dishing out justice, or what we sincerely hope is justice, in a month's time,' Lady Violet said to Unsworth as they walked away. They had encountered each other many times from the distance of their respective courtroom places but both were conscious of never having had a private conversation.

'There will always be crime, I imagine,' said Unsworth. 'But what we see as crime and what the Germans might see as crime are probably different things.'

'I would not like to be on that bench in those circumstances. What would I do if . . . well, for example, those local chaps this morning were apprehended laying booby traps?'

'From what's happened in Europe I don't think the Germans bother about magistrates' courts in circumstances like that.'

Her keen eyes went down the main street. 'I have to get the bus,' she said. 'I don't feel, in these times, I can come to court by car, especially in the Rolls, but that's all we've got. Sometimes I thumb a lift. There's a lot of army traffic and the soldiers are very sporting. Short of coming on horseback, it's the bus.'

Unsworth grinned and said he would be glad to give her a lift. 'I'm almost going by the Manor. I have to go and see a food officer about these ration books.'

'A miserable theft,' she said. 'I almost preferred the

skinny one with the banner. You wouldn't think he was strong enough to lift a banner, would you?'

'He was very nearly lynched, from what I hear,' said Unsworth. They reached his car and he helped her in. They began to drive through the summer forest. 'Everything seems so wonderfully enhanced this year,' said her ladyship. 'The colours brighter, the air sweeter.'

'People are too,' he said. 'Enhanced, you might say.'

'I know exactly what you mean. It's almost as if the disasters have added a zest to their lives. There was an open-air concert in Southampton last week, you know. Beethoven. There must have been two thousand people in the park.'

'The coppers in the police station are reading,' he nodded over the steering-wheel. 'And not just their notebooks. They've discovered these pocket books, paperbacks. I saw a constable reading a novel by D. H. Lawrence yesterday.'

'I've had eight small evacuees,' she said. 'From Jersey. Poor little souls. They've gone on now to some reception centre. I accommodated them for a couple of nights when they came off the boat.'

'My sister-in-law has just come from Guernsey,' said Unsworth. 'She left her husband behind looking after their tomato farm. She seems to believe he'll join the resistance. God knows what she thinks he can do. The place is too small to resist. He might throw a few rotten tomatoes at them but that's all.'

They were driving through a thatched village. Children shouted in the playground of the tiny school and a dog barked among washing on a garden line. 'I'm afraid I found it difficult to handle the eight little children from Jersey,' sighed her ladyship. 'They were so excited they wouldn't go to bed. Two helpers came with them but they were exhausted and it was left to me in the end. I gave each child a good glass of port. They really enjoyed it and it put them out until the morning.'

Unsworth laughed. 'The trouble was,' she said, 'they wanted it again the next night.'

As they turned off the main road and down the lane to the Manor she said in surprise: 'Something's going on here. Look at those men.'

Unsworth had already seen them. They were spread out across the open forest land behind the rear sloping lawn of the house. Unsworth stopped the car. 'They're clearing the gorse,' he said.

'Why would they be doing that?'

'At a guess, I think you're going to have the air force moving in.'

He drove on to the house and they saw he was right. A grey-blue car was parked outside. Two men had just got out, one in uniform. 'Here's one of them now,' said Lady Violet. 'And that man from the council who always looks rather ill.'

Unsworth pulled up behind the RAF car. 'Lady Violet Foxley,' said the council man. He looked red and pale in patches and his heavy spectacles were misted.

'Mr Jenkins,' said her ladyship. 'What brings you here?' She glanced at the air force officer, stubby and pink. 'Defence of the Realm, is it?'

'I'm afraid so,' said Jenkins. He eyed Unsworth and thought he recognised him from Lyndhurst court where Jenkins sometimes appeared to give evidence against people who had not paid their rates. Perhaps Lady Violet had got wind of what was happening and had brought her solicitor. 'This is Detective Sergeant Unsworth,' said her ladyship. 'He is not here to investigate, he kindly gave me a lift.'

Jenkins rubbed his face and looked as if he were still unsure. 'This is Flight Lieutenant Shawn,' he said.

'I am an RAF billeting officer,' said Shawn as though wanting to get it over. 'I'm afraid we are going to have to requisition your house, madam. Hopefully it may not be for too long.'

Lady Violet took the news easily. 'There is only my daughter Penelope and myself,' she said. 'And Mainprice. The other servants have gone now. He can go into the village and we will move into the gardener's cottage. Will your fliers be taking over?'

'Yes, madam.'

'Lady Yarborough, you know, gave Benfleet Grange for a hospital for wounded servicemen, and they burdened her with cholera suspects from some foreign ship.'

Shawn smiled. 'I promise we won't do that,' he said. 'The area behind your house has long been earmarked for a landing ground and it seems as if we are going to need it. And the house. You will, of course, be entitled to compensation.'

'I'm relieved that someone has actually planned *something*,' said Lady Violet. 'I was beginning to think the Government were making it up as they went along. Come on in and see what you're taking on. It's a touch damp in places.'

Unsworth said he must go. Lady Violet extended a gloved hand and thanked him, then strode into the house ahead of the two men. He started the car and drove thirty yards on, past the stableyard. There he braked and thoughtfully backed. Standing in full view through an open double door was the missing gun from the Brockenhurst war memorial.

By the beginning of July 1940 the inhabitants of the two extremes of the country could glance towards Europe and know that they were between the pincer points of an iron trap; Britain was like a nut in a nutcracker. Opposite the Shetland Isles the Germans lay a few grey sea miles away on the Norwegian mainland; from Cornwall the enemy waited in Brittany across the mouth of the English Channel.

Behind the coastal fortress there remained a feeling of unreality, almost of disbelief, that danger, so near yet so out of sight, could truly be threatening. The factories were turning out aircraft, guns and armoured vehicles at a good rate but at the same time they were producing unofficial badges and brooches, trinkets, rings, coal scuttles, pokers, bread bins, door knockers and foot scrapers.

These were fashioned during periods when the main production lines were paused and they were worked on the available machines from scraps of metal left over from shells, bombs, bullets and other war materials. Women faithfully wore brooches designed like the service insignia of their loved ones, and men had patriotic buttonhole badges made from unconsidered fragments of copper, steel and brass. Simultaneously there was an urgent nationwide salvage drive for pots and pans, church and park railings and other metal which, it was mistakenly believed, would help to build munitions. Housewives urged to sacrifice their cooking utensils were puzzled that they could still buy replacements in shops. The enthusiastically gathered metal was rarely of any use and most was eventually dumped.

Molly's wedding dress was fashioned from parachute silk.

'You look lovely,' said Bairnsfather as they met at the altar steps. He and Ugson, his best man, had walked. The clergyman had not yet arrived. Air-raid sirens had been howling on and off all day over Southampton.

'It's only an oddment,' whispered Molly who felt guilty. 'No good for a parachute.'

Bairnsfather's mother, owing to her arthritis and the disruption of wartime rail travel, could not be there but she had sent her own wedding ring. The bride had arrived at the church, blushingly, by ambulance accompanied by her fellow nurses from the Voluntary Aid Detachment who intended to form a guard of honour at the door after the service, making an arch of crutches and walking-sticks.

The guests were filling the front half of the church and the back was crowded with the members of another, separate wedding, including the bride. The groom was pacing and muttering in the porch.

'On account of the si-*reens* keeping going,' explained the churchwarden, 'we said to them to come early or they might never get here if there's a warning on. And our vicar's a fire-watcher.'

He was standing before Molly and Harry. 'Ladies and gentlemen,' he called over their heads to the congregation. 'If the si-*reens* should go I have to tell you that although God is bomb-proof this church is not and it is up to you whether you stay or clear off quick, either one at your own risk. There's a crypt but it's full of the dead and you might not like it down there.'

Although the air-raid warning and the all-clear had successively sounded all through the Saturday forenoon, there had been no sign of raiding aircraft. The sirens, plump canisters, were placed on the roofs of police stations or balanced on the top of high metal poles, like hammers on their handles. 'They've just got the jitters,' said Harry. He was reluctant to be away from the gun, even for his wedding or on his one-night honeymoon, although he would not have confessed it. They had a score to settle for Purcell.

The organ was droning but there was no choir. Archie had brought his gas mask in its cylindrical tin. 'I bet he puts it on his mug,' said Ronnie, hair savagely parted and wearing a stiff, long-trousered suit.

'Just let him try when he's giving his daughter away,' muttered Mrs Warner. She had made her daughter's bouquet from flowers picked in their small garden, and a few guiltily from the park.

When the vicar appeared he was equipped with both gas mask and steel helmet. 'I have to go fire watching later,' he explained. He placed both articles in the choir stalls. 'If there is a proper air raid,' he warned Molly and Harry, 'if the enemy is overhead . . .' He painted upwards, evangelically. '. . . We may have to discontinue the service.'

He wanted to get through it quickly. Ugson could not remember in which pocket of his battledress he had put Bairnsfather's mother's wedding ring and the vicar tutted while he searched. They were responding to the vows, and Molly was just promising to love, honour and obey, as her mother and her grandmother had done without question, when the siren sounded again. It was still howling when a high-calibre anti-aircraft gun on a nearby football pitch opened fire.

The church shuddered and everyone ducked. Molly and Harry found themselves on their knees together with the crouching vicar, heads bent like dice players. Harry was hugging his bride to him. Shrapnel fell with the clatter of heavy rain on the church roof. The vicar muttered: 'God help us,' but not in a pious tone. Another explosion shook the church. Plaster and dust fell and the cross standing on the altar toppled. 'I don't like the look of that,' said the vicar. Harry hauled Molly to her feet. 'Finish it off, padre,' he said.

'I now pronounce you man and wife,' gabbled the

priest. 'Sign the registers some other time.' There was a third discharge of the gun and he turned and scampered for the back of the church, vestments flapping like wings, picking up his gas mask and helmet on the way. The second wedding in the back pews shouted for him to stop. Harry and Molly headed for the door followed by their family and guests, ploughing through the waiting wedding as they went. The organist played a saraband.

Bairnsfather and Molly were at the front of the exiting crowd. He halted her at the porch and scanned the sky. It was blameless, patches of summer blue and placid yellow clouds with smudgy buds of smoke drifting from the anti-aircraft fire. The all-clear, a long level moan, began to sound. Ugson said: 'Trigger-happy buggers.' The bridesmaids produced two handfuls of round paper scraps from the public library hole puncher and threw them over the couple.

The ambulance which had brought the bride had vanished. Bairnsfather looked along the street which glinted with shell fragments. At its end a narrow road tunnel ran below the main railway. 'Let's make a dash,' he said to Molly.

He took her bouquet from her and they began to run, the wedding crowd following headlong. Ronnie was whooping and beating his hip like a cowboy on a horse. Into the tunnel they streamed. Then the air-raid warning sounded again. Bairnsfather pulled up at the exit holding Molly's hand. 'What a bloody wedding,' she laughed.

The whole party was packed into the dank passage, laughing and excited. Ronnie began to sing:

'Here comes the bride,
All fat and wide.
See 'ow she wobbles,
'er big fat behind.'

His mother clutched him. 'Shut up or I'll throw you out to the Germans.'

The guests remained crushed together in the short tunnel but there was no further gunfire. Apologetically the all-clear again sounded.

Out they streamed into the July sun, along the street, the bride and groom at the fore. People came out of their front doors to cheer and wish them good luck. In the Warner's house two rooms had been cleared and tables laid for the wedding reception. 'Look at that,' said Bairnsfather as he and Molly went into the first room. 'It looks a treat.'

A three-tier white wedding cake, with the tiny figures of a bride and groom on the summit, stood at the centre of the table. It was made of cardboard. The Ministry of Food had prohibited the icing of cakes. Bairnsfather and Molly cut a sponge sprinkled with sugar.

'Nobody,' said Bairnsfather when he had to make his speech, 'can say we've had an ordinary wedding. And nobody has *ever* had a bigger cake, even though we couldn't eat it.'

He looked around the tight tables and through the open door into the next room. Forty people in their best clothes had been crammed into the house. Ronnie and the other children had been put to eat in the air-raid shelter. Ronnie had picked up a piece of shrapnel six inches long which was still warm.

'Thanks for the wedding presents,' continued Bairnsfather. 'The butter, the cakes, the sandwiches, and the beer and wine. The girls at the library who contributed their sugar coupons and made the confetti. And I'd like to thank Archie, my new father-in-law, for the three big tins of ham which were sold to him by a mate who just happens to work at Southampton docks.'

* * *

They set out on their few hours of honeymoon on the top deck of a corporation bus. Molly was wearing a tailored suit she had bought in 1938 and a hat lent by one of her bridesmaids. She was pleased the suit still fitted. Her mother had noticed anxiously that she had lost weight during the first weeks of the pregnancy. The two bridesmaids, giggling from unaccustomed German wine which someone had stored in case of an invasion, sat on the bus with them. Archie paid for everybody's fare. Ronnie, who had sampled his first alcohol, ushered the bridesmaids to the upper deck with the popular radio catch-phrase: 'Get up them stairs.'

Southampton was full of afternoon sunlight. People kept undercover by the day's warnings and gunfire were hurrying to reach the shops before they closed. Council workmen were sweeping up shrapnel in Commercial Road. 'Call that an air raid,' said the youthful bus conductor. 'You wait till we get a proper pasting. They won't just be sweeping up after it.'

'You know all about air raids then?' said Archie handing him the coins.

'Seen them at the pictures, haven't I? All we got today was one plane, one Jerry doing some reconaissance according to a copper I had on. There was a tom-cat killed at Totton, that's all.'

'It's not altered the course of the war then?'

'It's used up a lot of ammunition, that's all I know,' sniffed the conductor. He was young enough to be a soldier but looked anaemic. 'Wasted it. These ack-ack blokes just blaze away for fun. They never hit anything. Call them gunners?'

'This gunner feels like hitting something,' muttered Bairnsfather from the front seat.

'Don't you dare,' nudged Molly. 'You could end up spending our honeymoon in the police station.'

He squeezed her hand and made sure the conductor saw his Royal Artillery shoulder flashes and A.A. Command arm badge as they left the bus at the station. 'Keep spreading the good news,' Bairnsfather said.

His comment was not lost on the man. He shouted from the platform: 'I'm joining the LDV.'

'Look, Duck and Vanish,' said Bairnsfather quietly. He called out: 'You fight to the last woman, mate.'

Molly giggled and pulled gently at his arm. 'We'll miss the train.' She saw a grey woman, sad and aimless, standing in the booking hall. Taking the bridesmaids' bouquets from them she gave them to the woman who nodded with a bleak smile: 'I'll take them up the cemetery.'

When they were seated together on the train and the waving was done she saw that the grey woman had joined in, wagging the two bouquets. There was only one other passenger in the carriage, a boy with a school cap and red knees who was staring out of the opposite window. Molly hugged Bairnsfather and, with a glance at the boy, her husband kissed her. 'What a wedding,' he grinned.

'We'll remember it,' she sighed getting as close to him as she could. 'For ever.'

The train stopped and the boy got up. 'Have you got any Hovis?' he asked.

'Not on us,' replied Bairnsfather. 'Why?'

The boy pointed to a poster on the station platform which said: 'Ask for Hovis,' and displayed a loaf of brown bread. 'It's only a joke,' he said.

They laughed as he went. No one else got into the carriage. Outside the window they could see the masts and funnels of the ships in the port, loading, unloading, preparing for sea and the prospect of the U-boats. A freighter, a glad signal of smoke escaping from its funnel, was entering the safety of the dock.

Then the train travelled through the southern part

of the New Forest. 'Our guns are just over there,' he nodded. 'The other side of those trees, not that far.'

'They've been like a family, haven't they, your mates,' she said. 'Poor Peter Ugson. Why do they call him Ugly?'

'Ugly Ugson,' he said. 'It just fits. He admits he is.'

'He looked very spruce today.'

'Except he couldn't find the ring.' He took her finger and patted the wedding ring gently. 'The best man never can,' said Molly. She looked down. 'It fits. It fitted your mother and it fits me.'

'Well, the old man's been gone ten years, she thought she ought to pass it on. It's just a pity she couldn't be there.'

Molly said: 'When we can, as soon as we can, we'll go and see her.'

He kissed her cheek gently. 'Shame about the war mucking up our day,' he said. 'Cardboard cake, confetti from the library, people giving us their rations and all that. No church bells.'

'We had gunfire. When the war's over maybe we could have another wedding. A proper one.'

He patted her skirt. 'We'll take the kids.'

'Not a word,' she warned. 'On your honour.'

'Honest injun.'

'Nobody need even know we're just married. We don't want people watching us coming down to breakfast.'

He grinned. 'We'll only be coming down to one breakfast.'

'I know. But it's still our honeymoon. Promise?'

He promised.

There was a solitary taxi waiting outside Bournemouth station. 'Just married then,' said the driver.

* * *

'Just married, are we?' said the woman behind the reception desk.

'Oh, a long time ago,' laughed Bairnsfather. He had put his army pay book on the desk with Molly's identity card. Three small pieces of library confetti fell from the book. 'How did that get in there?' muttered Bairnsfather.

They signed the register as Mr and Mrs Harry Bairnsfather. 'You'll need to get you name changed on the identity card,' said the receptionist. 'It says it's Molly Warner.'

When they were in their room and Molly was sitting on the bed taking her shoes off she said: 'We've got to go back to the church soon and sign the register. Otherwise it may not be legal.'

He laughed wickedly and drew her to her feet. 'In that case I've brought you to romantic Bournemouth under false pretences.' They moved to the big bay window overlooking the evening sea front.

'See those rocks out there,' he said. 'They're called Old Harry Rocks.'

She kissed him. 'I'm going to be married to you until you're Old Harry.'

'It'll be the end of the century,' he said.

'It is romantic though, Bournemouth.'

'Those lovely tank traps.'

'And there's the tank to go with them,' said Molly. A low Bren-gun carrier came clanking along the front. 'A matching tank.'

It was nine thirty when they walked along the promenade. The coastal dusk was still light and warm. The pier was strung with coils of wire and there was a gun emplacement at its extreme end, overlooking the sea. All the peacetime fun had gone leaving only the fading notices for the ice-cream stall, the rock shop, the fortune teller and the final theatre playbill: 'Old Mother Riley', 'The Two Leslies' and 'Afrique' who did impersonations of Churchill. There were some bleached flags stiff as cardboard and the Bournemouth gulls squawked.

Standing close, Bairnsfather and Molly peered through the wire. He had changed into his civilian suit with a white shirt, a tie and Oxford shoes. He had been uncertain about wearing them but Molly said he should. 'I've never seen you properly dressed before.'

'Just as long as nobody hands me one of those white feathers.'

'You don't even *look* like a coward.'

'I could always hit them, I suppose,' he grinned. 'Then they'd know I'm not a conchie.'

Looking through the barbed screen and along the deserted pier, she sighed. 'We used to come here in the summer. It was fun then and it always seemed to be sunny. It's funny how you never remember the rainy days.'

Bairnsfather was trying to see the gun emplacement. For a better view he moved along the front, away from the barred entrance to the pier. 'What d'you think you're doing?' said a small man who appeared by the shuttered ice-cream kiosk, tugged by a dog.

'Looking at the gun out there.'

'In that case I'm going to report you,' said the man bravely.

'Come on, Patty,' he said to the dog. They trotted off.

'He meant it,' warned Molly. 'I told you you'd be spending our wedding night in a cell.'

Bairnsfather made a face. 'Silly old bugger. I was just thinking I wouldn't like to be one of the gun crew.'

'It's a long walk back,' she said measuring the pier.

'Run, more like it. I was thinking what a target you'd be, stuck out there, out on a limb.'

They continued walking, bending sometimes to look through the defences at the level sea. The beach was flat too, undisturbed by humans as a desert island, its only indentations the marks of the seabirds and one set of dog footprints. 'What you up to then?' asked a voice. It was a policeman on a bicycle, wearing an armband which read 'Special'. The short man with the dog was standing at a safe distance pointing them out. 'This gentleman says you were staring down the pier.'

'I was,' said Bairnsfather. 'I was trying to get a look at the gun.'

'Why would that be?'

'Because he's a soldier, a gunner,' said Molly quickly. 'We're on our honeymoon.'

The policeman regarded them less sternly. 'I thought you might be,' he said. 'Not many spies take their wives with them when they're spying.' He seemed pleased with the deduction. 'Have you got your papers?'

Bairnsfather handed over his army pay book and the constable examined it. He had remained on his bicycle and was now astride the crossbar. 'Right you are,' he said handing the book back. 'It's just that you're in civvies.'

'And staring,' put in the man with the dog.

'I'll try not to stare,' promised Bairnsfather. 'Is it your dog who's been on the beach? Those paw marks?'

The man stood up to his full shortness, almost on his toes. 'It jolly well wasn't,' he said. 'He wouldn't do that.'

The constable was surveying the footprints below. 'That animal's lucky to be alive,' he said. 'The beach is full of mines.' He levered himself up from the crossbar to the saddle and adjusted his 'Special' armband. The man and the dog both shuffled away. The constable said: 'Good luck,' and prepared to pedal off. 'Do you know somewhere we could have a meal?' Molly asked quickly.

He paused and pursed his lips. 'There's not much to choose,' he said, 'Now you can only have one meat course. There was a wop place in Old Christchurch Road but it's been burned down. There's a café just over the street from there. That's not bad.'

He waved the arm with the band and pedalled away. The man who had reported them went in the other direction tutting disbelievingly.

'I swear his dog was shaking its head too,' said Bairnsfather.

Laughing they walked until they came to the centre of the town. There were only a few pedestrians about. They passed municipal gardens and flowers, touched by late sunlight. On one of the lawns a silver barrage balloon, huge and jovial, was at its mooring. Two WAAF girls sitting on a bench were being teased by a pair of airmen.

They found the Italian restaurant, gaunt and charred, the windows shattered. The counter and some of the overturned tables and chairs were visible, but one table remained covered with a red-and-white checked cloth on which was a carafe half full of red wine.

'Done by a mob,' said the owner of the English café across the road. 'Bloody disgusting. All the Nazis arc not in Germany, believe me. Those people have never done anybody any harm. The wife, Angelina, was born in Bournemouth. Smashed and burned the night Italy come into the war, or Mussolini did anyway.'

'What happened to them?' asked Molly.

'If you promise not to tell . . .'

'We won't tell,' said Bairnsfather.

'They're working in my kitchen. It's the least I can do. But the police have been around. Luigi thought they had come to investigate the fire, to blame someone, arrest them, but it was about interning *them*. And we talk about persecution.'

The main course was macaroni cheese, and after the meal Bairnsfather and Molly walked back silently. It was a warm, luminous night with the Needles Rock lighthouse a pinpoint blinking along the otherwise dark coast and leading them back to the hotel.

When they were in the room together they embraced. Molly said: 'It's odd not having to be nervous any more. No more air-raid shelters.'

'I quite liked the shelter,' he said.

She laughed. 'I wonder how many babies have begun in them.'

'In a few years' time there might be some kids around wondering why their middle name is Anderson,' he joked. He sat on the bed and begun to unlace his shoes. 'These feel like gloves after army boots.'

The blackout curtains had been heavily drawn in the room. 'Let's put the light out, Harry,' she said. 'There's a moon.'

He switched out the main light and went across the room to pull aside the two layers of curtains. 'They didn't intend the Germans to spot this place,' he said tugging at them heavily. As he did so the moonlight flowed into the room giving a sheen to the worn carpet and rolling across the faded quilt on the bed. 'Lovely,' she said.

She went to the window with him and they stood, arms around each other, surveying the sea and the town clothed in moonlight. It glinted on the curves of the barbed wire, swept sweetly across the mine-sown beach and touched the round bellies of three barrage balloons hanging low and in line like elephants, one behind the other.

Bairnsfather lay on the bed and watched Molly as she undressed in the moonbeams. She was in silhouetted profile, her face slightly tilted, her neck slim, her breasts lifted, her stomach displaying the slightest swelling. 'Is Anderson showing yet?' she asked.

He laughed: 'Anderson? It couldn't have been there, in the shelter. That was New Year's Eve.'

'I still think it's a good name. What's the name of the other air-raid shelter, the indoor one? Morrison. Morrison, that's it. It might start a new fashion in boys' names.'

'Why don't you come to bed,' he said.

She was still wearing her knickers. 'Feel them,' she invited. He did so.

'Parachute silk,' she said. 'There was a bit left over so the seamstress made them for me.' Taking them off she raised them in her hand, dropping them so that they fell lightly through the moonlight to the floor.

Naked they lay with each other on the dowdy quilt, the light across them like a gauze. He kissed her breasts and she gently caressed his bottom. 'Making love doesn't feel different being married, does it, Harry?'

'Not so far,' he said.

'We'll have to find another way to do it when Anderson here gets too big.'

'Never let your kids come between you, my mother used to say.'

Molly touched her wedding ring. 'It was lovely she sent this.'

'They try to help. Your old man wanted you to bring your gas mask.'

Molly giggled. 'I brought it too. It's part of my trousseau.'

'Don't put it on,' he said. 'I like you as you are.'

They lay quietly while the moonlight shifted. 'I hope we find we can sleep,' said Molly eventually. 'I mean, we've never actually *slept*, have we, properly, with our eyes closed. It's always been such a rush. You don't snore, do you?'

'Nobody's complained so far.'

'Stop it.' They came together again, and afterwards lay a little apart on their backs, their hands touching. 'I wish this rotten war was finished and we could look forward to a proper life,' she said. 'So we wouldn't have to worry, so our baby could be safe. Everything's going to be lovely after the war. No more wars, just peace.'

'And I'll go back to being a baker's roundsman.'

'You won't,' she said firmly. 'You'll have your own bakery, at least.'

'Bairnsfather's Bread,' he smiled.

They slept entwined. She woke once when it was almost dawn. She kissed his arm and closed her eyes again.

At seven a spindly lady in a black dress, crackling apron and lacy cap brought a tray of tea in to them. They had crept below the bedclothes as the night had cooled. Now the day was spread outside the window. 'You didn't have the blackout up,' said the lady.

'We're afraid of the dark,' answered Bairnsfather from under the quilt.

'As long as that's all you're afraid of,' she said. 'I'm afraid of dropping the bloody tea tray. I'm seventy-eight. I'm only doing this because of the war.'

They left the tea in its warm pot and made love again. 'I'm only doing this because of the war,' said Bairnsfather.

As if he had prompted it, the air-raid siren sounded. Molly poured the tea and they sat looking out from the bed while they drank it. 'Look,' he said suddenly. 'Look out there.'

'That ship,' she said. 'Those puffs of smoke.'

'It's being strafed.' He put his shirt on and went to

the window from where he could clearly see the planes diving over the lone merchant ship. Bombs sent up spouts of water and a column of black smoke began to climb from her stern. Her guns were firing, rattling over the sea, echoing against the town. People were standing on the promenade below the hotel watching and pointing.

Bairnsfather returned to the bed and kissed his wife. 'We'd better get back to the ruddy war,' he sighed.

Shipping in the Channel was frequently bombed during July. The Germans also raided Swansea, Falmouth and Dover.

'I reckon they be scared,' said Catcher as the forest men sat in the Hut. 'Scared to come any further. They drops the bombs and turns tail fast as they can.'

'Or maybe they ain't got proper maps,' said Tom Dibben.

It was meant to be a joke but the others merely nodded. 'I don't think they be as clever as they make out,' Catcher said. 'Otherwise why ain't they come over? Why ain't they sitting 'ere in this pub right now?'

'I wouldn't serve 'un,' said Rob. 'I'd rather turn on the taps and let the beer run off into the trees, though 'twould be sad.'

They were in their Home Guard uniforms, such as they were, khaki overalls of a single large size, so that little Catcher was swamped in his and needed four safety pins. Tom's forage cap was perched like an upturned boat on his big head. 'Even at 'ome, I 'as it on indoors.'

'In bed?' asked Rob. 'Does the missus like 'un?'

'I never arsked 'er. But you never know when they Jerry buggers is going to strike.'

Churchill himself had renamed them the Home Guard. There were now a million of them, watching the coast and vulnerable places inland, freeing the real army for reorganisation training and re-equipping. Enthusiasm among the national volunteers often overran discipline and common sense. British pilots had been shot at while descending by parachute. Cars which failed to stop at checkpoints had been summarily fired upon and their drivers killed, a garroting wire meant for enemy motorcyclists had proved all too effective, other vehicles had fallen down anti-tank pits and several guards officers were killed in East Anglia by the unscheduled blowing up of a bridge.

America had sent a consignment of army rifles unused since 1918 and when the cases were opened they were revealed sunk in thick yellow grease.

'Never did see the like of that,' said Catcher. 'T'was like treacle.'

'Preserved 'un though, d'in it,' said Tom. 'Twenty years they'd 'ave got rusty.'

'Took my missus three days to boil,' said Catcher. 'Clean as a whistle now. A proper job.'

He glanced fondly at the rifle standing in the corner of the bar with the others, each labelled with its new owner's name. They also had ten rounds of ammunition each.

'I wonder if we could shoot a moving Jerry?' said Tom looking fondly at the old rifle. ''Tween the eyes loike.'

Catcher looked affronted. 'Well, *I* could, Tom Dibben,' he said. 'Bein' a dead shot as I am.' He leaned confidingly. 'You see they made the new airfield for they Hurricanes back of the Manor. Well, they w'unt be able to ha' done that without me gettin' rid o' the rabbits and foxes and birds . . .' He paused. '. . . and vipers.' He leaned even closer. 'You can't ha' vipers on a runway.'

Tom nodded. 'No, you'm right there. Planes would run them over.'

The landlord said: 'What about our big gun that 'er ladyship still got?'

'In the stable, where we put 'un,' said Catcher confidingly. ''Er says to me that 'un's better there for the time bein'. After all we can't do much except wheel 'un about, can we. We can't fire 'e. We don't even know how 'e works.'

'It's just to froit they Jerries,' nodded Rob. 'Make 'em shit.'

They silently handed up their pewter tankards and he filled them. There were rarely strangers in the tight bar. The men were jealous of their places. 'I don't reckon Hitler's goin' to come at all,' said Tom. ''Ow's 'e going to get over the water, just tell me that. Swim? And even if they get across, 'ow do they get ashore? You got to 'ave special boats, flat bottoms, to get up these beaches. We'd pick 'un off, easy.'

'Parachutists,' suggested Catcher. 'And they gliders.' He looked suddenly disappointed. 'Don't tell me they ain't turning up after all.'

Rob eyed them. 'Patrol after,' he said. 'Up on the head.'

'On the tractor?' asked Catcher hopefully. 'We looks more businessloike.'

'I can get the tractor. All we want is some action, don' we?'

They agreed that they did.

The slow ships appeared from the shadow of the Isle of Wight just before two o'clock in the afternoon. Bevan watched them through his field-glasses from the observation post which was now in the round room of the turret on the end of Southerly. He wondered what Major Durfield was doing now. Somewhere, perhaps drunk in a deck-chair.

He turned the glasses inland. It was a cloudy but warm day and in many of the bungalow gardens facing the water he could see people drinking from tumblers and cups, one group under a sun umbrella, healthy-faced elderly people stationed there daily in the hope of viewing some of the war. A few had binoculars and he could see they were trained on the materialising convoy. One man had an ancient telescope on a stand. The Government had requested that field-glasses and telescopes should be surrendered to help the war effort, but not many people had complied. Now they were ready for action.

The convoy consisted of ten merchant vessels with two corvettes as escorts. Bevan guessed they were moving out to rendezvous with other ships, from Liverpool and the South Wales ports, in the Western Approaches, before together undertaking the Atlantic crossing.

There were barrage balloons hanging over the freighters and he wondered how much that slowed them. Going steadily through the afternoon sea they crept clear of the Needles. Then, through the field-glasses, he saw the German planes, a line of dots like a stave of music. Gunner Brown was standing beside him at the alarm. 'Action stations,' ordered Bevan quietly. Brown pressed the Klaxon and below them the gun crews tumbled from their huts or ran from the grass where they had been playing cards. The air-raid warning howled along the coast. The people in their gardens stirred in anticipation and began pointing excitedly. No one made for cover. They all wanted to watch.

The convoy was three or four miles out and unless the enemy planes came towards them Bevan knew that his Bofors crews would be as fixed and useless as the retired gin drinkers on their lawns.

Bevan watched as the planes droned and circled. He could see by their humped backs that they were Stukas. The guns on board ships opened fire and the sound of their salvos shuddered across the water as they began to put up a smokescreen; the wind was from the west, however, and they were sailing out of its cover even as it belched.

He glanced down. Runciman was with the gun crew. Laurel and Hardy were in command of the second gun. The sergeant glanced with a helpless expression up to the observation tower and Bevan spread his hands. There was nothing they could do.

The dive-bombers began to break their circle and one by one drop with their screeching descents on to the convoy. 'Just like in Norway, sir,' said Brown. 'Except then we was nearer.'

The first planes pulled out of their dive and they saw the bombs explode sending up spouts of sea water. At once a blaze erupted on one of the merchant ships. A barrage balloon burst into flames and faltered like burning paper. Then another caught fire and zigzagged madly as if trying to escape its cable. The guns from the corvettes were firing savagely but the Stukas fell on the ships and rose without harm. 'They ought to wait, sir,' said Brown. 'Like we did. Wait until they climb. When they're slow. You'd think they'd know by now.'

'Perhaps nobody's told them,' said Bevan.

'Come on, come on,' urged. Brown. 'Come on this way, Jerry. Come to us. We'll give you what for.'

But the attack continued like a slow and distant dance. The Stukas circled, then dived in almost prim fashion releasing their bombs and pulling away. Two ships were now on fire and another had stopped and was slewing around. Some of the planes remained at a height and Bevan guessed they were the escorting fighters. He wondered how long they could stay, how long their fuel would last.

From the bungalows there was now silence, a silence even obvious over the staccato noise of battle out at sea. Briefly aiming the field-glasses that way Bevan saw that the people had become a coloured frieze, a bright line strung between the garden fences; now they were motionless, their drinks idle, their talk stilled, stiff faces turned towards the blazing ships.

He turned his attention to his own gun crews, standing just as impotently, looking, waiting, willing one German plane to break away and come towards the land. Hignet sat on a chair outside the orderly room. Runciman looked up and shrugged towards Bevan. Bevan went to the window and shouted: 'What's Bombardier Hignet doing? Sunbathing?'

'Manning the telephone, sir,' Hignet called.

'Man it inside,' Bevan snapped. Hignet retreated.

A yellow bulb of flame was now growing from one of the corvettes. 'They've hit the escort,' said Bevan to Brown.

'Sitting ducks, sir,' said Brown morosely. 'Where's the RAF, I'd like to know.'

Then, miraculously, the question was answered. A flight of three Spitfires shrieked low overhead, followed by another and another, tearing vengefully towards the battle. The elderly people started to cheer lustily and the gunners spontaneously joined in. The roar of the fighter planes drowned the cheering for a moment but Bevan could see the people raising their arms. 'Bloody good,' he muttered. 'Get at them, boys.'

It was a massacre. The escorting Messerschmitts turned away as soon as the Spitfires appeared leaving the cumbersome Stukas to their fate. They were like pelicans, swift and sure in the dive, but almost idiotic in their recovery and slow in level flight. The Spitfires began their own circular dance above the now silent ships, initially standing off, then picking first one and then another of the dive-bombers as they continued the attack.

'The Stukas don't realise the Messerschmitts have gone home,' said Bevan.

'They soon will do, sir,' said Brown.

One by one the dive-bombers staggered flaming to the sea, the water engulfing their fire. On land there were exultant shouts. There was no escape for the raiders. When they turned and tried to head for France the speedy Spitfires caught them at will. Fourteen Stukas were destroyed that sunny afternoon. The last one, as though it had been blinded, flew towards the land. Both Bofors swung. The bungalow people ducked, still clutching their drinks. But the plane was losing height and slow oily smoke curled behind it. Bevan could see his gun crews eager for the order but it never came. Runciman and the two junior officers on the other gun knew there would be no need.

The plane banked just off the beach, coughed and spluttered, and dipped over the headland to the west. Bevan ran down the stairs from the turret. Laurel and Hardy were already standing by the fifteen hundred-weight. Bevan pointed to the thin one. 'Lieutenant, take three men and go and see what you can do.'

Laurel saluted. Three of the spare gun crew scrambled aboard the platoon truck and it clattered out on to the road and headed west. It had scarcely gone when Bevan was astonished to see three cars crammed with excited faces setting off from the bungalows and heading in the same direction. He called Bairnsfather and they got into the Ford. 'Let's get there before these old codgers get in the line of fire,' he said. 'Those two Germans, if they've lived, may not be in the best of tempers.'

Catcher Hurrock, Tom Dibben and Rob saw the Stuka crash into the sea. They were on the headland, Rob and Catcher riding in the trailer behind Tom who was driving the tractor. There were only stony tracks among the gorse out there and they had reached the end of the point where the wind always blew and they could hear the sea breaking below. They were staring out three miles to the convoy battle, as helpless as all the other land-bound spectators, when the Spitfires arrived. The three country men waved their old American rifles frantically as they saw the German planes one after another drop flaming into the Channel.

When the final Stuka roared over the headland they all ducked. 'Coming down, 'un is!' shouted Catcher. 'We'll get the bugger!'

They lifted their old rifles but the aircraft overshot the headland, smoke streaming behind it, then made an almost graceful turn and lost height before ploughing into the bay just below them. After a speechless moment they fell over each other with excitement. 'Round t'other side!' bellowed Rob. 'Us'll be first there! Capture 'em!'

As they rushed an uncertain figure rose from the gorse and Tom Dibben fell over him. It was the Reverend Goodenough. 'Christ!' said Catcher. 'The vicar.'

Tom picked himself up. 'What you doin' up 'ere, reverend?' asked Rob.

'Bird-watching. I often come here. It's so wonderfully empty these days, lots of birds.' He wore baggy khaki shorts held up by a boy's snake-buckle belt, and a creased khaki shirt.

'We could 'ave shot you,' said Rob.

'We might ha' thought you was a spy,' said Catcher.

Reverend Goodenough became testy. 'Well, the only things I'm spying on are terns and oystercatchers,' he said. 'What's happened anyway? What's all the fuss?'

'There's a Jerry plane crashed right down below,' said Rob.

'We're off to capture 'em,' said Catcher. 'If they's alive.'

The vicar sniffed. 'Then I had better come with you. To see fair play. You can't just climb down there anyway, you should know that. There's wire and the beach is probably mined.'

'Vicar's right,' nodded Rob.

'But, as it happens, I know a way through. There are nests on the rocks down there.'

'Oh, right then,' said Rob. 'You'd better get in the trailer, reverend.'

Catcher and Rob waited for the clergyman. 'It niffs a bit,' apologised Tom over his shoulder. 'It's been used for muck spreading.'

Goodenough said: 'Get going, man.'

Tom started the tractor and turned it through the gorse. 'Be careful,' said the vicar. 'There are several nests along here.'

The churned-up gorse made Rob sneeze and the clergyman muttered: 'Bless you.' Tom drove the tractor, snorting smoke, as hard as it could stand. Stones flew as it bounced along the cliff-top path. 'Look, there 'e be!' he shouted. The plane was lying like a winged bird in the gently rolling sea. A single yellow-jacketed figure was in the water beside it. ''Un's alive,' said Catcher. ''Un's swimmin'.'

Tom drove frantically along the path, the trailer bounding over the rocky ground, its occupants clutching its sides. 'Oh!' exclaimed the Reverend Goodenough. 'Oh dear, oh dear.'

'Where, vicar, where?' demanded Tom. 'Where we'm stop?'

'Keep going,' said Goodenough. 'Just beyond this next outcrop. You can get down the path from there.' Tom braked the shuddering tractor where the vicar had indicated. There was a steep way edging down the incline to the beach. The German airman, in his life-jacket, was splashing feebly towards the land. There was no sign of the second member of the crew. 'I'll lead the way,' said the vicar. 'I've been down here before.'

They followed him tentatively down the zigzag path. 'No mines this way then, vicar?' enquired Rob.

'A few only.'

The men exchanged glances. The German airman appeared to be resting, floating as they scrambled down to the beach. 'There's a way through the wire,' said Goodenough confidently. 'You can unhook it.'

'And there be no mines?' asked Rob again.

'Not many.'

In single file they followed him. There was a gull's nest on a shelf of rock and Catcher, from habit, peered into it.

Treading carefully between the strands of barbed wire which the vicar held aside, and then fearfully, almost daintily, along the wet level sand, they reached the water's edge. The yellow life-jacket was keeping the German afloat. Tom and Rob waded out and pulled him to the shore. 'Can't take this 'un prisoner,' said Tom sadly. 'He'm dead.'

'God rest his soul,' said the clergyman.

All the sash windows of the Manor were open on to the gardens and the slightly faltering sound of a gramophone record with a woman singing 'Smoke Gets in Your Eyes' filtered on to the lawn where two young pilots, pale bodied and in sagging shorts, played inexpertly at badminton. The falter of the singer slowed until it became a yodel.

They stopped their game. 'Somebody! Anybody! Wind that thing up, will you!' one called.

From the shadowy room came an answer and the song began to gather pace again. It was a close, cloudy afternoon. Hurricanes were parked below their camouflage netting, their propellers nosing the surrounding trees. 'Would you like the record changed?' enquired Lady Violet putting her head from the window. 'It's been on rather a long time.' The badminton players halted with embarrassment. 'Oh, sorry, madam,' said the one who had shouted. 'We thought one of our chaps was in there.'

'One is,' said her ladyship in something of a whisper. 'But he's asleep.'

'Don't worry about the record,' said the second airman. 'We'll be coming in soon.'

There was the sound of a plane far up, going through manoeuvres that varied its sound. The volume increased as the aircraft came through the cloud blanket and they heard backfires and then a long whine. 'Tubby,' said one of the players. They stopped and squinted up into the heavy sky. 'There he is,' said the other. 'Playing silly buggers.'

Someone in the room turned the gramophone switch to 'fast' and the vocalist began a comical gabble. A fresh face appeared framed by the window. 'Does that suit you?'

'Turn it off, Henry, old boy. We thought you were asleep.'

'Just snoozing.' They could only see his face; the rest of his body was lost in the dimness of the room. 'Dreaming of home.'

'Women more like it.'

The two stopped their game. There would be no combat today. Not with the weather as it was. The best German fighter, the ME 109, only carried enough fuel for forty-five minutes over southern England. 'Doubt if they could *find* England today,' said one of the airman.

There had still only been sporadic engagements. Apart from the attacks on harbours and shipping the Luftwaffe had seemed tentative, unwilling to come out and fight. Even the bombing of ports soon ceased. The Germans realised they might need them undamaged when they invaded. Three enemy planes had appeared over the New Forest and been attacked by a solitary British pilot who continued to engage them even though his plane was blazing. James Nicholson earned a Victoria Cross that summer day.

The badminton players watched the performing plane over the airfield disappear once more into the funnel of clouds and then drone down, flipping its wings, until it flattened out and tore along the length of the airstrip, scarcely clearing the treetops. Airmen sitting on the lawn of the Manor watched the plane sardonically. 'Tubby's showing his belly,' said a youth lowering his *Picture Post*, then following the fighter's curve upwards towards the swollen clouds.

The plane described a wide circle and lost height, eventually stuttering across the treetops and landing uneasily on the airstrip which had a hump in the middle and another at the end. It taxied to the fringes of the trees, where the mechanics' workshops were under tents. A sergeant and an aircraftman waited for it. The engine was switched off and the propeller feathered. There was still music coming from the house. The pilot, chubby faced and grinning, climbed down. 'Seems to be ticking over now, sir,' said the sergeant.

'She does everything but shag, sergeant,' grinned the young man. 'Thanks.' He unfastened the buckle below his flying helmet and took off his goggles. 'Christ,' he said as he walked towards the house. 'They're not still playing that moony song.'

The two men watched him go. The sergeant was old

enough to be his father. 'He's like a kid with a new bike when he's flying,' said the aircraftman.

'You can always get off a bike.'

Cartwright straightened up from digging the latrine. 'Look at that,' he said to Ugson who held the wheelbarrow. Both surveyed the newly cropped runway, the planes below the trees and the airmen sitting and lying around the gardens of the house. 'They get fourteen and a tanner a day.'

'They might 'ave to earn it soon,' said Ugson. 'I wonder if they get free fags.'

'Fourteen and six and all found.'

'Including a coffin,' sniffed Ugson. 'I wouldn't go up in those things, not even if there wasn't no war. All that empty air underneath you.'

That day they had moved their anti-aircraft gun to the edge of the emergency airfield, and the men were billeted in tents below the trees. They had been promised a replacement for the weapon they had left at Dunkirk.

'What about that?' said Runciman when the Ordnance Corps men arrived with the new Bofors in the early evening. It was to be positioned at the opposite end of the runway to cover the approach from the north. He pointed to the barrel on which were a black cross and a Nazi swastika. 'It's a ruddy German.'

'We've got three of them,' said the RAOC sergeant. 'Pinched by those Norwegian partisans. They got them on the last ship before we scarpered.' He patted the barrel. 'Brand new, that is, from Sweden.'

'Poetic justice,' said Bevan. 'We left one of ours for the Jerries and now we've got one of theirs.'

'Fair is fair,' said the ordnance man. 'They're all more or less the same, these Bofors. The Swedes must be doing all right out of this war one way and another.'

Their first night under canvas was strange. Zooming insects and other night creatures moved among the trees once it became dark. The cookhouse was established down a forest track, and water piped to it from the manor house. 'Like being a kid again,' said Bairnsfather looking at the tent roof. 'Did you used to go camping, Ugly?'

They were in their sleeping-bags on the ground. Hignet had procured a camp-bed and lay a little elevated from the others. He interrupted. 'I once considered joining the Woodcraft Folk.'

'I camped in our back garden,' said Ugson. 'But the neighbours complained about me peeing on their rhubarb. It's reckoned to do it good.'

They drifted to sleep. Cartwright was on guard, the duty shared with the other army units in the vicinity, and with the RAF men. In the early hours Ugson felt himself being nudged and his hand went nervously from his sleeping-bag to touch something warm and soft and breathing. He pushed Hignet. 'Higgie. Something's after me.' Hignet sat up complainingly. 'For God's sake, Ugly . . .'

'Listen, I can hear marching,' said Ugson.

Bairnsfather woke. 'Marching,' relayed Hignet. 'Ugly can hear marching.'

They listened. 'There it is,' said Ugson. 'Hear it?'

The soldiers crept from the tent. Hignet tripped over a guy-rope and cursed. Three New Forest ponies noisily crunched the nearby grass. The men went back to their sleeping-bags.

'Marching,' muttered Hignet. 'You're having hallucinations, Ugly. You could get a medical discharge.'

'Could I? I might try for that.'

By the following day they had consolidated the camp and both guns, one each end of the runway, were ready for action. 'At least we'll get something to shoot at here,' said Runciman. 'Something we can *see*. If they strafe the airfield they've got to come in low.'

The camouflaged Hurricanes remained like fish camouflaged in nets. At their distance the gunners watched the young pilots sitting in a ring on the lawn of the house listening to their squadron leader. Two or three times they collectively laughed. At lunch-time they brought their food out into the warm day. Some had wine. They always wore their flying kit, and carried their helmets and goggles wherever they went. No German planes crossed the coast. In the evening some of the airmen strolled to the Hut and stood in line with the soldiers and a few locals, to get their beer before going out the back to drink it on the grass. Sometimes they would share banter with the locals; quips about mole-eating from one side and propellers driven by elastic bands from the other. The soldiers watched and laughed.

Bevan sat on an ornamental seat in the Manor garden with Penelope Foxley. She looked weary with her pregnancy but her face remained composed, beautiful in a different way. He found himself strongly drawn to her and at night in his tent below the stirring leaves he imagined how they might be together, wondered what they would be like.

'If the Luftwaffe bomb us then I'm staying put,' said Penelope. 'I haven't got the energy to run.' She laughed and lightly touched his arm. 'My mother has been concealing a gun, a piece of artillery, in the stables.' He reached out for her fingers and held them briefly. She coloured a little and smiled towards him.

'I can imagine her making preparations for guerrilla warfare,' he said. 'Where did she get it?'

'God knows. The police turned up to take it away this afternoon. Mother said vaguely that she had found it in the forest and thought she ought to hand it in, as she put it.'

'It might come in useful,' he said.

'Do you think it will?'

'Who knows? If I did I'd be Chief of the General Staff. But I can't see the Germans leaving us to lick our wounds undisturbed. Not now they've got us cornered. Two things are going to stand in their way, two major things, the navy and what we're looking at now.' He nodded: 'Those fighters.' Their eyes went towards the Hurricanes. The evening was ebbing and men were moving around the planes, adjusting their covering nets as if tucking them up for the night. 'Hitler has to destroy the RAF,' said Bevan. 'And he has to deal with the navy. But that's not to say he won't try.'

They sat quietly while the dusk gathered around them. He asked if she were cold but she shook her head. 'I feel very comfortable with you,' he said without looking at her face, without emphasis.

'I know. I feel the same.' Her smile was a shadow. 'It's very complicated, isn't it, James. As if the world in general weren't fraught enough, here am I waiting for this fatherless child . . .' Her voice diminished.

'My wife was expecting someone else's baby when we parted,' he said.

She put her hand to her mouth. 'Oh, James,' she laughed. 'You do pick them.'

'I know, I know. My life has been one long saga of unrequited love, if love is what it was in the first place. It's hard for me to tell.'

She said: 'It's getting chilly.' As she stood he took off his battledress blouse and put it about her shoulders. She thanked him. They were close now and there was nobody about. He kissed her and she quietly returned the kiss.

* * *

Every day in the winter of 1919 more than a quarter of a million coal fires were burning in London, blazing, glowing, smouldering in homes and rented rooms, in offices, hotels and restaurants, public houses and public baths. Each sent its own smoky spiral up a brick chimney and out into the metropolitan sky where, joined by gritty clouds and vapours from the thick Thames, it hung over and often descended on the streets and the inhabitants. There were days of fogs, icy days, days of grubby snow and dripping cold days; painters travelled from abroad to capture the eerie light.

The office where James worked was only a street from the river. It was on the third floor and there was a window through which little could be seen on those winter days, only the tops of city churches. Horses, cars and buses moved invisibly below; the clerks could hear the trams from the Embankment and the public clocks chiming the murky hours.

Inside it was cheerful enough. There was a comforting fireplace with a blaze in an iron grate. A uniformed porter appeared punctually on the hour with a scuttle to replenish the fire and brush up ashes. Nearest to the warmth was the chief tobacco clerk at his big polished table. In front of him was a rank of unpolished tables at which worked the superior clerks, five of them, the most senior in the middle nearest the chief clerk and the fireplace. The other clerks perched on stools at desks which had been occupied for many years, marked and carved with dates and initials which went back to the 1870s. They wrote in pen and ink and there was a separate room where six upright lady typists struck their upright machines.

To most of the clerks the work was merely dealing with invoices and bills of lading for cargoes of tobacco but to James there was a vicarious romance concerned with figures and signatures from Savannah and the West Indies, shipments from hot, exotically named ports. Clerks worked from nine to five thirty, six on Friday, and on Saturday morning. James was paid three guineas a week.

The tobacco was brought into the Port of London, Bristol and other harbours and eventually found its way into the cigarettes, cigars and odorous pipes smoked by a great majority of the city's population. The smoke drifted up from the streets, from the open tops of buses, from public places and private chimneys. Many of the cigarettes had fanciful names, the dreamy Passing Clouds, the nautical Capstan, the rural Woodbine. London was known as the Smoke and many of its inhabitants had chronic coughs and wheezing chests.

James believed that he had found a happy security and private domesticity at last. His room at the Elephant and Castle was comfortable and cost him ten shillings a week. It had a small fireplace and each evening on his return from work across the Thames he would light a fire, turn up the wick of the oil-lamp and settle into an archaic armchair. He was able to have a sixpenny meal in the middle of the day in the company's dining-hall. At night he boiled eggs in a small saucepan on the fire and made toast against the glow.

On these winter evenings he read books about travels in England borrowed from the free library and wondered how long it would take to walk from Kent to Cornwall.

Once a week he saw Agnes. They would exchange childish coded postcards to arrange the meetings and often on a Friday went together to the cinema or the theatre. Agnes had theatrical friends who gave her tickets. She loved their meetings as much as he did.

'We are catching up on our whole lives,' she said as

they were walking arm in arm beside the misty shop windows of Oxford Street.

'I think we are,' he said. 'It's taken enough time.'

They went over the past piecing together names and memories. They talked about the present and the future. Agnes wanted to be famous. 'I want to sing on the stage,' she breathed. 'The music-hall, imagine the West End. Or if my singing wasn't good enough I could be a dancer, or the knife-thrower's assistant, anything.'

James simply wanted to walk across the south. 'When I get my week's holiday in July,' he told her, 'I'm going to start. From the Elephant and Castle, south-east into Kent and then see how far I can walk, going west. Then next year I'll take up from the place I left off.'

'Perhaps you will fall in love before then,' she said. 'Or meet a lady on your journey.'

He laughed. 'I don't seem to be very good at it.'

'I'd like to be in love with you,' she said.

He kissed her on the cheek as they walked. 'Are you going to have a jolly Christmas?' he asked. 'It's only three weeks.'

'Three weeks and two days. We will spend it together. Like we did when we were children.'

'Haven't you got other arrangements? You have a lot of friends. I don't mind being on my own. I thought I might take a practice hike. In two days I could probably get to Canterbury.'

'You are not walking across the country at Christmas,' she said decisively. 'You are coming to stay with me. I'll take you somewhere really strange on Christmas Day.'

Agnes had two rooms. The first was a small parlour with a wooden chair and a scratched table upon which stood a stubby Christmas tree. 'One day I'll have some nice furniture to put in here,' she said. She struck a ladylike pose. 'A *chaise longue*, I think, and a picture of the ballet.'

In the other room she had two mattresses on the floor, one each side of the fireplace, and a high-backed chair with patched upholstery. She insisted he sat while she kindled the fire. When the smoke began to run up the chimney she got from her knees. 'That will soon flare,' she said. 'I'll serve tea.'

A home and a fire. He smiled. She brought the tea on a wobbling wooden tray. The teapot and cups bore the words 'Salvation Army'. She sat on the edge of one of the mattresses, carefully covering her knees with her dress. 'I nearly had a baby once,' she said.

He stopped with the cup at his lip. Suddenly he felt desolate. 'When was that? You're only seventeen now.'

'Going on eighteen,' she argued; she did not look at him but stared into the tea. 'I wanted to tell you. I was running around a bit then, when I first came to London, but I've slowed down now. The baby frightened me. Nothing was so exciting then, James.' He put his cup down and knelt on the worn rug before the fire, in front of her, closing his arms about her. Her cup got between them and he took it from her and laid it on the floor. 'You should have told me.'

'You were in France. I couldn't bother you with that.' Her eyes were wet. 'It was only a matter of getting . . . disposing of it. But it made me feel very bad.'

'You poor little girl.'

She rose and picked up the cups. 'I was getting money for it,' she said. 'A prossie really. No prossie thinks she is one.' She took the cups to a small sink in the corner where she washed them under the single dribbling tap. 'You have to boil the kettle if you want a wash,' she said.

'But all that's finished now?'

'I can't live on hats,' she said. 'But I'm choosy.'

Slowly he sat back in the chair. The fire had diminished in the grate. She put four pieces of coal on it, carefully, weighing up the size of each piece. She rubbed her fingers together and then wiped them across her damp cheeks. He grinned at the coal smudges, took out his handkerchief and rubbed them off.

'I didn't think it was so terrible,' she said. 'Not while the war was on. Lots of girls did it. After all, being in service, being a maid, is not that different.' She paused: 'And the money's better.'

Tenderly he put his hands around her face and she pressed her forehead against his knees.

'Remember how you used to toboggan down the stairs.'

'On that tray,' she mumbled. 'I always was a bit crazy.'

He smiled. 'You were always brave.'

She patted him. 'Are we going to be close now?' she said. 'Just the other side of the river.'

'I'm going to have to keep an eye on you,' he said.

She rubbed her face into his legs. 'And me on you.'

They slept on the mattresses, close to the floor and the fire. James could feel the heat. He woke in the night and in the glow saw her face peaceful and pretty, her lips moving as she dreamed.

On Christmas morning she decorated the small tree with oddments, a golden streamer, some coloured cigarette cards and a bright star made from toffee wrappings. 'That's me,' she said. 'The toffee paper star.'

He had bought her a diary and she gave him an expensive-looking tie-pin which she said she had found lying on a bench in Hyde Park. At noon they boarded an omnibus.

The wide West End streets of London were almost

empty. Broom men were sweeping bottles from the gutters, the remnants of the previous evening's celebrations.

Agnes had refused to say where they were going. She took his hand and led him along the tight side-streets.

'In here,' she said. There was a notice saying: 'Stage Door. Keep Out.'

He followed her into a low passage, its whitewashed walls grey, its ceiling dangling with cobwebs. 'It's much better inside,' she said. She ran up some roughly carpeted stairs and pushed open double doors like someone making an entrance. James followed her. They were in one of the boxes overlooking the expansive stage of the theatre. The curtains were open and on the lit stage were twenty or more animated people in costumes, sitting in chairs or on the floor, surrounded by hampers, boxes and bottles. There was a girl dressed as a cat, two soldiers, a woodsman with an axe and a king with a crown. Half a dozen conversations, plays almost, were being acted out. 'Happy Christmas, everybody!' called Agnes from the box. 'I've brought my big brother. He's back from the war!'

The war had been over for more than a year. James put a restraining hand on her arm as an extravagant cheer went up from the people on the stage. 'Come on down!' called the king waving his crown.

Excited as a child Agnes caught James's hand. By the time they reached the lower level and the stalls the people on stage had begun to sing heartily. As brother and sister walked, slowly and hand in hand, down the wide aisle, the girl dressed as a cat, the head like a hood thrown over her back, was leading the song: 'When Johnny Comes Marching Home Again. Hurrah! Hurrah!'

James felt himself redden. The people in the white lights of the stage were as animated as if the scene were part of their pantomime. Agnes led him up on to the stage.

He always remembered it. The players in their coloured costumes, the raised glasses, the fun and theatrical laughter. 'Sorry that had to be a Yankee song,' said the king in his booming stage voice. He shook hands heartily. 'But they don't seem to have composed any welcome-back songs for our army.'

'Only songs to send them off to the trenches,' said the cat in high boots. She held out a fur paw and James laughed as he shook it. She said: 'It's our dress rehearsal. We open tomorrow.'

He and Agnes sat among them, the liveliest people he had ever known. There was food from the hampers and wine was handed around by the bottle. 'We always have our Christmas dinner here,' said the coachman, swaying as if rehearsing his part. 'We open on Boxing Day so we mustn't drink too much.' He emptied his wineglass at a swig, then said reflectively: 'Aye, we've felt ashamed, some of us. Guilty about the war.' The others listened. He put his hand on James's shoulder. 'Here were we, in the limelight, and you were in the trenches.'

James said: 'When I got to France the war had almost ended.'

'Ah, but you went,' said the king. 'One of those war poets said he would like to see a tank driven down through the stalls of a London theatre.'

'We tried to keep people happy,' said the coachman lamely. 'And ourselves safe.'

'Enough of this!' called Puss in Boots. 'The war's over! Rule Britannia!'

It was sufficient to make them happy again. Agnes, with her arm around a juggler in tights, came to James. 'Aren't I lucky,' she said, 'Having friends like this.'

'Agnes is going to sing!' announced Puss in Boots. 'Centre stage for Aggie!'

Agnes covered her mouth with her fingers but her eyes were glittering. 'I couldn't. Oh, I couldn't.'

The pantomime cast chorused: 'Oh, yes, you could!'

'Oh, all right,' said Agnes. She flung her pale arms wide. Her happy eyes went to James who smiled for her. 'If you insist.'

'I'll play,' said the king. He made for an upright piano in the wings. Two scarlet soldiers helped to move it squeakily. 'Audience,' said Puss. 'Agnes must have an audience.'

The players clattered down to the stalls. James's hands were caught by two chorus girls and they put him in a seat in the front stalls. The actors were sitting either side of him and some had gone further back along the aisle. The king in his crown remained at the centre of the stage. He announced: 'Ladies and gentlemen, Miss Agnes . . .' He halted.

James called up: 'Bevan. Agnes Bevan.'

'Miss Agnes Heaven,' said the king and they all laughed, 'will give us her rendition of a popular music-hall song. You have our performer's permission to join in the chorus.'

There were cheers, then silence. In the stark stage lights Agnes was ashen. To James she looked as small as she had ever been. The king at the piano pounded out an introduction. Agnes missed the cue once and he started again. Then she began to sing:

'Daddy wouldn't buy me a bow wow.'

The cast all joined in: 'Bow wow.'

'Daddy wouldn't buy me a bow wow.'

They shouted: 'Bow wow.'

Her voice was high and thin:

'I've got a little cat,
And I'm very fond of that.
But I'd rather have a bow, wow, wow . . .'

Her face was shining with happiness, her arms called to them to join in and they did. James would always remember that moment: the bright stage, the song, the audience in the dark, and Agnes, his lovely sister, Agnes the star.

In the months following the First World War an influenza epidemic spread from Asia across the world. Millions died, a greater number than had perished in the conflict. There were many deaths in Britain, more in one week of 1919 than births.

Agnes caught the flu on Boxing Day. She went to bed beside the fire and that night she began to sweat and shiver. In the early hours she cried out that she was cold and she opened her sweat-soaked sheets so that he could climb in with her and keep her warm. As they lay close she began to talk and cry. 'James, I wanted to be the lady who kissed the sheik at the Bioscope. Do you remember? I wanted to be in the pictures, a star. I wanted my face to be twenty feet high.'

'You would have been wonderful,' he told her. 'There is still time.'

'No,' she said. 'My chance has gone. I can't sing in tune, even on the stage.'

He kept the fire going through the night and brought cloths to cool her. At seven he ran down the echoing street to knock on the doctor's door. The doctor, a fat and sad man, came to see her. 'She will have to go into the hospital,' he said. 'She is very poorly. That's if there is room.'

At the hospital James heard the porter say: 'There's room, all right. They come in and they go out.'

James was frightened. Agnes was in the corner of a bleak brick-walled ward crowded with flu patients. She stared at him from the bed. He promised he would not leave her.

'I must pay you,' he said to the doctor. 'I understand it is five shillings.'

He handed two half-crowns to the man who handed one back. 'Let's see what occurs,' said the doctor.

James had waited all day and into the night in the dispiriting lobby of the place, walking up and down to keep warm, watching the comings and goings, the weeping people. God, he could not lose her now he had found her again. He thought of her laughing, singing, trying to look beautiful, full of hope and life. Surely someone like that could not die, not just in a few days. The porter wordlessly brought him tea. Agnes died as he was drinking a cup at three in the morning. They came and told him.

She was buried on 1 January, his birthday. It was rigid weather. Although she had had so many friends no one came with him to the cemetery except for the hospital porter who said it was his day off because he was Scottish. The ground was so hard that the men had barely been able to dig the grave and needed to be paid extra.

James went back to his room not knowing what he would do, except weep which he did through the night. At his work he was dumb with sorrow and in the evening he walked in the gaudy West End as though he might see her. Once, gazing blindly into a shop window, he saw a reflection of a young woman and thought it was Agnes. The reflection smiled and he turned. The girl invited him home for five shillings.

After a week he gave in his notice at the tobacco company and the chief clerk said that work was slack and he could go immediately if he liked. He said he would. After another bleak night he set out at the first lifeless light to begin his walk south.

He hardly knew where he was going, or why. All he wanted was to separate himself from the cold sorrow of London. If only he could have looked after her from the start. If only they could have stayed together. He thought of her being pregnant. Poor little Agnes. Now there was no one to care where he went, not even himself.

In his rough overcoat, with a single bag on his back, he trod a steady and stony five miles a day. He slept in slum lodgings and hostels. He scarcely wanted to eat. His money would not last long. He did not care.

There was thin snow falling on Canterbury. He went to a lodging house outside the town where he shared a room with three others who came in late at night, drunk and rowdy, one of them trying to ride a donkey. The rider fell from his mount outside the door and James went down to help the other two carry the man to his bed. The light was dim in the room, just a single gas jet, and the man was stubble-jawed and grimy, but as he helped to lay him on the narrow bed, James looked down into his face and realised he was looking at his father.

'Did he recognise you?'

'He wouldn't have recognised anyone at that moment.'

Penelope had baked two big fruit cakes, larger than anyone should have baked in wartime. 'I found the ingredients lying around,' she said. One she took to the young pilots and the other to Bevan's gun crew. 'Thanks for the cake, miss,' said Ugson. He took in her pregnancy. 'Missus.' She and Bevan had a slice each with their tea in the garden. It was a very English afternoon.

It had been a day of low clouds. The planes were resting below the trees as the light lessened, still waiting for the Luftwaffe. Someone had wound up the gramophone in the house and a soprano was singing: 'A Nightingale Sang in Berkeley Square.'

'I know for I was there,
That night in Berkeley Square.'

The song drifted towards the soldiers. 'Where's this Berkeley Square?' one asked.

'London somewhere,' said another. 'The posh part.'

'Lying in the same room all night,' Bevan continued, 'I could hear this man grunting and snoring. The moon came through the window and I got up and scraped the pane so that I could look at him better. But there was no mistake. His face was creased and he had lost most of his hair but he was my father all right.'

'Didn't you want to run away while he was still asleep?'

'I was tempted. I thought if I slipped out early and went on my way nothing would be changed, for him anyway. He wouldn't know that he had slept in the same room as his son. But I couldn't do it. I had to stay.'

In the past few days they had positioned two new barrage balloons close to the shore and two more just inland to protect the westward side of the Supermarine Spitfire factory in Southampton. The oval balloons with their fat tails were outlined in the late light, floating at a few hundred feet, the evening wind humming in their mooring ropes. Penelope said: 'I think they should keep the balloons after the war, just to entertain people.' She turned her face to him. Her eyes were always alive. 'How long did he take to wake up?'

Bevan laughed. 'God, hours. Even then he was in no state for me to tell him. It was an icy day and the men hung around until the last moment in the hostel. But you had to leave by a certain time, nine o'clock, if I remember, and be on your way, walking to the next hostel where they would let you in at six in the evening. There were hundreds of unemployed, destitute men whirling slowly about the country like some wandering tribe. They just kept walking until the next place. And I was one of them.'

As he spoke he could see his own men moving among the tents below the trees. It was Cartwright's birthday and some of the men had taken the slices of Penelope's fruit cake down to the Hut, to eat with their beer. Cartwright had received birthday cards from each of his women. 'They both love me,' he said. 'And I don't blame them.'

Bevan said to Penelope: 'Just as we were about to leave the hostel, as we were going through the door, I put my hand on his and said I wanted to tell him something. He looked at me, then turned away, then looked again, sideways, and then he beckoned me to follow him out into the cold. We began walking together as the men did, keeping company. After a whle we came to a stone bridge over a stream. The water was frozen with just a narrow, free channel. He asked me to fill his water bottle saying the water in the hostels was poisoned to cut down on the number of tramps. I took the old army water bottle from him and went down by the stream and filled it. When I got back we sat on the wall of the bridge and he took a drink before offering it to me. I drank a mouthful. It was so cold it made my teeth ache. Then he put the top on the bottle and said: "You're my son. I know you."'

Penelope's hand had reached for his and she held it lightly. She wore a smock over her stomach. Bevan said: 'It was very simple, really, nothing dramatic. I had not seen him for ten years and yet he didn't seem to realise. "Your mother's dead," he said. "She had a bad end didn't she, poor old Vera. Her and her violin."

'I told him Agnes was dead too, that she had only died a couple of weeks before. At first he seemed to have trouble placing her, at least I thought so, but then a dribble of tears ran down his rough cheeks and he wiped them with his coat sleeve and said: "I shouldn't have left."

'Then he stood and said we ought to be moving because otherwise we would be frozen to the bridge. It was the oddest thing because although we walked all day together it was too cold to talk. He never asked me what I was doing on the road, a tramp. He marched alongside me and kept pace. In the middle of the day, we stopped at a canteen which some women were running for the likes of us. We had a sort of stew, and we sheltered in their church hall for as long as they would let us. I told him about being in the army in France but he didn't seem very interested and even when I talked about Agnes again he appeared to have difficulty paying attention.'

Penelope said: 'He had no excuses?'

'He came out with a sort of excuse,' replied Bevan. 'While we were eating the stew out of the tin bowls with the others – you never heard such a noise – he suddenly asked me what my mother had done with the parcel of his clothes he had sent. I said I didn't know. I remembered they'd gone in the dustbin. "They were good clobber," he said. Then he said that his life had been ruined by the overturning of the Royal Yacht.'

She laughed. 'That *is* some excuse.'

'It actually happened. I've looked up the newspaper reports. It was in January 1900, only a couple of days after the start of the century. The Royal Yacht was undergoing some sort of overhaul and it turned turtle. According to my old man everybody blamed him. He was one of the contractors, he was working for a

Southampton shipwright. He said his life of failures had begun then.'

In the garden it was almost dark now. She had a shawl about her shoulders. 'I think I must take us indoors,' she said patting her stomach.

'Don't you think you ought to go somewhere safer?' said Bevan. 'Living on the edge of an airfield wouldn't be recommended by a doctor.'

He walked her to the door of the cottage. 'Mother's still in the officers' mess,' she said. 'She enjoys the company of those young men. She is going to miss all this.' He moved against her and kissed her deeply. 'You must mean it,' she whispered. 'With me in this state.'

'I mean it,' he said. 'I love you.'

'Touch me,' she said. 'I want you to touch me.' She took his hand and led it to her breasts and then over her swollen stomach. She seemed about to cry. 'I'm sorry about this. It's very inconvenient. But I do love you too. Thanks for finding me. I hope it's not too late.'

'It's not too late,' he said.

As they had trudged, father and son, through the bone-chill countryside, little was said between them. Vincent appeared less than amazed that they had met again after so many years. Perhaps, thought James, he was used to changes in his nomadic life. They marched doggedly side by side; his father kept pace with him without trouble for one of the few constants in his existence was tramping.

The older man had a matted overcoat which reached to the ground, an army balaclava covering his head and a canvas pack, which appeared to be empty, on his back. James carried his own sparse bag in his hand.

In the grey air their breaths puffed out, sometimes in unison, like smoke signals. Otherwise there was little communication. From time to time his father would halt and soundlessly point out some view that he had seen before, perhaps at a kinder season. He knew a barn where a farmer's charitable wife always left fruit and they ate some cold apples.

The countryside was almost colourless, the sky flat with scarcely a crow in it. On the road they were occasionally passed by snorting horses pulling wagons and less frequently by labouring motor cars but only in the villages and the small towns did they encounter people and then very few. It was too cold to be out.

That night they got drunk on cider which they were to pay for by chopping wood for the landlord the next day. It was the first time James had tasted cider and the first time he had ever been drunk. The older man laughed at his attempts to stay upright as the inn on the Kent border with Sussex seemed to spin from one county to another.

But before that, as though the time were proper, they had begun, at last, to talk. He told his father what had become of them after their mother had died so abruptly; of his own army days and some of the story of Agnes. Every now and then Vincent's rheumy eyes would roll up and James thought there might be the slight dampness of remorse in them. But then there would be a shake of the shaggy head and his father would mutter: 'If only that Royal Yacht hadn't overturned. If only . . .'

After a couple of pints of cider and some bits to eat, Vincent changed to cheerfulness and told his son: 'You were made, conceived as they say, in the very first minutes of this century.' He picked at his ear as if this might assist his memory. 'Or it might have been the end minutes of the last century. No, the first. It was gone midnight. It was an exciting night, that.' His face lit: 'You should have been there, you'd have enjoyed it! Bands at the corners, dancing in the streets. And singing of course. There was a dance called "The Turn-of-the-Century Two-step". Oh, what a night. Then your mother and me . . . Vera, yes, Vera and me . . . went back to our marriage bed and made you, George.' James did not correct him. 'One of the few evenings, I might say, when our home wasn't shredded with the squeals of the violin. Christ, I wonder did *any* of them learn to play? I wonder if your dear mother ever learned.'

The landlord brought them another flagon of cider. There was a lot of wood to be chopped the next day. 'So that's where you began,' said Vincent pointing directly at James and sniffing the aromatic tankard. 'At the very out-start of this century. Which makes you . . . where are we now? . . . What year is it?'

James told him it was 1920. 'So you're twenty,' sighed his father. 'That's easy enough to estimate. And here we are tramping England together.' He shook his untidy head as if it were all too difficult to understand.

The landlord allowed them to sleep in a stable which they shared with a flatulent horse. The straw made a warm bed, although damp in patches. On their staggering way from the pub to the stable he pointed out the dark mountain of wood which had to be chopped.

James's head was going in circles and his father's voice echoed like a warning, so that it seemed to be repeating things over and over again. James could only remember two things. When they had stretched drunkenly in the straw an owl began to cry outside in the frozen moonlight and Vincent said: 'It's no good, this life, being on the road. It's all right for you, you're young. But I have to look to my future.'

The other thing he could remember was when his father paused in his snoring and muttered: 'Good night, my son.'

James managed to reply: 'Good night, Dad.'

When he woke in the grey morning Vincent had gone leaving his son to chop the great pile of wood. And he never saw him again.

11

In that August of 1940 what became known from its earliest days as the Battle of Britain was painted on the skies of southern England; it was the first battle in history that all could watch and hear at their leisure, civilians standing in their streets and sitting in their gardens, children pausing in the parks and playgrounds. It was so lofty, so far away even though so visible, that life below went on much as usual. There were few bombs dropped for it was a fight in the skies, for the skies. The high and whirling vapour trails, spreading to feathers against the blue, the glint of silver as the planes looped and dived, the echoing of celestial machine-guns. The targets were the airfields of southern England so there was no necessity for people to cower in the air-raid shelters and they observed it from their front porches. It happened day after day. Civilians, still nine-tenths of the population, sedately drinking cups of tea watched the combat, saw the stricken falling of the planes, followed the course of parachutes, sometimes three or four at once, drifting like flowers to the ground. The countryside was littered with wrecked aeroplanes.

The gunners, waiting with the two Bofors at opposite edges of the airstrip, could only eye the eager Hurricane fighters take off, roaring over the pines, heading for the lofty fight. 'We seem to spend a lot of this ruddy war watching everybody else fighting it,' grumbled Sergeant Runciman.

'We've had our moments, sarge,' said Bairnsfather. 'So far we've bagged a Stuka and two motorcycle combinations.'

'At least the British can now *see* what's going on,' said Hignet. 'It's not some place with a funny name in Norway, it's not even France, it's here.' He had fashioned a square of plywood like a cricket scoreboard. The planes shot down that day, according to the figures broadcast on the news, were displayed as they might be at a game. 'Luftwaffe 165 all out. RAF 43.'

'If Hermann Goering is trying to shoot our fliers out of the sky then he's not doing terribly well,' said Lady Violet. She made it her duty to tour her former property every day, visiting the Bofors positions, the fuel depot where the bowsers waited to replenish the fighter planes, the mechanics, the armourers and other ground crew, and the cookhouse, always ending her tour in what had been her own dining-room, the officers' mess.

There the young pilots, in their flying kit and life-jackets, were noisily on stand-by. There was a darts game. As he waited to throw, one pilot twisted his dart like a spiralling plane. Casually they drank coffee, and two trays of sandwiches had just been brought in by a sturdy WRAF girl in her shirtsleeves, to common-room cries for both her and the sandwiches, when the black telephone on the table sounded. At once there was silence. The next dart remained unthrown. Wickens, the twenty-eight-year-old squadron leader who always stood next to the phone, picked it up. He listened and said: 'Understood. Thank you. We're on our way.'

Lady Violet felt her heart move in the sudden hush of the room. 'Scramble, boys,' said Wickens still not raising his voice. 'Krauts heading for Portsmouth.'

There was a dash. So far, although they had lost two planes, they had suffered no deaths. Both pilots had parachuted, one landing conveniently half a mile away, suspended in a tree. His friends had stood below laughing like children while he hung from his harness.

Now the room was cleared in a moment, the young men rushing to get to their planes, getting jammed together in the door as they hurried. 'After you, Claude,' said one with exaggerated politeness, using a current radio catch-phrase. The other bowed: 'No, after you, Cecil.'

There was one pilot left, the fair-haired Tubby. He picked up a dart and threw it disconsolately at the board, hitting the bull's-eye. 'There,' he said to Lady Violet. 'And they say I can't see.'

She looked at him as his mother might have. 'Why can't you see?'

'This,' he said turning a reddened right eye towards her. 'Bee sting. Snoozing under your hollyhocks. And now they won't let me fly because they say my vision isn't right.' He threw another dart. It nestled in the bull beside the first. 'Damned nonsense.'

'Perhaps it will be better soon.'

'The show will be over then,' he grumbled.

She sat on the arm of her sofa, worn and sagging, she noted, from its recent extreme use.

'We haven't been introduced,' she said. 'I'm Violet Foxley.'

'Yes, I know, of course.' Tubby appeared embarrassed. They shook hands self-consciously. 'I'm Edward Fingest.' His round face became creased by a half-grin. 'The others call me Tubby. I don't know why.'

'Ah yes, Fingest. You must have been at Eton with my sons, Arthur and Horace.'

'Yes, I was. I played rugger with both of them. How are they?'

'Serving. In this country now. They're in the army.'

'I think I'll volunteer for a transfer,' he sniffed wryly. 'Perhaps your eyes don't have to be so perfect.'

'It must be important when you're flying.'

'Reactions one-fifth quicker than normal,' he said proudly. 'That's until you get stung by a stupid old English bee.' He shot an embarrassed glance her way. 'Sorry, it must be one of yours.'

'Not a personal bee,' she said. 'They come and go as they please.'

She offered to make a fresh pot of coffee but he declined. 'I'd better write to my mother,' he said. 'As I've got nothing else to do.' He laughed. 'My father is training to be a secret resistance leader. He's fifty. If all this doesn't work and we're occupied he's going to blow up bridges when Huns are crossing them.'

She left him and walked out on to the lawn. Penelope was deadheading geraniums. She had to sit on a stool to do it. 'My war work,' she said.

'I'd be happier if you did your war work in some other part of the country,' said Lady Violet. 'Perhaps a visit to the Fitzroys in Derbyshire.'

'I'd prefer to face the Luftwaffe than the Fitzroys,' said Penelope. 'In any event, you wouldn't want to have to travel to Derbyshire to see your first grandchild, would you?'

'Poor old Fitzroy. He's dying of something, you know.'

'Yes, he's in hospital. In wartime you tend to forget that people still die of ordinary things.'

Slowly they went around the garden together picking the finished flower heads. 'That chap in there, he's a young Fingest, you know. He went to Eton with your brothers.'

'Why isn't he flying?'

'He was stung by a bee. On the eye. He's very fed up about it.'

'As long as he can recognise a Messerschmitt,' said Penelope.

A skein of vapour trails from a distant dogfight drifted like strands of wool across the amiable afternoon sky. The garden was sleepy. The pilots had left their books and chairs and plates and cups strewn on the grass; the air was quiet, birds sang unafraid.

When the planes came back they did so with a swagger, rocking their wings as they approached. One after the other they landed on the humped runway, each one snorting and describing a gentle circle, before taxiing beneath the trees. Ground crew ran to meet them. Propellers feathered and stopped. The pilots began to climb excitedly from their cockpits. They had all come back.

There was almost uproar in the mess. 'What a picnic!' 'What a party!' Tubby sat miserably as they described it. Forty unescorted Stukas had suicidally attempted to attack Portsmouth. Eighteen had been destroyed. 'Like shooting down delivery vans,' said Wickens the squadron leader, without elation. 'They didn't have a prayer.'

In the middle of the afternoon, five thousand feet below the dogfights, Unsworth drove to the police station. He had travelled through lanes and woods crammed with summer. It was hard to believe that a battle that could finish the war and his country, was going on over his car roof. People were standing in their doorways, in a rustic clutch under the church lych-gate, every face elevated; children pointed to planes drawing in the blue then white trails that would for ever be the trademark of the battle. One man watched from below an umbrella.

'At last everybody can *see* the blinking war,' said Police Sergeant Linnet, wearing his steel helmet, legs astride, arms behind back, on the police station steps. He examined the sky from below the helmet's rim. The crackle of machine-guns filtered softly down; you could even smell the smoke. 'I've just popped out for a breath of fresh air,' said the sergeant. He nodded over his shoulder: 'We've got a couple of Jerry pilots in the cells.'

'Pilots?' said Unsworth quickly. 'You're sure they're *pilots*?'

'Looks like it. They're done up like pilots. Goggles and everything.'

Goering had promised Hitler that the Royal Air Force would be eliminated by his Luftwaffe in four days. On what he dubbed 'Eagle Day' his pilots flew massed missions against airfields and, at first, against harbours and targeted secret radio location posts. At Ventnor on the Isle of Wight the tracking post was bombed but none of the dozen other establishments – the secret weapon of radar – strung across the south was put out of commission and they were able to pick up the German planes as they came. The four promised days became eight, then ten, then two weeks, then an indefinite period. German aircraft losses were heavy.

Unsworth had been searching since daybreak after mysterious, abandoned parachutes had been found in fields and German broadcasts had boasted that fifty spies had been dropped into Britain and were being hidden by people with Nazi sympathies, the fifth-columnists. In the Spanish Civil War, two years earlier, Franco's troops converging on Madrid in four columns boasted that within the city was a secret fifth column.

'I don' reckon we got *any* o' they fifth-columnists,' said Catcher Hurrock as he trudged up the police-station steps after Unsworth had gone in. Rob followed, helping to hump a parachute through the door. They had brought it in by tractor. 'Nobody I know'd anyway.'

Unsworth stared at them coming into the lobby. 'You found one,' he said. 'Where was it?'

'Middle of a cornfield,' said Rob. 'Down by Sway.'

'No sign of who came down on it?'

Catcher said: 'We reckon there *was* nobody. It were lying there in the corn . . .'

'. . . But ne'er a footstep round it,' said Rob. Catcher glanced at him annoyed that he had completed the sentence. 'Not a stalk broke,' he put in quickly. 'Whoever 't was who came out o' that field could *fly* over the corn.'

Rob laughed. 'So why would they be needing a parachute?'

Unsworth said: 'I'm sure you're right, boys. The Germans have been dropping these, empty, all over the country, making out they're infiltrating.'

'They not doin' any infiltrating 'ere,' said Rob stoutly.

'Wouldn't let 'un,' said Catcher.

Sergeant Linnet came into the room. They heard a truck outside. 'It's the army come for the Jerries,' said the sergeant.

'You got Jerries in 'ere?' said Catcher in a low voice, his little eyes lifting.

'Can we see?' asked Rob. 'Ain't never seen a live Jerry. That 'un we found at the beach, 'e was dead.'

The request was fulfilled at once. Two tall young men in oily flying suits, their goggles hung under their chins, their pistol holsters empty, their boots loud on the police-station floor, walked through. One looked sheepish, the other disdainful. They were escorted by two stiffly excited constables.

'What d'you think of our Spitfires then?' Catcher suddenly demanded. It was as if he were seizing his only chance.

'And our Hurricanes?' blurted Rob.

Oddly the procession halted. The sheepish German said: 'The Spitfire is a nice aeroplane.'

The second pilot regarded the forest men arrogantly. 'The Hurricane is a nice aeroplane to shoot down.'

By early evening Unsworth had decided to go home. He was putting his gas-mask case and his steel helmet on the back seat of his car and adjusting the clumsy revolver under his arm, when a blue vehicle turned into the yard. It had 'RN' above the windscreen and his first thought was of Alan. To his relief Alan himself got out of the front seat. He was dressed in naval dungarees. His cap was pushed up from his forehead.

'Caught you,' he grinned. 'Had an easy day?'

'Very,' said his father glancing at the sky. 'Nothing doing down here. Have you been home?'

'No, I can't. I'm on escort duty. A bloke who went off with the NAAFI takings and one of the NAAFI girls to Swanage.'

'Romance lives on,' said Unsworth.

'So this is unofficial,' said Alan. 'I hope the prisoner doesn't tell on me.'

'Well, there are the air raids. And you could always say that you stopped at the police station for directions.'

'The perfect alibi.' Alan looked about them. They were almost at the centre of the car park. The droning in the sky had stopped, the vapour trails were drifting away, it had the promise of a fine evening. 'Here's as good as anywhere,' said his son. 'Dad, I'm being commissioned and posted abroad. Fleet Air Arm. Canada, probably Flying Training. Just tell Mum quietly, will you. She'll worry when she doesn't hear from me. I'll write when I can.'

Unsworth nodded. 'I'll tell her.' They shook hands and patted each other's shoulders. Then his son was away. Unsworth got a glimpse of the prisoner, waving cheerily from the back seat alongside the second escort. They drove off and he climbed into his car.

When he reached home he found Ellen and her sister Kath sheltering below the kitchen table. 'What are you doing down there?' he asked.

'Taking cover,' Ellen said irritably. 'I said we should have had an air-raid shelter.'

'One of them came right across the house a couple of minutes ago,' said Kath remaining under the table. 'One of theirs by the sound of it.'

'And something's landed in the back garden,' said Ellen.

'I thought it was all finished for the day,' he said wearily.

'Well, it's not here.' Ellen was sitting on the floor. 'It hasn't stopped. Firing and bangs and aeroplanes screaming around, very low too, some of them. A boy just came to the door with a bag full of bullets. He wanted to ask you if they were dangerous. Then there was this terrible bang. I hope Alan is all right.'

Unsworth said: 'Let's go and see what's in the garden.'

He went towards the back door, aware of the gun under his armpit. Ellen and Kath came from beneath the table and followed him timidly. He unlatched the door. 'We locked it in case it was a Jerry pilot,' said Kath.

Unsworth opened the door and went into the familiar garden. He saw it at once. Projecting, standing upright, from the patch that he had meant for a vegetable plot was part of the tail fin of an aeroplane, bearing part of a black Nazi swastika. 'Now there's a souvenir,' he said.

'We ought to get it framed,' said Ellen.

At one in the morning the church bells rang. Unsworth sat up abruptly in bed and said: 'They're here.' He put on the light and his eyes went to his gun lying in its shiny holster on the chair with his shirt, pants and socks.

He thought Ellen had not heard him. 'Parachutists,' he said. 'They're ringing the bells.'

'At this time of the night.'

He was already out of the bed. 'I'll make some tea,' sighed Ellen. She began to climb out also. 'You can't go out without something.'

On the landing Kath stood in her quilted, rose-smothered dressing-gown. 'I thought I was dreaming about a wedding,' she said. She had been sleeping in Alan's room.

'Alf's got to go out,' said Ellen. She nodded towards Unsworth as if her sister might not know who she meant. He was already on the telephone.

'They sent the code word,' said the sergeant at the police station. 'Cromwell.'

Unsworth was almost dressed. He tugged on his brown pullover and strapped the gun on top of it. When Ellen arrived with the tea, the cup primly balanced on its saucer, he was wearing his sports jacket. 'You can see the bulge,' Kath pointed out.

'I'll tell the Jerries it's my lunch,' he said.

'You'll be home by lunchtime, I hope,' said Ellen. 'I'll worry otherwise.'

Unsworth, then realising, looked at them, two helpless middle-aged women in their floral dressing-gowns. They returned the uncertainty. 'If anybody knocks,' he said, 'don't answer.'

'What if they keep knocking?' asked his wife.

He had to think. Then he said: 'Shout through the door. Don't open it.'

'What do we shout?'

He had to think again. 'Shout "*Hausfrau*",' he said eventually. 'That's it – "*Hausfrau*".'

'*Hausfrau*,' repeated Ellen and Kath said: 'That seems sensible.'

Unsworth pushed aside the blackout curtain covering the door. 'I've got to go.' He kissed Ellen and then Kath with less emphasis. 'Be safe,' said his wife. He did not look her in the eye.

He opened the door and went out. The women stood for a few moments. Then Ellen muttered: '*Hausfrau*,' again. She turned towards the kitchen. 'I'm not talking German for anybody.'

She returned carrying a garden fork and an axe. Kath's hands went to her face. 'What are those for?'

'That's for you,' said Ellen giving her the chopper. 'You aim for the base of the skull, so I believe.'

Weakly her sister took it. 'And that,' she said nodding at the garden fork, 'is to stick in their tummies, I suppose.'

'Guts,' corrected Ellen. 'Their guts.'

It was a fine night for an invasion: calm, with a clear and placid sky and a steady moon. Ideal for a parachute landing. Unsworth eyed the moon suspiciously as he drove. The bells had stopped.

In the dim slits of the car headlights he suddenly, by instinct, realised there was something in the road ahead. All at once the car was caught in a mesh of wire, the barbs scraping across the paintwork and climbing like claws up the windscreen. He cursed and braked. Figures were rising from the roadside ditch.

'Sorry, Mr Unsworth,' said Rob as Unsworth climbed angrily from the car. 'We thought you was them invaders.'

'Parachutists,' confirmed Catcher Hurrock. There were a dozen men carrying American rifles and wearing Home Guard dungarees.

'What's a parachutist doing in a bloody Austin Seven?' demanded Unsworth.

'Might have been stole,' said Tom Dibben.

''Fraid you got a puncture,' said Catcher nodding at a front tyre. 'Devil for punctures, this barbed wire stuff.'

'You can mend the damn thing then,' said Unsworth. He surveyed the contrite men. 'Have you seen anything?'

'Nothin',' said Rob. 'We been lookin' hard too.'

'What about the bells?'

'Vicar rung 'em,' said Catcher. 'And Ted the verger.'

'They're still in the church,' said Rob.

Unsworth strode towards the lych-gate with Rob, Catcher and Tom close behind. Rob told the other volunteers to stay and guard Unsworth's car which was still enmeshed in the wire.

The three forest men closed up, almost clutching each other, as they hurried through the churchyard. Unsworth opened the big squeaky church door. Everywhere within was dark but he saw a shaving of light coming from the vestry.

He found the dressing-gowned vicar inside with Ted the verger wearing an overcoat over his pyjamas. They had opened a bottle of communion wine. The vicar looked shaken, pale and guilty behind his spectacles.

'Who gave orders to ring the bells?' demanded Unsworth.

The Reverend Goodenough pointed wordlessly towards the verger who said: 'They called me on the blower.'

'Who?'

'Dunno rightly. But they gave the code word.'

'Wellington or something,' mumbled the vicar.

'Cromwell,' said Unsworth.

The Home Guards and Ted all agreed: 'Cromwell.'

Ted said: 'There was other bells ringing. Down Lymington way, I reckon, and I thought I'd better ring ourn. So I got the vicar out to 'elp.'

'Damned bell ropes,' Goodenough snarled to the surprise of them all. 'I was up in the bloody air twice. Frightened the life out of me.'

'You got to know when to let go,' said Ted sagely.

There was a movement at the church door and they all turned quickly. It was one of the Home Guards. 'Soldiers outside,' he said. 'Ourn.'

Through the door came Bevan with Hignet. 'What's going on?' Bevan asked. He was relieved to see Unsworth. 'Who rang the bells?'

'We had the code word,' said Ted firmly. 'Honest.'

'Cromwell,' muttered the vicar. He was still hunched on the chair.

'Everybody's yapping about Cromwell,' said Bevan. He moved towards the door. 'No more bell-ringing,' he warned over his shoulder.

'To hell with the bells,' the vicar called back.

Outside the church Bevan said to Unsworth: 'This looks like a panic for nothing.'

'Nobody's seen any Germans,' said Unsworth.

They walked down the church path. 'I've been trying to get through to Divisional Headquarters,' said Bevan. 'But they're engaged.'

Unsworth grinned in the dark. 'All about Cromwell.'

'Cromwell, as I understand it . . .' said Bevan. He stopped when he saw the car still ensnared in barbed wire. 'Is that yours?'

'Yes.'

'You're lucky they didn't shoot.'

'We thought about it,' said Rob seriously. 'Didn't we, boys?' Catcher and Tom nodded in the night.

'Cromwell is the warning that *conditions* are right for an invasion,' continued Bevan. 'It doesn't mean it's *started*. Everyone's panicked.'

Hignet was standing by the platoon truck. There were

two soldiers in the back. 'Hitler won't come tonight,' Hignet said as if they were to take his word. Bevan ignored him. He said to Unsworth: 'Come with us if you like. We're going to check this area. If there'd been a landing by sea we'd know all about it by now. A parachute drop is still a possibility. Can we give you a lift?'

'Anywhere near Lyndhurst,' said Unsworth. He turned his eyes on Rob. 'I'll come back in the morning for my car.'

'Right, sir,' said Rob. 'We'll get that puncture mended. Provided we can untangle 'un from that wire.'

The code word 'Cromwell' had been widely misinterpreted. All over the country bells were rung, shots were exchanged, there were casualties and mishaps, bridges were blown up. In the police station at Lyndhurst Unsworth spent the rest of the night trying to reassure people who came in crowds to the door demanding to know where the enemy troops had landed and refusing to believe him when he said they had not. At daybreak a police car took him home.

He knocked on the window and called to Ellen. Tentatively she pulled aside the curtains and then unlocked the door. She embraced him tightly. 'I was worried all night.'

'They didn't turn up,' said Unsworth kissing her. 'It was all a false alarm. A big one.'

'Kath's gone to bed,' said Ellen.

His eye caught the axe lying on the table. 'What's that for?'

'Chopping wood,' said Ellen.

In the early September morning Brown relieved Cartwright on guard duty at the gun. The second Bofors, with its crew under Lieutenants Laurel and Hardy, was at the distant end of the runway. The dawn broke later now, the paling stars were still visible. It had been a close night with some showers before midnight but serene after.

'Nothing doing, Brownie,' said Cartwright by way of reporting. 'You'd think there would be, wouldn't you.' They were desperate to use the Bofors.

'It's like everybody knocks off at the end of the day,' agreed Brown. 'Clock off and go home. It's more like a factory than a war.'

Cartwright unloaded the round from the breech of his rifle and Brown moved prudently out of the way. 'Why do we 'ave one ready up the spout?' asked Brown. 'We've got to ask for permission before we shoot anybody. Don't make sense.'

'There's a lot don't,' said Cartwright. He did not seem anxious to get back to his blankets in the guard tent. Eighty yards down the lane they could see the pacing RAF sentry. 'Do they have the same stags as us?' said Cartwright. Brown had brought some tea in his flat mess tin which they shared, drinking from the corners. It was thick and sweet. 'Every two hours?'

'Ask 'im,' suggested Brown.

Cartwright walked down the forest track. The airman was startled at first but then saw who it was. 'Don't creep up like that,' he said. 'I thought you was one of them Storm Troopers.' Cartwright apologised. 'Is your relief coming?' he asked. They had been eyeing each other during the night but apart from a reassuring wave they had not communicated. Shouting would have woken others.

'He's late,' said the RAF sentry. His belt, bayonet and ammunition pouches were identical to the soldiers'. He was a bulky youth with hard country hands and the rifle did not look heavy. 'Always is late. I don't mind that much because I like to see it getting light. I used to get up early to go fishing.'

'Me as well,' said Cartwright. 'Fishing's good.' He studied the other sentry's blue uniform. 'They ought to put you in khaki for sentry go,' he said. 'You can be spotted a mile off in that clobber.'

The airman said: 'I don't want to be in the cake, mate. I'm in the cream. Anyway, you're supposed to be able to *see* a sentry.'

Cartwright sniffed. 'What if you have to hide, take cover? Where did you fish then?'

'Devon. My old man was a water bailiff. Still is. Should have retired but the war came. He used to take me out even when I was a kid. Out there, early, by a pool.'

'What river was that?'

'River Dart. Bloody good trout fishing. And salmon. Round here they go on about the Test and the Avon but it's the Dart for me every time. What about you?' His relief, wiping gritty eyes, appeared. 'Sorry, Ben,' he said. 'Didn't wake up.'

'Near Bristol,' said Cartwright. He hesitated. 'Sort of private fishing. I used to go in the middle of the night.'

One day when the war was finished, the airman promised he'd take him down to the Dart. Cartwright went back to Brown. 'Everywhere's been bombed,' he grumbled looking about him at the peaceful dawn. 'Everywhere. Every bloody airfield in England, even up Newcastle and places. All the landing grounds around here and Surrey, Kent, Essex. Everywhere but this bugger. Why don't the sods come here so we can have a go?'

'Maybe we ought to wave to them,' said Brown.

Hignet appeared sleepily from the guard tent. 'We've bombed Berlin,' he said. 'That will be a smack in the eye for them. The BBC said last night that the Germans couldn't believe it, *us* bombing *them*. They're saying our planes got through their defences because they were painted with invisible paint! What a laugh.'

Cartwright sniffed: 'Berlin? I told you, everywhere's being bombed but here.'

By that first week in September both air forces were heavily depleted. At the beginning of August the Luftwaffe had about two thousand eight hundred aircraft against which the RAF had six hundred and fifty front-line planes available for combat at one time. Enemy plane losses had been copious, although not as extensive as the British newspapers and the BBC claimed. Inept, indecisive planning failed the Germans. Unsuitable aircraft, so successful in the easy conquest of the Continent, found themselves no match for the British fighting above their own fields. The Messerschmitt 110 was clumsy in the acrobatic fights, the Dornier, Heinkel and Junkers bombers unsuited to their task, the Stuka indefensible and the swift Messerschmitt 109 handicapped by the ninety minutes it could remain in the air without refuelling. German aircraft production was languid; factories were still working a casual six-hour day. Losses quickly overtook replacements.

The British had a crucial shortage of pilots. More than three hundred had been killed by the end of August, or were missing or wounded although some had parachuted to fight another day. Fighter planes which had crashed had been recovered from the countryside and cannibalised for usable parts.

'We've lost two pilots, both twenty-four years of age, in three days,' said Wickens, the squadron leader, to Bevan. They were having breakfast at a card-table set outside the Manor. All around them the airfield was being prepared for another day. Men were wheeling out the planes, wiping the dew from them, mechanics and armourers made their checks, fuel bowsers filled the tanks, fire wagons stood prepared. There was a smell of bacon and eggs in the pine air of the forest. Men were having breakfast.

Wickens said: 'We've now lost four chaps. The planes are replaced, they only have to come up the road from Supermarines at Southampton, and they're tested and operational in no time. But the pilot casualties throughout Fighter Command are bad. It's all right for Churchill to make a speech about the gallant few to whom everybody owes so much. They're only *few* because we haven't trained enough.'

'My men have just been standing around,' sighed Bevan. 'It's a pity they can't fly.'

'Their time will come,' said Wickens. He was slight and fair haired with a narrow face and tired eyes. His nose looked cold in the early air. 'We're having to make up the shortfall of pilots with all-sorts. We've had some replacements just arrived who've been trained in Fairey Battle bombers, for Christ's sake, and you can't get anything more different than a Fairey Battle and a Hurricane. And there are other odds and sods, army pilots and so on. We give them a few days' training in a three-hundred-and-fifty-mile-an-hour fighter aircraft and then send them up to get on with it.'

It was seven thirty. Bevan and Wickens shook hands and the soldier went back to his gun crew, the airman to his pilots. It was going to be a big day.

The Hurricanes took off at ten o'clock. 'They keep gentlemen's hours,' said Cartwright to Hignet. 'They're always back for lunch.'

'If they live long enough for lunch,' put in Runciman.

The planes returned in an hour, refuelled with the pilots still in the cockpits, their foreheads resting on the controls, and took off again. To Bevan, the ordered routine of the young men's perilous lives was amazing. Their planes had a tough beauty, an encouraging sound, as they went across the pine tops. They called them kites and spoke of every battle as a joyride. At lunch they returned, still with no one missing, and recommenced the fight at two o'clock. By three, two of them had been shot down in flames.

In the late afternoon the Germans, at last, arrived to attack the airfield. Hignet, who was the lookout, had scarcely time to shout and press the Klaxon before the first plane screamed over the trees.

It fired a burst from its machine-guns like an afterthought, as if the pilot had been surprised by the suddenness of his target. The bullets cut a tree in half two hundred yards beyond the Bofors at the southern end of the runway and it cracked and tipped over like a severed man. Almost at once the plane was followed by a second, straddling bombs. They shook the ground and pounded the ears. Lady Violet covered hers and murmured: 'What a noise.'

The men on the Bofors had kept it at a low angle but the attack was so abrupt they had no time. The gun at the far end of the runway fired too late. Runciman was cursing, the gun layers were turning their handles madly. 'Aircraft north!' shouted Hignet. They did not need to get a bearing because there was only the channel through the trees. 'Fire!' bellowed Runciman. Bevan stood behind the gun. 'God damn it!' he shouted at the roaring Germans. The planes were too fast again.

One of the fuel bowsers began burning at the side of the runway. It was apart from the other vehicles and they could see the crews running to drive them further away. 'Just like in the films,' said Ugson.

Next time the Germans came back the other way,

again close against the treetops. They heard the other Bofors open fire but in a split moment there were two Messerschmitts tearing towards them. 'Fire!' shouted Runciman. He managed to be heard above the huge noise. Bairnsfather pressed the trigger pedal with his foot, the gun fired, shuddered and recoiled. They missed again. It was too quick. 'Get the bastard next time,' said Runciman like an order.

'I'm going to,' said Bairnsfather. 'Definitely.' He pushed back his steel helmet. He was the one who pressed the trigger. 'I'll get him.'

Ugson and Cartwright were carrying the ammunition in clips of four from the dump on the other side of the forest path. The gun, said to fire at 120 rounds a minute, realistically could fire only eight because it was manually loaded. The supply dump was only a dozen steps away but they had to dash from the cover of the trees. Carrying the clips of shells they ran like rabbits across the open ground. The Messerchmitts came back again. There was a bruise of smoke over the airfield, the fuel bowser was still burning and two aircraft on the ground were on fire. The Germans came through the smoke. The first roared in with its machine-guns sparking. Around the Bofors the trees were cut as though a high-speed saw was going through them. The gun recoiled as it released another salvo. Again there was no time. Bevan was cursing below his breath, Runciman was swearing aloud. They choked on the erupting dust.

Then they saw that Ugson had fallen in the middle of the path, sprawled on his face, a full clip of shells lying by his right hand, his helmet rolling away like a hoop. Bevan shouted and ran out into the open followed by Cartwright. They held on to Ugson together, shielding him. Then the Germans came again. Machine-gun fire raked the path. Bevan felt the heat like the lash of a whip and the force turned him over. Choking he staggered to his knees. Runciman was tugging him into cover. Cartwright was lying on his side, a beam of mocking sunshine across him.

The gun crew stopped, caught like a frieze, horrified. Bairnsfather felt his face shake. To his surprise he began to weep. The Messerschmitt, only one this time, made a last run. Bairnsfather looked up and held his fire. This time he had to be sure. Curiously there seemed to be plenty of time. He stilled his trembling and wiped his cheeks with his hand. The gun was ready. The others turned and watched. There it was, the Messerschmitt, coming at them, tracer bullets streaking. Bairnsfather sat like a man in a seaside deck-chair. 'Now!' he bawled to himself. He fired.

The wing of the German plane almost casually spun away. It flew off and dropped among the distant trees. They heard the aircraft crash and saw the bauble of flame. 'Got you, you fucking bastard,' sobbed Bairnsfather. He lay forward over the gun calling without looking: 'Is he all right?' he called to the men around Cartwright. He could not see Ugson. 'Where's Ugly?' he shouted. 'Ugly.' Stretcher-bearers were running across to the gun site. Cartwright was lying, almost lounging against a tree, bleeding from his chest. 'Bugger it,' he muttered before he died.

Ugson was below another patch of trees. A splinter had gone through his cheek. 'Give us a fag, mate,' he said to the first stretcher-bearer. Someone handed him a lit cigarette. His eyes were blank, almost dreamy. He drew on the cigarette and exhaled. The smoke drifted out of the hole in his face.

As the rosy afternoon moved towards evening the Hurricanes began to return, one by one, circling the trees, coming in from the north and landing on the runway in which the bomb craters had been filled only half an hour before by a gang of cheerful Irish navvies and two Southampton Corporation lorries which had miraculously appeared full of earth.

As usual the planes were counted in. The ground staff and the pilots who had already returned or were resting, ticked off each one as it appeared and touched down with a short curtsy. The young fliers had to be helped from the cockpits like old men. It had been another gritty and gruelling day. By seven o'clock six of the aircraft had come home. There was one missing. Tubby Fingest.

'He'll be OK,' they assured each other standing in the garden outside the mess. It was a velvet evening, the trees of the forest scarcely stirring. The guns were resting, the soldiers sat speechless.

The pilots told each other that they had seen Tubby over the Channel, flying low but apparently without concern. At tea-time he had claimed a Fokker Wolfe but then his radio went dead. He should have been back by now. The talk diminished and then ceased. Lady Violet and Penelope stood with the youths, scanning the sky, waiting. Then they saw him.

A boisterous schoolboy cheer went up. Hats were waved, gins and tonic were spilt, faces beamed as though someone had scored a winning try. Squadron leader Wickens grinned with relief and said he would have a drink after all. 'We're all accounted for,' he told the mess barman who said: 'He's not the sort to stay out, sir.'

Bevan stood with Runciman at the gun site watching the plane come in. Ugson was in hospital but his wounds were slight. They were sickened by Cartwright's death. They would miss him. The men moved around the gun as slowly as ghosts. Nobody had eaten their tea.

'Well, we got one of theirs,' said Runciman as if it might

be some sort of consolation. 'There wasn't much left of him, was there?' Bevan nodded, sadness overwhelming him. He would have to write another letter; two in Cartwright's case. 'A life for a life,' he said quietly. 'Another day of this bloody war.'

'He's going around again, that pilot,' said Runciman. 'Wonder why?'

They watched the Hurricane. It banked awkwardly over the pines and came in again. The airmen outside the mess had stopped cheering and watched. On the final approach it almost clipped the trees above the other Bofors gun. Then it dropped on to the runway, rocking a little as if nervous. It touched down. A relieved cheer began from the men on the lawn. Lady Violet sighed: 'Well done, God.'

She had hardly said it when the plane tipped on to its nose, somersaulting over and over and finally bursting into a flower of flame. It fell finally on its back with an emphatic explosion. A silence like death itself fell over everyone, everything. Then the airmen began to run towards the wreck. The fire-engines were already on their way.

'Christ almighty,' said Runciman. He and Bevan remained struck with horror. 'I'll be glad when today's over.'

Molly and Ronnie stepped down from the bus almost outside the Hut. It was only a walk up the grass slope to the little thatched building and Bairnsfather was there to walk down and meet them. Ronnie was wearing a steel helmet and both had their gas-mask cases. 'I'm her escort,' he said almost before his sister and her husband had embraced. He looked away with embarrassment as they did. 'You ought to pack that up now you're married,' he said.

They strolled up the slope. It gave Bairnsfather an odd fatherly feeling walking like that. It was six in the evening. For ten days they had kept in touch by postcards. For a penny stamp, the message would be delivered the next day, despite battles, despite bombs.

'Ronnie wanted to come,' said Molly, her arm around Bairnsfather, his around her. She was halfway through her pregnancy now. 'He said he would defend me from any Germans who happened to be about.' Bairnsfather laughed quietly. 'He can't go to school,' she said. 'They closed it while they repair the bomb hole in the roof. The kids are pleased as anything.'

Bairnsfather glanced at her anxiously. 'You had bombs that close?'

'They dropped some on the Spitfire factory the day before yesterday.' She sat on a bench in the calm air; evening birds were singing carelessly. 'They missed mostly but they dropped a bomb at the end of our street and one through the school. Fortunately it was Saturday. Nobody was hurt much in the street but it demolished the Phillips's house. You should have seen little George Phillips pedalling around the wreckage on his three-wheeler.'

Bairnsfather sat down heavily. 'We don't get that news,' he said. 'You must have been upset.'

'I try not to be because of our Anderson.' She patted her stomach. 'And it had its funny moments. Dad went in the house to get his gas mask. We were all in the shelter. When the bomb dropped the ceiling came down on him.' She began to giggle. 'Oh, Harry, you should have seen him.'

'Like a snowman,' confirmed Ronnie. He had come back from exploring the woodland. 'He's looking for souvenirs,' Molly had said.

'I've got bits of parachute, shrapnel, masses of that, a

few bullet cases and a button,' said Ronnie. 'I reckon it's a Luftwaffe button.'

'It's a bus conductor's,' said Molly, 'according to dad.'

Bairnsfather went to get the drinks. For three days there had been no attacks. By the middle of September the German air force had admitted defeat, at least in that battle. London had been bombed, the beginning of the long autumn and winter of the Blitz. But the countryside had quickly reverted to its peace, as though the seasons had merely changed.

'Run out of ammo, they 'ave, that's what,' said Catcher Hurrock from his corner in the Hut.

'Run out o' planes, the rate our lads knocked 'un out of the sky,' said Rob serving Bairnsfather.

'Jerry's just 'aving a breather,' said Tom Dibben. 'They'll be back, you see. 'E ain't finished yet.' He looked at Bairnsfather. 'What you reckon?'

'Don't know. They never tell me anything.'

'You lost a lad t'other day, didn't you? So we 'eard,' said Rob.

'That's right. On the gun.'

'Gets like bein' a family, I s'pose,' said Catcher. 'Like a brother.'

'Yes, he was.'

He went back out into the blameless evening. Ugson had come back from hospital. He knew Cartwright had died saving his life. He did not, could not, speak to anyone. They were going to send him home on leave.

'We lost Carty,' Bairnsfather said to Molly as he gave her her drink. 'You know Cartwright.' It was hard to imagine a more gentle evening, a more serene place. Molly looked shocked. She spilt her lemonade. 'Can't you find him?' asked Ronnie.

'He was killed,' said Bairnsfather simply. Ronnie tipped

his steel helmet back and said he was sorry. The soldier sat on the bench beside his wife. Ronnie announced that he was going back into the woods. 'It was bloody terrible,' said Bairnsfather. He wiped his eyes. 'End of last week. The Jerries strafed us. Ugly got hit . . .'

'Oh, God, no.'

'He's all right. Just a splinter. Through the cheek of all things.' He laughed wryly. 'Christ, he was sitting smoking and the smoke was coming out of the hole.'

'But Cartwright . . . I don't remember him.'

'We used to go together to the canteen when you were there. He was with us when I first met you. It was a bastard, believe me. Captain Bevan, the sergeant, everybody's so demolished . . . It was a nightmare. We managed to get one of the planes, but what's that?'

Molly put her hand on his. 'When is it all going to be over?'

'Wish I knew, love. Not for a long time yet.'

They sat silently for a while. Then music began to drift over the trees, strings sounding in the late air. 'Where's that coming from?' she asked.

'Oh, they've got a sort of cheer-you-up concert up at the Manor. I saw them getting the stuff out of a furniture van. These people go around playing at service camps, airfields and that. It's outside the house. They've lost some pilots. One tumbled all the way down the runway on fire. It was sickening.'

'Isn't it strange, this war. People getting killed, all the awful things, and then you get a perfect time like this, and music coming through the forest.'

'Some of our blokes have gone to listen,' said Bairnsfather. He squeezed her waist gently. 'But I've got the best seat. We can listen from here.'

Ronnie appeared through the ferns at the bottom of

the slope. He was carrying a boot. 'Now what's he got?' said Molly.

'Look at this,' said Ronnie triumphantly scrambling up the bank. 'A flying boot. German.'

Bairnsfather took it. 'Looks like it,' he said. 'Could be the plane we brought down.'

Ronnie almost grabbed it back. 'What a souvenir!' he gasped. 'None of the other kids have got a Nazi flying boot. It was wedged in a tree. I had to climb up.' He peered into the long leather boot. Molly grimaced. 'I was wondering if any of his foot was left in it,' said Ronnie.

Bairnsfather took the boot again and looked. 'Nothing doing,' he said.

The musicians played until it was almost dark. On the cello there was an elderly, thin man with wispy hair, who wore a black evening suit; he was accompanied by two girls in black dresses playing violins and a big woman, also in black, who had a mother's face, playing the oboe. In the absence of lights they merged with the deepening of the house in the dusk, their faces like coins.

For almost two hours they performed as they had done for two months in different and distant places, tonight their music mixing in the trees and the breezes. They played Saint-Saëns, Debussy, Delius, Elgar and 'Dusk' by Armstrong Gibbs.

There were few words among the people listening, only the cadence of applause, the deep sense of quietness at least for a while. The war would continue tomorrow. Tubby's Hurricane, and the others burned in the German raid, had been towed away, the fuel bowser had been taken off, and a foreman from Southampton Corporation had said he was pleased with the filled bomb craters.

At intervals Bevan glanced habitually towards the gun. It was resting and he could just see the sentry moving.

Laurel and Hardy had remained with their Bofors at the far end of the runway, in case of a raid, but the day had been unsuitable for combat; low cloud and rain showers. He and Penelope sat side by side on chairs from the kitchen. Their elbows were touching and they spoke little. On the other side of him were Unsworth and Ellen, invited that morning at the magistrates' court by Lady Violet. Ellen was content because Alan had sent a letter. He was away from England. He, at least, was safe.

There were other civilians in the audience and a few soldiers from the guns, Hignet and Brown among them, but they were mostly airmen, sitting on the grass, standing, listening.

Eventually the grey cellist stood and said: 'I think we must finish now. We cannot read the music.' Everyone laughed. 'We will conclude by playing the National Anthem.'

After all the fighting, the death and utter sadness of the past few days, they stood and sang 'God Save the King'. The sound floated over the trees to Bairnsfather who had just seen Molly and Ronnie on to the bus. The baker's roundsman of a year before was now a soldier, a husband and would soon be a father, and he had killed several men who were strangers. As he thought how his life had changed the volume of the anthem increased, perhaps by a shift of the evening breeze. Without embarrassment he stood at solitary attention in the fringe of trees, and loudly sang the banal words. In the Hut the forest men heard the anthem too and without a word between them, put their tankards down, stood as upright as they could manage and sang it as well. 'You'm out o' tune, Catcher,' said Rob at the end.

'Allus was,' said Catcher. 'Allus will be.' He put his beer mug on the counter in front of Rob. Wordlessly Tom Dibben put his alongside it.

* * *

They had to perform in Norwich the next day so the musicians could not stay long. They slept on mattresses in the back of the furniture van.

Before they went the thin-haired man did his party piece, sitting at the upright piano and thumping out songs, sung in the same way as they had always been, with laughter, sentimentality, and drinks all around. Some of the young airmen got helplessly drunk and had to be taken to their quarters. There was more laughter than necessary. A pilot was sick on the lawn.

'I think I must go now,' said Penelope quietly. Bevan walked with her across the courtyard to the cottage. He put his arms around her middle. 'It will soon be just me,' she said.

'That will be fine,' he said. 'We'll be three then.'

'You won't mind? It will be strange for you.'

'Nothing matters. I love you.'

'It was wonderful tonight, wasn't it,' she said. 'The music. Miraculous in a way after all the terrible things.'

The air of the September night was mild. 'Listen,' she said. They could hear the wind in the wires of the barrage balloons. 'More music.' She stopped walking and gave a small grimace. 'Something is moving,' she said.

Bevan held her anxiously and looked around for help. 'Your mother will be ...'

'No, don't worry. It's all right for the moment. You just stay with me, James, please. Don't go.'

'I don't intend to.'

They reached the cottage. 'Come and see where we live now,' she said. She seemed to have recovered and she unlatched the cottage door. 'It's not so grand as the Manor, but it's cosier.'

He had to lower his head to get below the door lintel. Beyond the step he followed her directly into the stone room. She went to the two windows and, despite his attempts to help, pulled the heavy curtains, then lit a tall brass oil-lamp, the light warming her face. She adjusted the wick and the glow steadied. 'You look very beautiful,' he said. 'Lovely.'

'You're kind,' she said quietly. He took a pace towards her and kissed her. 'And gentle,' she said. 'You're a gentle, good man. I've never met a man like you. Stay here for a while and talk to me.'

'This room reminds me of the cottage where I lived before the war,' he said.

'With your wife.'

'My first wife. In the early thirties.'

'How did she die?'

'A silly accident. She was riding her bicycle in the dark, she hit something.'

'And then you married Eve.'

'Several years after. I had a letter from some solicitors. About our divorce. It's odd isn't it how in the middle of all this mayhem, men being killed, you can still get a letter about a divorce.'

'Did you feel badly about it?'

'I'm conscious of a sense of failure.' He smiled at her. 'But I feel that, in spite of the war, things are going to be all right from now on.'

'Failure? I think you are an amazing success. You are a real man, James. Just talking to you, the things you've told me, we've talked about . . .'

'You are good for me,' he said.

She had sat on the single armchair in the room. She took his hand. There was a sofa, which had once matched the armchair. They were old now. An oak table was against the wall so that it did not take up too much space. Above it was a portrait of a man in uniform. 'Your father?' asked Bevan.

Penelope rose and picked up the oil-lamp putting it close to the picture. 'Lieutenant Colonel Sir Robert Foxley,' she said. 'How he would have loved this war.'

She was anxious that he should stay. 'Your chaps won't mind if you're out late, will they?' she joked.

He laughed. 'I'm always afraid the guard will shoot me in the dark. I make a point of singing "There'll Always Be an England".'

'It was awful you losing that young man,' she said.

'I know. Terrible, terrible. We've all felt it. We've just got to get over it.'

He held out his arms to her and hugged her gently. He kissed her and as he did so she said: 'Oh, James. I think something's happening.' She moved towards the chair and he helped her sit. 'Oh, God,' he said.

He helped her on to the worn sofa.

She was sweating in the lamplight. 'It feels very odd. Please don't go.'

He pulled a chair alongside her. 'Hold my hand, will you,' she said.

'I'd better get her ladyship.'

'No. No, stay with me, keep holding my hand.' Her face tightened.

'But someone should.'

'Someone will be here in a moment. I am all right as long as you hold my hand. Talk to me.'

He did. He kissed her. 'Take it easy,' she grinned. The spasms were coming more quickly. He tried to talk about anything, the concert, the weather, the prospects for peace, all the time looking towards the cottage door. At last Lady Violet came through it. 'Oh, dear,' she said. 'We're on the way, are we.' She put her head out of the door.

'The blackout, Mother,' warned Penelope.

'Hitler's gone home.' Her ladyship's head was still

outside. They heard her call: 'Ah, you, yes, young man. Are you an airman?'

'I am,' came the surprised reply.

'Then fly for the medical officer, will you, please. Tell him to hurry.'

Lady Violet returned to the room. Bevan was still holding her daughter's hand. 'Good,' said her ladyship looking at them. 'I am glad.' Her eyes went around the room as though checking resources. 'I don't know whether this medical chap has any experience with childbirth,' she said. 'But he can start now. I'd get Mrs Hewings, the midwife, but she has to come by bicycle.'

The air force medical officer came in. He had a bright bald head and was in a tiger-skin dressing-gown. 'Oh, goodness,' he said pleasantly. 'Well, this is a nice change.'

'I'll telephone for Mrs Hewings anyway,' said Bevan. He felt he ought to get out of the room. He kissed Penelope and released her hand. She smiled. 'Thank you for staying with me, James.'

'It was a pleasure.' He grinned. 'Say hello to the baby for me.'

Bevan went back to the main house. The mess waiter found the telephone directory and he called Mrs Hewings. Squadron leader Wickens was still in the bar, alone and listening to the radio. 'Unemployment has gone down. It's on the news,' he said. He sent a car to pick up the midwife.

Bevan had a Scotch with him. They talked about what they would do after the war. Wickens said: 'Personally, I'd simply like to go home again.' The car with the midwife had just come back. 'Life's very exciting just now, sir,' said the RAF driver to Bevan. 'It never stops, does it.' In the fine night Bevan walked down the slope towards the Bofors. He could see the guard shifting. There was no moon but the sky was settled. The barrage balloons were floating over the shore and he could hear their wires singing.

He paused and looked about him. This was England. Everything would be all right in the end.

Then he thought he heard a baby's cry.

Also by Leslie Thomas

DANGEROUS DAVIES AND THE LONELY HEART

In this, the fourth of Leslie Thomas's novels about Dangerous Davies, the last detective, Davies is retired from the Metropolitan Police and has set up as a private eye in an office above the Welsh Curry House, Willesden, North-West London. Cases are hard to come by until he is abruptly thrown into two mysteries – the murder of women answering lonely hearts advertisements and the disappearance of a young girl student with a secret worth millions. They bring him into contact with some typically eccentric characters, including Sestrina, a beauty who likes sex with a dagger in her hand, and Olly, whose expensive Harley Davidson motorcycle is stolen while he is collecting his dole.

Mysteries and escapades are all interwoven into a highly original detective story that is as ingenious as it is touching and funny in true Leslie Thomas fashion.

'Thomas's skill in yoking unlikely elements together is little short of hilarious. Dialogue skips along, people are roundly sketched, places set a vivid mood. Thomas . . . midway between Archer and Amis, keeps on giving fiction a good name' *Mail On Sunday*

CHLOE'S SONG

From the prison cell where Chloe Smith, 43, is awaiting trial for the merciful murder of the only man who ever loved her with honesty, she recalls the men in her life who lied to her.

She remembers her adored father, who drank too much; the loss of her virginity at Stonehenge to a schoolboy; her marriage to petty crook Zane Tomkins, the Isle of Wight ferryman who said he was a lonely deep sea sailor, the young priest who said he loved her but left to establish a church for men, or the lighthouse keeper who shouted in his sleep – all these men, and many others, have let Chloe down.

Chloe's Song is the story of one woman's quest to get what every woman wants – a man who tells the truth.

'Thomas is that increasingly rare kind of writer, the old-fashioned storyteller' *Sunday Times*